W9-AMX-344

CORMORANT'S BROOD

OTHER BOOKS BY INGLIS FLETCHER

The White Leopard
(*A Tale of the African Bush*)

Red Jasmine
(*A Novel of Africa*)

The Scotswoman

CAROLINA SERIES

Raleigh's Eden
Men of Albemarle
Lusty Wind for Carolina
Toil of the Brave
Roanoke Hundred
Bennett's Welcome
Queen's Gift
The Wind in the Forest

Cormorant's Brood

BY INGLIS FLETCHER

J. B. LIPPINCOTT COMPANY
Philadelphia & New York

SECOND IMPRESSION

Printed in the United States of America

Library of Congress Catalog Card Number 59-11142

It will be borne in mind that Eden, Burrington, and Everard, in fact the government officials, were then generally not North Carolinians, but needy adventurers, who came over here to seek their fortunes at the expense of the colony—a Cormorant's brood not equalled in America.

Prefatory Notes X, Volume 11
Colonial Records of North Carolina
William L. Saunders, Secretary of State

Tell me where all past years are.

JOHN DONNE (1573-1631)

CONTENTS

FOREWORD

THIS is a novel with no real hero or heroine, a novel about a quiet time, in which there were neither battles nor wars. It is a story of people—villagers, soundside planters, yeomen along the rivers and creeks, craftsmen and artisans, bond servants and Negro slaves. The events of the years between 1725 and 1729 have been somewhat compressed, but they are the events of history, enacted both by real men and by men of fiction.

Even though this period did not see the stirring events of war, great changes were taking place in the Albemarle. In the province of North Carolina, among the Englishmen who had come to the New World there grew up a deep love of the land and its development, a love that was to move men forward in their search for freedom.

It was in 1663 that England's Charles II paid the great debt he owed to eight of the noblemen who had helped him regain the throne of his father, the martyred Charles I, by granting them, their heirs and their successors, a vast dominion in America, made up of the fertile districts between the Albemarle Sound and the River St. John. Thus it was that Henry Hyde, Earl of Clarendon; General George Monk, Duke of Albemarle; William, Earl of Craven; Lord Ashley-Cooper, later Earl of Shaftesbury; John, Lord Berkeley; Sir William Berkeley; Sir John Colleton; and John Granville, First Earl of Bath, became the true and absolute Lords Proprietors of the Carolinas and the Bahamas, their only obligation to the Crown an annual payment of twenty marks of lawful English money and one-fourth of all the gold, silver and pearls to be found in their domain.

The Proprietors were forward-looking men, who hoped to create a just and liberal government in their land. Its constitution, inspired by the Earl of Shaftesbury, was drawn up by the great John Locke, and although the provision it contained for the establishment of an order of hereditary aristocracy proved inappropriate in this new, pioneering land where strength and energy, far more than family prestige, were the marks of a man's worth, it was in all other respects a just and wise document. Under it, the people of the Carolinas could have been honestly and fairly governed in liberty and freedom. But the governors sent to enforce this constitution were a weak and sorry lot, more concerned with lining their own pockets than with honoring their trust, and the period of this cormorant's brood hastened the time of the final break with England.

For, with the very air of the New World, the settlers were breathing in new hopes and aspirations. They had been granted independence and justice by Locke's Fundamental Constitution. They would cherish these as they cherished the land itself—the people's land, given them to hold and to develop and to defend.

Book I

Chapter I

THE VILLAGE

THE SUN was just beginning to lighten the clouds in the eastern sky when the blare of the hunting horn split the quiet, chilly air. The western gate of the village swung open, and through it galloped a party of riders, dressed for the chase in high jack-boots, tight breeks, leathern jackets bordered in braid, and large beaver hats with trailing plumes. They were singing at the top of their lungs:

"Oh, the bonny Earl of Moray
Came sounding through the town . . ."

Governor Burrington rode at the head of the other five hunters. The slaves, with the morning's kill of two bucks and a fawn, brought up the rear. They galloped down Queen Street and wheeled sharply into Broad. At the turn, one of the horses kicked a dog, and it ran yelping into the driveway of a house. But the horsemen did not pause, nor did they take any heed of the irate householder who, thrusting his head out of a window, shook his fist angrily after them, and muttered imprecations at their departing backs.

When they arrived at Government House, Burrington jumped from his saddle and flung the reins to a slightly built Negro who had come scurrying out from the kitchen.

"Come in, lads, come in! We have earned a drink, and then breakfast!"

Laughing and talking, the men jostled their way into the house, threw their hats on the hall settle, and trooped into the governor's office to warm themselves by the crackling red flame that was already blazing in the fireplace.

The governor went to the door, looked quickly down the

hall to the back of the house, and called out impatiently:

"Taphy! Taphy, you lazy good-for-nothing! Hurry up and bring the rum! We're cold, and we want warming in our bellies! Taphy! Aren't you even awake?"

A white-haired Negro hurried into the room, his shirt-tails not yet tucked in, the sleep still showing in his eyes. The glasses and the squat decanter on the tray he carried clinked noisily with every step he took. He had barely set the tray on a table near the desk when Burrington started to fill the glasses. The men reached for them avidly and smacked their lips in satisfaction as the burning liquor coursed down their throats.

"Tell cook to make up a big breakfast," Burrington ordered. "And have her hurry with it. We've been out three hours, and are hungry as the very devil."

But they had time for two or three more glasses of the strong West Indies rum before Taphy came in to announce that breakfast was ready. At his words, the men crowded into the large dining room, where they filled their plates with the ham, bacon, eggs and corn-meal mush that had been set out on the hunt board. Then they seated themselves at the long mahogany table and ate heartily.

The sheriff, a robust man of wide girth, took a second helping.

"Eat up, eat up," he said to the gaoler, poking him in the ribs. "A man needs food after a deer drive like that."

"I'll have the animals skinned and cleaned," Burrington promised. "We will all have venison for dinner tonight."

"Better send a double portion to the sheriff, sir." A smile crossed the gaoler's face. "He'd eat that and more."

The others laughed noisily and, encouraged by their response, the gaoler told a long anecdote about the sheriff's notorious appetite; the sheriff himself seemed to appreciate it more than anyone else. When the tale was finished, Dr. Carter stood up, sighing and patting his full stomach.

"I'd better go," he announced. "I have a woman about to give birth. Her tenth, but she wants a doctor anyway. I'd say the devil with it, but then she would take her brats' aches and pains to Norcomb, and I need the patients more than he does."

"By God, you'd better go quickly, or she'll drop it before you get there." Burrington slapped his crony on the shoulder. "But take a glass of brandy first. Rum is all right when you're cold, but brandy is a real drink. I have some in the office."

As the party moved into the hall, the governor discovered his six-year-old son and four-year-old daughter leaning over the stair rail. Wakened by the shouts and loud laughter, they had run out of their rooms dressed only in their nightclothes. Burrington reached over and gave the boy a sound smack on his little bottom. "Get you back to bed, lad. This is no hour for respectable folk to be up and about." He laughed and turned to the doctor. "It's different for old reprobates like us, eh?"

"I want to see the deer. Did you get one with antlers?" The boy's eyes shone with excitement.

"That I did. You can see it later. Run, now, run!" He made as if to reach over the banister.

"Oh, don't!" the little girl cried out, and the two children scampered quickly up the stairs.

"Fine children. Fine children." Carter's tone was approving. "As healthy as little pups."

"Aye. And at times, as annoying."

The governor turned to the rest of his guests, who were already at the door.

"I'll send over some meat for the prisoners in your gaol," he said to the gaoler.

The man grinned broadly. "You know I have no prisoners, sir."

Burrington slapped his thigh. "What do you think of that, doctor? No prisoners, he says, and yet the people call me a sorry governor. The fools don't know a good man when they have one. They would prefer a Charles Eden, I suppose, who dealt with pirates, or a Seth Southal, who sold them as slaves to the Indians."

"Well, what do you expect of ignorant country folk?" the doctor asked as the door closed behind the other members of the hunting party.

Burrington led the way back to his office. He poured a glass of brandy for himself, motioned Carter to take one, and sat down behind his desk.

"Many of the people here think very well of themselves and their manners," he said, narrowing his pale blue eyes until they were mere slits in his craggy face. "All the Council members seem to think themselves better bred than I." He laughed. "But I cannot believe they would do very well in London society, or even in one of the Crown colonies, where there are real ladies and gentlemen, and a real society. I cannot believe the governor of South Carolina has to go hunting with his sheriff." With an abrupt movement, he stood up. "Well, that's neither here nor there. If you want to be on hand when that wench has her child, you had better move along."

The doctor tossed down his brandy and started for the door. As he opened it, he nearly collided with Burrington's secretary, David Elton, a pale, slightly stooped young man, with good features and a sensitive face.

"Ah, there, Elton," Carter said. "Remind the governor to take you with us the next time we go out hunting. Build you up a little." He gave the young man a playful tap on the stomach and walked out, laughing. In a moment, there was the sound of the front door closing behind him.

Elton remained standing where he was.

"Was it a good hunt, your excellency?" he asked.

"Not bad, not bad," Burrington yawned several times and stretched vigorously. "I'm going up to take a nap. Call me at dinnertime, if I am not up by then." He crossed to the door and paused. "Oh, yes. You might write up a draft of my speech to the Council next week. That will keep you busy for the morning." He walked out, slamming the door so hard the whole house shook.

David clicked his tongue. The noise was loud enough to have aroused the frail Madam Burrington, as well as Miss Dierdra Treffry, the children's governess.

The villagers, awakened before their time, rose reluctantly from their beds to begin the new day, grumbling because the governor's hunting party had robbed them of their last hour of sleep.

Martin Trewilliger, the farrier, muttered as he heated a bar of iron in the charcoal fire. He loved those last minutes of rest, when one lay stretched out, half-dreaming, half-awake. And he was no admirer of Burrington at the best. When the governor had thrown him into gaol because he refused to get up in the dead of night to shoe a horse so that his excellency could go out riding with his friend Dr. Carter, Martin had lost all hope that this new man would be any better than his predecessor, Charles Eden. It was nearly a year ago, but the memory still rankled: four days in gaol "to think it over" in addition to a fine of ten shillings—no small sum for a poor artisan. Martin hit the hot iron an angry, ringing blow with all the power of his strong arm.

At the King's Arms Inn, the servants were already at work, sweeping out the common room, washing off the tables, making ready for breakfast. deVoe, the landlord, a sullen, swarthy Frenchman with anxious, darting eyes, stood by the bar shouting orders to the potboys and waiters.

"There's a ship coming in today from England. I have some goods on her. I want two boys down at the wharf when she docks, to unload my stuff. Joan," he called out to the maid in the upstairs hall, "see that the balcony suite and two bedrooms are readied up. There are travelers from London on that ship. They must be gentlemen of importance; one of them is bringing a valet." He turned back to the men. "I'm going out to talk to the hostlers about the gentlemen's horses. See that you step lively, now."

He had no sooner left the room than the work came to a virtual standstill. The servants hated him; rumor had it that deVoe had been a member of a pirate ship that had its rendezvous off Ocacoke Island.

Merchants and artisans stood in the doorways of their shops, watching their servants take down the shutters, sweep the floors, and set up the displays of their wares outside the store fronts. Joseph Castleton, the barber, whose shop was just a few steps from the Green, took the cloths off his chair and set long wooden blocks in the window, to hold models of the latest style of wig: full-bottomed, brown or white. Actually, he had little call for such elegant appointments; except for the governor, the Council members and one or two others, the men of Edenton eschewed them, and wore their own locks, long, or cut short after the Cromwellian fashion.

In King Street, Goldsmith Coltrane raised his head from his goosefeather pillow to find his man, John, standing beside the bed, in his hands a silver tray on which were a china pot of chocolate and a delicate cup.

"Master, you ask me to wake you early this morning. The *Flying Fish* is coming in today, and you say you expect important letters."

Coltrane sat up slowly, rubbing his eyes, sorry to break off his pleasant dream. "Thank you, John. Put the tray on the table and hand me my wig, please."

He had a long day ahead of him; as town banker, Mr. Coltrane carried the financial problems of the entire precinct on his shoulders, and these problems always seemed to increase with the arrival of the London mail. Sighing, he took off his muslin nightcap and put his brown wig on his shaven poll. Then he reached gratefully for the steaming cup of chocolate.

In her large, double-galleried house on Broad Street, Mistress Penelope Lovyck rang the bell for her Negro maid. The morning was chilly, and the fire had not yet been lighted. She, too, had a busy day ahead of her. Her husband would be returning tomorrow from his trip to Virginia, and she wanted the house to be in perfect order when he arrived. Then, there were the clothes she expected on the *Flying Fish:* two new dresses from her London manteau maker, a pretty pair of slippers, and a fashionable hat. And she was having guests for lunch: Madam Gale, the wife of the chief justice; Mistress Peterson, whose new home on the Virginia Road promised, when it was completed, to be the most up-to-date in the precinct; and Mistress Moseley, the wife of the surveyor-general.

The village of Edenton was awake. A ship day always brought excitement—there were the London journals, personal mail, new clothes for the ladies and farm equipment for the yeomen of the countryside. Every house and shop was alive with activity. Every house save one—the lewd house, across from the shipyard. There the girls buried their pretty faces deeper in their pillows or hid them under the counterpane. Sunrise was not for them.

At high tide, the *Flying Fish*, commanded by Captain Thomas Blackwell, crossed the bar at the entrance of Albemarle Sound and moved slowly westward, under full sail. By eleven o'clock, she had reached Edenton Bay.

At the rail stood the ship's only passengers, Richard Chapman and Anthony Dawson. The two young men had met on the long journey across the Western Ocean, and had become firm friends. The voyage had been fair, with one stop at the Azores, to fill the casks with fresh water and to wait for an easterly wind. But now the trip was at an end, and adventure lay ahead.

Dawson was a striking figure of a man—well over six feet, with broad shoulders, a narrow waist, and a soldierly bearing. His black eyes and hair and his olive skin bespoke his Norman blood. Chapman was shorter than his companion, and fairer: he had brown hair, a rosy complexion, and the blue eyes of the Saxons. His forebears had come to Virginia in 1614, and settled at Bermuda Hundred, on the James River, where his father now planted a thousand acres of rich land. But Dick had little desire as yet to follow in the older man's footsteps. Four years at William and Mary College and a year's travel in England and on the Continent had made him restless and eager for excitement. He was still young, the whole world was before him, and he saw little reason to settle down so soon to the life of a moneyed planter.

And so he had begun his journey home in a mood of depression, which had grown more severe when, on shipboard, he met

Anthony Dawson. Here was a man who had everything Dick wanted and admired: a sophisticated manner, a detailed knowledge of London's most fashionable circles (he apparently knew any number of important people, among them, Lord John Granville, Palatine of the Lords Proprietors of North Carolina), a brave and honorable record as a colonel of His Majesty's forces in the Low Country Wars. And, probably most enviable of all, Dawson's future held the promise of further excitement and adventure. For the Englishman was coming to the New World to purchase land along the unsettled reaches of the Chowan River in North Carolina, to clear it, and to build his home there. Such rugged pioneering was much more to Dick's liking than the placid existence of a James River planter, and he pleaded to be allowed to accompany his new friend.

Anthony was amused and flattered by the Virginian's obvious admiration, but more than that, he had developed a warm affection for this eager, open-hearted youth. Dick was the kind of easy-going, pleasant fellow who was bound to make a good companion. He might prove a valuable ally, too, in the event that one should be needed. And this was entirely possible; Anthony had other plans in addition to the ones of which he had spoken.

He had, therefore, quickly fallen in with Dick's suggestion, and when the *Flying Fish* put in at Yorktown, in Virginia, the two young men persuaded Mr. Chapman to give his consent to the enterprise. Dick had been in high spirits ever since that day, and now he whistled gaily as he scanned the shore through his glass.

"Not much of a village here, Tony," he reported. "No more than forty dwellings, and most of them quite small at that. No mansions to compare with those along the James."

"You are a true Virginian, Dick." Anthony smiled. "Nothing good south of the Virginia border, eh?"

"I didn't mean that. I meant that it seems much less settled here. More exciting. If you want to hear North Carolina insulted, you should talk to the South Carolinians."

Dick's eyes were still glued to the glass when the ship came to anchor at the Dram Tree, near the middle of the bay. "Tony, I believe the whole town is down at the edge of the Green to watch us. Oh, and say—there are some pretty girls there."

"I thought we came to look at land, not girls," Anthony said. "Give that to me. I want to see the town."

Dick shook his head and grasped the glass more firmly. "Wait a minute." He paused. "There's a girl coming onto the dock now . . ."

Laughing, Anthony took the glass from him. "Come on, Dick. The girl can wait."

He put the instrument to his eye. Behind the long curve of the beach, shining white in the midday sun, were clusters of houses. A broad street, cut by narrower ones, ran north from the water's edge to the stockade gate. On the Green was a large building with a portico; a flag flew from its roof—it was probably the courthouse. Beyond the village was a heavy forest of primeval pines and oaks, while along a creek was a pocosin, leafless cypress trees growing deep into its waters. The ship swung around into its anchorage, and Government House came into view; a pleasant building with a Jacobean overhang and a cupola, set in a large garden behind a paling fence that ran close to the water.

So this was North Carolina! Anthony felt a thrill run through him, but he kept his voice steady.

"The countryside looks like a French painting. I think I am going to like it here, Dick."

Dick reached for the glass. "The girls look like paintings, too." He laughed. "Especially that blond girl standing with the grey-haired man. It is she I saw walking toward the dock."

Captain Blackwell had come down from the poop deck and was standing beside them. "The man is Yeoman Killigrew from out on the Virginia Road. He has a fine property, I'm told. I have plows and cultivators for him. He's an impatient Cornishman, and I imagine he will want his goods off before anyone else."

"Who is the girl?" Dick asked. "I've seen lots of yeomen, but very few young women as pretty as that."

"His daughter, I presume. He has one, I know." Captain Blackwell peered ahead to the shore. "I see deVoe is on the dock too. He's the landlord of the King's Arms, where you will be staying. He has two of his hostlers with him. They should be a help in getting your horses off the boat; they have had experience with restive animals before."

"I suppose that's the inn, up at the head of the Green?" Anthony took his eye from the glass.

The captain nodded, and walked off to direct the landing operations. The seamen were taking down the flapping sails and making them secure, and barefoot sailors were already lowering small boats over the side and letting down the rope ladders.

Anthony turned to Dick. "Why don't you go ashore now and warn the hostlers about the horses? They might as well know they've a difficult task ahead. You remember how much trouble we had with Black Douglas in Virginia. I'll stay here and oversee things at this end."

"What about Smalkins?" Dick asked, nodding his head in the direction of Anthony's valet, who was standing further up the deck, keeping a careful eye on the sailors as they prepared to lower the young men's boxes into one of the small boats.

"Take him with you. He can go ahead to the inn and see that our rooms are ready."

Dick turned and made his way across the deck. He spoke briefly to Smalkins, and the two men descended the rope ladder into a boat, which moved smoothly through the waters of the bay to the shore.

As the brown-haired young man picked his way among the piles of shingles and barrels of tar on the dock, the villagers, who had gathered to watch the ship's arrival, eyed him with interest. Who could he be? Tongues wagged. Not many young gentlemen came to Edenton on the London ships. Matrons and young girls looked covertly at him. It had been a long time since any personable young man had come to the village, and today two were arriving: this one, and the dark-haired gentleman, still on the boat.

Tamar Killigrew left her father's side and ran over to Dierdra Treffry, who was walking across the dock, Governor Burrington's youngsters holding firmly on to her hands.

"Good morning, Tamar," Dierdra said. "I should not have expected to meet you here. Children, say good morning to Mistress Tamar."

"Good morning." The children spoke in unison. The boy made a small, jerky bow and the little girl spread her skirts daintily in a curtsey.

"Good morning, William. Good morning, Ann." Tamar smiled.

William turned to Dierdra, his eyes pleading. "Please, Mistress Treffry, may we go down to watch the sailors unload?"

"My father is there, waiting for his equipment," Tamar put in. "He will see that nothing happens to them."

Dierdra glanced over to the side of the dock, where Yeoman Killigrew stood, an earnest expression on his wind-reddened face. A pang of homesickness shot through her; in his leathern jacket and wide-brimmed hat he looked like a hundred yeomen she had seen in her native Cornwall.

"All right, children, you may go." Dierdra spoke gently. "And William, I depend on you to help Yeoman Killigrew take care of your sister."

"Oh, I will. Come on, Ann!" And the two children raced happily off.

Dierdra watched them until they reached Killigrew's side, and then turned back to Tamar. The two girls made a pretty contrast as they stood there. Tamar, tall and blond, had small, pert features and eyes as tawny as a leopard's, the color of yellow wine with flecks. Dierdra, equally tall, with shining black hair that molded her well-shaped head like a satin cap, and deep, sparkling blue eyes, was wearing a bright red cape which seemed to add a glow to her ivory complexion, and to heighten the sculptured delicacy of her fine, classic features. There was amusement in her voice as she said:

"Well, Tamar, I still do not know what brings you here."

The blond girl laughed. "Oh, you know it perfectly well. Things are so dull at Lilac Farm, and something always happens in the village when the ships come in." She looked over her shoulder toward Dick, who was speaking earnestly to one of deVoe's hostlers. Then, turning back to Dierdra, she continued in a lower voice. "Have you seen that young man who just came onto the dock? There, right in front of you. No—turn your head a little to the left. That's it." She waited until Dierdra had caught sight of him. "Isn't he the handsomest thing? I noticed him while he was still on the boat. I think he noticed me, too. I wonder if he will be staying here?"

Dierdra smiled. "He is very pleasant looking."

"Pleasant looking! Is that all you can say?" Tamar turned to bring Dick into her line of vision. Her eyes danced with excitement. "Look, he's smiling at us. He looks like a real gentleman. So elegant! Oh, Dierdra, wouldn't it be wonderful if he stayed here for a while? He does not seem to be alone; he was standing with another young man on the boat. A dark one. You can see him now." She nodded her head toward the *Flying Fish*. Anthony was at the rail, watching the sailors as they strapped the horses into heavy harnesses, preparatory to lowering them over the side.

"Yes," Dierdra said. "I see him." She narrowed her eyes and her expression grew thoughtful. "The ship is still too far away for me to be sure . . ." She paused. "But there is something about him. It's the way he stands, I think. He looks familiar. I have a feeling I know him."

Tamar stole another glance at Dick, still deep in conversation with the hostler. "It would be wonderful if you did! Then we would be sure to meet them. I never thought such good-looking men would come to this poky little village!"

Dierdra smiled. "I only said I thought I knew him, Tamar, not that I did."

But Tamar chattered on, oblivious. "Two handsome men! And I nearly died of boredom all winter. Maybe the spring will be better."

"Now, Tamar, stop building castles in the air!" Dierdra shook her head and sighed. "Probably they are only passing through. Probably I do not know the young man at all." She paused. "I must go now. It's time for the children to be home. William! Ann!" she called.

Reluctantly, the children left Yeoman Killigrew's side and returned to her.

"We watched them unload Mr. Killigrew's cultivator," William said, his eyes wide. "He promised we could come out to Lilac Farm and see how he uses it. Won't that be fun?"

"And he said to tell you he is ready to leave now, Mistress Tamar," Ann put in. "He said he would meet you on the Green, on the side where the cart is."

Tamar threw a glance toward Dick, who had just started across the dock with the hostler. Did she imagine it, or was he smiling at her? She tossed her head. Then she hurried to catch up with Dierdra and the children.

Chapter II

THE GENTRY

Four old friends were sitting around a table in a private room of the King's Arms Inn, having their midday meal. Except for Goldsmith Coltrane, none of them lived in Edenton; they had come in that morning from their plantations along the Sound to pick up the mail and London purchases that had arrived on the *Flying Fish*, and were taking advantage of their visit to the village to spend a little time together. There was Chief Justice Christopher Gale, from Strawberry Hill, about two miles away; Edward Moseley, the surveyor-general, whose home, Moseley Point, was over four miles distant; and Thomas Norcomb, the surgeon, whose place was some miles beyond Moseley's.

The surveyor-general, who was also Lord John Granville's representative on the Council, was a tall man with strong features and a quick, incisive manner. He took the last bite of his roast mutton, pushed his plate away, and spoke.

"I shall have to leave you in a few minutes. I want to speak to Anthony Dawson, one of the young men who arrived on the ship today. Lord John wrote me that he plans to take up property here."

"I saw the lads when they came in," Goldsmith Coltrane said. He patted his thin lips carefully with his napkin. "They seem pleasant-looking fellows."

A smile crossed Dr. Norcomb's bland face, and his blue eyes twinkled. "It takes more than pleasant looks, it takes stamina. Particularly if you have to break land and clear the forest. I've seen several pleasant-looking young men come here, in my time. I've seen them go, too."

Chief Justice Gale nodded. He had a long face and an arched, high-bridged nose; in his London clothes and brown wig he was the perfect picture of a gentleman. "And if he does stay, where is he going to get the land from? There is practically no open property left in Chowan Precinct. Between planters on the sound and yeomen along the Chowan and Roanoke, most of it is gone."

"Oh, I don't know," Norcomb laughed. "Moseley, here, might give up some of his. He has taken up more grants than anyone in the whole province."

Moseley smiled, but his grey eyes were serious. "A surveyor-general has some privileges. And what about you? You've more acreage than a doctor needs."

"I wish that were true. I need all the land I have. I was thinking only this morning that I make more money out of planting and fishing than I do by doctoring."

Goldsmith Coltrane pushed his chair back from the table and stood up.

"You are fortunate to have a profession," he said. "When the yeomen have a bad year, they don't make a penny."

But Norcomb had lost interest. He turned to Moseley.

"When is John Lovyck's case coming up?"

"The memorial is to be read at next month's Council meeting." The surveyor-general ran his fingers through his long hair. "I told John he was foolish to write Governor Eden's will, even if the old man did want him to. It is bound to look bad when the man who writes the will inherits all the property."

"I imagine Mistress Lloyd is counting on that. After all, Eden was her brother. Nearly eight thousand pounds, I hear, and none of it to her!" Norcomb shook his head.

"Eight thousand pounds!" Coltrane exclaimed. "I had no idea it was that much. None of our governors ever left anything like that. It almost makes one believe that Eden *did* have dealings with Blackbeard."

"Almost! For a man who handles financial affairs so astutely," Moseley said, laughing, "you certainly are naïve. Have you forgotten what I discovered when I raided the home of Eden's secretary of state, Tobias Knight? The papers I found then proved beyond any possible doubt that Knight and his master were in partnership with Teach, or Blackbeard, as you call him. Not only that, I used to see ships of all kinds landing at the Eden House pier to discharge contraband cargo. Molasses, sugar, rum—they made Eden a rich man. Remember, the governor was my neighbor. I know that he was crooked as a snake's back!"

"I cannot believe he left anything like eight thousand pounds," Gale put in. "But that is hardly the point."

Norcomb sighed. "It makes one lose faith, it does. An English governor who dealt with pirates! But you know what the Greek philosopher said: people get the rulers they deserve."

Gale lit his pipe and drew thoughtfully on it. "We must be a pretty bad lot, then. I cannot say Burrington has made too good an impression on me. He has been here over a year already and he has not yet begun to do any of the things he should."

"And so much needs to be done!" Moseley started to tick off the items on his fingers. "There's the dividing line with Virginia. It simply must be settled; as it is, the people on the border do not pay taxes to anyone. When the Virginia men come around, they say they live in Carolina. And when *our* collectors go after them, the same folk insist they live in Virginia."

"You have to give them credit for being clever rascals, at any rate." Norcomb laughed.

"Clever?" Gale frowned. "They should be brought to court. But more than that needs to be settled. The tobacco tax, for instance. And the law that all our goods must be shipped in English bottoms, even though the French and Dutch ships have served us so well. And the rents. This demand that they be paid in cash! Why, we've always paid the government in pork and tobacco."

"Well, it would be splendid if we could count on Burrington," Moseley said. "But I fear that is a hopeless wish. Have I told you that a friend in London wrote me he was arraigned at Old Bailey for hitting a woman in a drunken brawl."

"Was he convicted?" Norcomb asked.

"No," Moseley shook his head. "But . . ."

"Now, that is precisely the kind of thing that makes trouble," Coltrane interrupted. "Spreading rumors like that. You know

Aesop's story about the boy who cried 'wolf!'" He sighed and shook his head.

"All right, all right. I apologize. I never should have said it." But Moseley did not sound contrite. He took his turnip watch from his brocaded waistcoat pocket and looked at it. "I must go now, and make my call on our new settler."

He closed the door behind him, walked briskly across the common room, where town folk and country yeomen were drinking ale and playing at darts, and made his way up the staircase to Anthony and Dick's suite.

"Come in," a voice called out as he knocked on the door.

He entered to find the two young men in their sitting room. The remains of the chicken deVoe had sent up for their luncheon were still on the small table in front of the fireplace.

"Mr. Dawson?" Moseley asked, looking inquiringly from one to the other.

"I am Dawson," Anthony said. "And you are Mr. Moseley, I take it. I've been expecting a call from you. This is my friend, Richard Chapman. Mr. Moseley is the surveyor-general, Dick, the man who will help us find our land."

"It is nice to meet you, sir. Do sit down." Dick smiled and pulled up a chair for the older man. "Can we order something for you?"

"No, thank you," Moseley said, "I've just eaten." He spread the tails of his long blue coat and took a seat. "Lord John wrote me that you were coming to North Carolina to look for land with the idea of settling here. What kind of property had you in mind?"

Anthony rose. "Frankly, I am not quite sure what I want. Mr. Chapman and I looked about a little in Virginia on our way here. But it is far too settled there for our tastes. We were hoping to find some undeveloped property. Lord John told me you are his personal representative here. He said you know more about North Carolina than anyone else in the province. I hope you will be able to help us."

Moseley nodded. "I do not think it immodest for me to agree

with Lord John. I've been here over thirty years and have traveled pretty well through the country." He took out his pipe and lit it. "Let me look at my maps and see what property is open. Sometimes land that has been taken up by grant becomes free when there has not been sufficient work done on it."

There was a knock on the door, and Smalkins entered. He was carrying a tray.

"Beg pardon, Mr. Chapman, but the hostler tells me your horse is acting up. He wondered if you would want to go down and take a look at her." The valet crossed the room to the table and began to clear it.

Dick picked up his waistcoat from the back of a chair.

"Poor Star! She has never been on shipboard before, and she is a nervous creature, anyway. Will you excuse me, Mr. Moseley?"

"While you are there, Dick," Anthony said, "will you take a look at Black Douglas, also? I do not believe animals ever get used to sea voyages."

When the door had closed behind Dick and Smalkins, Anthony turned to face the surveyor-general.

"I am glad we have this chance to be alone, sir. Mr. Chapman does not know my real name, or why I am here. As a matter of fact, except for my man, who was my corporal in the army, you are the only person in North Carolina who does." Anthony smiled. "And I did want to talk with you in private."

Moseley laughed and made a low bow. "I am at your service, Mr. Granville."

"I have not been called by that name since I left England, more than two months ago," Anthony said. "I had almost forgotten it." He walked over to a side table, on which stood a decanter of wine and some glasses. "Can I give you a little port, Mr. Moseley?"

"I'd like that."

Anthony poured the wine from the decanter. "Frankly, I do not know how much Lord John has told you about my mission, so it is a little difficult for me to know where to begin."

Moseley sat down on the divan and took a sip of his port. "Well,

I know that your mission is a secret, and that you are here under a pseudonym. I know that your real name is Anthony Granville, and you are Lord John's cousin, and that means that you are one of the Proprietors of North Carolina. I know, too, that the Granvilles hold more land here than any of the others, and have taken considerably more interest in the province than the rest."

Anthony nodded. "Right. Not that we were granted more land, but Christopher, the son of the Earl of Albermarle, one of the original eight, died without heirs, and he left his share of the grant to my ancestor, the Earl of Bath."

Moseley set his glass down on the end-table next to the divan. "And I know the property has been no unmixed blessing." He pulled at his pipe, frowned, and spoke thoughtfully. "They must have had some notion, back in Charles' days, that the New World was like the Indies Columbus set out to find—all gold and precious stones. At least, so it seems from the terms of the grant. The Proprietors were supposed to give the crown one-fourth of all the gems found here, were they not?"

"Lord John and I have laughed over that provision many times. As a matter of fact, we were talking about it only a little while before I left England." Anthony's expression became serious. "But we are much less concerned about precious stones than we are about the land." He clasped his hands behind his back and began to pace the room. "The property has been in the family for over fifty years now, and not one penny has it returned. And we cannot understand the reason."

Moseley took another sip of his port before he spoke. "The land is fertile, and the people are hard-working. It should be profitable. I have my own ideas about why it is not, and I will tell them to you when we have more time. I take it that is the question that interests you most."

Anthony stopped pacing and turned to face his guest. "That is one of them. But there is another."

Moseley looked at him inquiringly.

"Well, Mr. Moseley." Anthony's voice was firm. "Since the land has not earned a penny, the other Proprietors have been talking about selling their shares. The Crown wants to buy. Perhaps we Granvilles ought to consider selling, too."

Moseley set his glass down heavily and sat for a moment, unmoving. Then, suddenly, he stood up. His face was red and angry.

"I had not realized things had gone that far, Mr. Granville. To sell North Carolina to the Crown! Why, part of the reason I came here—and there are many others like me—was that I felt I would have more freedom in a proprietary colony. A sale to the Crown! Great God!" He sat down and spread his hands in a gesture of helplessness.

"It is by no means certain that we will sell, but there is that chance." Anthony was delighted at Moseley's reaction, but his voice was calm.

The Carolinian looked up. His expression was set and hard. "I know what is wrong here, Mr. Granville, and I have written Lord John about it many, many times. The real problem is the governors whom the Proprietors send. We will never attract enough settlers to make the province prosperous when it is so badly ruled. I do not know how Burrington behaved to the lords when he met them, although I am sure he can put on a good display of London manners when he thinks it to his advantage. He even treated us to courteous behavior when he first arrived." There was contempt in his voice. "But the fact is, he has done nothing at all for the province—unless he has helped by drinking up every bottle of wine that pirate Charles Eden left in the cellar at Government House."

"Lord John hinted to me that you were not precisely fond of Governor Burrington." A wry smile crossed Anthony's face; the Palatine's exact words had been, "The man seems to make a habit of hating governors," but Anthony saw no point in quoting. "Mr. Moseley, I am going to be very candid with you. We do not know what is wrong here—whether the problem lies with the governor, or the people, or the very fact of proprietary government, or with the difficulties that arise because England is so far off. Whatever it is, I mean to find out. I have not yet met the governor. When I do, I intend to form my own opinion of him. I have not met any of the people except you, either. But I am going to get to know them, too." Anthony walked over to the window and, pushing the curtain aside, looked out at the Green for a moment in silence. Then he turned. "I *am* sure of one thing, however. We Granvilles have done our best to see that North Carolina is properly governed, and that only responsible folk come to settle here. But in spite of that, the land has done us no good at all." His voice softened, and he smiled. "I do not doubt your word, Mr. Moseley. Lord John has the highest regard for you, and the utmost confidence in you; if he did not, he would not have made you his representative on the Council, and he would not have taken you into his confidence about me. But if I am to perform my commission properly, I must investigate the situation with an open mind. You do understand that, don't you?"

The older man nodded. "I suppose I did speak rather sharply. But I am not a diplomat, and I was shocked by what you said. I know that when you have looked into things, you will come around to my point of view. And until then, you can depend on me not to say a word to anyone."

There was the sound of footsteps in the outside hall. The door opened, and Dick entered.

"Well, that was a needless worry. Star calmed down quickly enough."

Moseley rose from the divan, took his watch out of his waistcoat pocket, and examined it. "I am afraid I must be off. It has been a pleasure meeting you gentlemen. I am always in my office in the courthouse on Fridays, Mr. Dawson. If you come over there, I will be able to tell you whether I have found any open land you can take up."

"That will be fine," Anthony said. He went to the door and held it open. "I will see you Friday, then."

As the door closed behind Moseley, Dick said: "He seems a nice fellow, Tony. The hostler was telling me the townspeople think very well of him. 'Mr. Moseley doesn't mince his words,' he said. 'But he's an honest man, and we always know where he stands.' "

Anthony laughed. "That is the impression he made on me, too. Mr. Moseley does not seem to be one to beat around the bush."

Shortly after the ship had docked, Anthony had sent his man, Smalkins, to Government House, with a letter of introduction from Lord John. Mr. Dawson, the letter said, "is a young man of good family, late of His Majesty's Army, desirous of settling in North Carolina." Smalkins had returned to the inn carrying a note requesting the pleasure of Mr. Dawson's company at tea.

The sound of the big brass knocker was still echoing through the house when an old Negro with white hair opened the door.

"Sir, step inside and rest yo' hat. The governor he waiting in the office."

Anthony found Burrington seated at his desk. The older man rose and extended his hand in greeting.

"Glad to welcome you to Albemarle, Mr. Dawson," he said, cordially. "Lord John sent me a most enthusiastic report on you. He says you are precisely the kind of person we need in the province. We are delighted to have you. And you could do much worse than to settle here, much worse. But sit down, and be comfortable." He waved Anthony to a chair and turned to the butler. "Taphy, bring in a bottle of Madeira. We must drink to your success, sir."

The door opened and a young man came into the room. "Pardon me, your excellency, will you sign these letters? Captain Blackwell is sailing again first thing in the morning."

"This is my secretary, Mr. Elton, Mr. Dawson. Will you excuse me while I look these over? You will find that the English mail is very important to us in this province, sir." He took up the papers. The young man bowed and quietly left the room.

While the governor was occupied, Anthony studied him with some care. Moseley had no use for him, and Lord John had indicated that the surveyor-general was not alone in this opinion. If one could judge by the man's looks, Burrington was no weakling; imposing and even handsome, he was strong and robust, with heavy shoulders, a large head, a thick neck and craggy features. His pale blue eyes protruded slightly. A marksman's eyes, Anthony thought.

He was dressed in the approved London style: a long blue coat with silver buttons, a brocade waistcoat, light brown small-clothes and silk stockings. There were silver buckles on his square-toed shoes. The lace at his sleeves and throat was of fine Mechlin. He wore a brown wig. Gold seals hung from the watch in his waistcoat pocket. The gold snuff box on his desk, confirmed Anthony's impression that he was something of a dandy.

Burrington finished his task and rang for his secretary. When Elton left the room, he turned to Anthony.

"As I was about to say, sir, Lord John writes of you with a great deal of enthusiasm. Do you know him well?"

"I have known him for some time," Anthony said. "I believe he is considered an excellent statesman."

"So I understand. I've only met him very briefly, but I have had considerable correspondence with him. As Palatine of the Lords Proprietors, he is my immediate superior."

The butler came in, carrying a silver tray on which were a bottle of Madeira and two long-stemmed glasses. While they drank, the governor talked about the country.

"A vast land to be cleared and cultivated. But it goes very slowly. We do not have enough yeomen or artisans, even though the Proprietors have made an earnest effort to obtain them through advertisements. The soundside planters are a stiff-necked lot, from Devon and Cornwall, mostly; although many of them are cadets of noble families, very few of them are what I call real gentry."

"I do not understand, sir," Anthony put in.

"Well." The governor sat back in his chair and gazed reflectively at the ivory letter opener in his hand. "Something seems to happen to people when they arrive here. The lower and middle classes forget their places, and think they are the equals of those of better birth."

"Don't the gentry object?" Anthony asked.

"Some do. But many do not, and seem to be in favor of this

intermingling of classes. And no matter how they feel on this matter, all the settlers—yeomen, planters, gentry and artisans—think it their right to run the government. The governor has no easy task, Mr. Dawson, as I have found out this last year. I thought it would be fairly simple when I first came: administer the law justly, and everything will be smooth. But I have discovered it is not as easy as that. The governor must keep control with a heavy hand, lest the settlers wrest all authority from him, and even fall to fighting among themselves."

"It must be a delicate situation," said Anthony. "But I know very little about government." He did not want to pursue this subject now. "As Lord John wrote you, I have been soldiering most of my life."

Burrington sat back in his chair. "The Low Country Wars?"

"Yes. I served in Poland and Austria."

"I should like very much to hear about it in detail, but that will have to be later. My wife is waiting for us to have tea. Shall we go?"

He led Anthony to a small, paneled drawing room, which was bathed in the warm glow cast by the fire burning in the grate and the flames of the tall, slender candles on the tables.

Madam Burrington, a delicate-looking woman of about thirty-five, greeted her guest with a charming smile as he kissed her hand.

"It is a great pleasure to meet you, sir. This is my friend and the children's governess, Miss Treffry," she gestured toward a young woman seated across the tea table.

Anthony raised his head from Madam Burrington's hand to look into the deep blue eyes of Dierdra Treffry. A shock went through him. Although he had not seen her since she was a child, he knew this girl: she was the sister of his old friend, Roger Treffry. Roger and he had gone to school together in Bideford as boys, and had served in the same regiment in the army. What was Dierdra Treffry doing here? Had she recognized him? And if she had, would she give him away? If he did not handle himself properly now, he might as well return to England immediately. Noticing the puzzled look in her eyes, he spoke quickly.

"I am happy to see you, Miss Treffry. I was a fellow soldier in your brother's regiment, and you and I have met before. But you were very young, and I imagine you have forgotten that gawky lad, Anthony Dawson." He emphasized the last word slightly.

She looked at him closely. "But you are Anthony . . ."

"Yes," he flashed a quick look at her. "Anthony Dawson, of Bideford."

"Anthony Dawson, of course. Pardon me for not recognizing you at once. It has been such a long time."

Anthony breathed an inward sigh of relief.

"I am the one who would not have recognized you. You were only a child when I saw you last." He turned to Madam Burrington. "At that time I spent a few weeks with Roger at Penzance. This young woman had no interest save running along the beach and waiting for the fishing boats to come in with a load of pilchards, or riding her pony across the Bodmin moor, so fast you would think the devil himself was after her."

Dierdra laughed. "I must have been a frightful tomboy. Roger always said I was more like a brother than a sister."

"He was lucky indeed to have such a delightful brother." Anthony smiled. "I quite envy him."

Dierdra handed the governor a cup of tea. He took a sip and set the cup down on a small table. Then he walked over to the mantel and leaned against it.

"Mr. Dawson," he said, "you can do Madam Burrington a great favor. I know she must be starved for news about London people and fashions."

Madam Burrington was stirring her tea. She looked up.

"I would love to hear, Mr. Dawson. But do not let the governor impose you for a moment. The truth is, he is at least as interested in the doings of London society as I."

The governor frowned and flicked an invisible speck of dust from his sleeve.

"Well now, my dear, Mr. Dawson has not been here long enough to have discovered how very cut off we are from the world. You know yourself there is no real society in North Carolina."

"And I must confess I find it a relief in many ways." Madam Burrington smiled at Anthony. "Whenever we come back from a visit to Virginia, where the people are always giving parties or going to them, I take to my bed for at least a day. I have never seen so much social activity! I come from Scotland, and we lead a rather retired life there."

"I stopped off in Williamsburg for a few days on my way here," Anthony said. "In many ways it seemed much like London in the season."

"Did you meet my good friend William Byrd?" the governor asked. "He is really the greatest of the Virginians."

Anthony shook his head. "Unfortunately, I did not have that pleasure. He was away when I arrived. But I hope to pay another visit to Virginia soon, and I shall certainly try to see him then. Everyone in London speaks highly of him."

Taphy entered.

"Beg pardon, your excellency," he said. "Chief Justice Gale is here. He say he have an appointment with you."

Burrington snapped his fingers. "By God, I had forgotten. I shall have to leave you now, Mr. Dawson. I hope to see you soon again." He turned and left the room.

"I should be going, too," Anthony said. He bowed to Madam Burrington. "Thank you for the tea, Madam."

"I am delighted you came. I, too, shall be looking forward to seeing you soon again. Dierdra, will you please see Mr. Dawson out?"

Dierdra and Anthony walked down the hall in silence. At the door, he said:

"Thank you for not mentioning my name. I could see that you recognized me. But I do not think you were any more surprised to see me than I was to see you. I never knew you had left England."

An expression of sadness crossed her face for a moment. It vanished quickly, and she laughed. "I never knew you had left, either, or that you had changed your name to Dawson."

"Well, now you know both. Perhaps we will be able to spend an hour or two alone, and we can tell each other our stories."

"That sounds delightful. I must confess that mine is rather dull. But I am sure yours is an intrigue—and we Treffrys always love intrigue."

Anthony smiled. "I am sorry to disappoint you so soon after we meet again, but there is very little exciting in my tale."

"I cannot really believe that; Roger always told me that excitement followed wherever you went."

He bowed and kissed her hand. "Well, I shall let you decide for yourself." His smile faded and his expression became serious. "I consider Roger my close friend, and I hope I can say the same thing of his sister."

He stood for a moment on the stoop after the door was closed. It was dusk, and the old lamplighter was making his way across the Green, lighting the candles in the iron lanthorns on the lamp posts. The frosty air danced in their glow.

The day's impressions crowded Anthony's mind; things had been happening since the very moment of his arrival. First, his meeting with the outspoken Edward Moseley. The chances were strong that the Granvilles would not sell their land, no matter what the other Proprietors chose to do. "You know," Lord John had said to him when they were discussing his mission to the New World, "we have a saying in the family that goes back nearly to the Conquest: 'The Granvilles buy land; they never sell it.'" Anthony had, therefore, been glad to see Edward Moseley's reaction; with its indication of support for proprietary government among the settlers. Of course, Moseley's opinion might be his alone. . . .

Then there was the governor. Moseley said Burrington drank too much, but he had not downed his wine with the nervous haste tipplers so often displayed. Anthony had to confess that the man had made a good impression on him. He was suave, polished; he could hold his own in any gathering of London gentlemen. Yet Burrington was not a simple person, by any means. He was a complex character, one that did not yield itself up to immediate understanding. . . .

And then there was Dierdra Treffry. . . . She had grown into a very pretty girl—Black Cornish, with the proud look. He was sure she had the quick, flashing temper of her brother; he hoped she was as loyal. In any event, it was good to know there was an attractive, well-born young woman in Edenton, with whom he could be friendly. Too well born, he suddenly realized, for her work. He would have to find out more about her.

As he made his way slowly across the Green, toward the lights shining in the windows of the King's Arms, Anthony sighed with quiet elation. It seemed to him that his adventure was getting off to an exciting start.

Chapter III

THE COUNTRYSIDE

EARLY ONE AFTERNOON, Anthony and Dick mounted their horses and rode out through the Northern Gate to explore the countryside around Edenton. The hostler had suggested they take the Virginia Road, which ran not far from the Chowan River.

Even though it was late in March, the weather was still cold, and a chill, damp wind blew from the northeast. As they rode along, the two young men could see icy patches dotting the brown, barren earth on either side of the road. The trees had not yet begun to bud; they loomed gaunt and skeletal against the overcast sky. Every once in a while, a rabbit darted out of its burrow and scurried across the road, but except for these little creatures, there were no other signs of life.

"Not a very cheerful sight, is it?" Dick said.

"It must have been a bad winter," Anthony replied. "If it does not warm up soon, the farmers will have a very late planting—which will not please them at all."

"You sound like my father." Dick laughed. "The weather and the crops are his favorite topics of conversation. Except for politics, of course."

But Anthony was not listening.

"I was beginning to believe no one lived here. But now I see a house." He reined in Black Douglas next to a gateway marked by brick posts. At the end of a long, curved drive bordered by maple trees stood a large house. It was obviously not yet finished; the boards were still bare of paint, and planks and carpenters' horses were lying about in front. A small brass plaque had already been attached to the gatepost. On it was the name Enar Peterson.

"It looks as if it will be as handsome as some of the James River mansions," Dick said. "It is much larger than any of the houses we saw from the boat."

Anthony nodded. "We must be near the river, now. I imagine there is a path through this property. But with no one around, I do not think we should ride through."

"There's a bend in the road a while ahead," Dick pointed to the left. "Perhaps it will take us to the river."

The bend brought in view another gateway and a long avenue of bushes, now denuded of greenery. A man astride a brown moor pony was riding out toward the gate. Dick drew Star up close to Black Douglas and whispered excitedly into Anthony's ear.

"I say, Tony, I recognize that man. Captain Blackwell said he was the father of that beautiful blond girl we saw on the dock the other day."

"Hush, he will hear you." Anthony reined in his horse and touched his hat with his riding crop. The man drew near, pulling his forelock.

"Good afternoon, sir," Anthony said. "Can you tell us if there is a path to the river nearby?"

"There is no open path about here, but there is one through my farm." He paused. "You be the young men who came in on the *Flying Fish,* ben't you?" He put his hand behind his ear in order better to catch Anthony's answer.

"Yes, sir. I thought we'd seen you on the dock. My name is Anthony Dawson, and this is my friend, Richard Chapman."

"My name is Owen Killigrew, sir, and this is Lilac Farm." Killigrew dismounted from his pony and opened the wooden gate. "I do not know the name Dawson, but I've seen the name Richard Chapman many a time in my day. There's a shipyard in Appledore, in Devon, owned by a Richard Chapman. It's been there since Elizabeth's time, I'm told."

"And owned by the Chapmans since then," Dick said. "I've never seen it, myself, but I've heard about it from my father. Those Chapmans are connections of ours, he says. But we have been in this country for quite a while. My father was born here. Our home is in Virginia, at Bermuda Hundred."

Killigrew nodded. "There's good, rich land along the James River." He turned to Anthony. "And you, sir? Be you Virginian, too?"

"No, I come from England. From Cornwall, originally, although I've lived in London a great deal."

"So you be a Cornishman. I be Cornish, myself. Ride in, gentlemen. Ride in my gate, and I will show you the path to the river, through Lilac Farm." He fastened the gate after them, and mounted his pony again.

Tamar was gazing listlessly out of the kitchen window when her father, with Anthony and Dick, rode by on the way to the river. A wide smile brightened her discontented face, and she wheeled to face her mother, a plump, pleasant-faced woman who was kneading dough on a board.

"Do you know who just passed? That young man I saw when the *Flying Fish* came in. He and his friend. They were with Father."

Mistress Killigrew looked up. "Oh, that's nice, dear."

"Can I invite them for tea?" Tamar spoke in a rush. "I'll have to fix the table. Phenny never gets anything right. I will never understand why you can't teach her to lay a table properly." She smoothed her golden hair and pinched her cheeks, to bring the color to them.

"Of course we can ask them for tea. Go and set the table to your liking." Mistress Killigrew's voice was placid. "I'll have Phenny lay a fire in the hall, so that we will have a warm place to sit. The parlor is much too cold these days."

Mistress Killigrew watched her daughter run out of the room. She sighed and shook her head. Tamar was eighteen years old, and still such a baby! Always dreaming, or moping about, or turning over the linens in her marriage chest, or spinning stories about the handsome, well-born young man her heart yearned after. Things had been different when she was young. But what could a body do, when Killigrew doted on the girl, and could refuse her nothing. She looked just like his dead sister, he said. That was true enough; Mistress Killigrew only hoped the resemblance did not go too deep. . . .

She called to Phenny. "Would you get some gooseberry preserves from the locked cupboard, Phenny? And see if the Devonshire cream is ready. Two young men will be coming for tea. They are with Mr. Killigrew now. I've a mind to give them gooseberry tarts for a sweet."

Phenny, the bondwoman, was tempted to refuse. She had made the gooseberry preserves herself, and she was loath to set them out for the young folk, who did not really appreciate what they were eating. But she got the keys from their hiding place in the old blue Canton teapot in the pantry, and set the jar down on the kitchen table with a bang.

"You should save it for real company, mistress."

Mistress Killigrew was accustomed to the bondwoman's reluctance to part with the preserves, and it took more than that to upset her tranquility. She only smiled.

"This *is* real company. These young men are newcomers. They came in on the *Flying Fish* yesterday. Mistress Tamar saw them. Would you lay a fire in the hall? We'll have our tea out there."

As Phenny left, Tamar came hurrying back. She spoke breathlessly.

"The table is all set. I'll run upstairs and change, and then go down and invite them for tea. I imagine Father has taken them to look at the river. They were riding in that direction."

"I have not seen you so excited since your father bought you that gold locket."

The girl threw her arms around her mother and kissed her. "I wasn't half as excited then!" Her tawny eyes sparkled. "I shall wear my brown wool; everyone says it is my most flattering dress."

"Be sure to take a cape with you. 'Tis cold outside," Mistress Killigrew called as her daughter dashed out of the room.

Tamar did not hear; she was already on her way upstairs. In her room, she changed her clothes hastily, leaving her discarded garments in a heap on the floor. She drew a comb through her blond locks, inspected herself in the mirror, flung a cape over her shoulders, and dashed downstairs and out of the house.

She slowed her pace to a sedate walk as, crossing the barn lot, she saw two horses tied to the hitching post and, looking ahead, caught sight of her father and his guests standing on the high bank of the river. As she approached, she could hear one of the young men speaking.

"Does the river ever freeze all the way across?"

"It doesn't happen very often," Killigrew replied. "The last time was in '17. That was a bad winter, very bad." He shook his head in recollection. "It was terrible cold, and the Tuscarora Indians rose up that year, too, and they killed some of our best men."

By now, Tamar was not far away.

"You must not say things like that, Father! You will frighten the young men away."

The three men turned to face her. Dick's grin stretched almost from ear to ear.

"There's my daughter, Tamar," Yeoman Killigrew said. "This is Mr. Dawson and Mr. Chapman. What brings you down here, daughter?"

"Good afternoon, sirs. Welcome to Lilac Farm." Tamar curtsied. Her voice was demure. "Mother asked me to come," she continued. "She saw you passing, and she asked me to invite the gentlemen for tea."

"Now, your mother knows I would have done that myself. You'll catch your death with only that thin cape on. You'd best hurry back to the house. We will be along in a little while."

"It *is* cold," Dick said. His shiver was exaggerated. "I'm a little chilly myself."

"Would you like to come back to the house with me now?" Tamar's voice was sedate, but an impish grin crossed her face.

"If you don't mind, sir?" Dick turned to Yeoman Killigrew.

"As long as you take care of my golden girl. She's my pride and joy."

"My father is my greatest admirer," Tamar said.

"That may have been true once," Dick said as they walked off, "but no longer."

Yeoman Killigrew watched them leave and then turned back to Anthony.

"Would you like to go in now, sir?"

"No indeed. You had just begun to tell me about the river. I am most interested. I'm thinking of taking up land here."

"Well, now, let me see." Killigrew gazed out over the choppy water. " 'Tis not very wide here," his eyes strayed to the great pocosin at the other side of the stream, where the cypress trees marched straight into the water. "But it's two miles from shore to shore in Bertie Precinct. 'Tis a purely beautiful sight in summertime. South is the confluence with the Roanoke River, at the head of Albemarle Sound. And there," he pointed north, "is the island where Sir Richard Granville's men had trouble with the Chowanoke Indians. 'Tis the legend here that Sir Richard Granville, the great sea lord of Elizabeth, sent ships up our river long ago, in 1585. The seamen camped on this land, and their fight with the Indians was at the far end of this farm." He smiled meditatively. " 'Tis strange, is it not, sir, that men of Devon and Cornwall first looked on this land, and now a Cornishman owns it?"

A surge of pride swept through Anthony, but he kept his voice calm. "It proves that the world is small, sir, very small."

Killigrew pointed upstream. "Across the narrow, by the Reach, are our nets. My son, Allin, is out there now, pounding in fresh stakes. 'Tis lonely work, but he likes it. He's a solitary one, my Allin, and a great thinker." A troubled expression momentarily darkened his cheerful face. "Anyway, that work must be done, so it's fine he enjoys it. The herring run will come soon, and we must be ready. Fishing is a money crop for us planters. We sell fresh to the markets and we ship to Virginia. We smoke fish and salt fish for winter food." He sighed with satisfaction. "The water of this river is almost as important to us as the land we are standing on."

The two men stood silently for a moment, and then Killigrew spoke again.

"I tell you, sir, I feel downright proud to know this is my land.

And it's virgin land, sir, all of it. In the old country, there's nothing to compare with it. But the thing I like most is that it belongs to me. I've always farmed land, and so has my family, for generations. But we could never have owned it. And here I am, with near five hundred acres." He looked searchingly at Anthony. "I suppose you would not understand, sir. Begging your pardon, but you look to me to be a gentleman, sir, and you must be used to owning property."

Anthony smiled. "My family does own land. But in England, I never thought very much about it. I can see that things are different here. Perhaps because it is virgin land, and a man can see it change and develop under his eyes."

"That's it, sir, that's it," Killigrew nodded enthusiastically. "Why, I've still got three hundred acres that is just timber and pocosin. But even so, I've got my eye on a hundred more, up against my north pasture. It belongs to Mr. Moseley, the surveyor-general, but he has taken up more open land than he can do the work on, and he probably will not be able to hold it according to the law. It will come up for sale in the autumn court session."

"So that's the way you get land. Not by grants."

"Oh, you can get it by grants, too, if you have influence with the Lords Proprietors, in London. That's the way most of the soundside planters got their acreage. But there's still another way. They give you one hundred acres for yourself, another hundred for every man you import, and fifty more for every woman. That's how I got my land. My grandfather's seventy-five-year lease in Kilkhampton ran out, and the owner of the property did not want to renew it. I saw one of the advertisements, and decided to come here. I brought five people with me—three indentured men and two women—and so I got five hundred acres."

Anthony was looking out over the river. After a silence, he spoke.

"Yes, I think I would like to have some land here."

Killigrew's eyes lit up with interest. "You will never regret it. I know of two places already lapsed. Three hundred acres on the river, by the bend, that was seated by Moseley. Nothing has been done to improve it. And there's another place in Pasquotank. Belongs to a man named Matthew Caswell. Four hundred and eight acres."

"Why doesn't Caswell improve it?"

Killigrew shrugged his shoulders. "Caswell has a number of plantations across the sound. Doubtless he took this land hoping to make some money. But Pasquotank is slow in developing, and the land is free now." He sighed. "That is my only objection to the planters and the gentry here. They are impatient. They snap up the land and they do nothing with it. Sometimes I think they be more interested in speculating than in developing the land." He pointed a finger at Anthony. "And that is where the future lies, sir, in the land. In the twenty years I have been here, I have seen it change so you would hardly recognize it, and things are not moving half so fast as they should. If we only had more honest, hard-working Cornishmen . . ."

"Why are things slow? And why don't people come?" Killigrew's opinion, Anthony was sure, would be valuable. His honesty shone through every word he spoke. This was the best of the yeoman stock: shrewd, intelligent, with a real love of the land. It was impossible not to like and respect him.

"Ah, that is a big question, sir. Different people say there are different reasons. Some blame the governors; there's always been a lot of trouble with them. And people hear about it over in England. I heard things myself, before I came. Others say things would be better here if we were a Crown colony." He paused. "We had better go in now, sir. 'Tis time for tea." He turned to the river, put his cupped hand to his mouth, and hallooed loudly. "Allin, Allin, come ye in for tea, now." Then he turned back to Anthony and started to lead him toward the house.

"You were telling me why North Carolina has not done too well," Anthony said as they crossed the barn lot.

"Well, sir," Killigrew's voice was reflective. "There's another thing people mention. Our shore line. It is difficult for the large ocean-going vessels to put into port here. The *Flying Fish* is quite a small boat, you know. But the bigger ships, that can carry a heavy cargo, cannot navigate past the long sand banks that shut us off from the ocean. That works all manner of hardships on us. For instance, our tobacco is the very best. But it has to be shipped through Virginia, where every pound is taxed. By the time it gets abroad, its price is much higher than the Virginia leaf." He shook his head. "Aye. There be many thorny problems, sir. But we will not solve them now. And here is the house." He nodded toward the long, low, double-galleried building in front of them.

They entered to find Mistress Killigrew in the hall, throwing a stick of wood on the fire. She turned and brushed her hands on the white apron that covered her green cloth skirt. She wore a white mull scarf and a fluted mull cap, in the old Cornish style. She smiled at her guest and made him welcome.

"It is not often that we have visitors from abroad. Your friend, Mr. Chapman, told me you were straight from London, sir."

"But from Cornwall originally, Mother," Yeoman Killigrew said. He looked around. "Where is Mr. Chapman?"

"Tamar has taken him out on the gallery," Mistress Killigrew replied. "Ah, here is Owen." A husky, blond young man of about twenty entered the room. "This is our son Owen, Mr. Dawson. Mr. Dawson and his friend Mr. Chapman just arrived here."

Owen bobbed his head. "Welcome to North Carolina," he said. "Is your friend with you today?"

Anthony smiled. "It is a pleasure to meet you. Yes, my friend is here. He is with your sister, I'm told."

"Oh, he must be the young man who . . ." Owen fell silent in response to his mother's warning glance.

"Why don't you take Mr. Dawson up to your room, Owen?" Mistress Killigrew put a hand under her son's elbow. "He may want to tidy up a bit after his ride."

The others were already seated at the table when Anthony and Owen returned. Mistress Killigrew motioned them to their places. Phenny came in, bearing a platter of Cornish meat pasties. Her calico skirts rustled importantly. A smile had broken through her somber face, and her black eyes snapped with pride. Like Mistress Killigrew, she relished fine company, and the look she had stolen at Anthony through the kitchen window gave weight to Tamar's assertion that these young men were real gentry. She stood quietly, and with dignity, holding the large platter in her outstretched arms, as Yeoman Killigrew bowed his head in prayer.

"May the good Lord bless these folk and give them grace in the New World."

As he was speaking, a dark-haired young man arrived and slipped quietly into the one vacant seat. Anthony could not avoid raising his eyes. This must be Killigrew's son Allin. But how did such a Black Cornishman come into such a blond family?

His difference from the others was all the more conspicuous by his taciturnity during tea. For the others it was a gay meal, the elders giving over to youth. Tamar quizzed Dick and Anthony at length about the reigning London beauties.

"I've seen portraits of some of them," she said. "They are so much more beautiful than any of us here."

"Oh, that's not true!" Dick's voice was so earnest that Anthony could barely restrain a smile. "I cannot understand why it is," the Virginian went on, "that we Americans always think the people in England so much more elegant than we. Before I went abroad, I was afraid I would feel most uncomfortable there, and that everyone would soon discover I was only a country bumpkin." He laughed. "But I soon found out that we can be quite as elegant as our English cousins."

Allin raised his dark eyes from his plate for the first time.

"But only if we have their advantages." His voice was quiet, almost expressionless.

Yeoman Killigrew took a gulp of his hot tea and wiped his mouth on the back of his hand. Then, suddenly remembering, he picked up the fringed linen napkin and glanced up to see if anyone had noticed the lapse of the manners his wife had taught him. But, to his relief, he found that no one was looking at him. He spoke hastily.

"Now, then, Allin, you know I've been after you to go up to William and Mary College. There are advantages to be had there, I am sure. And I know a serious boy like you could make good use of them."

"There probably are advantages. But they will not help me to be a better yeoman. And that is what I am, after all, a yeoman."

Owen looked at him with pride. "And a very good one. Why, do you know," he went on, turning to Anthony, "we were the only folk on the river last year who made anything from the herring run. No one but us had their stakes in on time, or their nets mended and ready. So they lost half the run. Allin knew the run would be early, and he warned them. But they would not listen."

A wry smile crossed Allin's face. "And you think if I'd gone to college they would have?"

"They would have if you were more sociable," Tamar put in. She turned to Dick. "That brother of mine is the most solitary man in Chowan Precinct, and the shyest. If he is not out working, he has his head buried in some silly book or other. I never saw such a one for reading."

Allin blushed, but he spoke quietly. "You make it sound as if there was something wrong about reading."

"Well, when you do it so much," Tamar said. "And such dull books—all about science and philosophy and things like that."

"I cannot see anything wrong with that at all," Anthony put in. "I think it is admirable."

Dick laughed. "I do, too. But I must admit I've never been much of a one for reading. You would have a fine time at William and Mary, though, Mr. Killigrew, if you are so devoted to books. The men are expected to do a great deal of reading there, as I found out to my sorrow. I don't think I have read as much in my whole life as I did in the years I was in college."

"Oh, were you there?" Tamar looked from Dick to her brother. "Then you must go, Allin."

"Allin shall go if he wants, and not if he doesn't," Mistress Killigrew said in her placid voice. "We shall be satisfied with him whatever he does."

At that moment, Phenny came in with the gooseberry tarts and a china bowl of Devonshire cream. As she set them on the table, Anthony rose, made a deep bow to Mistress Killigrew, and kissed her hand.

"Madam, your meal has been a delight in every respect. And

now, to top it all off with the fine cream of Devon! If I had known I could find that here, I would have come to North Carolina a long time ago."

Mistress Killigrew's smooth cheeks grew pink with pleasure.

"Mistress Peterson lays claim to being the best housekeeper in the precinct," Yeoman Killigrew said, smiling. "But I don't believe she can make a tart to compare with my wife's, and I am sure she does not even know about Devonshire cream."

"Now, then, Owen, you be fair." Mistress Killigrew's blush deepened. "What would they know about Devonshire cream in Maryland? Patience Peterson comes from there, you know," she explained to her guests.

"Peterson?" Anthony's tone was inquiring. "Isn't that the name we saw on the gate-post a short way up the road?"

Tamar nodded, her brown eyes sparkling. "And did you see the house? It is going to be just beautiful! When I am married, that's the kind of house I want to have."

"Lots of houses in Virginia are even bigger and more beautiful," Dick said.

"Really? Allin, you simply have to go to William and Mary. Then I could come to visit you and see those houses."

Dick smiled. "You could visit with my family, too."

Tamar looked at him from under demurely lowered lids. "If I went to Virginia, I might meet a young man and fall in love with him. And we would live in one of those big houses."

Dick looked at her earnestly. "I don't see why you should not marry a Virginian. I think it a good idea, myself."

Chapter IV

THE GOVERNESS

DIERDRA TREFFRY sat at her dressing table brushing her heavy dark hair. When she had finished, she plaited it into two braids and wound them around her head like a coronet. The reflection of her face was distorted in the wavy glass of the mirror.

"I look like a witch," she said, aloud. Her hand flew up to cover her red lips and she quickly made a sign with her fingers to ward off evil. One did not talk of witches or devils, for fear of a visitation. Her old Cornish nurse had told her that, and she still half-believed it.

She stood up, tall and slender, in her stays and three muslin petticoats. She slipped a sprigged kalikut dress over her head, taking care not to disturb her braids. Next came a muslin tucker, to fill in over her neck and shoulders.

" 'Tis a pity," she murmured, studying her white neck.

Her brother Roger would have laughed to see her, so demure, so quiet, and he would have teased her as he recalled the days when they used to race over the wild moors on their tough little ponies, or swim boldly in the waters of the Lizard. A true Treffry she was, spirited and zestful. But now she had pressed herself into the mold set out for governesses in the best English county families. . . .

Certainly, at the time it had seemed the best thing to do. And even now she was far from sorry. After all, Roger was committed to the army for the next six years, and those last months in England, before she had left, had been worse than lonely. Her London aunt had been wonderful, had tried to comfort her in every way, and to keep her from brooding and unhappiness. She was grateful, and had done her best to smile and to seem her usual cheerful self. But the shock had been too much: her parents and her fiancé, the three dearest people in the world, drowned at the same time, in a freak storm that had sunk the boat on which they were returning to England from Spain, where her father had been the British Consul and her fiancé his secretary. She herself had escaped death with them only because she had gone back home a month earlier, to purchase her trousseau for the wedding that would now never take place.

And so, when she met her aunt's friend, Madam Burrington, and learned that this frail Scottish lady was having difficulty in finding a governess for her children when they took up their home in the New World, Dierdra had eagerly volunteered her services. It might not be the conventional thing for a girl of her class to do. But the Treffrys had never been conventional. And it would be an adventure.

Of course, there had not been very much adventure so far—unless you wanted to include the governor's occasional bouts with the bottle. Dierdra still could not understand why this polished gentleman should so often lose himself in liquor. Sometimes drink made him jovial; then it was not too bad. But at other times he became abusive, and then only his wife could hold him in check.

Dierdra shook her head, sighed, and sat down on an ottoman to lace up her soft, flat kid slippers and to tie the ribbons around her slim ankles. When she stood up, she surveyed herself once more in the looking glass.

"Demure, very demure," she whispered. And suddenly she raised her skirts ankle high and whirled about in a dance.

She still had some free time; last night Madam Burrington had said she was going to take the children for a drive that morning and Dierdra would have a few hours to herself. The dark-haired girl sat down at the little desk under the window, took her journal out of the locked drawer in which she kept it, and started to write. She had not touched it in some days, and there was much to report.

29th March, 1725. The other afternoon, the governor had a visitor, and after they had talked for a while, he brought him in to have tea with Madam Burrington and me. He was introduced as Anthony Dawson, but when I took a good look I could see he was not Dawson at all, but Anthony Granville, a good friend of my brother Roger's. There is certainly something mysterious going on, for when I looked at him, on the verge of speaking his true name, he cut me off in such a way that it was clear he did not want Burrington to know who he really is.

He is an extremely handsome and self-confident young man. A trifle arrogant—or perhaps it is only that he is an aristocrat, and used to having his own way. I have met several young men like him in London, but there are none here, young or old. Not even Chief Justice Gale, who is every bit as well born as he, has Granville's air of assurance. It is hard to picture him staying here in this little village, or to imagine why he came in the first place. This quiet, simple life hardly seems the one he would choose. He must be up to something. Roger always said that Anthony was born for intrigue. I am bursting with curiosity. Thank goodness, before he left the other evening, the mysterious Mr. Dawson promised to tell me his secret. I can hardly wait.

A knock on the door interrupted her. She slipped the journal back into its drawer and locked it before she answered.

The children stood in the hall, their faces downcast.

"Good morning," Dierdra said. "What makes you look so unhappy?"

"Mother has a headache," William said, "and cannot take us for a drive."

Ann interrupted. "But she said we could ask if you would mind please taking us for a walk along the quay, so we could watch the fishing boats."

"I would love to take you for a walk. You run to nurse and fetch your coats, and I will go in and see if there is anything I can do for your mother. We can have a contest to see who is ready first."

The children scampered off, and Dierdra walked down the hall to Madam Burrington's room.

Poor thing! she thought. She gets the headache so often.

The elder woman did not look well. She was pale, and her pallor was intensified by the grey streaks in the brown hair that tumbled loose over her shoulders, and by the feverish light in her dark eyes. Her skin seemed to be drawn tightly across her delicate features. But she insisted she only needed rest.

"The biggest help will be to know that the children are having a good time with you." She smiled weakly. "And I hope you are not too disappointed at losing your morning. I'm sure I will feel better after lunch, and I have promised to take them for their drive later on. That will give you back the time I am stealing now."

"Now, you must not worry about me or the children. We will have a fine time. I am much more concerned about you."

"If that is your concern, you can go with a light heart. I promise I will be entirely well by the time you come back."

Dierdra and the children walked down to the water and sat on a wooden bench between the docks. The fishing boats were coming in, their sails furled. The air was full of noise and confusion: boats sliding against mooring spars, lines being thrown, loud voices calling, fishmongers waiting to carry away the morning's catch to their shops in Cheapside. Dierdra felt a swift surge of nostalgia. It was like home, only here the waters were quiet and no cliffs rose out of the sea.

"Oh, see the fish squirming," Ann cried out. "They're not dead, the poor things," and she began to cry.

"No matter, little Ann," Dierdra said soothingly, as she dried her tears. "They soon will be dead and made ready for the table. That is what fish are for, to give us good, tasty food."

"I thought they were made to swim in the sea," Ann sobbed.

William looked at his sister scornfully. "What a silly you are! Isn't it better to be eaten by us than to be gobbled by a shark or a monstrous whale?"

Ann stopped crying and grabbed hold of William's hand, and the two ran down to the water's edge, the better to watch the unloading.

"A very sensible young man, Master Burrington. That was a fine solution."

Dierdra looked up into the sharp eyes of Anthony Dawson. He was dressed for riding, a crop in his hand. He smiled warmly, looked at her inquiringly, and, as she extended her arm in a gesture of welcome, sat down on the bench beside her.

"I saw you crossing the Green with the children and came at once to thank you."

"To thank me?"

"Yes. For the other day. You did not say my name or ask a single question."

"You have a right to use any name you like," she said, hoping her voice masked her curiosity as well as did her impersonal words.

His eyes twinkled. "I do have a right to Dawson. It is my mother's name." He broke into a grin. "And if I had wanted to be really mysterious, I could have used my grandmother's name and been a Spanish adventurer."

"You had a Spanish grandmother?"

"Indeed I did. My mother's mother. And think how much more romantic I should have been if I had used her name! But no matter," his voice grew serious. "It was most discreet of you to remain quiet, and I am really grateful. I am only afraid that when I tell you my secret, you will be disappointed to discover how small it is."

"I'm sure it cannot be too small. But please do not feel under obligation to tell me anything you would prefer me not to know. I shall be perfectly happy to leave things as they are, and to know you only as Anthony Dawson."

"Miss Treffry . . ." A puzzled look had come into his face. "Now I do not know what to say. I would like you to know. There is no one else here in Edenton whose friendship I value as much. After all, you and I have known each other for many years, and I am sure we understand one another. But I do not wish to impose on you . . ." His voice trailed off.

Dierdra sat silent, her eyes on the glistening water ahead of them. She did not want to urge him. After a moment, Anthony stood up.

"I should feel foolish keeping something from Roger's sister," he said. "And it is really very simple. I have come over to look into things for my family. The Granvilles are among the Proprietors of North Carolina, and I want to find out how our property is being managed and what kind of tenants we have. But when people are being inspected, they put on their best manners. If they were to know who I really am, the folk here would not be natural with me."

"No, I suppose not," Dierdra's expression was thoughtful. She had forgotten the Granvilles' connection with North Carolina, and now that it had been recalled to her, she was not sure whether Anthony's presence boded good or ill for the province. It was not easy to believe that this London aristocrat would have sympathy either for the people or for their erratic governor.

"But not knowing who I am," Anthony went on, "they are as open and honest as can be. Governor Burrington seems to be a gentleman. And the other day I met a perfectly splendid yeoman. Killigrew. Do you know him?"

Dierdra nodded.

"He and his wife are fine people. Simple and hard-working. Just the kind of folk for a new land like this. If all the North Carolinians are like the Killigrews, I would say my family need have no concern about its tenants."

Dierdra was relieved at these words. "I am extremely fond of the Killigrews myself," she said.

"Their daughter is a pretty thing," he said. "She seems a little silly, but I suppose silliness is the privilege of young girls. And my friend Dick Chapman does not think her silly at all. He is quite smitten with her."

"Is he the brown-haired young man?" Dierdra asked.

"Yes. Blue-eyed and a little shorter than I."

"I thought so. The children and I met Tamar when we went down to see the *Flying Fish* dock." Dierdra smiled. "She seemed rather taken with him, too."

Anthony shook his head. "I thought I noticed that when we

were out at Lilac Farm. Well, I hope things do not go too far. They certainly cannot be married. I met Dick's father in Virginia on our way here, and he is not the kind of man who would want his son connected with a yeoman's family."

Dierdra's relief gave way to a swift surge of anger. "I think you have forgotten what country you are in, Mr. Dawson. In one generation, a yeoman from Devon can become gentry here."

"I suppose so." Anthony rubbed the side of his nose. "I fear it will not be easy for me to become used to that idea. When the Killigrews started talking about sending their dark-haired son to college . . ."

Dierdra turned on him, her eyes flashing. "Allin, I suppose you mean. And why should he not go to college if he wishes to? I think it a very good idea. I am glad you told me about it. Allin is very intelligent. Much more intelligent than many of the London dandies I have met."

Anthony laughed. "You look just like Roger now. I should have remembered the Treffry temper." He paused; when he spoke again, it was in a conciliatory tone. "Allin did seem intelligent. Perhaps in time I will come around to your point of view. I can see that you have become a real American. And that reminds me: I never did find out what brought you here."

Slowly, Dierdra told him. When she had finished, he took her hand in his.

"I am very sorry," he said. An expression of pity crossed his face. "I had not heard. It has been so long since I've seen Roger. What a terrible thing!" He shook his head and sat silent for a moment. Then he smiled. "I hope that one afternoon, when you have some free time, you will come out for a ride with me. We can gallop, as I remember you did across the Bodmin moors."

"I would love that." Dierdra's voice was wistful. "I do miss the wildness of my youth." She laughed. "Sometimes I find it difficult to believe that this prim governess is really Dierdra Treffry."

"Prim? That is hardly the word I would have used. Proud, perhaps, and a true lady. Perhaps you were a tomboy once. But tomboys often grow into ladies, and when they do, they make the most delightful ones."

Dierdra felt a blush rise to her cheeks. She turned quickly, to conceal it.

"I feel I shall have to leave you now, Mr. Dawson. I must take the children home. And I hope you will not worry about your secret. I promise it will be perfectly safe with me."

At three o'clock that afternoon, Dierdra, dressed in her dark green riding habit, asked Taphy to send for a horse. She was going to ride out to Lilac Farm.

She always enjoyed visiting the Killigrews—the sturdy old yeoman and his comfortable wife reminded her of the folk she had known in her own Cornwall, and Tamar and Owen were gay and cheerful and good-hearted. But today she had a special reason for making the trip. She wished to talk to Allin.

She had not known, until Anthony told her, that Yeoman Killigrew wanted to send his older son to college; the more she thought about it, the better the idea sounded. Why had it never occurred to her? More than any of the other young men she had met in North Carolina, Allin seemed cut out for the role of a cultivated, educated gentleman.

Dierdra had been drawn to this silent lad from the first time she met him, and although they had never been intimates, she felt sure Allin liked her, too. She found his reticence attractive; her fiancé, too, had been quiet and somewhat shy. Yet Allin remained something of a puzzle to her. His reserve and studiousness contrasted as sharply with the easy, outgoing warmth of the rest of his family as did his shock of unruly black hair with their blondness. It was hard to believe that such utterly different people were so closely related. Of course, if Allin were to go to college—and Dierdra hoped she could persuade him to—he would be even more unlike the rest of the Killigrews. But he owed it to himself to take advantage of the opportunity. Dierdra hoped her words would have some influence on him.

She reached the stable yard to find the groom holding the reins of a young bay stallion. The boy spoke apologetically.

"I hope this feller be all right, miss. The governor, he take his horse, and Mr. Elton, he take another. Black Knight got a sore foot, and Millie be about to foal. So that leaves only this rascal."

"Do you think I can handle him, Tom?"

"Yes'm, if you be careful. You ride better than anyone here, even the governor. You have a gentle hand. Ride him on the snaffle, please. He go plumb crazy when he feel the curb."

For the first two miles, Dierdra had a difficult time. The stallion pulled and danced, shied and ran, his silky neck lathered with white foam. She did her best to calm him, but it was no simple task.

"Easy, now, lad, easy. We have more than four miles before you get a drink of water and a bit of hay. Steady, now, steady. It's only a snake crossing the road. Nothing to be nervous about."

When he had finally settled down to a quiet, steady trot, Dierdra looked about her. She loved the open fields beyond the town. Now that the weather had become milder, the earth was turning from winter brown to tender green as the delicate grass shoots pierced its crust.

When she turned into Lilac Farm, she saw a horse tied to the rack. A bond servant, old Enoch, came to take her animal.

" 'Pears like he's been running some, miss. He be all of a lather, and sweating fit to kill."

Dierdra laughed. "I had a hard time holding him down, Enoch. He certainly wanted his head."

"He be young. Young uns always want their head—animals and humans alike. But he be no ladylike horse, miss." He led the stallion off, shaking his grey head in disapproval.

Dierdra ran up to the house and banged on the brass knocker. Tamar opened the door.

"Oh, Dierdra! I am so glad to see you. Dick Chapman is here. He is that handsome young man I saw on the dock."

"I heard you had met him." Dierdra was taking off her little riding hat, with its long blue plume. She stood before the small oval mirror, framed in gilt, that hung above a narrow table in the hall. "I met his friend Mr. Dawson this morning, and he told me."

"Mr. Dawson is very elegant." Tamar stood on tiptoe, looking over Dierdra's shoulder into the mirror. She smoothed her blond hair as she spoke. "Mr. Chapman is even handsomer than I thought at first. And I think he liked me, too."

"Mr. Dawson had that same impression," said Dierdra as the two girls moved through the great room on to the gallery.

The men rose as the young women entered. Dierdra greeted Mistress Killigrew and smiled at her host. After she had said a few words to the brothers, she turned to Dick.

"You are Mr. Dawson's friend, Mr. Chapman. I am delighted to meet you."

"Do you know Tony?" A smile lit up Dick's face. "I admire him tremendously."

"So does my brother Roger, who is a good friend of his. They served in the army together, and Roger says that Anthony is one of the bravest men he has ever met."

Mistress Killigrew rang for Phenny, who brought in a place setting and a chair for Dierdra. She sat down between Allin and Owen. When Yeoman Killigrew had said grace, Phenny filled the cups with tea and passed around the freshly baked meat pasties.

"When I was taking the children back from their walk this morning," Dierdra said, "Mr. Castleton, the barber, told me that a merchant would be coming here in a few days. He is from far away, I hear, and he has bales of satins and kalikuts and a hundred other things."

"What name does he bear, do you know?" Yeoman Killigrew asked.

Dierdra picked up her tea cup. "Ali Hassan. Mr. Castleton says that his bazaar is like a breath of the East."

"Ali Hassan!" Mistress Killigrew exclaimed. "How fine that he comes again. I'm fair put to have a good meal cooked for want of pots and pans."

"And we need bridles and some leather goods," Owen put in.

"I've a mind to see if he has any good Turkey carpets," Killigrew said to his wife. "You've been honing for some for years."

"I don't give that for pots or pans or bridles," Tamar announced, pouting prettily. "What I want is lots of pretty goods for dresses. And maybe some beads."

"And you shall have all you want," her father said.

Dierdra glanced at Allin, who had not yet spoken.

"You must want something from Ali Hassan's treasures," she said to him. "What is it, I wonder?"

"My father and Owen seem to have mentioned everything we need."

Dierdra laughed. "I was not thinking of necessities, but of something you would want for yourself."

"Oh!" Allin's face grew thoughtful. "Well, let me see. If the merchant had books . . ." He smiled. "I know what I would like. To talk to him. When he was here last, I knew nothing about his part of the world. But since then I have read a little, and learned something about it. There were many famous philosophers and thinkers in the East. One man, for instance, a Persian astronomer named Omar Khayyam. If the merchant could tell me something more about him . . ."

Owen laughed. "I have never seen such a one for learning and books. Now, what good will some old Persian's ideas about the heavens do you?"

"A great deal of good, Owen," Dierdra said. "The heavens have a lot to do with the things that happen to us."

"You mean our fate is in the stars?" Tamar asked.

Allin smiled. "Probably not in the way you mean, Tamar. But we farmers depend a great deal on the heavens. We make up our calendars from them, and know when to expect the tides . . ."

"Well, anyway, you can see that Ali Hassan has something for everyone!" Owen's laugh was infectious.

After tea, the young folk walked down to the boathouse, to see the first day's catch being dried. The sun lay along the horizon, and across the river, the trees of the great pocosin cut sharply into the golden sky.

"Let's row out to the fishing boat," Tamar said. "The water is so beautiful and still."

"Why not sail up to the entrance to Rocahock Creek? I have time before dark." Owen looked at the others inquiringly.

"Oh, yes. That's even prettier. And very romantic." Tamar darted a glance at Dick.

He smiled. "I say Rocahock Creek."

At the dock, which smelled of wet wood and fish, Owen untied a large boat, while Allin placed in it the mast and sail he had brought from the loft. When the boat was ready to pull out, Dierdra spoke.

"Do you think it will be overloaded with all of us?"

Allin looked at her. "I suppose it might be." He hesitated for a moment. "Would you like to come with me in the canoe?"

Dierdra smiled. "That would be very pleasant."

"We'll go ahead, then," Owen called, as he took up the oars. Dick handed Tamar into the boat. A short distance from the shore, they caught a southwest breeze. Owen stepped the mast into the thwart and ran up the small square sail.

Allin had disappeared. Presently he came out of the boathouse with a canoe. He got in and poled it around to where Dierdra was standing.

"Mind you step in the center, lest you upset the canoe," he said, as he extended a hand to help her in.

"I have known how to get into a boat ever since I was a child," she replied, smiling. "I went out often with the fishermen in Cornwall."

From her seat in the canoe, Dierdra could not see Allin. But she was intensely aware of his presence, and she sat silent, wondering how to broach the subject that was on her mind.

The sun, now low, was flooding the great river with molten gold. Fish jumped from the water, lured by the dragonflies skimming along the surface. So gentle was the movement of the little canoe that its passing did not disturb the waterfowl, standing at the edge of the dark cypress swamp. The rhythm of the dipping paddle was even; its faint plash as it cut the water only intensified the stillness around them. Dierdra closed her eyes and breathed in deeply the delicate scents carried on the quiet evening breeze. When she opened them, she saw that the canoe had entered a swamp, one of those small streams, canopied over by the branches of trees, whose waters were sweet and black and full of mystery.

The boat scraped onto the shore, and Dierdra caught a flash of white against the dark water as a flock of egrets rose from the stream and flew into the blackness of the swamp.

Allin stepped out of the canoe. "Come," he said, holding out his strong, brown hand, "come."

As he pushed the small boat up onto the beach, out of the reach of the water, Dierdra looked around her. She was standing on what seemed to be a platform of hard-trampled earth that gave way to a tangle of thorn bushes. Grapevines fell from the cedar and pine and cypress trees around them. At the edge of the clearing was a cone-shaped building, made of branches and rushes. In front of it were a crude log table and a couple of benches.

She turned inquiringly to Allin.

"An old Indian camp," he said, as he sat down on one of the benches. "There is a town further up. They say it goes back to 1585."

"It is a wonderful spot," Dierdra spoke softly. The egrets had flown only a short distance into the swamp; she could see them now, some standing in the black water, others perched on the bare branches of a dead tree that tipped crazily into the creek. The motionless birds formed a strange picture, grotesque and eerie.

She wondered what was going on in Allin's mind. Somewhere beneath this impassive façade, she felt sure, deep emotion and deep sensitivity were hidden. Nothing could mask his fine looks. His features were almost classic. His black hair lay in unruly curls on his strong, bronzed neck. His shoulders were wide and muscular under his worn leathern jerkin. His long legs were strong, too. How elegant he would look in a brocaded coat, satin buckles and silk stockings!

She sat down on the bench beside him. "You must have read my mind," she said, smiling. "How did you know I wanted to talk with you alone?"

He looked at her from under quizzical eyebrows. "I did not know. But I thought you would like to see this old spot."

"I am delighted we came here. Allin . . ." She paused. Then, taking a deep breath, she spoke rapidly. "I hope you will not take this amiss. But I am concerned about your future. It seems a shame for you to be only a yeoman."

"Only a yeoman? But that is what I want to be. As fine a yeoman as my father."

"Oh, your father is a fine yeoman—and a fine person, too." Dierdra's voice was soft. "I respect him a great deal. But you are different from him and the rest of your family in many ways."

"No," Allin said, his eyes averted. "They are my family, and we are all alike. He's a yeoman, and I am a yeoman's son."

"Allin," Dierdra laid a tentative hand on his shoulder. "You talk as if you were still in England, where people stay all their lives in the classes they were born into. Things are different here."

"Are they?" He turned his piercing gaze on her. "Governor Burrington certainly does not think they are. And many others agree with him. They believe that yeomen are yeomen and gentry are gentry, no matter where you go. And, for aught I know, they may be right."

"But it just is not true, Allin. People here can make themselves into gentry, if they want to. In England they cannot."

"You see all kinds of differences I do not," he said, stiffly. "Differences between me and my family, even though I am a part of them. Differences between this country and England, even though this is a part of England." Abruptly, he turned away. "I do not know what you are driving at. Perhaps we had better drop the subject."

But Dierdra was not to be deterred. "You have a fine mind, Allin, and that is just as important as a strong body. Mr. Dawson told me your father wants you to go to college—to William and Mary, I imagine. I think that is a wonderful idea. When I think of how much you have learned, all by yourself! I told Anthony that you are far more intelligent than many of the best educated men I met when I was still living in England."

Allin's reaction startled her. She had never seen him angry before, and his expression was almost frightening. His eyes blazed in his ashen face, and he spoke through tight lips.

"I'm a grown man. I may not be an educated one by your standards, or by Mr. Dawson's, but I am quite old enough to make up my own mind about my own life. I am not ashamed that I am a yeoman's son. And I have no desire to be what you would call a gentleman. I am not so impressed with Mr. Dawson's London manners and elegant airs as you seem to be."

Dierdra tried to stem his rush of words. "It has nothing to do with Mr. Dawson, Allin. That isn't what I meant at all."

"I am not concerned with what you meant, but what you said, and the way you have been acting."

"But I have only been trying to do what I think is best for you." It was not easy for Dierdra to keep her voice calm.

"I am the one who has to decide what is best for me, not you. And it is high-handed and patronizing for you to interfere at all. If being a gentleman means being inconsiderate of other people's feelings, as you have been of mine, I certainly want no part of it." He paused. "I thought we were friends, and I believe friends should respect one another's wishes. I asked you to drop the subject."

Dierdra was silent. Allin rose from the bench and strode over to the edge of the clearing. His back was to her, and she had to strain to catch his words.

"But now, since you have brought it up, you might as well know how I feel. I want no part of being a gentleman, as you call it. From what I've heard, the English gentry think they own the earth, and do not care how they treat yeomen and their families. Order them about. Uproot them from their land. Why, many of them, I'm told, even leave yeomen's daughters with noisy, bawling souvenirs of their attentions."

Dierdra was thunderstruck. When she had seen how much her words hurt Allin, she had regretted them. But now regret was turning to anger. He was as narrow-minded as Anthony Dawson, even though their ideas were so different. She should never have bothered to speak to him in the first place.

"I do not know what you are talking about, Allin," she burst out. "It has nothing to do with what I was saying. Nothing at all. It isn't even the kind of thing one talks about. You sound like Tamar at her silliest." Her hand flew to her lips. How could she have said such a cruel thing!

He turned to face her, his expression set and angry.

"Now that you have insulted my sister, I hope you are satisfied." He strode toward the canoe. "We are going back now. You had better get in."

Dierdra walked blindly toward the shore and stepped into the little boat. He neither helped her nor looked at her, but sat there silently, holding the canoe steady.

"Allin," she said, and then stopped. She wanted to apologize, but she could not meet his angry eyes.

The canoe turned out from the creek into the river, into the full light of the dying sun. On the trip back, neither of them said a word. When Allin had brought the canoe up to the dock, he offered her his hand to help her out, but still he did not say anything. Dierdra could see that his expression had not softened. He started up toward the house, but she placed a restraining hand on his arm. She must speak.

"Allin," she said softly, "I'm sorry for what I said about Tamar. Truly sorry. It was cruel and uncalled for, and I was dreadfully wrong." She searched his face for some sign of friendship, but it was still hard and set. "I apologize, I really do. But please don't say those things about yeomen and gentry. They simply are not true in this country. I certainly do not believe them. I want to be friends, as we were before."

He seemed on the verge of saying something, but just at that moment the large boat came in. As she was getting out, Tamar caught sight of them.

"Where have you been?" she cried. "We lost you. Or did you run away?"

"I took Miss Treffry to see the lagoon," Allin said stiffly.

Tamar's hand flew to her mouth. "The lagoon! Oh, Allin, it is an evil place!" She turned to Dierdra. "I hope you were not frightened."

Dierdra had no time to reply; at that moment Owen and Dick, who had been taking down the sail and making fast the boat, came up to join them. Tamar turned to Owen.

"What do you think? Allin took Dierdra to the lagoon. You know it's haunted."

"Haunted?" Dick's voice was interested. "By whom?"

Owen was casual. "Oh, you know those old wives' tales. This

one is like all the others. A lovely Chowanoke Indian maid and one of Sir Richard Granville's men. She ran away to be with her lover on the white man's ship, but the Indians followed her . . ." He stopped, his eyes lured to the river.

"And then what?" Dick prodded him. "You can't leave us hanging in mid-air like that, you know."

"Oh, she came to some sad end. They always do, in those stories."

"Come on, now," Dick laughed, "let us have all the gory details. We promise not to be frightened."

Tamar took up the tale, her golden eyes big. "Oh, it's very sad. They carried her in their canoe to the lagoon and tied her to a tree and left her there to die."

"And I suppose she comes back to haunt the spot?" Dick asked. His blue eyes twinkled.

"You must not scoff." Tamar's earnestness was out of character. "People have seen her searching through the lagoon for her lover. She weaves a spell over the folk who go there."

"A love spell?" Dick asked hopefully.

"An evil spell," Tamar said. Her voice was hushed and sober. "It brings nothing but tragedy to anyone who may happen to go near."

A feeling of desolation swept over Dierdra. True, the story was only a legend, but her quarrel with Allin hinted that it might be true. Suppose a spell had been cast over the mysterious lagoon. Did that mean Allin would never forgive her? Why, oh, why had she continued the conversation when he asked her to stop? She would have given anything to recall her words.

She stole a glance at him. He was standing quiet, unmoving, expressionless.

"I have a matter to discuss with Father," he said. "I probably will not see you again before you leave, Miss Treffry, so I will say good-bye now." He strode off.

Chapter V

THE COUNCIL SITS

THE DAY of the council meeting dawned warm and sunny, and as Penelope Lovyck sat drinking her breakfast chocolate at the small table beneath the window in her sitting room, she could see most of Edenton's morning activities spread before her: the workmen on the docks, the fishing boats putting in with their catches, the carpenters building Mr. Harnett's new home at the curve of the land, the housewives, with their market baskets, on their way to make the day's purchases. Had she turned her pretty little head just a trifle, she could have seen the lower part of the Green, and the courthouse, where the Council sat.

In her pale blue taffeta peignoir, with its huge lace frill cascading down the front, her pale blue satin slippers, tied about her trim ankles with blue satin ribbons, and her small lace mobcap, perched at a coquettish angle on her red-brown hair, Penelope looked like a little girl playing at being grown up; her worried expression only emphasized the youthful delicacy of her features.

The butler was pouring her second cup of chocolate when her husband, John, came into the room.

"You are late this morning, Johnny." Penelope held up her cheek for him to kiss. "All the boats have docked and the fish are already unloaded."

"I know, my dear. I had to wait while Abraham took a spot off this coat and mended a lace sleeve ruffle. The governor insists we dress formally for the Council meetings, you know." He poured chocolate from his cup into a saucer, and set the cup carefully on a little glass tray.

"Well, you look very elegant." Penelope's voice was abstracted, and she sat for a moment in silence. Then she burst out:

"Oh, Johnny, I dread this meeting! If only you had not written my stepfather's will!"

He leaned over to pat her hand, which was lying on the table. "There, there, my dear. You must not worry. We have weathered storms before."

"Yes, I know. But Burrington hates you. I believe he is jealous because you can think faster than he. And many people disliked my stepfather so much they would be willing to use this case against him, even though he is dead."

"Now, now. There is nothing to worry about, I tell you. And besides, they are only going to read the memorial today. And then they will probably assign a time for me to put in my answer. Nothing more."

"But two days from now every precinct in the Albemarle will know about it and everyone will be mouthing your name and wondering."

She was right, John knew. Even though he had done nothing wrong, all the speculation that had sprung up when Penelope and he were married, some years earlier, would now be revived. The people of Edenton, no less than John himself, had found it difficult to understand why such a beautiful young woman as Penelope Maule, who had spent more time in Williamsburg, Annapolis and London than at Black Rock Plantation in Bertie Precinct, should have chosen as her husband a man whose only claim to distinction was that he was secretary to her stepfather, Governor Charles Eden. Even at the time, there were rumors that John Lovyck had some mysterious power over the governor and his family, and the news that the secretary had drawn up Eden's will and was his sole legatee was sure to add new fuel to a fire that had flickered, but never quite died out. Actually, it was to prevent these rumors from being revived that John had attended to all the legal details surrounding his wife's stepfather's will so quietly.

"Let them wonder," he said now. "Everything will come out all right. We have done nothing wrong. The will is perfectly correct in every way. It was witnessed by two respected citizens.

And when your stepfather died, I took it to the courthouse and had it probated. We have not committed even so much as a blunder."

"I know, Johnny, I know. And when I think of all this trouble for a few hundred pounds that we do not even need . . ."

"Now, stop worrying." John patted his wife's hand again and, rising from the table, went over to the long mirror on the wall opposite. "I must have the wigmaker take in this lining. A tuck will do it. It doesn't fit to suit me now." He pushed the brown wig back from his forehead.

Penelope went over and stood beside him. She grasped his arm and looked up into his face, her blue eyes anxious.

"Johnny, I want to go to the meeting. I want everyone to know that I stand beside my husband."

John bent his head to kiss her. "My dear, my dear," he said, softly. "Of course you shall come to the meeting if you like. I will be proud to have you there. But the memorial will not come up before the afternoon session. No need to come with me now." He kissed her again, then turned abruptly on his heels and left the room.

Penelope sat down at the breakfast table. She took a sip of her chocolate and made a little *moue;* the drink was cold. "Poor Johnny," she murmured as, looking through the window, she caught sight of his tall figure walking to the courthouse. Her eyes clouded with tears. She blinked to clear her vision and noticed the merchant, Ali Hassan, and his boy, crossing to the far side of the Green where, on his arrival in Edenton a few days ago, he had set up his bazaar. Perhaps she ought to go over and look at his wares. That might take her mind from the troubles that lay ahead. She rose from the table and made her way upstairs to dress.

Ali Hassan sat cross-legged on a Turkey carpet, drinking a little cup of thick black coffee. His serving boy had erected a shelter for him, a tent covered with vines and rushes, to protect him from the sun. It had the look of a bazaar in Spain or Morocco, and the peddler's green turban of Mecca and the striped robe that covered his angular body heightened the carefully calculated exotic effect.

Utensils of brass and copper for cooking; pierced brass bowls and plaques for ornamentation; candlesticks, single and seven-branched; baskets woven of reeds; long strings of amber and red seed pods—these made up an important part of Hassan's wares. But there were also bolts of silk from Italy, brocades from Greece, thin velvets and delicate laces from Venice, and piles of soft printed cotton from Egypt. There were, in addition, leather shoes and slippers and portmanteaux from Morocco, and beaver hats and silver paste buckles for ladies' and gentlemen's shoes.

It had been five years since Ali Hassan had last been in Edenton. Before he came he knew that by now the people must be starved for his wares and for that breath of the strange unknown he brought with him. This would be a profitable visit; he could feel it in his bones.

He rubbed his hands and watched the boy place the leather sitting pillows in the proper position, near the mother-of-pearl-decorated taborets of sandalwood. Hassan knew all the tricks of selling, not only to women, but to men as well. A customer must be comfortable. First, a cup of Turkish coffee, freshly made; then a smoke. After that it was easy to draw the conversation around to silks and velvets, and last of all to his superfine Turkey and Persia carpets.

The best thing was to let the customer bring up the subject of buying. The years had taught Ali Hassan a great deal about human nature. The women, he knew, would bargain over small things, but it was the men who bought his finest rugs and rare jewels. Only a favored few were permitted to look at the fine amber and turquoise and amethyst, and even fewer were privileged to see the rubies and emeralds; they were reserved for men of high estate: great plantation owners, members of the assembly, the governor himself. Such gems were perfect gifts for one who wished to surprise his lady, or to make up for some misdeed.

Ali Hassan was a peddler par excellence. He could bargain with a yeoman or a craftsman with waving hands, abrupt gestures, and a high-pitched voice, or spread his jewels on a piece of velvet for the gentry, praising their beauty and rarity in a hushed tone that bespoke his reverence and awe.

His wares had not yet all been set up when Dierdra Treffry and her little charge, Ann Burrington, came into his tent. Ali Hassan bowed low from the waist, his arms crossed in the long sleeves of his striped aba.

Dierdra saw a tall, thin man, dark complexioned as a Moor, with brown, curly hair and beard. He had the liquid, almond-shaped eyes of a Persian, his nose was thin and aquiline, his lips were full, and deeply indented at the corners. His teeth, when he smiled, were even and very white. Dierdra was puzzled. She liked to place people, and this man eluded her. She tried to make out his origin, but all she could tell with certainty was that he must be from the East—he might be an Arab, a Persian, or an Egyptian. She had spent some time in Persia; when she was no older than little Ann, her father had been Consul there, and she still remembered the noise, and the color of the bazaar.

Ann was running about, lifting up coffee cups and plates.

"Miss Treffry, can I buy this for my father?" she cried, holding up a dagger with a curved blade.

"Ann Burrington!" Dierdra exclaimed. "Have you forgotten why we came here? You said you wanted something for your mother's birthday." She took the dagger from the little girl and laid it down on a table.

"Of course. I forgot. Do you think I could buy these?" She pointed to a long string of amber beads.

"I am afraid they will be too expensive," Dierdra said.

Ali Hassan smiled. Burrington was the new governor's name, was it not?

"I think we can arrange something for the little lady. How much money do you have, little miss?"

"Three shillings. That's not very much, is it?" Ann's eyes were anxious.

"It is just right. Here, take them." He put the string into her hands. The sun shining on the beads transformed them into little balls of fire. "They bring good fortune, little miss. They ward off the evil that comes to the throat of the wearer."

Ann was delighted. "Oh, Miss Treffry! Perhaps they help the headache, too." She turned to the merchant. "My mother has the headache very often. Will these be good for her?"

Ali Hassan shrugged. "Who can tell? The amber is lucky in many ways."

Ann thrust the money into his hand and, clutching the beads to her, danced out of the tent.

"That was very kind of you," Dierdra said. "Those beads are worth much more than three shillings."

"The first sale of the day always brings good fortune," he replied, rubbing his hands together. "Perhaps I can carry some bolts of silk and brocade to the little lady's mother? Lace from Venice, perhaps?'

"I'm sure she would be delighted," Dierdra answered, smiling. "It's right there," she nodded in the direction of Government House. "I will tell her to expect you."

Dierdra turned around.

As she and Ann were making their way across the Green, Penelope Lovyck stepped out of the door of her house. She caught sight of Dierdra and called out:

"Dierdra! Dierdra Treffry! Could you wait a moment? I'd like to talk to you."

Dierdra turned around.

"It's Mistress Lovyck," Ann said as Penelope hurried over to them. "Look what I bought for my mother's birthday present." She held out the string of beads.

Penelope managed a smile. "Very pretty, dear, very pretty."

"Why don't you run ahead, Ann? I will catch up with you in a moment." Dierdra could tell from Penelope's expression that something was worrying the young woman.

"All right. Wait until William sees my present! I'm sure his isn't half so beautiful," Ann said as she scampered ahead.

Dierdra turned to Penelope. "You look troubled, Penelope. Is there anything I can do?"

Penelope was silent for a moment. When she spoke, her voice was strained.

"Dierdra, may I ask you a favor?"

Dierdra looked inquiringly at her.

"Roderick Lloyd and his wife, Governor Eden's sister, are about to sue my husband. The memorial will be read today, at the Council meeting. I want to hear it, but I dread going alone."

Dierdra frowned. "I have the children's lessons at ten. I suppose I could postpone them . . ."

"This will not be until the afternoon. At about three. I dislike to impose on you, but . . ."

"Then I shall certainly come," Dierdra interrupted. "I will be happy to."

"Oh, Dierdra, you have no idea how much I loathe this whole affair. It's so hard for poor John." Penelope touched her eyes lightly with her lace-trimmed handkerchief. "He turns it aside to keep me from worrying—but somehow that only makes me feel even worse."

She was silent for a moment, then she went on: "John is such a good man, Dierdra. He filled all the legal requirements about the will—probated it and everything. He is much too honest ever to do anything wrong. And he did not even want to write the will in the first place. He told me so any number of times. Not only that, Mary Badham told me. She was at Government House when it happened, and she says that John protested over and over again, but the governor simply would not listen to him. He made John write it, and Mary witnessed it. My stepfather was a stubborn man, and he liked to have things his own way."

Dierdra felt helpless. "Everything will be all right, Penelope. Wait and see."

"I pray so. And Dierdra, I hope you will not be prejudiced by Governor Burrington's attitude. He should be impartial, of course, but I'm afraid he will not be. He dislikes John; he thinks him too outspoken." She shook her head. "John can be very direct at times. Like Edward Moseley and Chief Justice Gale. Burrington dislikes them, too, and they are also on the Council." She looked at the dark-haired girl remorsefully. "I suppose I should have asked one of the others to come with me, Mistress Moseley, perhaps. But she is so much older." She sighed. "It really is unfair to you. Even though you are not an ordinary governess, you are a member of the governor's household."

"I'm a friend of Penelope Lovyck's, too," Dierdra said. "But I must hurry now; it's nearly ten. I will meet you at the courthouse a little before three."

The Council met in the small chamber off the assembly room. This afternoon there were only a few spectators, and most of the seats were empty, but Penelope and Dierdra chose places at the back, near the long window that gave on the bay.

The Council members were already present and seated at the Council table, but Burrington had not yet returned from his midday meal. The men were impatient; Edward Moseley had laid his watch on the table in front of him and he glanced at it, frowning, several times. It was three-fifteen before Burrington entered, took his seat in the high-backed chair at the head of the table and, with a sharp rap of his gavel, called the meeting to order.

The governor made an impressive chairman. His manner was dignified and his appearance fastidious. He wore a long puce-colored coat with silver buttons. His waistcoat was a bright scarlet. His breeks were satin, and his stockings heavy white silk. His pointed shoes had handsomely embossed silver buckles.

"You may call the roll," he said to Will Badham, the clerk.

The little man's eyes darted to each of the Council members in turn, and each, as his name was called, responded "present." The full Council was there: William Reed, Christopher Gale, Edward Moseley, Richard Sanderson, John Blount, Thomas Pollock, Thomas Harvey, Arthur Goffe, and John Lovyck. When the roll call was completed, Burrington picked up the top sheet of the pile of papers in front of him.

"The first order of business for this afternoon is the memorial of Roderick Lloyd, Esq., on behalf of his wife, Ann, and her daughter, Margaret Pugh, in the matter of the will of the late governor, Charles Eden. Mr. Badham, will you read the memorial?"

Badham rose to his feet and began nervously to read. His voice was low and monotonous; Penelope and Dierdra had to strain to hear him. The stilted legal language was not easy for them to follow, and the clerk's drone robbed his words of whatever meaning they might otherwise have had. But one sentence leaped to their attention.

"And whereas the said John Lovyck, secretary to the said governor, hath possessed himself of said estate by pretext of a pretended will . . ."

Penelope's eyes flew to her husband. He half-rose from his chair, and a look of astonishment, followed by swift anger, flashed across his long, thin face. He shot a glance at his wife. Her face was pale, but she shook her head slightly and he sank back into his seat. Badham's voice continued:

". . . bring before your honor a just and true account and inventory, on his oath, of the said governor's effects . . . particular value in sterling money . . . before the proper courts of Great Britain . . . that justice may be done."

Burrington, who had been riffling through the papers in front of him during the reading, adjusted his wig and rapped his gavel. His voice, when he spoke, was brusque.

"It is therefore ordered by the governor in Council that the said memorial be entered upon the record of the general court of this province, and that the said John Lovyck be ordered to put in his answers on the first Monday of October, at the regular general court of the province. The next order of business . . ."

There was a gasp from the spectators and the Council members, and Edward Moseley leaped to his feet. His face was livid. "Is there to be no discussion of this memorial?"

"The question is out of order, Mr. Moseley. Be seated." The governor rapped his gavel again.

"Your excellency." It was Christopher Gale, the chief justice. "I protest. Should not Mr. Lovyck be given a chance to make his answer to the Council? The memorial was addressed to us, not to the court. This is a most unusual procedure. It is—"

"It is my procedure. Mr. Lovyck will have his opportunity to answer. In the courts, as I have directed." Burrington's voice was icy.

Moseley was still on his feet. He trembled with anger. "This is an outrage!"

"Mr. Moseley!" A look of distaste crossed the governor's face. "I have already said these comments are out of order. If necessary, I shall adjourn the Council meeting. Mr. Badham, you will read the next petition."

The clerk's voice was even lower than before; only the Council members could hear what he said.

"Petition of William Maule, of Bertie Precinct, showing that an Indian slave of his is now being detained at the Indian King Blount's town, in Indian Woods, against the will of his master."

Moseley was on his feet and speaking almost before the clerk had finished.

"The Council hereby orders the Indian King Blount to deliver up the slave according to the articles of agreement with this government, or show cause why he should not."

There was a loud chorus of ayes, and Moseley went on: "I ask the clerk to enter that the motion was passed unanimously by the Council." As he sat down, he shot a look half-venomous, half-triumphant, at Burrington.

The governor's face was mottled with rage, but his voice was calm. "The Council meeting is adjourned." He gathered up his papers, rose swiftly from his chair, and left the room. The Council members observed the forms of decorum; they rose with him, waited quietly until he had gone, and then took up their belongings and made ready to depart.

Anthony, who had come in when the meeting began, had watched the entire proceedings with amazement. Shaking his head doubtfully, he went over to pay his respects to Dierdra, who was still standing with Penelope Lovyck.

"Mistress Treffry," he said, "it is always a pleasure to see you, and especially here, today. We need feminine faces to brighten this rancourous masculine atmosphere." He smiled and looked inquiringly at Penelope.

Dierdra looked up. "Mr. Dawson!" She turned to Penelope. "Have you met Mr. Dawson yet? He is a new settler here in

North Carolina and an old friend of my brother Roger's. This is Mistress Lovyck, Mr. Dawson."

Anthony bowed. "I am delighted to meet you, Mistress Lovyck. Although I am sorry the occasion is not more pleasant."

Penelope smiled wanly. "And here is my husband," she said, as John approached. "Do you know Mr. Dawson, John?"

Lovyck's long face was still angry. "I have not yet had that pleasure." He bowed slightly. "But Mr. Moseley has told me of your arrival. We can use new settlers here, sir, and we are delighted to welcome you." He turned to Dierdra. "Mistress Treffry, I want to thank you for accompanying my wife. It was an act of real friendship." He offered Penelope his arm. "Shall we go, my dear?"

"Poor Penelope," Dierdra said, gazing after the Lovycks' departing backs.

"Yes. It must be very difficult for her." Anthony's face was somber. "But I am afraid I do not understand the entire affair. Why should a will arouse so much feeling among people who have nothing to do with it?"

"Well, I'm not very clear about the legal details, myself," Dierdra said. "But I know it has made Penelope dreadfully unhappy. I hate to see that. I am fond of her. And it all seems quite unnecessary. I know she does not need the money, however much it is. Mr. Maule, her father, was one of the richest men in the province, and he willed several plantations to her."

Anthony looked thoughtful. He stood for a while in silence. Then he snapped his fingers.

"I say, I have an idea. When I met you on the dock the other day with the children, you promised to come out riding with me some afternoon. Why not make it today? The weather is wonderful. You could tell me what you know about this case as we go along. That is, if you care to."

"That sounds very pleasant." Dierdra smiled warmly. "I have no duties this afternoon, and it will not take too long for me to change into my riding clothes."

They had been standing on the courthouse steps as they spoke. Dierdra hurried off, and Anthony remained for a moment in thought. Suddenly he heard a loud voice behind him.

"Damned insolence! It's time he had his lesson!" Anthony turned to look into Edward Moseley's angry eyes. "Oh, it's you, Dawson. I thought it was Reed."

"That was certainly a stormy session." Anthony kept his tone light.

"That man is a disgrace to decent government, that's what he is!" Moseley shook a finger in Anthony's face. "Now you have some idea of the kind of things that go on here."

"I saw what happened. But I do not understand it." Anthony laughed wryly.

"There is nothing to understand. It is simply that your friend Mr. Burrington thinks he is the law, and the Council is there to do his bidding. I suppose he believes himself too elegant to be bothered with country folk like us."

"The Council members did not appear to me to be country folk."

Moseley nodded vehemently. "And no more are they. They are fine gentlemen; Burrington is not fit to lick their boots."

Anthony shook his head. "Now, that's a little strong, Mr. Moseley, don't you think?"

"I do not. The man is mad. I can tell you this, Dawson," Moseley pushed a warning finger into Anthony's chest. "No governor is going to run high-handed over this Council, no matter who he thinks he is. We have as many constitutional rights as he. The Proprietors gave them to us. I hope you will report this outrage to Lord John." And the surveyor-general strode off without giving his companion a chance to answer.

Chapter VI

THE STORM

ANTHONY AND DIERDRA rode out through the Northern Gate. Neither of them spoke until they had passed the Red Lion Inn, Edenton's last outpost. Then Anthony broke the companionable silence between them.

"If it is not imposing on you, I would like to hear more about the Eden Will case."

Dierdra patted her horse's neck and spoke reflectively.

"It began before I arrived here—that is, the will was made out then. Apparently, Governor Eden left all his money to John Lovyck, who was his secretary and is his step-daughter's husband, and because John drew up the will for the governor, Eden's sister claims he forged it. It probably seemed strange to her that she did not receive a single penny. She certainly must have expected something."

Anthony shook his head. "I still do not understand. The law here must be similar to the law in England. When a will is drawn up, it is witnessed, and when the person who made it dies, it is filed for probate. Then all the records are available to any interested party."

"I am not familiar with the legal requirements," Dierdra said, "but Penelope told me this morning that John had filed the will for probate and that Mary Badham, Will Badham's wife, was there when the governor made John write it out. Perhaps she was a witness."

Anthony sighed. "It becomes more and more confusing. If the will was witnessed and probated, Lovyck should not object to having the case go to court. Nor should any of the Council members. But perhaps it should be heard by the Council first."

"I am not sure I should say this to you—" Dierdra's voice was soft—"since you are a Granville. But I expect you have already noticed that there is very little love lost between the governor and the Council members."

"I knew there was some friction. But I had no idea it went as deep as this. It appears to me that the Eden will case has been turned into a struggle for authority between the governor and the Council. And the Lovycks are simply pawns in the game. Probably if this issue had not arisen, another one would."

Dierdra smiled wryly. "Well, you wanted to see how your property was being managed." She sighed. "I care less about politics and government than I do about people. And quarrels like this . . . It will be difficult for Madam Burrington, too. The governor has a hot temper."

They rode on in silence for a while. Suddenly Anthony reined in his horse.

"That breeze," he said. "It seems rather stiff. Stop for a moment, and you will feel it."

Dierdra brought her mount to a halt. "It *is* blowing up. Look," she pointed to the trees that lined the road. "The branches were barely stirring before. Do you think it will rain?"

"Nothing worse than an April shower, I should imagine. But we can turn back now, if you'd like."

"No, no, a little rain never frightened a Treffry." She spurred her horse and it broke into a canter. "Come on," she called back over her shoulder.

Anthony followed close behind. Suddenly the sky became black as night and a strong wind arose.

"I fear this will be more than an April shower." He had to shout to make himself heard over the howling wind.

"It certainly seems that way." The first large drops of rain fell. "We will be drenched."

"It's coming from up ahead. If we turn back, we can race it. Run before the storm."

They wheeled their steeds around and spurred them on.

"What fun!" Dierdra cried. Her hair came loose from its confining net and the braids tumbled down over her shoulders.

"You look like a little girl again," he shouted.

She laughed, but did not answer. The horses' hooves and the heavy drops of falling rain beat a tattoo on the hard-packed earth.

"I see a barn ahead," Dierdra called out, "under that great oak tree."

They turned off the road and made for the tall, narrow building, an empty tobacco barn, just as the storm broke with swifter violence. The dark heavens seemed to open, and the rain poured down in a heavy sheet, beating against the ground with a fury that drove it back upward, into their faces, nearly blinding them.

Anthony lifted Dierdra from her horse and, holding her to him, struggled against the howling wind until he reached the barn. He had to exert all his strength to push the door open. She stumbled into the dark building and he ran back to the horses to lead them to shelter at the side of the barn, where he had seen a post. He tied them to it, and the animals shivered against one another, fearful of the heavy roll of the thunder, now breaking close about them. Flash followed flash of forked lightning.

Anthony reached the barn to find Dierdra standing with her arms clasped around a wood support. She was trembling.

"You're soaked through," he said. "Let me help you off with your coat."

She stood quietly as he pulled it off her shoulders. The rain had wetted her through, and her shirt was plastered close to her body. In the dim light, she seemed almost naked. Her freshness and youth were even more vivid in the dank, musty atmosphere of the old, deserted barn and it was almost with a sense of shock that Anthony realized what a desirable woman she had grown into. It seemed to him that he was seeing her for the first time.

Suddenly the silence between them was shattered by a violent crash of thunder. Dierdra screamed and flung herself against him, burying her head in his chest.

He felt the quivering of her slim body and its pressure against his, and his heart began to pound and the blood to rush through his veins. Instinct overcame him; he bent his head to hers and put his arms around her. As his fingers began to caress her back, he felt her body stiffen and, with a sudden movement, she pulled away from him. For a moment neither of them said a word. Then Dierdra spoke.

"I am sorry to have been such a coward." She laughed tremulously. "But it was so loud." Her hand went to her hair in a futile effort to arrange it.

Anthony did not answer; the surge of passion that had swept through him when her warm young body was molded to his had not yet subsided. Finally he managed to speak.

"It's all right."

A flash of lightning, twisting in through the window, made the building blindingly bright and sent them reeling to the wall. A deafening clap of thunder followed; hard on its heels came an ear-splitting roar as a tree crashed into the barn wall, splintering it into a thousand pieces. The very earth seemed to tremble, and they could feel the building shiver and quake. The noise stopped as suddenly as it had begun, and in the profound quiet that followed, the terrifying whinnying of the horses was eerie beyond description.

Anthony grasped Dierdra around the waist and they ran out of the building. The sky was black; not until the next flash of lightning came could they see the gaping hole that had been torn in the barn wall by the crown of the fallen oak, lying now not six feet from where they had been standing.

Dierdra had stopped crying, but she was shaking from head to foot. Her eyes were wide and staring, her face white as parchment.

Anthony led her to a fallen log and they sat down.

"Don't cry, sweet, don't cry." He spoke softly. "God's mercy, we are safe." He took off his jacket and put it around her quivering shoulders. He started to put his arm around her, but withdrew it. They sat in silence as the rain and the wind and the storm beat in on them.

After a time, the storm's violence passed. The thunder and lightning stopped. Although the rain continued, it was gentle and mild.

"Shall we try to go on now?" Anthony asked. "I think the rain will keep on like this for quite a while."

She nodded. "The horses—what about them?"

Anthony walked around the corner of the barn. Dierdra's horse was standing quite still. But Black Douglas lay dead, crushed by the heavy branches of the fallen oak. Gently, Anthony freed Dierdra's mount from the tangle of twigs and small branches in which she had been trapped. He spoke softly and soothingly to her until she had calmed down. Then he led her over to the log.

"Come, let me help you up. I'll walk beside you. It cannot be too far to the Red Lion. We will be able to dry off there."

She turned her frightened face to him. "Is Black Douglas dead?"

As he lifted her to the saddle, he nodded. "Death must have come with merciful swiftness."

They made their way to the inn in silence. Dierdra's mind was in a turmoil. She had heard from Roger of Anthony's reputation, and of his affairs with many of London's fashionable ladies. Was he trying to add her to his string of conquests? Was he really so arrogant as to believe that all he had to do was to snap his fingers, and any woman would fall into his arms? Well, she had shown him that was not true of Dierdra Treffry, at any rate.

But suppose it was not that. Her rebuff had been fairly gentle, and he had accepted it immediately. A philanderer would have tried to press his advantage. . . .

Perhaps he really cared for her. This was a new and disquieting thought; it had never occurred to Dierdra to think of Anthony except as her brother's friend, a gay and pleasant companion, but no more. Even if she could feel deeply about Anthony, she would not want to; he was too self-assured, too self-sufficient to understand the meaning of love to a woman, who would want not only to be desired, but needed, as well. And there was Allin. If ever he forgave her . . . She raised her head at the sound of Anthony's voice.

"I think we are there now."

At the Red Lion, the landlady took Dierdra to her own room to find some dry clothing. As she led the girl upstairs, she clucked sympathetically.

"There, there. It's a blessing you were not hit by those lightning flashes. I can't remember a worse storm since the one in 1700."

Groggins, the landlord, a short, plump man, took Anthony to the common room, where he laid a fire on the grate.

" 'Tis lucky we have some logs in the house. The stack outside must be soaking wet. You'd best dry out here. Nothing of mine will fit your long length. But a hot posset will warm you while you wait." He hurried off to the kitchen to prepare it.

By the time Anthony's clothes had dried, the rain had stopped, and the two young people made ready to leave. Since they had only one horse, Groggins insisted on hitching up his gig and driving Dierdra to Government House. Anthony followed on her mount.

It was early evening. The sky was washed in purple and red, and the air smelled fresh and clean in the aftermath of the rain. Puddles had formed in the road, and the gentle plop of the horse's hooves made a rhythmic accompaniment to Anthony's thoughts.

He was deeply disturbed, and in a way that was foreign to him. The feeling Dierdra had aroused had been too sudden, too unexpected. He certainly had not planned for it to happen, or even wanted it to. And it was not a feeling he could toss off lightly; it had taken a real effort of will to prevent himself from making love to her. He could have overcome her resistance, he felt sure. An ironical smile crossed his face as he thought of the number of well-born, beautiful women who could testify to that. After all, a woman was not supposed to give in too quickly.

Then why had he stopped? Could it be that he was falling in love with her? He hoped not, fervently. He did not want to feel deeply about any woman yet; he was only twenty-five, he had plenty of time. True, his thoughts of the future had always included marriage, but the image of a wife that had appeared most frequently in his mind had been that of Tomasine Gorgas, a sprightly redhead, whose family was as old as the Granvilles', and nearly as rich in land. Marriage to Tomasine would be pleasant, sensible, and advantageous to both of them. It would be right and proper and logical; a fulfillment of everything he had been born into. Marriage to Dierdra, with her unconventionality, her quick temper, her ideas of social equality . . .

The groom caught sight of the gig and the horse as they came up to Government House, and ran around to the front gate to take Dierdra's mount. Anthony pressed some money on Groggins, who was at first reluctant to accept it, and then went to the door, where Dierdra was waiting.

"Will you come inside and have a cup of tea?" she asked, as he opened the door for her. "You must be chilled."

Anthony stepped inside. He wanted to go back to the inn and try to sort out his tangled emotions, but he did not want to seem brusque.

"I think perhaps I had better leave," he said.

At that moment, the door to Burrington's office opened, and the governor came into the hall. Even in the dimly lit vestibule Anthony could see that his color was unusually high.

"Is that you, Dawson, with Miss Treffry?"

Anthony nodded. "Good evening, your excellency."

Burrington walked toward them. He was unsteady on his feet.

"You two young people got caught in the storm, eh? Must be drenched." He threw back his head and laughed. Then his face sobered. "Shouldn't laugh. Suppose you were hurt?" He shook his head and pointed a long finger at Dierdra. "You go right upstairs, Miss Treffry, and have my wife's maid draw you a hot bath. That will warm you up. And you," the finger was now directed at Anthony, "you come in and have a drink with me. Liquor to warm up a man, eh?" He smiled and, taking Anthony by the arm, led him down to the office before the young man had a chance to protest.

Anthony shrugged and followed quietly. There was no point in arguing with a man so deep in his cups.

In the office, Burrington poured Anthony a glass of brandy from the decanter on his desk. Then he leaned back in his chair, facing his guest. His smile had vanished, and a look of anger crossed his face.

"I saw you at the Council meeting today, Dawson. What did you think of that exhibition? Outrageous, I say."

He did not wait for an answer, but went right on.

"The Proprietors put me in charge here. Me." He pounded his chest with his fist to emphasize his words. "If somebody comes to me with a charge against a citizen of North Carolina—Council member or anyone else—I say that man has a right to have the charges heard. That's simple justice. And I am here to see that justice is done. Eh?" He half-rose, his hands on the arms of the high-backed chair.

Anthony did not know what to say. He nodded noncommittally.

"Every one of the Council members is a friend of Lovyck's. How do I know he would get an impartial hearing from them? They might acquit him even if he was guilty. Although between you and me, Lovyck is too much a coward to have done anything wrong. But where money is concerned, you can never tell." He shook his head portentously. "Safer in the courts. Jury there. I trust the jury." Suddenly he threw back his head and laughed. "Have good reasons."

"Our English courts are fair," Anthony felt he had to say something; this seemed as innocuous a remark as any.

"I told you about these people the very day you came here," Burrington went on. "Remember? The trouble is Carolinians . . ." He sank back in his seat and his expression became crafty. "The Carolinians are so touchy. They rebel whenever the governor exercises his powers." He shook his head. "Roderick Lloyd is Governor Eden's brother-in-law. He must be a respectable man. He has a right to be heard." He paused. "You know what worries me, Dawson?"

Anthony shook his head.

"I'll tell you. In confidence. But I can tell you because you're a gentleman." He closed his eyes. "Suppose they have me recalled? My friend William Byrd has warned me about that over and over. 'They've thrown out a dozen governors,' he says. 'Better watch your step, George.' That's what William Byrd says. He thinks this colony should be sold to the Crown." Burrington sighed. "It's a fine line to walk here. The governors of the Crown colonies have a much easier task. The settlers cannot influence the Crown the way the Carolinians can influence the Proprietors. Have another glass of brandy."

Anthony rose. "I think I had better go now, sir."

On the deserted Green, the overhanging branches of the maple trees cast dark shadows. Only the inn was lighted. Anthony walked slowly. Moseley had been right; Burrington was a drinker. But there was some merit to the governor's argument, drunk or sober. Lloyd was entitled to his day in court. Charges that were made publicly should be answered publicly. The Council members were all friends of John Lovyck's; perhaps they would be prejudiced in his favor. Perhaps the case should be heard in court rather than by the Council. But what did Burrington mean when he said he had "good reasons" to trust a jury?

Anthony shook his head. Things were far from simple. He paused for a moment and then walked briskly on. It was still not too late to have a talk with Ali Hassan, who was also staying at the King's Arms. It occurred to him that the merchant might prove a valuable ally. Anthony was just changing into fresh clothing when Smalkins, whom he had sent to invite Ali Hassan, knocked on the door of his bedroom.

"The merchant says he will be delighted to come, sir. He'll be here in a short while."

"Fine. Will you bring us some wine, Smalkins?"

A few minutes later, Ali Hassan arrived. Anthony advanced to him, holding out his hand. The thought crossed his mind that never before in his life had he extended his hand to a merchant. This new idea of equality seemed to be infecting him, too.

"It is good of you to come. Do take a seat. And will you have some wine?" Anthony walked over to the table, on which stood a decanter and two glasses.

"No, thank you. I am a Mohammedan, you know. A follower of the Prophet. We do not drink wine or spirits."

"Yes, of course. I should have thought. Please pardon me."

"No pardon is necessary. And I hope you will not deprive yourself on my account."

Anthony poured himself half a glass of wine. "I will be frank with you, sir. The people of Edenton think I am here to buy land—and that is true enough, as far as it goes. But I have come for another reason, as well."

Briefly, he outlined his mission. When he had finished, he looked steadily at the merchant. Hassan, who had been sitting quietly, moved a trifle, but the expression on his face did not change.

"This is all very interesting, sir. But I am afraid I do not understand why you have honored me with this confidence."

"Hassan, I believe you can help me in my work. You travel. You talk to people, not only here, in North Carolina, but in Virginia and South Carolina as well. They tell you the things that are on their minds. And I must know these things if I am to do what is right." Anthony rose and paced the room restlessly.

"I have no interest in political matters, sir," Hassan's voice was cool.

"Believe me, this is not information of a political nature, in the usual sense. Political events are outside my ability to control, even if I should want to. And now that I see how complicated the situation is, I certainly have no desire as much as to try." Anthony looked at the merchant earnestly. "If the other Proprietors want to sell their land to the Crown, no action of mine will prevent them from doing it. Most of them have no real interest in the people of North Carolina, whose lives and opinions make very little difference to men who live in England and have never even visited here." He smiled. "That would have been true of me, as a representatative of the Granville family, too, before I came here, even though we Granvilles have always been more concerned than the others and have never really expected to sell. The land and land-owning have always had a strong hold on my family." He paused for a moment and tossed off the balance of his wine. "And this land and its people have begun to cast a spell over me, as I have heard your part of the world does over those who go there. I may very well settle here permanently. But with things as they are, with the Crown, the Proprietors, the governor, the Council—all pulling in different directions . . . There was a Council meeting today . . ."

Ali Hassan nodded. "I have heard about it."

"Yes. A perfect example of what I mean. No good can come from this kind of thing. But if I can see the picture clearly, I may be able to do something to help the people of the Albemarle as well as my own family."

The merchant sat silent for a long moment. Then his dark eyes brightened, and a smile crossed his face.

"I, too, would like to help the people of the Albemarle. I have known them for many years, and my respect for them grows." He rose and bowed slightly. "And my respect for you, too, sir."

"Thank you, Hassan, thank you." Anthony smiled.

"What I need to know, more than anything else, is how the ordinary people of North Carolina feel about the present government and whether they would welcome a sale to the Crown. Do they honestly believe that would solve their problems? Or are they in favor of proprietary government? Or do they disagree about this, too? It will not be too difficult for me to talk to the people around Edenton. I have been here a while now, and they know me, and, I think, trust me, too. But I do not know the people in the other parts of the province, whose opinions are quite as important as those of the men in Chowan Precinct."

Hassan smiled. "These people know me very, very well. And I believe they trust me. I shall ask them what you want to know, and when I come back from my next trip, toward the middle of the summer, I shall have a report for you. I will be happy to do my share to help North Carolina."

Chapter VII

ALLIN'S STORY

THE PETERSONS were giving a party to celebrate the completion of their new home on the Virginia Road, and Mistress Peterson was determined to make it the outstanding event of the season. After all, the house was the largest and most handsome in the precinct: two full stories and two one-story wings. In addition to the sitting room, dining room and family bedrooms, there were a drawing room, a library, four guest rooms, and a small chapel with an altar, where Mistress Peterson, who came from Maryland and was a Roman Catholic, could make her devotions. The furnishings, too, were elegant: Turkey carpets from Bokhara, heavy mahogany tables, a Chippendale mirror and chairs, and one hundred and ninety-six ounces of silver plate complete with crest, which had come from the lady's family home.

Patience Peterson was a tall, statuesque woman, whose boast was that she was the best housekeeper in the province. Her ham and bacon, smoked over hickory and persimmon wood, had a tang and sweetness all their own. Her dairy was the freshest and cleanest: every day one of the bondmen drove the cows to the pond to scrub them down thoroughly. From her weaving rooms came the finest linens and woolens. Her candles were the best bayberry and her house servants kept the heart-pine floors shined to the highest polish. Everything in Mistress Peterson's home reflected pride as well as hard work: she was a connection of the Calverts, and she aimed to conduct herself as befitted a member of that important clan.

Her husband, Enar, had come to the New World from Norway, and he had neither his wife's connections nor her social aspirations. Enar was a stout, easy-going man, who had grown rich through his love of the land. He had once owned the acreage on which Edenton was built, and although he had not at first wanted to sell it, Edward Moseley and John Lovyck had persuaded him it was his patriotic duty to do so; its location on the bay made it the ideal spot for the provincial seat of government. And it had occurred to Enar himself that dividing the property into town lots would bring him considerable cash, which he was not at all averse to having. He had used some of the money to buy other land, and had taken up a great deal more through grants from the Lords Proprietors. He worked and cultivated every acre he owned and kept up with all the assessments; as a result, none of his property had lapsed, and now he owned more than any other man in the precinct save the surveyor-general and the governor himself.

Peterson's bond servants were his friends; he was generous and fair to all of them and they knew that when they had worked out their five-year indentures, they would receive the land that was due them. The town merchants, too, spoke highly of him; many of them were indebted to him for loans of credit in England, which had seen them through the lean years, when crops were thin and cash unobtainable.

The planning of the house-warming party had not been without its difficulties. Patience discussed every problem in the most minute detail with her husband, who regarded the entire affair with the amused tolerance of the busy man for the trifles with which women occupy themselves. When Mistress Peterson arrived in the library for tea with her husband one afternoon in late April, carrying a large sheaf of papers in her hand, he sighed in anticipation: another long discussion was about to begin.

"I have two problems, my dear," she said, as she took the cup of tea the bond maid had handed her.

"Speak, my little dove. Perhaps I can help you."

Patience had tried hard, over the years, to break him of calling her "little dove" or "little nightingale," but without success. Her only consolation was that these were less vulgar than "little cabbage," which had at first been his favorite term of endearment. Her name had always been a burden to her: "Patience" had a tinge of the Friends' sect, and even though William Penn himself was quality, the Quakers were not the sort of folk with whom Mistress Peterson liked to be associated.

"It is about the guest list," she said. "Shall I or shall I not invite the Killigrews?"

Enar set his cup on the table with a clatter, and his large blue eyes, usually kind, seemed to turn steel grey.

"Of course you will invite them. Killigrew is one of my closest friends."

"Yes, yes, I know," she said impatiently. "But I am only inviting plantation people, and the most important of the town people. Men like Goldsmith Coltrane and the Lovycks. I am not asking any of the yeomen at all."

"And what, my dear Patience, am I? A yeoman, I've always thought."

"Why, Enar, you are a rich man, and a plantation owner." Her tone was shocked. "There's a very great difference. A vast difference. To put Enar Peterson in the same class with a man like Killigrew! And my sister and her husband are coming down from Maryland to be with us for the occasion. I want them to see that we have a society here, too."

"Patience," he said, "we have been through this before." The warning note in his voice and the stern set of his jaw told her she had lost; Enar could be pushed so far and no further.

"Oh, very well, if you insist, I will ask the Killigrews." Mistress Peterson gave in with the best grace she could muster. "I certainly am not going to argue about it. After all, we have more important things to discuss." She consulted her list. "For instance —I want two striped marquees to put up in the garden. The house-warming will be late in May, and then it will be warm enough to serve out of doors. You can buy the tents in Norfolk town, can't you?" She laid a slim hand on his arm. "You and Dusty can go over tomorrow and be back in the evening if you start early enough."

Reluctantly, Enar agreed. "I did plan to have a talk with Coltrane tomorrow. But I suppose I can postpone it." He sighed. "That's going to be expensive, I imagine. I presume you must have large ones?"

"Yes, indeed. Red and white striped canvas. That will be very elegant."

The day of the garden fete was warm and cloudless; a gentle May day that was perfect for an outdoor party. Everybody of any account in Chowan Precinct was present, and folk had come from as far away as Bath Town and Norfolk. There must have been close to a hundred people scattered in colorful little knots on the lawn, and there were more inside the house, where many of the women were wandering from room to room to view the furnishings and inspect the display of plate. Tables had been set up outside under the striped marquees; behind each one stood a serving man, ready to ladle out cups of refreshing rum punch from the huge cut-glass bowls. An orchestra—three fiddles and a violin—provided a melodic background for the gay conversation and the bursts of laughter.

The governor and his lady had seats in high-backed elbow chairs on a raised platform, which pleased his excellency enormously. He nodded graciously to the guests as they approached to pay their respects to them. Burrington was resplendent in a long coat of purple brocade with large buttons of Spanish paste, white satin smallclothes and sleeve ruffles and scarf of fine Mechlin lace. His shoes were of the latest style, with high red heels and large paste buckles. Madam Burrington wore a gown of shell-pink embroidered mull, which came from London, and her brown hair was dressed in curls that cascaded over her bare shoulders.

Enar Peterson, in a black broadcloth coat with large silver buckles, greeted his guests with warmth. He was as proud of the handsomely bejeweled gold snuff box he carried as he was of his new home and his wife's elaborate party preparations.

"My people in Norway sent this to me," he told everyone, smiling, "as soon as I wrote them we were having a house-warming. Isn't it beautiful?"

Mistress Peterson, in a pale blue taffeta dress with wide floating skirts, presented her sister and brother-in-law to the governor and Madam Burrington and then, taking her sister's arm, led her through the crowd to introduce her to the guests. Anthony was one of her prize displays; as she caught sight of him strolling across the lawn toward her, she whispered in her sister's ear:

"That young man came here from London a few months ago. He is taking up some land not far from here; it was the surveyor-general's, but he let it lapse. Mr. Dawson is most elegant; it is astonishing how many important London people he knows." She smiled as Anthony approached and greeted him with flutterings and a wave of her peacock fan.

"I am so pleased you were able to join my little gathering, Mr. Dawson," she said. "I have been telling my sister that since your arrival we have the beginnings of a real society. Mistress Gardner is from Maryland, you know. I fear they think us no more than provincials there."

Anthony bowed. "I am happy to meet you, Mistress Gardner. And to see you again, Mistress Peterson. This is most delightful."

Mistress Peterson waved a deprecatory hand. "Nothing compared to what you are used to in London, I'm sure. Nothing compared to what I was used to as a girl, in Maryland. You remember Father's big gatherings, don't you, Clara? All the Calverts used to come," she explained to Anthony.

As soon as he could escape from his hostess, Anthony made his way over to Dierdra, who had arrived with the governor and Madam Burrington, and was now talking to Dick and Tamar.

"I hope I am not too late to claim the first dance," he said, bowing.

Dierdra smiled. "Not too late at all."

Three pipers and a drummer had joined the other musicians, and two canvas-covered platforms had been set up on the greensward for the dancing. The first dance was a minuet. The governor led Mistress Peterson out and Enar Peterson escorted Madam Burrington. The Gales and the Moseleys made up the figure.

The young people moved quietly to the second platform, and Anthony led Dierdra through the dance. But the girl was not in a party mood. From the moment of her arrival, she had been searching through the crowd for a sight of Allin Killigrew's face. She had not seen or heard from him since the day they had quarreled at the old Indian camp. That was more than a month ago, and he had been in her thoughts many times since then. As she moved through the steps of the minuet, her eyes strayed to the lawn beyond the platform. Tamar had assured her that Allin was coming, but she could not see his tall dark figure anywhere.

When the dance was over, she made her excuses to Anthony and moved quietly away from the crowd and down the path to the river. She wanted to be alone. She had hoped so much that Allin would come and that she would be able to persuade him to forgive her and to be her friend again. She winced as she recalled her cruel words to him, and a wave of loneliness swept over her. Now that her parents were dead and Roger was in the army, she had no one, no one. . . .

She turned away from the glittering water and walked slowly back toward the house. The music sounded faint and far away, the laughter and the voices were muted. Never, since she had come to North Carolina, had loneliness so closed in on her. She turned off onto a small path. In a thicket, a thrush was warbling. A creaking windmill seemed to echo her heart's cry. Lonely, it said, lonely, lonely . . .

Suddenly she heard footsteps and the sound of approaching voices. She did not want to see anyone, and she stepped off the path and behind a great tree.

Thomas Pollock and Chief Justice Gale came into sight. Pollock was talking earnestly.

"Then it is all settled. I will get the signatures and send the petition to Lord John Granville."

"See that it is all done in a legal way, Pollock," Gale said. "We have a reputation for disliking governors here in North Carolina, so we have to be particularly careful. But the Proprietors should know that Burrington is drinking heavily and conducting himself in a most undignified and unbecoming manner."

"In addition to treating the Council shabbily."

"I do not know whether that point should be mentioned now." Gale shook his head.

Pollock laughed shortly. "It's the main reason we are sending the petition."

"But this is not the time to bring it up. Besides, I am not too sure how the Proprietors feel about such matters of government."

"Will you sign the petition when it is drawn up?"

"No, I cannot, in law, while I hold the office of chief justice. But William Reed will sign. Burrington has removed him from the Council, for no reason whatsoever." He paused for a moment. "And of course Moseley and Lovyck will sign."

"I don't think Moseley's name will help us," Pollock said. "He has a worse reputation for hating governors than any of us. And with this suit against Lovyck, I am not so sure his is a good name." He was silent for a moment, then he asked: "What about Killigrew? He stands well in the county. I should say he is the real leader of the yeomen."

"Good, a very good name. And you might try Martin Trewilliger, the farrier, and Elkin, the cordwainer, and Castleton, the barber. They all have cause to dislike Burrington." Gale halted, broke a twig from a sassafras bush, and began to chew the stem.

"What about Davis, of Carteret? He has come to grips with the governor more than once."

"Yes, Davis, by all means. He has powerful friends in London. He will be very valuable. And you might try Thomas Tinseley. He's hot-headed, and has never forgiven the governor for the sentence that was passed against his friend Atkins for sedition at the last court."

"What did Atkins do?"

"Have you forgotten that scandal? He had put in his bid for a piece of land up in Bertie Precinct, and Burrington managed to persuade the Proprietors to grant the property to him. Atkins was furious, and some of the things he said were quite outrageous."

"Then I shall definitely try Tinseley."

The chief justice threw down the twig and turned around. "We'd best start back. How soon do you think you can have all the necessary signatures?"

"Within a month, I hope."

The two men passed out of earshot, and Dierdra stepped out of her hiding place. She was greatly shocked by what she had heard. The Council meeting and her discussion with Anthony afterwards had made it plain that Burrington had many enemies, but she had not thought things would move so quickly. Nor had she realized that hatred of the governor was felt by so many different kinds of people, from the Council members and the rich plantation owners to the yeomen and artisans of the town. That Burrington was a difficult and erratic man, she knew only too well. Since the Council meeting he had been drinking more and more heavily, and spending more and more of his time with Dr. Carter, whom Dierdra had instinctively disliked from the very first moment she met him. On several occasions recently, she had been awakened by the governor's heavy footsteps and boisterous voice as he went unsteadily upstairs to bed after a night of carousing with the doctor. But much as his personal habits distressed and even shocked her, she had no real evidence that his conduct as governor was bad. Indeed, from what she had heard, Burrington was a fairer man than many of his predecessors; except for this affair with John Lovyck, she saw no reason for the Council members to be opposed to him.

She shook her head, sighed, and started back toward the house. She wished Anthony had been with her, and had overheard the conversation, too. Well, she would tell him what had happened as soon as she got back to the party. He might want to prepare Lord John for the petition.

She had just caught sight of the young Englishman, who was talking to Edward Moseley, when she heard the governor's angry voice. The sound came from the direction of the house.

"On your feet, sir, and draw. No man can use such words to the governor. Draw, you scoundrel, draw, I tell you."

She ran toward Anthony. "Come," she cried.

"Where are you going? This sounds like man's business. Stay here, away from it." He grasped her arm.

She shook herself free. "I must go to Madam Burrington. She will need me."

Together they ran to the long gallery, where the governor, his wig awry, his coat and brocaded waistcoat tossed on a chair, stood with a rapier in his hand, confronting a tall, thin man, who stood silently, his arms folded on his chest, a disdainful smile on his face.

"That's Thomas Tinseley!" Anthony cried. "I've heard he is the best swordsman in the Albemarle. Does Burrington want to commit suicide?"

"Stop him, Anthony, stop him!" Dierdra's eyes were wide. "Burrington is drunk. He doesn't know what he is doing. Tinseley has probably been goading him deliberately, because he knows he's in his cups."

Anthony bounded up the steps, two at a time and, at the top, collided with Enar Peterson, who had come dashing out of the house.

"You cannot fight here, governor, you cannot fight here!" Enar shouted.

By this time the entire company had converged on the lawn beneath the gallery, and was staring up at the scene in shocked amazement. A woman shrieked, and there were muttered curses from the men.

Anthony had placed himself between the governor and Tinseley, and he spread his arms. "Mr. Tinseley is unarmed, your excellency."

"Damn it! Let him borrow a blade then! If he's brave enough to call me names, he should be brave enough to fight."

Tinseley seemed imperturbable. "I am quite brave enough. But not so dishonorable. I am a better swordsman than you when you are sober. And now, you're drunk. Disgustingly drunk." He shot a contemptuous glance at Burrington.

The governor lurched forward, his sword extended. Anthony jumped out of the way just in time and, with a deft movement, grabbed Burrington's weapon from him.

"Get away! Damn it! I will not have some insolent young pup interfering with me!" Burrington shouted, making for Anthony. His voice trembled with rage.

The color drained from Anthony's face and he set his lips grimly. Dierdra could see the effort he was making to keep control of himself. Peterson pushed him out of the way and planted himself firmly in front of the governor.

"You should not have said that to Mr. Dawson, sir. He was only trying to help. And this is no place to fight. I am sure Mr. Tinseley meant no offense."

"I meant every word I said, every word." Tinseley's voice was not loud, but it was clear enough to reach every one of the guests crowded on the lawn. "I will not stand by and see my friend Atkins ordered into the pillory on the public parade, and then required to beg that creature's pardon on bended knee." He folded his arms across his chest. "And for what? For telling the truth about him. I agree with him: Burrington is a rogue and a scoundrel, and in no way fit to be the governor of this province."

A gasp went up from the crowd.

"Sir," said Peterson, "I shall have to ask you to leave. You cannot bring your private quarrels into my home. Governor Burrington is my guest. I will not have you insult him here."

"I won't put up with it, I tell you," Burrington made a lunge at Tinseley. He tripped against the railing, and would have fallen, had not Anthony grasped his arm and pulled him erect just as he was about to lose his balance.

"Sir," said Peterson to Tinseley, his voice cold. "I must ask you once again to leave."

The man looked fixedly at his host. "I wonder how you would feel if you knew what Burrington said earlier. I do not believe you to be a coward, Enar." He turned on his heel and walked down the steps and across the lawn. A tall, slender woman joined him. Mistress Tinseley. The crowd parted silently to let them pass.

At that moment, Madam Burrington stepped out of the door of the house. Dierdra hastened to her side. The governor's lady was pale and her hands trembled, but her voice was calm as she said to her husband:

"Come, my dear. It is time to go home."

Burrington neither spoke nor moved.

"It is time to go, George," she said again. "Give me your arm, dear." She led him to the door. Dierdra and Anthony followed.

"Mr. Dawson, would you mind calling the coach, please, and telling Taphy we are ready to leave?"

"Yes, indeed. And if you will permit, I will accompany you back to Government House."

Madam Burrington nodded and smiled weakly. "That would be kind of you."

Anthony hurried off.

There was a dazed look on Burrington's florid face. Suddenly he spoke.

"No man should call me those names. I will not put up with it. I will not, do you hear?"

"There, there, my dear. It is all right. We are going home."

Burrington shook her hand off his arm. "It is not all right." His strong features seemed suddenly to crumple. "Damn it, I'm the governor." His voice became louder. "They may not like me as a man, these country nobodies, but they will have to learn to respect me as the governor. If they do not, that will be their bad fortune. The law is the law. They are insulting the entire government when they insult me. Not one of them has the courage to come to me privately to make his complaints! Oh, no, they wait to make public displays of themselves. They have not a single real grievance; things have been better in North Carolina since I am here than they ever were before. They simply do not want any governor at all. They want to run things to suit themselves. Well, they will not! I'll see to that."

Madam Burrington patted his arm. "Be quiet, my dear. Everything will be all right."

Dierdra spoke softly to her. "Is there anything I can do?"

"No, thank you." The older woman smiled gratefully. "It will be all right. Mr. Dawson will see us safely home. You stay here and have a good time with the young folk."

By now the coach was in the driveway. Anthony and Taphy helped the governor in. Madam Burrington turned to Mistress Peterson, who had been standing quietly in front of the house.

"Thank you for a very pleasant afternoon. We wish you and your husband every happiness in your new home." Her step was dignified as she walked down the drive.

The coach drove off, and the spell of silence was broken. Enar Peterson called out to the musicians:

"Let's have something lively. A contra dance."

The fiddlers tuned up and the others followed. Everyone welcomed the diversion; as if to cover their embarrassment, the dancers moved with unusual energy, and those who did not join in formed a circle around them and clapped their hands loudly in time to the music.

Just as the dance was breaking up, Peterson cried: "To the punch bowl, friends. We'll drink a toast to His Royal Highness, the King of England."

The toast to His Majesty was followed by one to the Queen, another to the royal family, and still another to the Lords Proprietors.

"And now to supper, friends," said Enar.

"Wait a moment!" Chief Justice Gale's voice rose above the noise. "I have one more toast to propose. To our gracious host and hostess, and to their continued happiness in their new home."

There was a roar of approval. The party, which had threatened to collapse in confusion, took on new life.

While the dancing was going on, Dierdra stood listlessly at the edge of the crowd. When it was over, she turned to look for Dick Chapman. She wanted to ask him to escort her back to Government House. She had not gone very far when she felt a hand on her arm and she wheeled about to look into the dark eyes of Allin Killigrew, handsome and elegant in a dark blue coat and tan satin smallclothes, with lace ruffles at the wrists and neck.

"Allin! I did not know you had come."

"I just arrived. On the heels of the excitement. I saw the governor's coach leaving, and met Dick Chapman with my sister while I was looking for you. They told me what had happened."

"Oh, Allin, it was dreadful, simply dreadful."

His face was serious. "I can imagine. Burrington may not be too bad when he is sober, but when he's in liquor . . ."

Dierdra was silent for a moment. Then she spoke tentatively. "I think I would like to leave now, Allin. Will you see me home?"

"Must you go now? I want to speak to you. To apologize and explain."

"For the quarrel we had? I was inexcusably rude and I interfered in your affairs. You owe me no apology; I owe one to you."

Allin smiled, but his eyes were grave. "You have already made your apology. Now, it is my turn. Come, let's take the path to the river. Mistress Peterson has had a fine little pavilion built, high above the stream. You have no idea how beautiful the river is, when the sun begins to set. And twilight is coming now."

They walked silently across the lawn and down the path to the river. Once there, they stood on the high bank, looking down at the reflection of the setting sun in its waters. The calm seemed almost unearthly. A fish broke the surface of the water, leaving a circle of widening ripples, and then sank into the river depths again and the water returned to its mirror-smoothness. The quiet evening was full of its own special sounds: a whooping crane in the distance, an owl's triumphant cry in the dark pocosin, and the frightened whimper of a small animal, caught in its tearing claws.

Dierdra sighed. "I needed this moment of peace. Today has been too much for me, I fear. I was disappointed not to see you. And then I overheard something unpleasant. And that ugly scene with the governor. I'm glad you did not see it, Allin."

"I hope you can forget the governor for a while. Come here." Allin took her by the hand and led her along the river bank to the pavilion. "Sit down, will you?" He gestured toward the wooden bench inside. From his waistcoat pocket he drew a folded piece of paper.

"I want you to read this. Is it too dark? Would it be easier outside?"

"There is quite enough light here. My eyes are sharp." She took the paper from him, and he walked off, leaving her sitting alone in the little pavilion. The trees rustled above her, but all else was silence. She unfolded the sheet. It was old, she could tell, and had been read many times before; the creases in the paper were so sharp, and the paper itself so wrinkled. The ink was faded, but the writing was still legible.

"My little son," she read. "My first-born son. When you read this, you will be a big boy, living in another land. When you think of me, I hope it is without anger or wrath. I loved your mother. She was sweet and gentle and lovely. She quieted my wildness and held me in check. I came home from my months abroad, in the army, determined to marry her in spite of my father's displeasure, only to find that she was gone from me—forever, in death—but that she had left you in the care of her brother, Owen Killigrew, and his good wife.

"I was too heartsick to claim you and take you with me, but I thought I would be able to see you often; Killigrew lived so near my family's estate. Then the good yeoman and his wife decided to go to America, and I had to make my choice. It was not easy for me, little Allin. But I thought it would be better for you if I let them take you with them. In the New World, you will not meet the restrictions of the old. You will not see your father's bitterness and grief. For how can I help feeling responsible for your mother's death?

"There will be ample funds for you, paid quarterly through my solicitor. This is the only amends I can make to you.

"I want you to have a suitable education, to prepare you for the future. You have a proud heritage. When you reach maturity, the choice is yours: to remain in the new country or to return to the old. It may be that, God willing, I shall still be living; if I am, it will give me great joy to welcome you, and claim you as my son. But even if I should be dead, I have taken the legal steps necessary for you to have my name, if you do not think it does you dishonor.

"This will be my only communication with you, my son. I shall not beg or importune you. The next step will be yours to decide. Whatever your decision may be, I want you to know my heart is with you. Your father, Allin Gorgas. London: 18th October, 1705."

Dierdra slowly folded the paper and stood for a time without moving. So many thoughts raced through her mind! Here was the explanation of all Allin's strange behavior: his reserve, his resentment at her interference, his outburst against the gentry, his fierce loyalty to Killigrew, his unwillingness to do anything to better himself. How long had he known? And what would this mean for his future—and for hers? She knew the Gorgas name well; it was borne by a very old and powerful Devon family. It was as proud a name as Granville.

She turned and walked slowly over to him.

"So now you know," he said softly as she approached.

She nodded.

"And has it shocked you beyond measure?"

"Oh, Allin, what kind of poor creature do you take me for?" Dierdra laid her hand on his arm. "It has not shocked me, it has made me sad. For your poor mother, and your father, too. And for you, as well, Allin, to carry such a painful secret in your heart."

"My father needs no more pity. He's dead. Killed only a short time after my uncle brought me over here. He went back to the wars."

"I'm so sorry," Dierdra murmured.

"Now I am, too. Now, I would like to have met him. But when I first heard the story of my birth . . ." He was silent for a moment. "It was on my sixteenth birthday, and I remember every second of that day. My father—Killigrew, I mean—took me down to the work house with him. I was so excited. I thought he had some kind of special birthday present for me." He laughed bitterly. "It certainly was a special present.

"Dierdra," he went on, grasping her arm almost savagely. "When I first read that letter, I was blind with rage. If my real father had been there, I think I would have strangled him with my bare hands."

"Poor Allin," Dierdra's voice was gentle.

"Then Killigrew began to talk to me," Allin went on as though he had not heard her words. "He told me how sweet and gentle my mother was, how warm-hearted and gay. He told me how much my father loved her. He told me that this strong man wept like a baby when he heard that his Mary was dead." He began to pace up and down. "But I did not believe him, or my father's sweet words in the letter. Some of the anger went out of me, Dierdra, but some of it stayed." He turned to face her.

"It was not until a while after that day at the Indian camp that things began to become clear to me." He paused and stared off into the darkness of the pocosin. The sun had sunk nearly out of sight, and his face was half lost in shadow.

"I don't quite know how to explain this to you, Dierdra. When I recovered from the first shock of my father's letter, I made up my mind never to let anyone know my story, and to live my life as Owen Killigrew's son—to be a yeoman, just as he is. Tamar and Owen still think I am their brother.

"It has not been exactly happy for me, but it has not been too bad. After all, my uncle has done so much for me. I felt it would be like slapping him in the face to tell the world the truth and take advantage of my father's name and position. I never have thought much of that saying that a king's bastard is a family's honor. Especially when I know that people like Mistress Peterson, who lord it over me and my father—my uncle, I mean—would fawn on us if I were to use the Gorgas name. . . ." A look of distaste crossed his face.

"Killigrew urged me over and over to go to college and to take my father's name. But I believed it would be unfair—not only to him, but to Owen and Tamar, as well. I cannot imagine Owen in college. So I paid no attention to his pleas. And when you added yours, and tried to pull me out of that comfortable little shell I had crawled into—well, that was a terrible moment. For the sake of my pride I told myself that you were arrogant and a snob." He shook his head. "I am ashamed even to tell you this, Dierdra."

She smiled sympathetically. "You shouldn't be. I can understand."

"Well, that night, after our quarrel, I could not sleep at all. My whole world was turned upside down. I was in a rage. And it was not until several days later that I could admit to myself you had spoken as you did because you believed in me and wanted to help me. And then I had to admit something else: that I had been just as unfair to myself as I had been to you."

Dierdra looked puzzled.

"Because the fact is, I had always wanted an education, even before I knew about my father. And if I had been Killigrew's true son, I would have had no hesitation about asking him to send me to college. He would have moved heaven and earth to give me my wish, too. But since I was not his son, everything was different in my eyes."

"Oh, Allin, Allin! I wish I had known."

The young man stood silent for a long moment. When he spoke, his voice was soft.

"Dierdra, I think I have finally come to my senses. I am going to do what you and my uncle have asked me to, what I've always wanted to do myself. But it is not going to be easy for me. I will be so much older than the other young men at William and Mary."

Impulsively, Dierdra took his hands in hers.

"Allin, how wonderful! You're going to go!"

He looked at her searchingly, and his fingers tightened around hers.

"Dierdra, Dierdra," he whispered.

Suddenly she was in his arms. She pressed against his hard, firm body. His kisses were sweet on her lips. When finally he released her, they stood for minutes without speaking.

"Dierdra, will you wait for me?" Allin's voice was husky. "Will you give me a chance to prove myself? I know it is a great deal to ask, but I do have one thing to recommend me. . . ." A tremulous smile broke through his lips. "When I feel I have the right to ask you to take my name, I will be able to offer you two to choose from. That's more than most young men can—"

She did not give him a chance to finish. Her arms went around him and she raised her lips to meet his in a kiss that left her trembling with an emotion deeper than any she had ever known before.

Chapter VIII

THE WILL

ANTHONY MADE one attempt at conversation on the trip back to Edenton, but the governor merely nodded and although Madam Burrington smiled and replied, it was obvious that both of them preferred silence. The liquor and the argument had apparently exhausted his excellency completely; Burrington was asleep by the time the carriage arrived at Government House. It had been Anthony's intention to leave as soon as the Burringtons were safely home, but as he helped Madam Burrington out of the coach, she said:

"I hope you will not mind waiting for a moment, Mr. Dawson. I would like to speak with you, if you have a moment's time."

Anthony nodded. He and Taphy woke the governor and, supporting him under the arms, led him into the house. As they entered, David Elton came out of Burrington's office. The secretary took in the situation at a glance.

"Taphy and I will see the governor upstairs, Madam Burrington."

She smiled gratefully. "Thank you, David." She turned to Anthony. "Come. We can talk in the library."

Silently he followed her into the small, paneled room. It was dark, and she lit the candles on the long table.

"There," she said as the last flame danced into life. "And now a cup of tea and we will be quite comfortable."

She pulled the bell cord by the fireplace and her maid came in —a little round-faced country girl with big, curious eyes. She curtsied.

"Taphy is busy upstairs, Madam. Can I help you?"

"Yes, thank you, Lillie. If you would ask cook to send in some tea?"

The girl curtsied again and withdrew. Madam Burrington motioned Anthony to one of the two large chairs that flanked the fireplace and sat down opposite him. Her delicate face was pinched and drawn, and her long thin fingers moved nervously across her lap, smoothing the folds of her skirt.

"Perhaps it is unfair of me to bring you into this, Mr. Dawson." Her voice was hesitant. "But I really do not know whom else to turn to, and besides—"

"Please, there is no need to apologize," Anthony leaned forward. "If there is anything at all I can do . . ."

The little maid entered with the tea. Madam Burrington did not speak again until she had left.

"I hope the servants do not hear about this. Gossip spreads so quickly. Taphy is almost one of us, but the others . . ." She paused and then, looking earnestly at Anthony, went on. "I am sure you can understand how mortified I am over that dreadful scene at the Petersons'. Yet in a way I am not sorry it happened. It has brought things out into the open and given me an opportunity to talk with you about what is on my mind."

Anthony's expression was inquiring.

"Mr. Dawson, I am desperately concerned about my husband. A man who drinks too much is a problem to himself and everyone around him." She was silent for a moment. "I hope you will not misunderstand. I am not complaining, or asking for sympathy. That would be contemptible. I knew George's weakness before I married him, and I am devoted to him in spite of it." She smiled wryly. "At first, of course, I thought he would stop drinking when he had a wife and family to look after. There must be thousands of women who expect the same sort of thing: as soon as their fiancés hear the wedding bells, their faults will disappear. It is quite a disillusionment when you discover things do not happen that way. Perhaps even the fortunate young woman who marries you will have secret hopes of reforming you, although you certainly do not seem to me to need it."

"Oh, I imagine I could stand some small improvement." Anthony laughed.

"And who of us could not?" Madam Burrington shook her head. "If George's drinking were only a private fault, it would be different. But it is more than that. After all, the governor is a public figure." She stirred her tea thoughtfully, and a frown appeared on her forehead. "I do not know if you are aware of how many problems there are in the province."

Anthony smiled. "One cannot be here for more than a short time without learning at least something about them."

"No, I imagine not. When it comes to political matters, George is far from weak. He is perfectly well able to hold his own against opposition, when he meets it, and until recently he was doing quite well. The people liked him, even though they knew he was inclined to take a drop too many and disagreements were settled amicably. But that incident today . . ." She shook her head. "I do not know what Mr. Tinseley's motives were, but he should not have spoken to the governor as he did."

Anthony drank off the last of his tea and set his cup down on the table. "I can hardly imagine anything like that happening in England."

"I am afraid this will not be the end of it." Sighing, Madam Burrington poured herself another cup of tea. "Since this has happened, George is going to brood over it and become upset. And when he is upset, he drinks. And when he drinks," she shook her head and a hopeless expression crossed her pale face, "he is likely to do foolish things, things that are politically unwise, things he would not do if he were not angry and unhappy. The result is inevitable: the situation will become more and more difficult for everyone in the province. And George will simply refuse to understand why, and to see that he has to accept part of the blame."

Anthony was silent; there was nothing he could say.

"I wish you would talk to my husband, Mr. Dawson," the governor's wife said softly. "You are one of the few people here he trusts and respects. Make him see how wrong his behavior is, and how self-defeating. This Eden will case, for instance. I know there is a great deal of feeling about it. If it goes to court and

John Lovyck is cleared—and I am quite sure he will be—all my husband's enemies will use it as a weapon against him."

"But isn't it too late to do anything now?"

"I do not think so. If the case were to be brought back to the Council, rather than to the Court, that might satisfy everyone." Madam Burrington's tone was speculative.

Anthony rose.

"Let me see what I can do," he said. "I do not want to promise too much. But I too have heard reports that Lloyd's charges are glaringly false. Perhaps the affair can be smoothed over."

Madam Burrington smiled. "I knew I could count on you. I have learned to like and trust you a great deal in the time you have been here. And Dierdra Treffry has confirmed all my favorable impressions. She thinks a great deal of you, too." She paused. "Dierdra has been extremely kind in helping me out with the children. I am fortunate indeed to have her. But this is not the kind of life she should lead. The Treffrys were never meant to be governesses; I'm sure I do not have to tell you that. And now that Dierdra is beginning to get over her heartbreak about her parents and her fiancé, I think it is time for her to make plans to leave us and take up her own life."

Anthony smiled. So Madam Burrington would like to see him married to Dierdra. Well, he himself was beginning to think more of the idea every day. But this was not the time to speak of it.

"I shall be happy to talk to the governor about the Eden will case. But before I do, let me find out whether the will is legal or not. If John Lovyck filed it for probate, there should be a copy in the clerk's office in the courthouse. No doubt Will Badham will let me take a look at it."

The following Monday morning, after breakfast, Anthony made his way across the Green to the courthouse. He found Will Badham in his office near the back of the building. It was a small, shabby room, cluttered with the cabinets that housed North Carolina's legal records. The sunlight that filtered in through the window sent motes of dust dancing in the air and picked out all the nicks and scars on the clerk's old maple desk.

Badham jumped to his feet as Anthony entered.

"Mr. Dawson! What can I do for you, sir?"

Anthony smiled and closed the door behind him.

"Good morning, Mr. Badham. Do you have a few moments?"

"Why yes, sir, yes. Sit down, Mr. Dawson, sit down." Will hurriedly removed a pile of papers from the room's one spare chair and looked around for a place to set down his burden. When he had managed to make room for it on top of one of the cabinets, he moved the chair next to his desk and motioned his visitor to take a seat.

Anthony picked up the chair and turned it around. Then he sat down astride it, his arms resting across its back.

"Mr. Badham," he said, "you can help me with a very important problem."

"I, sir?" The clerk's voice was nervous.

"About Governor Eden's will," Anthony went on.

A worried look crossed Badham's face. "I wish I had never heard of that plagued thing. Please, Mr. Dawson, I would rather not even talk about it."

"Mr. Badham," Anthony looked at him earnestly, "I would not ask you to discuss it if it were not a serious problem."

Badham smiled wryly. "But the reason I do not wish to talk about it is precisely that it *is* serious. It is very embarrassing for me. John Lovyck is my friend and the governor is my employer, in a manner of speaking. I do not want to take sides for or against either one of them." He sighed and looked at Anthony. "I suppose that makes me sound like a coward. Well, perhaps I am."

"I know you are in a difficult position," Anthony said, feeling in his waistcoat pocket for his pipe. "And I appreciate your frankness. I don't think you're a coward at all, but I would not ask you to help me if I thought it would create trouble for you."

"But it must make trouble for me, Mr. Dawson, can't you see?" The clerk picked up his handkerchief and nervously started to wipe his spectacles. "I have done everything I can about the Eden will already. More than I wanted to. I witnessed it, I probated it for John Lovyck. Even—" he lowered his voice confidentially

—"tried to persuade the governor not to hear Roderick Lloyd's charges. What more can a man do?" He spread his hands in a gesture of hopelessness.

"The will is legal, then?" Anthony asked.

"Mr. Dawson, why do you keep after me? I am sick to death of hearing about the Eden will." Badham rose from his desk, walked to the door and looked down the courthouse hall to make sure nobody was listening. He locked the door from the inside as he closed it. "Yes, the will is legal. Lovyck wrote only what Eden wanted him to. I can even show you the papers that prove it. When that case is heard in court, Roderick Lloyd's barrister will go home with his tail between his legs. No doubt of it." He shook his head. "But the governor says he is obliged to hear any charges a British subject may choose to bring up."

"He is perfectly correct about that." Anthony paused. "Mr. Badham, what do you think of the governor?"

Badham peered anxiously over his spectacles.

"That's another reason I am so disturbed about this case. The fact is, Mr. Dawson—and not just because I work closely with him—Burrington is a good governor, no matter what Edward Moseley and some of the others may tell you. He is difficult, sometimes, but many people are difficult. And he is fair."

"But he would have been equally fair if he had let John Lovyck reply to the charges at a Council meeting. Suppose I could persuade him to bring the case back to the Council?"

"Suppose the moon were made of green cheese? The governor's mind is made up. He will not change it. Events will just have to take their course."

Anthony smiled. "Perhaps the moon is made of green cheese, Mr. Badham. I am almost positive I could persuade the governor to change his mind. That is, if you will let me see a copy of the probate and the will, so that I can be convinced in my own mind that John Lovyck is innocent. And, believe me, Burrington will never know you had anything to do with it," he added hastily, noting the worried look on the clerk's face.

"What makes you so sure you will be able to influence the governor?"

"I have my reasons, Mr. Badham. Good ones." Anthony rose and stood looking down at the older man. "You know as well as I that this is not simply a case of Governor Eden's will, but a struggle between the governor and the Council."

The clerk nodded. "I suppose it is."

"Perhaps the time will come for a showdown between them," Anthony gazed reflectively at his pipe. "But I do not think this is the proper moment. And if Lloyd has no chance of winning his suit, the governor will not increase his stock very much by appearing to be a partisan of his."

Badham looked up with a start. "I had not thought of that."

Anthony smiled. "But I have, you see. And I am perfectly willing to point it out to the governor. That is, if you will let me see the papers, so that I know what I am talking about."

"You're sure no one will know my part in this? If the governor does not listen to you . . ." Badham's voice trailed off.

"You have my word of honor," Anthony said as he knocked out his pipe in the tray on Badham's desk. "You and I want the same thing, sir. Justice and honor—and good feeling in the province. This is our chance to get all of them."

Badham was silent. Then he rose from his desk and, drawing a ring of keys from his pocket, went over to one of the cabinets. "Of course, these papers are a matter of public record. You have a right to see them if you wish. But I hope the governor will not think I gave you the idea of looking at them. He would be furious at me. I wish this entire matter had never come up, or at least that I was not part of it." He sighed and, unlocking one of the drawers, drew forth a sheaf of papers. "Here you are, Mr. Dawson."

Anthony examined the papers with care. Everything seemed to be in order; there was no room for any suspicion of illegality. As his eyes moved across the paper, he was startled to discover how small the estate had been. If Eden had divided the property between his sister and his son-in-law, they would have had less than three hundred pounds apiece—hardly enough to warrant all this fuss, especially between well-bred people. And the probate certainly gave the lie to Lloyd's claim that there was eight thousand pounds in the estate.

He finished reading the last of the papers and rose. "Thank you, Mr. Badham. You have been a great help. And you have nothing to worry about. I am sure everything will go smoothly from now on."

As he made his way down the hall, Anthony saw Edward Moseley approaching him.

"Good morning, Mr. Dawson," the surveyor-general cried jovially, "I hope you are well." He smiled. "Although I should be angry with you, I suppose. I had hoped to be able to keep up that Chowan property of mine, near Killigrew's. But now that you have put in your bid, I am afraid I shall have to resign myself to losing it."

"I particularly wanted that parcel," Anthony said. "The island in the river there is where my ancestor, Sir Richard Granville, camped with his men in 1585. I feel as if it had been in my family all along."

Moseley nodded. "Of course. I should have remembered. Well then, you are forgiven."

"Good," Anthony smiled. "Have you a moment, sir? I would like to ask you something."

"At your service. Come into my office," Moseley threw open the door to his chamber. It was larger, brighter, and better furnished than Will Badham's. "Have a seat."

Anthony sat down, leaned back in the chair, and crossed his legs. "It's about the Eden will, Mr. Moseley. What do you really think of it?"

"It's nonsense, that's what I think. Lloyd has no case at all. And I think the governor's action was simply unforgiveable, as I told you on the day of the Council meeting. He rode roughshod over all our rights." He walked over to the window and gazed reflectively out over the bay, which was dotted with small craft. "Let me tell you something else, Mr. Dawson. This case has turned many people against the governor who used to speak highly of him, even Council members. Of course, it did not surprise me at all. I have been expecting something like this from the beginning. And if it goes on much longer, the settlers will be so anxious to be rid of Mr. Burrington they may eject him forcibly. We North Carolinians have done that before, you know."

"Really?" Anthony asked. "When?"

Moseley returned to his desk. He sat down and began absently to play with a quill pen.

"1677 was one time. The man was not appointed governor in the first place. His name was Miller, and he was secretary to the legal governor, Eastchurch. The two men started here from England, and on their way they stopped off at the Island of Nevis. Eastchurch met a young Creole lady there, fell in love with her, and decided to remain for a while, to press his suit. He sent Miller on to North Carolina to govern in his place. Miller made himself so unpopular here that there was an armed uprising against him—Culpepper's Rebellion, it was called. He was seized by the people and imprisoned on a ship. And Miller's successor, who came over shortly afterwards, was so cordially disliked that he was forced to flee the province and exile himself in South Carolina. There should be some lessons for Governor Burrington in those events."

"I'm sure he knows of them," Anthony said. He looked for a long moment at the surveyor-general. "Mr. Moseley, what would you think of having the Eden will case brought back to the Council for a rehearing?"

"You want my candid opinion?" Moseley eyed his visitor warily. "I think it would help a little. But I do not believe it would solve our real problem here. You mark my words, Mr. Dawson, Burrington is going to find himself in deep trouble with the people of this province."

"Perhaps he will. That I do not know. In the meanwhile, however, there is the question of the Eden will to be solved. If the Council members would like to hear John Lovyck's answer . . ."

"Of course they would," Moseley nodded his head vigorously. "That is all we wanted in the first place: a chance to hear the whole story, so that we could decide whether or not the case should be sent to court."

Anthony picked up his hat and rose. "I think you will have your wish, Mr. Moseley."

Anthony went straight to Government House from Moseley's office. Fortunately, the governor was not occupied, and he seemed delighted to hear that Mr. Dawson had come to call. He rose from his desk as the younger man entered.

"You could not have come at a better time, sir," he said, cordially. "I have something I particularly wanted to discuss with you."

Anthony looked at him inquiringly.

"But sit down, Mr. Dawson, sit down. A glass of wine, sir?"

"No, thank you," Anthony said as he took his seat.

Burrington smiled. "Nor I. I seem to have had quite enough at Mistress Peterson's party the other day to last me for a while."

"Well, wine goes with a celebration," Anthony said, wondering what had prompted the older man to this unexpected confession.

"I have told myself that. But it does not help much. The fact is, Mr. Dawson, that I behaved most foolishly. No sensible man plays right into the hands of his enemies. And that is precisely what I did when I let myself lose my temper with Tinseley." The governor paused and his expression became angry. "All the same, the man was goading me. You would have seen it yourself if you had been in the room at the time. He knew I had had a drop too much, and he was deliberately trying to provoke me."

"I should not be surprised, sir."

"Let me tell you why I am saying this, Mr. Dawson. That scene at the party gives you some idea of the way these people treat their governors. I have reported incidents like this to Lord John several times before. Mr. Tinseley's was not the first attack. But although I am sure Lord John respects my word, I think he would take this matter more seriously if it were backed up by some impartial observer, someone he knew, someone who understood the situation here." The governor leaned forward and lowered his voice. "I have a favor to ask of you, Mr. Dawson. If you would write Lord John, too, and tell him what happened at the

Peterson party . . ." He raised a warning hand. "And I do not want you to gloss over the fact that I offered to fight the man, or even that I was in my cups. Everyone is entitled to a little human weakness. The important thing is that the Proprietors should know how shabbily their governors are treated."

So this was the reason for Burrington's frankness. Anthony realized he could use the governor's request as an entering wedge for his own. He kept his voice casual.

"I could write to Lord John, of course. But, if you will forgive me, your excellency, it seems to me that you have given the settlers cause for resentment recently." Burrington looked up sharply but Anthony went right on.

"I think you should know that the Eden will case has created a great deal of bad feeling. Everyone to whom I have spoken seems to think that John Lovyck should have been given a chance to present his answer before the Council. They feel that you acted arbitrarily in sending the case directly to court."

Burrington's expression was angry, but his voice was calm. "I acted firmly, not arbitrarily." He shook his head. "Sometimes these people baffle me, Mr. Dawson. If I were John Lovyck, I would welcome the opportunity to answer charges like these in open court, especially if I knew my case was strong. And Will Badham—I may tell you in confidence—has assured me that Lovyck's case is unassailable."

"Then why not let the Council pass on it, sir?"

"Because all those gentlemen are friends of Lovyck's. They would be prejudiced in his favor, and everyone would know it. If I were Lovyck, I would not want to be cleared by my friends, but by an impartial jury."

"Your excellency, I cannot disagree with anything you have said. But you must look at this from the settlers' point of view. You yourself have told me that these people are independent. You did not consult them on this case, you must admit that. And that makes them feel that you have been a tyrant."

Burrington rose from his desk and shook his fist angrily in Anthony's face.

"Tyrant! George Burrington a tyrant! How dare they?" He

set his hands on the edge of the desk and slowly sank back into his chair. A look of defeat crossed his face. "Oh, very well, Dawson. I still believe I did the right thing. But I want Lord John to know what goes on here, and I certainly will not let a trivial matter like this interfere with my administration. If John Lovyck wants to live under a cloud . . ." He shrugged his shoulders. "There are more important matters coming up, and I want to be here when they do." He nodded his head thoughtfully. "Much more important matters. The whole future of the province . . ."

The second reading of the Lloyd memorial took place at the Council's meeting on the following Thursday. Only a few village folk were present; it had not been generally known that the memorial would come up again, and there was no other business of sufficient interest to draw people into the courthouse on a beautiful spring day.

The governor was pleased to lay before the Council the memorial of Roderick Lloyd, Esq., Ann, his wife, and Margaret Pugh, her daughter, of London, England, in the county of Middlesex, on the subject of the late Governor Eden's will. The Council members listened in silence as Will Badham read the paper, accusing John Lovyck of undue influence over an old, sick man, and of taking possession of an estate of eight thousand pounds sterling by pretext of a forged will.

Burrington listened to the reading of the memorial unmoved. When it was finished, he addressed John Lovyck.

"Have you prepared an answer to these charges, sir?"

Lovyck rose and bowed.

"I have. Your excellency, court records will prove that I placed in the courthouse, at the time of Governor Eden's death, a true and perfect inventory of the late governor's estate, which was appraised by law and amounted in value to 560 pounds sterling, eighteen shillings and sixpence. I have obtained a copy of the probate, which I beg leave to present to you now. It leaves no room for any imputation that the estate was of larger size." He handed a sheaf of papers to the governor and stood back with his arms folded.

Burrington examined the documents carefully and passed them on to Chief Justice Gale, who sat at his right. When they had made the rounds of the Council members, Lovyck spoke again.

"I would also like to enter before the governor and the Council the testimony of two reputable persons who have made depositions, under oath, that they were familiar with Governor Eden's will, were present when it was drawn up, and acted as witnesses to it. They swear to the events and also to the fact that the governor was completely able and competent to make disposition of his estate."

There was a stir among the few spectators and Lovyck sat down.

"Mr. Badham, you wrote one of these depositions, did you not?" Burrington asked.

Will Badham nodded.

"Then perhaps I should ask someone else to read them. Mr. Moseley?"

Edward Moseley smiled as he walked up to the end of the table and took up the papers. He cleared his throat and began to read.

There was a slight movement in the back of the room as Penelope Lovyck stepped in and took a seat next to Anthony and Dick, who had arrived earlier. She greeted them and leaned forward, her eyes alight. John Lovyck looked at her, a slight smile on his lips, and she blew him a hurried kiss.

Moseley's voice was loud and clear.

" 'Deposition of Mrs. Mary Badham, wife of William Badham, Esq., of Edenton in North Carolina, who is sworn and sayeth that on the twenty-fifth day of December in the year 1724 she was in the house of the late Charles Eden, Esq., then governor of North Carolina, where she had been visiting for several days. The governor was then indisposed, but of sound and perfect mind and memory, and not confined to his bed.

" 'The governor spoke to her of his will. He showed some concern that John Lovyck, to whom he said he designed to give everything, should be so backward about writing it, and much wondered if he could not prevail on Mr. Lovyck to perform this service for him.

" 'The governor further stated that he desired the will to be written while deponent and her husband, William Badham, were present, in order that they would witness the instrument. The governor requested that deponent speak to Mr. Lovyck and urge him to write the will while she was there, for it would be the last will the governor would ever make.

" 'Deponent further sayeth that she was present when John Lovyck came into the room, and that the governor said to him, in her hearing, that he had often been at Mr. Lovyck to write the will, and although Mr. Lovyck had refused whenever he was asked, it would be a great favor to his excellency if it were done then. At this point, John Lovyck reluctantly consented. He sat down and by the governor's order wrote the will, which the governor signed, and deponent and her husband then witnessed.' "

Moseley handed the paper to the governor. "This deposition is signed by Mary Badham. I give it to you for your inspection."

Burrington examined the paper and passed it on to Chief Justice Gale. "You have another deposition there, I believe, Mr. Moseley."

The surveyor-general nodded. "This one is signed by William Badham, Esq." He adjusted his spectacles and began to read. Will Badham's statement bore out all the details of his wife's.

When he had finished reading and the Council members had inspected the paper, Chief Justice Gale arose and addressed the governor.

"Your excellency, Mr. Lovyck's evidence proves beyond the shadow of a doubt that there is no truth in the accusations that have been made in the memorial. Mr. Lovyck did not influence the governor in the making of the will. He did not forge any documents. He listed and itemized Governor Eden's holdings at the time of the probate, under oath and according to law. We have seen and examined all the documents he has presented in support of his case. I am of the firm opinion that the Council would be remiss in its duty if it were to pass these charges on to the court. I therefore move that the memorial be dismissed."

Thomas Harvey got to his feet. "I second that motion, and call for a vote of the Council."

Burrington's face was expressionless. "I await the Council's pleasure," he said drily.

The chorus of "ayes" that rose was deafening.

As the Council members arose and waited for the governor to leave, Anthony turned to Penelope Lovyck.

"This must be a welcome relief for you," he said.

There were tears of happiness in her eyes. She nodded mutely and a smile crossed her lips.

"You have no idea how much of a relief."

John Lovyck broke away from the little knot of Council members and townfolk who had clustered round to congratulate him, and hurried over to his wife. He took her hands in his and looked at her for a long moment.

"Well, Penny?" he said, his deep voice unsteady.

"Oh, John," she squeezed his hand, "the nightmare is over."

"You know it is his doing, my dear." He turned to Anthony. "Mr. Badham has told me, Mr. Dawson."

"I wish I could take the credit," Anthony said. "But I'm afraid I cannot. It only proves that if honorable men are willing to sit down and discuss their differences amicably, a great deal of trouble can be avoided."

"There's no question of that." A smile crossed Lovyck's long face. "I only hope everyone remembers it."

As they emerged from the courthouse, Dick said:

"You and Lovyck sounded to me as if you were talking in riddles, Tony. What was it all about?"

"If you had not been spending all your time at Lilac Farm, you might know," Anthony smiled at his friend. "Why, I don't think I have had a chance to say more than 'good morning' and 'good night' to you since the day of the Petersons' party."

"I'm afraid I have to plead guilty to that charge." Dick laughed. "But you cannot really blame me for being more interested in Tamar than in Governor Eden's will."

By this time, the two young men had reached the King's Arms. They crossed the common room and went upstairs to their suite. Dick hung his waistcoat over the back of a chair and flung himself onto the divan.

"You know, Tony," he said, "Tamar and I have made up our minds. We are going to be married."

Anthony sat down, a thoughtful expression on his face. "Do you really mean that, Dick?"

"Why else would I possibly say it?"

"Marriage is a serious step."

"Oh, come now, don't lecture me. I know all about the responsibilities of marriage. But with Tamar as the reward, I am perfectly willing to take them on."

"What about your families, though?"

"What do you mean, 'what about them'?" Dick stretched. "I certainly intend to tell my father."

"I do not think he will like it one bit. Or that the Killigrews will either."

Dick looked startled. "Why not?"

"The Killigrews are yeomen, after all."

"Tony, I am surprised at you." A red flush suffused Dick's cheerful countenance. "I never thought you would talk like that."

Anthony could see that his friend was becoming angry. "I don't want you to think I am interfering, Dick, but—"

"Well, perhaps you are. I cannot believe you take all this nonsense about yeomen and gentry seriously. It's, it's . . . old-fashioned."

Anthony shook his head in perplexity.

"I am sorry if my ideas seem old-fashioned to you, Dick," he said softly. "But I cannot pretend I do not have them. The question is not my feelings, however, but your father's and Killigrew's. I do not believe either of them will want to see their children marry out of their class. You and Tamar may think these social rules are out of date, but many people believe in them."

"In England, perhaps. Not here. I've already spoken to Killigrew, as it happens. And the only thing he dislikes is the fact that

Tamar wants to live in Virginia, far away from her family." He paused. "I am not too happy about it, either. I was looking forward to taking up property near yours."

Anthony was glad of the chance to change the subject. "Perhaps you can have property in both places."

"Perhaps." Dick stood up. "And that reminds me. I want to leave for Virginia in a few days. I had thought of writing my father about Tamar. But since she wishes to settle along the James, I may as well take the trip up and work out all the property details at the same time I give him the glad tidings."

Anthony looked at Dick thoughtfully; an idea had just come to him.

"How would you feel about having company on the trip?"

"You, Tony? I would be delighted, you know I would. That is, provided you do not lecture me on the responsibilities of marriage and the social standards of England."

"If you promise not to spend all your time sighing and mooning over Tamar."

"Done!" Dick extended his hand, smiling. "It's a bargain!"

Anthony grinned as he returned his friend's strong grip. He was not as sure as Dick that the marriage plans would proceed smoothly, but having issued his warning, there was nothing more he could do. If Mr. Chapman refused to give his consent, Anthony's presence would be some comfort to his friend. If, on the other hand, things worked out as Dick wanted, Anthony would be free to devote all his attention to the main purposes of his trip: conversation with the leading settlers in Virginia, and an inspection of the Crown colony. His recommendations to his family for their future conduct in North Carolina would be determined at least in part by a comparison of the respective merits of proprietary and Crown governments.

Chapter IX

MUSTER DAY

ANTHONY AND DICK arrived back in Edenton from Virginia in the early evening of the day before the annual Muster Day, which was set for the tenth of August. They found the town humming with activity. Flags were flying from galleries and rooftops. Booths had been set up around the Green. The public parade, long overgrown with weeds and brush, had had its annual cleaning. The town merchants had freshened their shops and put their best merchandise on display; farmers and planters came to town on Muster Day prepared to trade their produce for merchandise. The bay was crowded with craft, not only from across the river and the sound, but from as far away as the Outer Banks.

Performers of all kinds had already arrived; on the Green a small, bronzed man was stringing wire for wire-walking, and a couple of jugglers were practicing their act. A festive spirit filled the air, and Anthony found himself in the grip of homesickness; it all reminded him so vividly of one of the annual Devon or Cornwall fairs.

As soon as they arrived, Dick hurried out to Lilac Farm to see Tamar. Anthony's prediction had proved true; Mr. Chapman was bitterly opposed to his son's marriage to a girl of yeoman stock. But Dick had been adamant, and had finally wrested a reluctant consent from his father, who agreed to bestow his formal blessing on the match on the condition that Dick and Tamar make their home in North Carolina. Since this had been Dick's preference, the young man had offered no objection. Tamar might be disappointed, but she would get over it.

Anthony smiled as he watched his friend leave. He was remaining in Edenton; he had arranged a meeting with Ali Hassan for later that evening. The merchant would have information for him; he had been traveling through North Carolina for the last few months.

There was still an hour or more before Ali Hassan was due to arrive. Anthony rested for a while and then pulled up a chair to the small table in the sitting room and spread before him the map of Edenton he had made before he left. The houses on Water Street followed the line of Edenton Bay, from the long peninsula at Hayes Plantation, curving across the Green, and then forming a straight line to the shipyard, across from the Island of the Deep Pocosin. Behind Water Street was King Street, then Queen Street, then Church Street, where the vestry planned to build a church. Cutting across were Broad Street and Oakum Street, where the seamen stretched their ropes. Nearby was Rope Walk. Beyond were a few scattered dwellings, and beyond that, the countryside.

Anthony tamped the tobacco in his pipe, lit it, and sighed. The map was fine, as far as it went. Every single dwelling and shop in the village had been marked. But it was not the buildings that would tell the story; it was the people who lived in them. He thought back over the conversation he had had with William Byrd, of Virginia, whom he had visited on his trip. Byrd's words had not increased his confidence in North Carolina's future; the statesman had little use for its settlers.

"An ill-educated, shiftless lot," he had said. "They sit on their porches, rocking, when they should be working in the fields."

"There are educated men in Edenton, owners of soundside plantations," Anthony protested.

"A few, perhaps. But a very few. You can tell from the plantations themselves. They don't begin to compare with our James River properties. Your Governor Burrington is hard put to keep them in check. Dawson, it is my opinion that North Carolina ought to follow our example and go over to the Crown. A proprietary government will never succeed. Never. And at least one important person in your province agrees with me. You would be surprised how important."

Anthony tried to resist the impulse to fight the battle of North

Carolina, but he could not restrain one comment that had come to his lips. "What about the proprietary governments of Pennsylvania and Maryland, sir?"

Byrd waved his hand. "No comparison at all, Dawson. Absolutely no comparison. There is a world of difference between a government with one man ruling and a government that is in the hands of many—among them women and children—who have not even the slightest interest in the country. Governor Burrington tells me he has not been paid his salary once, and he has been in the province for over a year now. Not one single penny has he received in all that time."

As he pored over his map, Anthony made a mental note to tell Lord John about this conversation in detail. He had been writing him regularly, but now the time had come for a comprehensive report. Anthony had not yet made up his mind whether to put this final statement in writing, or to go back to London and present his conclusions in person. Actually, the decision was in Dierdra Treffry's hands, not his. All the time he had been in Virginia, she had not been out of his thoughts for more than a few moments, and the idea of settling down with her on the property he had purchased in North Carolina was becoming daily more appealing. He would speak to her very soon; if her answer was yes, he would start work on the new house immediately, so that they could be married near the beginning of the year. Perhaps they could take a wedding trip to England; then he would be able to supplement his written report to Lord John with face-to-face conversation. But that was a detail; the important thing was to see Dierdra soon and to settle matters with her. Actually, there should be no problem—Madam Burrington had all but told him his suit would be welcomed.

A knock on the door interrupted his thoughts. It was Ali Hassan.

"Good evening to you, sir." The merchant bowed.

"And to you." Anthony motioned his guest to a chair. "This time I remembered that you do not drink spirits, and I sent my man to learn the secret of preparing coffee as you like it. But I wonder if in this heat you would not prefer something cold?"

"A hot drink is always best on a hot day. Besides, I find conversation more companionable when I can take a sip or two of good Turkish coffee."

Anthony smiled. "At least conversation over coffee is likely to be sensible. Over wine . . ."

"True, very true. I fear that is the first lesson your governor has to learn."

"Is the governor still drinking? I thought he had stopped."

"Apparently not. There was some improvement about the time the Eden will case was settled, but the governor seems to be back to his old ways now. It does not increase his popularity."

Smalkins entered, carrying a tray on which were steaming cups of Turkish coffee.

"Thank you, Smalkins. You can set the tray down here." Anthony rolled up the map to make room on the table.

Over their coffee, Ali Hassan gave Anthony his report. He had spoken to townspeople and country folk, not only to those around Edenton, but to residents of towns as far distant as Bath. His information was thorough.

"Only about a third of the townspeople like the present form of government. All the others feel that North Carolina would do better under the Crown. Not only because they dislike Burrington; those outside of Edenton have very little feeling about him. But the majority of the people believe that the enormous strides Virginia and South Carolina have made since they went under the Crown are the result of that change, and they want to see North Carolina advance, too." Hassan took a sip of his coffee and sat back.

"What about the country folk?" Anthony asked. "Do they agree?"

The merchant shook his head. "By and large, no. Neither the planters nor the yeomen want the Proprietors to sell. They admit that they may be suffering economically under proprietary government, because the Crown Colonies discriminate against them. But they would not want to give up their political freedom and their voice in the government. They prefer things as they are."

"A most complicated situation." Anthony leaned back in his chair and stretched.

"Life itself is complicated," Ali Hassan smiled and rose. "But eventually it comes to an end, and we can look forward to Paradise and its pleasures." He bowed. "I wish you good night, sir."

When Anthony went down to breakfast the next morning, he found the common room overflowing with yeomen, farmers, and young town lads. Many of them were drinking their morning grog of rum punch, which was supposed to ward off the chills and agues of late summer. Potboys, barmen and waiters passed through the noisy, cheerful crowd, carrying trays with pewter tankards and stone mugs of rum and cider.

Anthony pushed his way through the press of people to the door. On the gallery men and boys were crowded around Jock, the old Negro fiddler, who was playing a gay tune on his squeaky violin. On the Green, Anthony could see two husky young men engaged in a boxing match with bare fists; an old yeoman nudged him with a bony elbow to explain that the winner would get a quart of rum, donated by deVoe.

Anthony nodded and smiled and slowly made his way to the small breakfast buttery that gave on the courtyard. He found a vacant table along the wall and sat down. Through the small-paned window he could see men and horses, carts and mules, hostlers and farm folk, all milling about in wild confusion. Stable boys were unhooking the carriage horses and leading saddle horses into the stables. Farmers in their brown butternut homespun coats, leathern knee breeks, and home-knit hose, were moving in and out of the crowd, caring for their mounts and cart horses. Men in militia uniforms were hurrying to the Green.

The waiter came up to take his order.

"I am glad to see you, man," Anthony smiled. "I'm famished. I want three eggs, two rashers of bacon, and a pot of China tea. And the faster, the better!"

"Yes, indeed, sir." The waiter hurried off.

As he waited for his breakfast, Anthony watched a game of fives that was being played in a quiet corner of the courtyard.

The players, a group of young men, had drawn a line along the wall of the stable, about a yard above the ground, and another line on the paving stone, almost ten feet from the wall. Two others, at right angles to these, marked the boundaries of the court. With much laughter and chaffing, the players tossed for sides, and the game began. The leader hit a ball against the wall with a bat; when it bounced back into the marked division, it became the property of the other team, one of whose members hit it back against the wall with the flat of his hand.

The waiter, who had returned with Anthony's breakfast, looked out of the window.

"They are playing for a quart of brandy. Liquor is the winner's prize for nearly all the games today. It's costing deVoe a pretty penny, and he is considerably annoyed about it."

Anthony laughed. "I'm sure he will more than make it up in the liquor that will be sold."

The waiter nodded. "It will be an exciting day, sir. What with the competition between different precincts, and every man drinking his grog, Edenton will be a noisy place before nightfall."

Anthony took a bite of his bacon. "What games will they be playing?"

"All kinds, sir. Wrestling, and bandy—"

"Bandy? I have never heard of that one."

"In England it is called cambuc, or goff."

"Oh, yes, goff. With a stick with a turn at the end. But that takes a lot of space."

"Yes, sir. They play it out on the Virginia Road, on the open space beyond the Red Lion. There's plenty of room there for long driving. But the big event of the day is the gander pulling. You must see the gander pulling."

Anthony did not get a chance to ask what gander pulling was; deVoe was calling loudly and angrily for the waiter, and the man hurried away, wiping his hands on his leathern apron.

Anthony was drinking the last of his tea when Dick Chapman entered.

"Ah, there you are, Tony. I've been looking all over for you."

"Good morning, Dick. You give me an excuse for another pot of tea."

Dick drew up a chair and sat down.

"I did not hear you come in last night," Anthony said. "You must have stayed with Tamar until all hours."

"It was late when I came back." Dick's face was somber. "I never will understand women, Tony. You would think the fact that we are not going to live in Virginia spells the end of the world. That was all Tamar could talk about last night. Not me, or whether she had missed me, or whether she loved me."

"Did you tell her about your father?"

"How could I? It would have hurt her feelings terribly. I simply told her I thought we would be happier here; that seeing Virginia again had made me realize how much I wanted to live in North Carolina."

"Well, don't worry. She probably feels a little frightened now that she is really faced with marriage. It was only a dream, before." Anthony smiled. "And don't even try to understand her, Dick. Tamar is a woman, and in a woman the mystery is half the fun."

"I daresay you are right." Dick's expression was pensive. He sighed. "By the way, your friend Dierdra Treffry was at Lilac Farm yesterday afternoon."

Anthony caught sight of the waiter and beckoned him to the table. After Dick had given his order, the young Englishman said:

"What was Dierdra doing there?"

"I imagine she enjoys visiting with the Killigrews." Dick paused for a moment. "And I can tell you that one of them enjoys having her there—and much more than a little. Allin. That young man is in love with her, I'm sure."

A feeling of unease came over Anthony, a quick tightening of the muscles of his stomach. He controlled his voice.

"Why do you say that?"

"Well, first of all, you have never seen anybody so changed. I have no idea what happened while we were away, Tony, but whatever it is, it has turned Allin Killigrew into a new man. He no longer has to be urged to talk. He's friendly, and he smiles. He even speaks about going to William and Mary College next month. Everything about him is different, even the expression on his face. And when Dierdra comes into the room . . ."

"And what does Dierdra think of him?" Anthony tried to keep his voice indifferent.

"I don't know. I am not sure. She is very quiet. But I am inclined to think she knows what is going on, and likes it."

"What makes you think that?"

"Well, she seems somehow aware of him all the time, even when she isn't looking at him."

Anthony's discomfort increased. Dierdra and Allin . . . But that was impossible! Quickly he changed the subject.

"Today seems to be a real holiday."

Dick smiled. "I hear there will be wrestling this afternoon. I think I shall enter."

"That sounds like a good idea."

"I'm not very good at it, but Allin is going to have a try, so I might as well, too. There's a professional wrestler here, from Bideford. The Old Bunger, they call him. Allin is good. Maybe he will even be able to throw the fellow."

"Where do you come in, then, Dick?"

"Me? Oh, I will only be in the preliminaries, to swell the number."

"I shall put a wager on you, lad," Anthony said.

"Don't. You will only lose your shillings. Wager on Allin. He was practicing with Owen yesterday, and from what I saw, he can really put a man on the mat."

When Dick had finished his breakfast, the two young men separated. Anthony walked down King Street and across Broad, dodging among the carts and gigs. On the Government House lawn he found Madam Burrington and Dierdra. The governor's wife was seated on a lawn chair, her knitting in her hands; Dierdra was keeping an eye on the children, who were running up and down the garden paths, playing tag.

"It is good to see you again, Mr. Dawson," Madam Burrington said. "We have missed you these months. I hope your journey to Virginia was successful."

Anthony smiled. "It has made me even fonder of North Carolina. If that is success . . ."

"It is success for us. We are delighted to have you back among us. Do bring up a chair and sit down. The governor is at the parade ground, inspecting the drill. He says we can see the parade from here, in comfort."

Anthony's eyes were on Dierdra. "I came to ask Mistress Treffry to walk up to the shipyard with me, to see the muster."

Dierdra hesitated, but Madam Burrington said:

"Do go with Mr. Dawson, my dear. The children can stay here with me. I will send for nurse if they get out of hand."

"Well," Dierdra sounded reluctant.

"Oh, run along, do. Dr. Norcomb and his wife are coming soon. They will be company for me. And the servants are here to look after my wants."

"Not Taphy," Dierdra put in.

"How is that?" Anthony asked. "Is something the matter with the old man?"

Madam Burrington smiled. "Taphy is at the parade ground, selling gingerbread."

Anthony raised his eyebrows inquiringly.

"Yes. It seems to be an old custom. Taphy always sells gingerbread on Muster Day. 'Gingybread,' he calls it. He and cook were up most of the night, baking."

"What does the governor think of the idea?" Anthony asked.

"He thinks it is amusing. 'Can't break precedent,' he told Taphy. 'What are you going to do with the money?' And when Taphy said, 'Sir, I earn it, and I will keep it,' he nearly burst with laughter."

"Well, now that I know about Taphy's business enterprise, I shall buy some gingerbread for Mistress Dierdra and, if I may, bring some back for the children."

"Oh, please, Mr. Dawson, don't bring any back. Taphy left the children far too well supplied. I am afraid they will both be ill tomorrow."

The Norcombs arrived just then and, after the greetings were completed, Anthony and Dierdra left. He put his arm under her elbow and hurried her off, bound for the lane that followed the water to the shipyard. He thought he had never seen her more beautiful. She was wearing a soft sprigged muslin with a full skirt and a narrow, pointed bodice that emphasized the gentle curve of her breasts. Her wide leghorn hat was wreathed with blue cornflowers, and she carried a small rose-colored taffeta parasol.

"I was afraid I would never get you alone," he whispered, as they crossed the lawn. "I've never felt the pressure of so many people closing in on me."

Dierdra looked up at him from under the curved brim of her flower-laden hat. She smiled, but her blue eyes were serious.

"You are very beautiful," he said. "I was away so long I had almost forgotten."

She moved away from the pressure of his arm. "You make rather an impressive-looking figure, yourself, Mr. Dawson." Her eyes swept appraisingly over his tall, supple form. A beautifully fitted coat, a handsome chamois waistcoat, smallclothes, and hose of white silk. "I am sure the buckles on your shoes are pure silver."

"You are teasing me, my girl," he laughed, pressing her arm close to his side. "But I was serious."

Again she moved away. "The worldly Mr. Dawson serious?"

A hurt look came into his eyes. Dierdra saw it, but she would not let it affect her.

"Come now, Anthony, remember what old friends we are."

He stiffened. "Of course. So we are. Old, old friends. Almost brother and sister, eh?" His voice changed abruptly. "Well, here we are almost at the shipyard. Have you ever seen such a motley crowd of human beings?"

She spoke sharply. "Don't be so superior, Anthony Dawson. These are fine, good people. I fail to find them laughable."

"I beg your pardon," Anthony bowed deeply, an ironic smile

on his face. "I had forgotten how much of an American you are. They are all fine, good people, out for a splendid, quiet frolic."

He looked pointedly at a group of young men, sprawled under a spreading oak tree. They were passing a bottle from one to another, each tilting his head as he took a drink. "A splendid, innocent frolic," Anthony said. They walked on in silence.

Dierdra ignored his remark. "Come over to the parade ground," she said. "I see the governor. He must be getting ready to review the troops."

"That's an extraordinarily fine horse he has there," Anthony said as they crossed the path and took up a position at the edge of the square. The crowd was packed shoulder to shoulder around the four sides of the parade ground; Dierdra had to stand on tiptoe to see.

The bugle sounded, there was a ruffle of drums, and the citizen-soldiers entered the parade. The men from Chowan Precinct were a good-looking lot: young, bronzed, vigorous and eager, they marched smartly. One of the officers wore the uniform of the Queen's Own.

"Not bad, not bad at all," Anthony murmured, as the parade passed Governor Burrington, each man saluting expertly.

Dierdra turned to him and smiled. "I am sorry I was so sharp, Anthony. But I do admire these people, and I'd like it if you did, too. I want us to be friends."

He smiled in return. "I admire them, too, and I am sorry if I sounded arrogant. We certainly are friends, Dierdra. Very good friends."

The company from Chowan gave way to the one from Perquimans. Next came the Bertie patrol; this newly-made precinct did not have a full company, nor did the men have uniforms. But the lack was more than made up for by the professional manner in which the company drilled, and by the spirited music produced by their fife and drum corps, which won loud applause from the crowd.

I could drill a fine army here, in case of need, Anthony thought. Farm lads make good soldiers.

Governor Burrington and his aides started to ride off the field and Anthony touched Dierdra's arm. "We had better leave now, before it breaks up. Otherwise we will be trampled to death."

"Yes, and I think it is time for me to be going back. I promised Allin Killigrew I would go to the picnic with him this afternoon."

Anthony left Dierdra at the Government House gate and made his way across the crowded Green to the inn. The merry-makers' voices and laughter sounded noisy and vulgar to his ears, and he barely nodded to Justice Gale and Edward Moseley, whom he passed on their way to take their places on the platform that had been set up in front of the courthouse, from which the governor and the village worthies were to review the troops.

At the King's Arms, Anthony forced his way across the common room and went upstairs. He took off his coat and chamois waistcoat, kicked off his shoes, looking with distaste at their handsome buckles, and threw himself on his bed. He felt defeated. What had happened to Dierdra? Madam Burrington had said she admired him. . . . Perhaps he should not have stayed in Virginia such a long time. He had given her a chance to forget him, and Allin Killigrew a chance to help her forget.

Noises from the crowded Green floated up to his window. An amateur band began to play, its tones discordant and raucous. Anthony got up and closed the window with a bang that all but shattered the panes. Better to suffer from the summer heat than from that racket!

It was almost four when he awoke. Dick was pounding on the door of his room.

"How can you sleep on a day like this? Hurry up and put on your riding clothes. The wrestling will begin in half an hour."

Anthony stretched and sighed. "All right. I have to watch you get beaten up." He went to the washstand and splashed water over his face.

Dick had taken off his jacket and tossed it on the bed. "Don't wear a coat. It's too hot. See you in a little while." He slammed the door behind him and raced downstairs, whistling.

Anthony dressed in doeskin riding breeks and a white silk shirt with lace ruffles and stock, over which he slipped on a sleeveless jerkin of brown cloth. He pulled on his high riding boots of brown leather. In the stable he found the brown mare, Chissy, which he had bought after Black Douglas' death. He saddled her and jumped up. The wrestling was to take place in an open field near the Red Lion; by keeping Chissy at a gallop, he was able to make the trip in about fifteen minutes.

Once arrived at the wrestling square, Anthony went first to pay his respects to Governor Burrington and his lady, who were sitting in raised seats under the trees. Then he walked over to the north side of the square, where Dick was talking with the ring officials. While he was waiting for them to finish their conversation, Anthony glanced at the other side of the ring. A group of small boys was gathered around a gigantic man, with heavy features, broad shoulders, and long arms that hung down at his sides like a gorilla's. He wore white canvas breeks and heavy boots. This must be Old Bunger, the Devon wrestler Dick had spoken about. His real name, Anthony learned, was Porkin.

Anthony wondered if any of the young farmers could stand up to this brute. Most of them, he knew, were trained in the Cornish manner, which allowed neither boots nor kicking. But the Devon style permitted both, and traditionally the Devon wrestlers' boots were soaked in bullock's blood and baked; their kicks could do violent damage to an opponent's shins. It was hard to believe that Old Bunger would not down everyone he met.

Anthony confided his fears to Dick.

"Don't worry about me," the Virginian said. "I will not last long enough to meet him."

A commotion broke out on the other side of the ring. The boys started to dance around and sing an old Cornish song, to tease the Devon man.

> "Chase water boobies up in a tree,
> Looking as whish'd as ever could be.
> Truro man strong as oak,
> Knock 'em down at every stroke!"

Scowling, Old Bunger started to break through the crowd that surrounded him, but before he could reach the lads, one of the ring officials ran over and sent them flying.

The early events, four rounds each, were fast over. Dick had drawn a burly farmer from Perquimans. He had no style, but his oxlike strength was enough. Dick was down in the second round, and he lay sprawled on the trampled ground of the square, a silly, dazed expression on his boyish face. Anthony dashed a bucket of water over him and dragged him out of the ring.

Allin Killigrew fared much better. He knocked down two opponents, and a split decision brought him up to the finals.

The noisy crowd sank into sudden silence as the Devon wrestler walked into the ring. He towered over Allin. A shout went up from the crowd, "Killigrew, Killigrew!" but Allin paid no heed. He went to his corner and sat down on a three-legged milking stool. Owen was in the corner with him. Both boys were pale, but there was a determined set to Allin's lips.

"Batter his stomach, Allin, where he's fat!" "Keep out of his way when he flails, then rush in!" The advice came from all parts of the crowd.

Old Killigrew made his way to the boy's corner. "Hit him square in the heart, lad," he said. "He will not be able to stand up against a long battering."

Allin looked up from under his heavy eyebrows. He smiled and patted the older man on the arm. "Thanks, Father."

Groggins, the landlord of the Red Lion, went to the center of the ring to make the announcement.

"In this bout, William Porkin, the Bunger, from Devonshire, will fight Allin Killigrew, winner of the amateur preliminaries. The match will be six rounds. The winner will secure the Carolina championship belt and purse. The fight will be according to Devonshire rules, which permit shin kicking and boots."

Allin had chosen to fight without boots, according to the Cornish rules, and a great shout went up from the crowd. "Get boots, Killigrew!" "Kick him in the groin!" "Grab his hair!"

Groggins rang a cowbell and the fight was on. The Bunger and Allin circled each other warily, like two fighting cocks. At first, Allin kept out of reach of the Devon man's long, heavy arms, and got in a few quick blows to his stomach. But although the crowd cheered as they heard the punches land, the wrestler only grunted. The man was iron. Allin kept dancing out of his reach, and the first round ended with Killigrew puffing, but untouched.

The next three rounds were much the same; having escaped injury thus far, by the fifth, Allin had become overconfident. He moved up close to Porkin, evidently in the hope of goading the wrestler to overreach himself, but he did not move back swiftly enough, and Porkin aimed a kick at his shins, so hard that the cracking of the bone could be plainly heard. Allin fell to the ground and the Bunger kicked him again.

An angry shout went up from the spectators, and Groggins and the other officials jumped into the ring and dragged the Bunger off. The crowd surged forward, but the constable and his men held them back, while a doctor hurried to Allin.

When the ring had been cleared, Groggins stood up and announced:

"Wrestler Porkin is the winner of the bout. He has asked me to follow the regular procedure and call for another challenger."

Anthony looked at Dierdra. She was sitting very still, her hands clasped tightly together in her lap, her eyes following the men who were carrying Allin to the inn.

Suddenly he made up his mind. He leaped to his feet and vaulted over the ropes that enclosed the ring. "I challenge!" he cried out.

From the crowd came groans and shouted comments. "You'll be murdered!" "Wait till he hits you with that fist!" "Are you crazy, man?" But from the far side, a voice cried out: "Hooray for the man from Tre-Pol and Pen!" Others took up the chant, and the air was filled with cheers.

Anthony turned to the officials. "I ask for fifteen minutes to change my clothes."

"Granted."

Anthony started toward the Red Lion, where rooms had been made available for the contestants to dress, and the Bunger sat down on his stool to wait. His granite face was expressionless.

Dick overtook Anthony and grasped his arm. "For the love of

God, Tony, are you mad? That fellow will break you in two. Look what he did to Allin."

"It will be all right, Dick, believe me. If you want to help, run to the stable and get the hostler to make a pair of skillibegs. Tell him to twist the hay strongly, and to make them long. They have to cover me from knee to ankle."

"Right. I'll second you, but I still think you are a fool."

At the Red Lion, Anthony stripped off his tunic and silk shirt; he would fight with bare torso. His riding breeks, which came to his ankles, would be some protection for his legs, but he counted mainly on the skillibegs. He buckled his belt around his trim, narrow waist, and bound a silk kerchief about his head to prevent the Bunger from getting a grip on his hair and snapping his neck. Now he was ready to meet the champion.

Downstairs he found Dick and the hostler, who was holding the straw skillibegs in his hand.

"Nate Trewilliger, sir," the man said. "From Newland, I am. I've seen the Bunger fight many a bout." He moved closer and spoke in a confidential tone. "Sir, he's big, but he's clumsy. Get a left arm hold. His arm's been broke, and he favors it. If you could bring it behind his back . . ."

"Thanks, Trewilliger. I'll remember."

When they got to the square, Anthony pulled off his riding boots and put on the skillibegs. The crowd gasped when they saw he was not wearing boots.

"Not skillibegs, boots, lad!" "Didn't you see what he did to Killigrew?"

Anthony barely heard the advice. As he waited for the bell, he examined his opponent carefully. Porkin was sitting slumped over in his corner. His massive frame seemed twice as big as Anthony's, but there were rolls of flesh around his middle. I can't win this on strength, Anthony thought, I shall have to outwit and outmaneuver him.

"The governor says he has five pounds on you," Dick whispered. "Not because he thinks you will win, but because you are a true sport."

Anthony smiled, and looked over toward the governor's party.

Dierdra was leaning forward, a frown on her pretty face.

Killigrew came to the ringside and grasped Anthony's hand. "Give him one for Allin," he said softly, "a perishing hard blow for my lad."

Groggins made the announcement, the contestants stood up, and Anthony saluted the governor as the bell rang.

The two men stood, palm against palm, each striving for a grip. Good, thought Anthony, my grasp is as strong as his.

Porkin lunged at him, trying for a hold, but Anthony slipped away. He tried again, and again Anthony eluded him, using a trick he had learned in the Greek classical wrestling, in which he had been trained. A puzzled look came into Porkin's little pig eyes. When the Bunger rushed him for a kick, Anthony moved aside; this maneuver he had learned in Spain, from a bullfighter. Just a slight shift of position, and the Bunger, propelled forward by his own impetus, landed on the ropes.

The crowd yelled and clapped. Here was something new in the ring.

The bell rang, giving the Bunger a moment of rest. Three backfalls was the match. By now Anthony knew that he could evade the fellow, but to get him on his back was different.

In the fourth round, the Bunger all but had Anthony in a flying mare, but the young Englishman jumped to his feet with such agility that Porkin had no time to follow through. Anthony's skillibegs halted him; the kicks, when they landed, slipped off the straw.

The crowd was shouting. Men were running up and down making bets.

Porkin grabbed for a neck hold. That suited Anthony's plans; with luck, he could kick the man's feet from under him and throw him on his back. The trick worked; the tactics bewildered Porkin, whose hand slipped off Anthony's shoulder. Anthony kicked at Porkin's legs and they flew out. The man fell with a crash that seemed to rock the earth. For a moment he lay without moving. Then he rose slowly to his feet, his hand on his back, a bewildered expression on his face.

"Count one for the challenger."

Both men were winded. Porkin tried to lift Anthony, but caught his leg. In an instant, Anthony was astride him, and the referee allowed a second fall.

Now Porkin went wild. He aimed a great kick at Anthony's groin, but the act was his undoing; the bullfighter's swerve sent him crashing to the ground. Anthony pounced and, turning the man on his back, won the third fall and the match.

Yelling and clapping, the spectators jumped the ropes and rushed into the ring. But Anthony did not wait for their congratulations or even for the announcement of the results; he slipped through the crowd and ran to the inn, where he dressed himself quickly. In minutes he was riding down the back lane to the King's Arms, the cries of the crowd still ringing in his ears.

Back in his room, he bathed and threw himself on the bed. He was exhausted and a pleasant weariness coursed through him. In seconds he was asleep.

It was dark when Dick came to wake him.

"That was a fine trick, running off like that! The whole county wanted to greet you. I think they were about to carry you around on their shoulders. And the governor wanted to present the purse."

"That was kind of him. But I am turning the purse over to Porkin."

"What? Giving that great booby fifty golden guineas? Are you moonstruck?"

"Not really. Porkin has lost a great deal today. After all, he has been beaten by an amateur. That's not good for a professional wrestler."

"Moonstruck! Well, I'm off to the governor's. You had better dress now—and in your best clothes. We have been invited for supper, and I am quite sure you will be the main attraction."

The lawn at Government House was crowded with people; from the water to the house itself guests were moving about, walking along the paths, or sitting at the little tables that had been set up for the occasion. Everyone stopped to congratulate Anthony; his progress across the garden was a constant series of interruptions. He smiled and bowed and murmured replies, but his manner was abstracted, and his eyes swept the crowd, searching for only one figure. Finally he caught sight of her: Dierdra was standing by the wicket gate at the far end of the garden. He made his way toward her.

"What are you doing here all alone?"

She wheeled quickly, a startled look on her face. "Oh, the great hero!"

"You know that is nonsense. This happened to be my lucky day, that's all."

"So it was, lucky. You did not have to fight the man until Allin had worn him down." Her voice was quiet and cold. "I wonder what would have happened if you had fought him first."

"That's hard to say. I think I still could have won, though. Not because I am so strong, but because I used my head. In any event, I have turned the purse back to Porkin."

"How generous! The true aristocrat! I think all you really wanted was to show Allin up."

"That is not kind, Dierdra." But the suspicion nagged at him that perhaps she was right. "How is Allin? He wasn't badly hurt, was he?"

She looked quickly down the lane. "He is still at the doctor's. He is putting a splint on his leg. It was broken."

So that was why she was here. Waiting for Allin—for Allin, whom she loved. Waiting to console him for his defeat. Anthony turned on his heel and started back up the path. There would be no wedding for him early next year. He might as well go back to London immediately and make his report to Lord John in person.

Book II

Chapter X

THE CASE OF MARY CATTEN

THE GENERAL COURT of Oyer and Terminer and Gaol Delivery was held at the courthouse in Edenton in late October. The courtroom was packed on opening day; the heavy calendar contained several cases of particular interest to the Edenton townsfolk.

The loud buzz of conversation that filled the chamber dropped to a quiet hum as Will Badham, clerk of the court, and John Manson, the bailiff, entered through a side door. The jurymen, mostly yeomen and artisans, trooped in behind them.

"Twelve good men and true," Martin Trewilliger, the farrier, whispered to his neighbor, Elkin, the cordwainer. "And not a single one that ever I have seen before."

"I'm not surprised at that," Elkin replied. "They come from every precinct in the Albemarle save Chowan. After all, we are too close to the government here. And to the governor, too. We might be prejudiced about the sedition cases." His voice dripped sarcasm.

"Oyez, oyez, oyez," Manson pounded three times on the reading desk. "The General Court of Oyer and Terminer is now in session. All rise for their honors, the justices."

With a scraping of chairs and a shuffling of feet, the jurymen and spectators stood up. The door at the back of the room opened, and Chief Justice Gale walked slowly and solemnly into the room, an imposing figure in his scarlet robes and curled white judicial wig. The two assistant justices, Adams and Wormley, followed.

When the jury had been sworn in, Chief Justice Gale consulted the sheaf of papers on his desk and said to Will Badham:

"The first case to be heard concerns Joseph Castleton. Mr. Badham, will you read the indictment, please?"

Badham's voice, though low, was clear.

"A bill of indictment against Joseph Castleton, barber, of Edenton, for publishing and declaring seditious words and speeches:

" 'Said Castleton did maliciously and contemptuously speak, publish and declare false and seditious words against the governor, Captain George Burrington, saying that he is a "damn rogue and dishonest to boot." Such words he said in the presence of witnesses who have appeared before the grand jury and sworn to the truth of their statements.' "

Chief Justice Gale leaned over the bench and looked down at the barber, a slight, dark-haired man.

"How plead you to this charge, Castleton? Guilty or not guilty?"

"Guilty, your honor." The little man caught his breath and then spoke rapidly. "But may I tell the story?"

Gale nodded.

"It happened like this. I was with some friends, your honor, at the inn, and I suppose I had a little too much to drink. We fell to talking about our affairs and I told my friends that I had lost some money that very day because the governor refused to pay me for a wig he ordered and took. I was fair gone in drink, your honor, and said some things I should not have. Nor would have, had I been sober. But the drink went to my head, and I was still angry. I was wrong to speak as I did, and I apologize most humbly, your honor."

Trewilliger poked Elkin in the ribs. "I was with him that night. He told me what Burrington said when he asked for his payment. Those were really false and contemptuous words. I would let no man speak to me like that. It must have been deVoe, that scum, who turned Joseph in. He was skulking about our table, smiling that greasy smile of his, and eavesdropping, I have no doubt." He paused. "Of course, it had its good results, too. Castleton finally worked up the gumption to join our guild. If Burrington had treated him fair, he never would have. He would never have come to a meeting, either, or signed that memorial for the governor's recall."

"Ssh," Elkin hissed. "The jury is coming back. It doesn't seem to have taken them any time to make up their minds. Let's hear what they have to say."

The jurymen straggled into the box and the foreman, Samuel Pagett, a rough-looking farmer, read the sentence from a slip of paper he clutched in his hand.

"My lord chief justice, it is the verdict of this jury that the said Joseph Castleton, having no visible effects against which to levy a fine commensurate with the severity of his crime, shall be compelled to stand in the pillory, on the public parade, at Edenton, for eight hours of the clock, and that he shall later beg pardon on his knees and at a public meeting of the Council, of Governor George Burrington. He shall also pay all costs and stand committed until this sentence is performed."

There was a gasp from the audience, and a murmur arose. "Pillory and gaol!" "The man was drunk once. Burrington is in liquor more often than not!"

Order was restored as the chief justice pounded his gavel on his desk and, taking up a sheaf of papers, cleared his throat and began to speak.

"The next case, which will be presented by William Little, Esq., is a bill of indictment against Mary Catten, for felony and misdemeanour. The clerk will read the indictment."

Badham adjusted his spectacles and began to read.

" 'To the Honorable Christopher Gale, Esq., chief justice, and the rest of the justices for the holding of general court:

" 'The jurors for our sovereign lord, the King, on their oath do present that Mary Catten, spinster, late of Bath Town, did by force take or steal two white cotton and linen shirts, of value ten shillings each, one window curtain, of value undisclosed, and one pound bill of public credit, all belonging to Roger Kenyon of Bath Town, against the peace of our lord, the King."

As Badham sat down, the bailiff led the defendant forward. Mary Catten was a tiny woman, who looked even tinier next to the tall, heavy-set Manson. Her dark kalikut dress and her white bib and apron were shabby, but neat. She wore heavy home-knit hose and there were wooden buckles on her sturdy shoes. Her face was frightened, and her eyes swollen and red from weeping.

Chief Justice Gale spoke to her gently.

"How do you plead, Mary?"

Her voice was barely audible as she replied, "Not guilty, your honor, not guilty."

William Little, the attorney-general, presented the case for the prosecution. His story was brief, and it added to the information in the indictment only the fact that Mary Catten had been the Kenyons' bondwoman. In Little's calm, deliberate manner the spectators could read sympathy for the accused woman. When he had finished speaking, he bowed and sat down.

"Are there any witnesses to this crime, Mr. Little?" the chief justice asked.

"No, your honor," the attorney-general replied.

"Did not the Kenyons come down to speak for themselves?"

Little shook his head. "They were asked to, but refused."

"Very well." Gale turned to Mary Catten. "Now, Mary, suppose you tell us in your own words your side of the story. You have no reason to be afraid. And speak up, so that everyone can hear you."

Her story, in its faltering delivery, was simple.

"Mistress Kenyon asked me to do some extra work for her, to weave a bolt of cloth. And she promised she would give me something for it, because she knew the work was outside my regular duties. The pound note, and the shirts, and the curtain were the payment." She paused. "But when Mr. Kenyon came home, she was afraid he would be angry with her for giving me anything." The little woman's frightened voice dropped even lower. "Mr. Kenyon has a strong temper, your honor, a very strong temper. So Mistress Kenyon told him I took the things. But I never did, I swear to that." She fell silent for a moment, and then resumed: "By God and my country, sir, that is the whole truth of it. May lightning strike me if it is not. I never stole a thing in my life, and I expect I never will. Stealing is wicked, and a sin. Mistress Kenyon knows this is the truth, your honor. That is the reason she refused to come down to speak against me. When her husband swore out the warrant, she even admitted to him that she had made up the story. But he said he did not care, that he had started this, and was going to see it through." She broke into quiet sobs.

"Now, now, Mary, you must not cry. You are in a court of justice and law here, and you have nothing to fear." Gale turned to the jury. "Gentlemen, you have heard the evidence in this case. Mary Catten says these goods were payment for extra work. The Kenyons accuse her of stealing them, although they have refused to come down and make their accusation in person. Therefore, all you can judge by is the grand jury's charge and Mary's explanation. It is up to you to decide where the truth lies." He was silent for a moment. "Felony is a crime, and punishable. But first it must be proved to your satisfaction that a crime has been committed." He paused and looked meaningfully at the jurymen. "If, however, you should judge this woman guilty, the court recommends leniency. She is a poor, weak thing, and the crime of which she has been accused involves only a small amount. You will now retire and consider your verdict."

As the jury trooped out, a hum arose from among the spectators. Sympathy for Mary Catten could be heard in every voice.

"Poor little thing," one man whispered. "She's no bigger than my ten-year-old Annie."

"And weaker-looking than Annie, too," his neighbor replied.

"They will let her go; they must." This from a woman in the last row.

"The chief justice certainly wants them to, that's clear," her companion answered. "Well, we shall find out. They are coming back in now."

Again Pagett read the verdict from a slip of paper.

"It is considered by this jury that the said Mary Catten is guilty of felony, and that she shall therefore be required either to give good security in the sum of one hundred pounds sterling, to all His Majesty's liege people, and further to pay all fees and costs accruing by order of her prosecution, or she shall be committed to the Edenton gaol for one month. At the end of that time, since the Kenyons are no longer willing to have this convicted felon in their home, it is ordered that Mary Catten shall be sold at auction by the provost marshal to the highest bidder, and the moneys received from this sale shall be paid to Master Kenyon as reimbursement for her bond and the goods she did unlawfully take from him. Mary Catten stands committed until this sentence is performed."

There was a stunned silence in the courtroom, and every eye was turned on the little, frightened woman, who sat transfixed, her large dark eyes searching the foreman's coarse face in startled horror.

"Where would a poor woman like me get a hundred pounds?" she finally said, in a dull and toneless voice. "You mean to sell me on the auction block!"

Her words shook the spectators out of their shocked disbelief, and a mutter of rage swept through the courtroom.

"A weak little thing like that in gaol! It will kill her!" someone cried. Another voice called out: "She's no more guilty than I am!" And still a third: "King's justice! By God, more like Kenyon's cash, Pagett!"

The chief justice pounded for order, but it was several minutes before his dry, cultivated voice could be heard above the angry words and muttered curses.

"Enough, enough! The jury has given its verdict. There can be no discussion. The court now stands adjourned. It is now twelve of the clock. The court will reconvene at two, to hear the case of Philip Lancer, known as Philander, against Thomas Harrow, Esq., executor for the estate of Thomas Sparrow."

Dierdra heard about Mary Catten immediately after the noon recess. She was walking in the garden of Government House when David Elton came up to her. The secretary was incensed by the verdict.

"It is so unfair, Mistress Treffry. If you had seen the poor woman, your heart would have bled for her."

Dierdra's vivid imagination had already re-created the scene at the courthouse; she was as touched and shocked as Elton himself.

"It is difficult to believe a jury could be so harsh. I wish I knew how to help the little thing."

"The men of the village are in a fury," Elton said, shaking his head. "There is to be a meeting at Elkin's, the cordwainer's, tonight, to see what can be done." He pulled at his ear. "I have never seen the people so wrought up, Mistress Treffry! I cannot vouch for what may happen."

Dierdra sighed. "I wish the governor were here. Perhaps he could do something."

"Well, it is too late for that. He and Madam Burrington and the children left for their visit to Virginia immediately after I brought him the news of the Castleton verdict."

"And they are going to be visiting with Governor Orkney for nearly a month, aren't they?"

Elton nodded. "Actually, it probably is best that the governor is away. The people are as angry at him as they are at the jury."

"I don't understand," Dierdra's voice was perplexed. "Why should the people be angry at the governor?"

"Although," the secretary went on as though he had not heard Dierdra's interruption, "I cannot imagine he had any feelings about Mary Catten's case at all. It was only Castleton's . . ." His voice trailed off.

"David—" Dierdra was impatient. "Stop talking in riddles."

"Joseph Castleton was tried for sedition. He admitted he had spoken harshly of the governor. The jury gave him a very heavy sentence. . . ." He paused, and when he spoke again, it was so softly that Dierdra had to strain to hear him. "That foreman, Pagett. The governor knows him, and I think he must have dropped a pretty heavy hint he would like to see Castleton punished severely. The governor is most upset about all the scurrilous talk there has been about him."

"But what can that possibly have to do with Mary Catten?"

Elton's voice was even softer. "I imagine Pagett decided that if Burrington wanted the jury to be severe in Castleton's case, he would want them to be severe in Mary Catten's case, as well."

The color drained from Dierdra's face. "But that means the governor has been interfering with the law!"

Elton smiled wryly. "Not interfering with the law, simply talking with an old friend. But I can tell you in confidence, Mistress

Treffry, that it was Burrington who had Pagett appointed to the jury. And that man enjoys seeing people suffer."

Dierdra bit her lip. "This is terrible. To bring politics into the court!"

"You know perfectly well, Mistress Treffry, that politics is in every court case in North Carolina. The Eden will—what else was that but politics?" Elton shook his head. "It is shocking to think that this sort of thing can happen in a British court!"

They looked at each other silently for a few moments. Finally the secretary spoke.

"I am going to go down to the Green now. The men were talking about breaking into the gaol and carrying the woman off. Truly, Miss Treffry, I fear for the peace of the town." Shaking his head, he made his way quickly down the garden path and out the gate.

After he had gone, Dierdra stood for a while, lost in thought. Even though it was late in the year, the weather was still warm, and in the afternoon sunlight the fallen leaves laid a vivid blanket of red and yellow and orange on the paths and the lawn. She kicked her foot absently, and a little pile of leaves rose in a whispering flurry of color.

What was to be done? She wished Allin or Anthony were here; she needed advice so desperately. But Allin was off at William and Mary, and Anthony had returned to England almost immediately after Muster Day. David Elton was intelligent and kind, but this situation called for strength and force, and these qualities he did not possess. She was still musing when Elton returned, tight-lipped, his eyes ablaze with anger.

"Things are even worse than I thought," he said. "Pagett tried to persuade the jury to have Mary whipped as well as imprisoned. The man must be an utter brute. He had his taste of blood in the Castleton case and now he is running berserk. A fine friend for the governor." He paused. "If it had not been for him, the jury would not have convicted Mary at all; I heard that most of the men believed her innocent. The sentence—selling her on the auction block like a Negro slave—is a compromise! A compromise!" He laughed bitterly.

"David, I simply cannot believe it."

"It is true enough. The townsfolk have heard, and now they are even more enraged than they were before. Then, they only *spoke* about breaking into the gaol. Now, I fear they may very well do it."

"But that would be mob law, David. It must be prevented."

"Well." The secretary ran his hand across his forehead. "I managed to convince them not to do anything for the next day or two. Mary is so weak and frightened that she would never be able to stand the excitement. She has to be left alone for a while, and given a chance to pull herself together."

"Thank goodness they were willing to listen to you." Dierdra sighed with relief. "At least we have a while to think about this problem." She frowned and stood for a long moment in silence. Then her face brightened and she laid a hand on David's arm. "I have the solution. I am going right out to Lilac Farm to ask Yeoman Killigrew to buy Mary when the auction comes up. She could not have a better home than with him, and if the townsfolk know she will be there, they will be less disturbed about the gaol sentence."

Yeoman Killigrew shook his head as he listened to Dierdra's story, and his good-hearted wife sighed and clucked her tongue in sympathy. But when Dierdra asked him if he would buy Mary Catten, Killigrew's rosy face darkened and he spread his hands in a gesture of helplessness.

"Mistress, I simply cannot. This has been a bad year, and a late one, and I have neither the cash nor the credit. Half my harvest has already been mortgaged to pay for goods and equipment I need."

Dierdra looked from Yeoman Killigrew to his wife.

"But something must be done!" Her expression was thoughtful. "I have a hundred pounds sterling I have saved from my wages. Goldsmith Coltrane is keeping it for me. If I were to give the money to you, would you buy Mary Catten for me? I would not want people to know I was her purchaser, so I dare not appear at the auction myself. And I am far from sure it would be wise to keep her at Government House. The governor probably would not like to have anyone in his household associated with this case."

"Even that I cannot do." Killigrew shook his grizzled head. "Or, to put it better, should not. As soon as my face is seen at the auction, the price will go up, and your hundred pounds will never be enough to buy her."

"That's true enough," Owen put in. He had been sitting silently listening to the conversation. "We Killigrews have a reputation as shrewd folk. If people knew that we wanted the woman, they would realize that she must be a good worker, and everyone would try to outbid everyone else."

"I wish Dick were here instead of down the river, working on our property. He would know what to do." Tamar sighed. Then her face brightened. "If she is as good a sempstress as Dierdra says, think what wonderful dresses she could make for my trousseau! We simply must have her here, Father!"

"How can you think of your trousseau at a time like this?" Mistress Killigrew's usually quiet voice was sharp and she looked at her daughter in stern disapproval.

"Wait a minute!" Dierdra cried. "Tamar has given me an idea. Mary Catten really should be here. If I can arrange to have someone else buy her with my money, would you put her to work? On Tamar's trousseau or anything else."

"Aye," Killigrew nodded. "But who would do the purchasing?"

"Shall I ask Dick to come back?" Tamar asked.

Dierdra shook her head. "I shall ask Martin Trewilliger, the farrier to do it. He is one of the men who is most outspoken for Mary. We will be doing everyone a great favor if we make him part of the plan. Then he will not spend his time stirring up trouble. David Elton told me that there was to be a meeting at the cordwainer's tonight, and those men are in a state of mind to do something desperate if they are not stopped in time. And if the governor were here to stop them, David says, that would probably cause even more trouble."

"Aye, they're hot-tempered. And there are many who dislike

Burrington. Joseph Castleton's friends, especially. Mr. Elton is right; they might well start something dangerous." Killigrew nodded his head. "You persuade Martin to buy Mary Catten for you, and you can tell him we will put her to work here, and gladly."

Dierdra rode quickly back to the village and went at once to the farrier's. Trewilliger was in the forge, shaping a horseshoe in the glowing charcoal fire. When he caught sight of her he stopped work and, rubbing his great hands on his leathern apron, came forward to greet her.

"Mistress Treffry," he smiled. "Always a pleasure to see you. But I hope your horse has not slipped a shoe."

"No, Martin," she shook her head. "Millie is fine. I came to talk to you about something else. Mr. Elton told me what happened to that poor woman, Mary Catten, and I want to help her if I can."

"Aye, the poor soul! She can certainly use help. But she will have it from us men, Mistress Treffry. That was a black scene this morning at the court. And the governor to run away at a time like this! But he probably knew what he was doing. We're in a mood for action, I tell you! When I heard that cruel sentence—and learned that it would not have been passed but for that Pagett!" The farrier ran his work-hardened hand through his hair. "But you have no cause to worry, miss. We will take care of everything. If we have to burst into the gaol to free her, why, we will."

"But that is precisely what I do *not* want you to do, Martin. That would be as bad as the jury. I have a little money, and I am willing to use it to buy Mary Catten when the auction comes up. I am sure she will be all right while she is in gaol; Mr. Elton told me she would. It is what might happen later that worries me."

"Buy her? But you would have to keep her at Government House. Burrington would not like that, I'm sure. It would be an insult to his friend Pagett."

"I have no intention of keeping her at Government House, Martin. Not because of the governor, but I have not enough work to keep the woman busy." Dierdra did not want the farrier to think she had any interest in the political aspects of the case. "But if you buy her, with my money, Yeoman Killigrew has promised to take her into his home and put her to work there. She can help make Tamar's trousseau. And I will be happy to know that Mary Catten has a good home. She will be much better off with the Killigrews than she ever was with the Kenyons."

Martin looked pensive. Then he slapped his great hand on his thigh and laughed.

"That's it, that's it! That would be fine all around. And a great joke on that Pagett." His face became sober. "Let me think. You wait here a minute, mistress. I'll be right back."

He went through the wide door at the back of the forge, and Dierdra saw him walk up the street and into the cordwainer's shop.

As she waited for him to return, she looked about her. Against one wall of the forge there stood an ironwork gate, as beautifully made as any she had ever seen in Cornwall. As often as she had been here before, to have Martin examine her horse's shoes, she had never noticed it. Why, he was a superb craftsman!

It was not long before he returned.

"Mistress, I think we will be able to work things out. How much money do you have?"

"One hundred pounds. Goldsmith Coltrane is keeping it for me. He will give it back to me whenever I want it."

"With that to start with, there will be no difficulty. Elkin and I will add anything that may be necessary. And if we have to call on Killigrew for a small amount, I have no fear he'll not give it. I know he has but little now."

"Oh, thank you, Martin, thank you! It is such a relief to know that Mary will be all right."

"We're the ones should thank you, mistress. You can go home with a calm heart. When you have the money, bring it to me. But tell no one, lest the price go up. As long as we are sure that Killigrew will take the woman if you buy her . . ."

"He gave me his word."

"And Killigrew's word is his bond."

"When do you think the auction will be held, Martin?" Dierdra asked.

"Market Day, I suppose. That will be a little over a month from now. And the town is crowded then. They likely will figure they can get a good price for her if they wait until that time."

Dierdra frowned. "But Martin, won't that mean the price will go up so high we will not be able to afford to buy her?"

He patted her hand. "Now you just stop worrying, miss." His voice was gruff. "I told you before, everything will be all right. We will find a way. By the end of next month Mary Catten will be sitting, peaceful and happy, in her new home at Lilac Farm, working away on Tamar's trousseau."

Dierdra walked home slowly. As she opened the gate, a little dog Allin had given her before he left for college came bounding down the garden path, yelping with joy, his tongue wagging wildly. Dierdra bent down and picked him up, and he began to lick her face in an ecstasy of love.

Suddenly, the full meaning of her actions burst on her. When the farrier appeared at the auction on Market Day and, with her hundred pounds, purchased Mary Catten's indenture, she, Dierdra, would have become the virtual owner of another human being. Mary Catten would in effect be her property. She stroked the dog absently. A grown woman—her property—just as was this little, helpless animal. She buried her face in his soft fur, trying desperately to hold back her sobs.

Chapter XI

DIERDRA AND THE BONDWOMAN

One cold morning in late November, shortly before Governor Burrington and his family were due to return from Virginia, a small Negro boy appeared on the steps of Government House.

"I have a message for Mistress Treffry," he told Taphy, importantly.

Dierdra could not suppress the smile that came to her lips when she saw the lad; he was much too tiny to support the weight of the dignified bearing he had assumed.

"Taphy says you have something to tell me," she said.

"Yes, mistress." The lad bowed jerkily from the waist. "The farrier say to tell you he'll fix your mare's shoe right now, if'fn you bring her over, mistress. That's the very words he asked me to say." His expression was earnest.

"Thank you."

As she rode up Broad Street toward Martin's shop, Dierdra wondered what he had to tell her; the offer to shoe her mare, she knew, was only an excuse. Probably it was something about Mary Catten. Had anything gone wrong with their plans?

She arrived at the forge to find the farrier deep in conversation with Elkin, the cordwainer, a thin, quick-moving man, as yellow as untanned leather—the result, he said, of the swamp fever from which he suffered every autumn.

"Good morning, Martin. Good morning, Mr. Elkin," Dierdra said as she entered. "The boy gave me your message. Tell me, how is Mary Catten?"

"Right as rain, mistress, right as rain." Elkin smiled. "I've never seen a prisoner to be so well treated."

The farrier nodded. "That's the truth, Mistress Treffry. Mary Catten has a much better home in the Edenton gaol than she ever did with those Kenyons. The women of the town have seen to it that she has plenty of good food; they take her soups and custards and fresh-baked bread. My own wife has been making an extra portion for every meal we have and giving it to Mary. Why, even the children have done their part. It would have done your heart good to see the little tykes, carrying late-blooming asters and Michelmas daisies to her. 'Tis a sight to make you laugh and cry at the same time."

"I have wanted to go over to the gaol so many times, Martin. But you always told me to stay away."

"Aye. And I knew what I was talking about. Mary Catten is a convicted felon. The gentry is not supposed to visit criminals. And besides, someone might have learned about our plan, and spoiled it."

Dierdra sighed. "I suppose you know best, Martin. But I am so sorry that I never visited the poor woman, have never even seen her. At home we always used to visit the needy, and the people who were put in gaol for debt, and others like them. We took them food and clothing, as the women have been doing here, so that things would be a little easier for them."

"Well, there's nothing more to worry about, mistress," Elkin put in. "Today Mary Catten is still at the gaoler's—you know, don't you, that when Mistress Burnett, the gaoler's wife, discovered that Mary is an expert weaver, she had her husband move the woman into their house so she could make a counterpane to keep the Burnetts warm this winter? But tomorrow afternoon, Mary will be at Lilac Farm. That's what we wanted to tell you. The auction will be in the morning."

Dierdra's face must have mirrored her concern, for Martin raised a quieting hand.

"Now, now, don't go into an alarm. Everything will be fine. We have it all arranged. The woman will be auctioned off at six in the morning, opening time. There will be only a few country folk there at that hour, and they won't bid, so we will be able to buy her cheap. You may even get some of your hundred pounds back."

"I'm not concerned about the money, Martin. You know

that." Dierdra shook her head. "I just want to be sure we get her. How can you be so positive? Perhaps people will bid. By now word must certainly have gone around that she is a fine sempstress and weaver. If nobody else has mentioned it, Mistress Burnett surely has."

Elkin fixed his piercing eyes on her. "Now, you stop worrying, mistress. Martin and me will take care of everything, we promise. She'll be bid in so quick nothing will have a chance to go wrong. I guarantee it."

"But the auctioneer?" Dierdra's voice was still troubled.

"He's a good friend of ours. He understands. We will have the woman bought and out at Lilac Farm in two winks. Young Owen Killigrew will help us. We have already made our arrangements with him."

"I wish I could be at the auction," Dierdra said, wistfully.

"Now, that would spoil all our plans! The price would certainly go up then." Martin's voice was sharp.

"I suppose so. But everybody else is doing so much, and I am doing so little. I feel ashamed of myself, putting all you people to such risks."

"You stop that right now, mistress," Elkin said gruffly. "You are doing more than any of us. And we perfectly well know it."

Early the next afternoon Dierdra went out to Lilac Farm. There she met her bondwoman, sitting at the loom in Mistress Killigrew's weaving house. Mary Catten was small and spare. Her features were delicate and her light brown hair was half hidden under a snowy white mobcap. Her expression was pensive, but her grey eyes were bright and alert.

As Dierdra entered, she rose from her stool and curtsied, her lips trembling. Dierdra was afraid the woman was going to cry or, just as bad, begin to thank her profusely. She spoke hastily:

"I hear you are an expert weaver, Mary, and that you sew beautifully, too. Perhaps you will be able to make a gown for me out of the material I bought from the merchant, Ali Hassan. I have had it since last spring; it is so fine I have been afraid to trust it to anyone in Edenton."

"Oh, mistress, I doubt you should trust it to these hands, then. They've become so rough, what with gaol work and hard water. They're not as soft as they belong to be."

The Cornish twist to her speech was unmistakeable.

"You must be from Cornwall, Mary!" Dierdra exclaimed.

"Indeed I am, mistress. From Kilkhampton. And it's an evil wind that blew the ship across the Western Sea."

"But it is almost as if you had come home, then," Dierdra said. "The Killigrews are from Kilkhampton, too."

A smile lit up the woman's forlorn face. "Aye, from right near me. I recognized Yeoman Killigrew as soon as I saw him. I remember him from my childhood."

"What did you do back home, Mary?"

"As soon as I was old enough, I worked at Stowe Barton, weaving for Lady Grace."

A sudden thrill shot through Dierdra. Lady Grace was Anthony's aunt, Lord John Granville's mother. The wide world seemed smaller every minute! But she kept her thoughts to herself.

"So you worked for the Granvilles of Stowe?"

"Yes, mistress, that I did. And Lady Grace counted on me and praised my weaving and sewing to the skies."

"Then why did you leave, Mary?"

With that question, the woman's last bit of reserve seemed to crumble. The tears flowed from her eyes and her story was interrupted by sobs.

"Ah, 'twas all my own fault, mistress. No one else is half as much to blame. And I did not leave because I wanted to, you may be sure of that." She paused. "He was a fine-spoken lad, and I met him by the lytch gate at the church in Kilkhampton one day. He invited me to go to the pasty shop with him, to have a bite. He was so pleasant and polite I didn't think there would be any harm if I went with him. I was a foolish girl, I was." She shook her head and sighed. "And I was even more foolish to go for a walk with him in the fields after we had eaten. I took a drink of ale out of a can he was carrying, and when I woke up again my stomach was churning and churning, and I was lying on a hard, bed-like thing in a small, dark room, and there were lots of other women there, too." She broke off and stood for a moment, staring silently into space. When she resumed, her voice was expressionless. "One of the women told me we were on a ship, bound for America. That was five years back, mistress, but it's still as alive in my mind as if it had happened yesterday."

Dierdra looked at her in horror. "I knew there were press gangs for men, Mary, but I never heard they had them for women."

"Well, they did," Mary sighed. "And that fine-spoken young man was in their employ, the pirates. You know, mistress, my bond with the Kenyons would have been up next year, and I was going to go home to Stowe Barton. I thought perhaps Lady Grace would take me back again. But—" a smile crossed her pale face—"I am not sorry things happened as they did with the Kenyons. I have never met such fine people as the Killigrews and you, yourself, Mistress Treffry. Mayhap the Lord meant for me to live with my own folk in a strange land. I am grateful if He did."

Dierdra arrived back in Edenton to find that the Burringtons had returned from their trip to Virginia a few days earlier than had been planned. As she rode up to the gate of Government House, she saw the children waiting for her. When they caught sight of her horse, they began jumping up and down in excitement.

"Hurry, hurry, Miss Treffry. I want to kiss you hello," Ann cried out. She looked charming, in her navy woolen coat and the little knitted red hood that framed her small, piquant face.

Dierdra dismounted and swept the little girl into her arms. Suddenly she realized how much she had missed these youngsters.

"Ann! William!" she exclaimed. "My, how good it is to see you again!"

She bent her head to kiss William, but an embarrassed look crossed his face and he turned away. With a stab, Dierdra realized he was growing up and felt himself too old to be babied. She lifted her head and extended her hand to him. He took it gratefully, and bowed from the waist.

When the greetings were over, the children pulled her into the house and up the narrow stairs to their mother's sitting room.

Madam Burrington was seated in a chintz-covered chair, beside the crackling fire. She looked tired, and the heavy rings under her eyes had grown darker—like smudges drawn with a sooty thumb. She smiled and held out both her hands to Dierdra.

"Come, sit by me, my dear. I have so much to tell you about our trip. But the journey back has exhausted me. It even made Nanny ill; she has gone to bed with a headache. All that jolting over the rutted roads! And once we were stuck in the mud; if not for a farmer and his sons who happened to be passing by, I do believe we would be there yet."

"I am sorry to hear you had such a difficult trip," Dierdra said. "But now you are home, and you will be able to relax a bit. Did you have a pleasant time in Virginia?"

"Oh, very pleasant. And so busy! I will tell you all about it at dinner. I have ordered it served up here. I hope you will eat with me. Oyster stew, with biscuits and some of Mistress Killigrew's fine pickles." She sighed. "After all that rich company food at Williamsburg, I long for something simple and homely."

As they ate, Dierdra listened to the gossip of the capital: The Byrds had been in residence at Westover, and the Burringtons had dined with them there one Sunday and had attended church in their chapel. William Byrd was a gay man, with a roving eye. Rumor had it that he had cut quite a swathe in London society. And why should he not with his mother's family wealth to draw on as well as his own? The Williamsburg gallants called him the Black Swan, but Madam Burrington had seen no evidence of his philandering; he was sedate enough under his wife's watchful eye.

The Carters and the Harrisons and the other James River families had been in residence, too. There was a definite society there, a small London, but Madam Burrington preferred it here in Edenton, where one could be quiet and peaceful, with no entertainment but teas and an occasional ball at one of the plantation homes.

"If my health were better, perhaps I should enjoy the excitement. But I am afraid I am not strong enough for it." She sighed. After a pause, she went on. "And I forgot to tell you that we met young Richard Chapman's father on our visit. He is most unhappy that his son is going to marry Tamar Killigrew. He begged me to try to dissuade the boy."

"But why?" Dierdra had not known there was any objection to the marriage.

"Well, my dear, the Killigrews are yeomen, and although the Chapmans may once have been yeomen too, they no longer are. They have quite a position in Virginia society. Mr. Chapman is a stiff-necked man, from what I saw of him, and a proud one. He feels it is beneath his son's dignity to marry into the yeoman class."

"I hope Tamar does not know this," Dierdra said.

"I cannot imagine Dick would be so cruel as to tell her." Madam Burrington patted her hair. "I certainly would not have presumed to quarrel with Mr. Chapman's views, but I did think it proper to tell him how highly the Killigrews are regarded here."

Dierdra felt the color rising to her face. "How can people be like that? I always feel so angry when I hear that kind of talk!"

Madam Burrington smiled. "I am glad you were not with me, then. It certainly would not have done for you to have been angry with Mr. Chapman."

Dierdra was just about to reply when there was a knock on the door and the governor entered.

"So you have bought yourself a bondwoman, Mistress Treffry," he said, without introduction.

Dierdra was startled. But it was certainly too late to try to conceal matters now. She managed to keep her voice calm as she spoke.

"Yes, sir."

"And sent her out to Yeoman Killigrew's?"

Dierdra nodded.

"That was a strange procedure. I hope you will do me the honor of explaining it. If it is not too much trouble, of course." The governor's manner was elaborately polite. "But I would be most interested to know why you bought the woman in the first place and why, once you did, you sent her out to Yeoman Killigrew's instead of bringing her here."

Dierdra was silent, unsure of what to say.

"Why don't you speak up, child?" Madam Burrington's voice was reassuring. "I am sure the governor is not angry with you. It is simply that he does not understand. Although—" and she looked at her husband inquiringly—"I do not know that we have any right to pry into Mistress Treffry's affairs, George."

Burrington looked at his wife coldly. "You may not know, Amelia, but I do. We have every right. As long as Mistress Treffry is here, living with us, eating at our table, teaching our children, she has an obligation to conduct herself as befits a member of the governor's household. And when she goes about behind our backs and purchases a bondwoman and sends her somewhere else to live—and all of this without even consulting us—well, it seems to me she has gone too far."

"But, your excellency, how could I have consulted you? You left for Virginia the very morning I learned about the poor woman."

"You could have written to us. You know perfectly well you could have. No, Mistress Treffry," the governor shook his head. "Your conduct has been strange, to say the least. Why was this not the first thing you told us about? And why did you ask others to make the purchase for you—and men who are known to be my enemies, as well? These are not the actions of a straightforward, honest person."

Dierdra could feel her temper mounting as he spoke. But she had managed to keep it under control until his last words. They were insupportable! To be accused of dishonesty!

"If you think so little of me, your excellency, perhaps I had best leave Government House." She spoke through thin lips. "I will pack my things right now." Holding herself steady and erect, she walked quietly to the door. She was just about to turn the knob when Madam Burrington rose hurriedly from her chair and ran over to her.

"Dierdra, Dierdra!" she said, gently disengaging the girl's hand from the knob and leading her back into the room. "There is nothing to be so upset about."

"I am sorry, Madam. But I'm not used to being called dishonest." Dierdra's voice was calm, but her lips trembled.

"I am quite sure the governor did not mean to say you were dishonest," Madam Burrington said.

"I will handle this, Amelia. I am perfectly well able to speak for myself," Burrington put in. "I know the facts. You do not. Suppose you let me tell you what your friend Mistress Treffry did, and then you can judge her honesty for yourself." He shot an angry glance at Dierdra. "In the first place, she did not purchase just any bondwoman. Oh, no, Mistress Treffry is too particular for that. She bought a very special one—a very desirable person. This Mary Catten—as I hear she is called—is nothing but a common thief. Convicted at the last court session." He folded his arms across his chest and glared at Dierdra venomously.

This was too much! A picture of the frightened, frail little bondwoman leaped to Dierdra's mind, and tears welled up in her eyes.

"She is not a thief! Mary Catten is as honest as you or I. She no more committed the crime she was accused of than—" She broke into a torrent of uncontrollable sobs.

"There, there." Madam Burrington put a consoling arm around her. "Try to keep calm, my dear. Here, take this," she drew a handkerchief from her sleeve and handed it to the girl.

Dierdra turned her tear-stained face to the older woman. "If you had only seen the poor thing. And heard her story." She dabbed at her eyes with the handkerchief.

"So tender-hearted! Touching, really. Look at Mistress Treffry, Amelia—how solicitous of a convicted felon and how unconcerned about the reputation of the man who pays her wages and supplies her with the food she eats!" The governor sneered.

"Now, George, stop it!" Madam Burrington looked at her husband angrily. "The girl is upset enough. If you gave her a chance to calm down, I am sure she would be able to explain the whole thing to your satisfaction."

"Well, I shall be very interested to hear her explanation. Very interested, indeed. What do you think this looks like to the townspeople? If I learned the story just a few hours after my return, it must have made the rounds of Edenton three or four times by now. My enemies are having a glorious laugh at my expense, I am sure. And all through the good offices of my own children's governess!"

By now, Dierdra had regained her composure. With a stab, she realized there was truth to the governor's last words. It did look as if she herself did not trust him, and as if she had allied herself with those of the townsfolk who were his declared enemies. But this had not been her intention at all. All she had wanted was to save Mary Catten! She turned a penitent face on Madam Burrington.

"I am sorry, Madam. I was not thinking of that at all. Well," she frowned slightly, "that is not quite true. I did think of it, in a sense. The most important thing in my mind was to help the woman. But I wanted to stop the people from taking action against the peace of the town and against the governor, too."

"Oh, I see," Burrington said sarcastically. "You did this all to help me."

"Mostly, I did it to help the woman," Dierdra looked at him defiantly. "Everyone who was in the court that day was shocked at the conviction. Why, they tell me that even Chief Justice Gale was horrified at the verdict, it was so unfair."

The governor poked an accusing finger in her face. "It was the verdict of a legally constituted jury."

Dierdra stood her ground. "It was the verdict the jury was forced to by your friend Mr. Pagett."

"George, Dierdra—" Madam Burrington looked helplessly from one of them to the other. Sighing, she sank into a chair. "You are still talking in riddles. This can go on forever. Will somebody please explain things to me?"

Dierdra ran over and dropped to her knees at the side of Madam's chair. She took the older woman's hands in hers and looked at her with pleading eyes.

"Let me tell you the story as I heard it. Then you will know that I did the only thing I could. Roger Kenyon and his wife—they come from Bath Town—held Mary Catten's bond. They accused her of stealing some trifles from them—a shirt, I think, and a pair of curtains and a one-pound note. But Mary Catten says that the goods were given to her as payment for extra work. It is her word against theirs. If you saw her, you would know how honest she is. Roger Kenyon did not even come to court to tell his side of the story. Most of the jury believed Mary innocent, but the foreman, Pagett, wanted her to be convicted and sentenced to a public whipping. Finally the others agreed to sentence her to be sold at auction." She held tightly onto Madam Burrington's hand. "How could I have let her suffer the risk of going to people who might be as bad as the Kenyons? I had to buy her, don't you see? But I did not want to bring her here—not while you were away. I was going to tell you about it tomorrow, after you were rested from your journey."

Madam Burrington patted the girl's hand absently. "There, there," she said. She frowned. "And you say the Kenyons did not come to court?"

Dierdra shook her head. "Attorney-General Little said they refused."

"That certainly is odd, George, don't you think?" asked Madam Burrington, looking inquiringly at her husband. "You would think they would have wanted to be there and give evidence in person."

The governor brushed her comment aside. "What is so odd about it? It is a long trip from Bath to Edenton."

"It's not that long a trip, George. If you or I had been in their place, we would have gone to court. That is a serious accusation, stealing."

"And the jury judged her guilty." The governor turned on his heel and walked over to the window. He pushed aside the curtain and stood staring down into the garden, at the bare hawthorn bushes and the sere brown earth.

"That isn't so. The jury wanted to free her. But the foreman insisted on a guilty verdict," Dierdra put in. "And the townspeople were ready to take any kind of steps to save her. They were even talking about bursting into the gaol. I know. And I know that woman is as innocent as you or I. She would not steal from anybody. She worked at Stowe Barton, in England, for Lady Grace Granville, Lord John Granville's mother. She is supposed to be a wonderful weaver and sempstress. And she did not come here of her own free will. She was pressed into service. Some young man who gave her something that made her fall asleep, and then put her in a boat bound for this country. A press gang, it was."

"A press gang! How dreadful!" Madam Burrington's voice was shocked.

But that part of the story did not seem to interest the governor. He stood silently at the window, and when he finally turned around it was to say:

"She worked for Lady Grace, you say?"

"Weaving for her," Dierdra said.

Madam Burrington looked at her husband thoughtfully. "George," she said, "I have an idea."

"Well?" he asked, shortly.

"Why should we not buy Mary Catten from Dierdra and bring her here to live? You would not object to that, would you, my dear?" she turned to the girl.

"And give her a chance to steal from us, too?" the governor asked.

"Now, George. The woman has served her sentence. And from the story Dierdra tells us, it is more than likely she was not guilty at all." He seemed about to interrupt, and she went on, hastily. "I am in great need of a living-in sempstress and weaving woman. And there is a cozy little room for her in the attic of the weaving house. That loom is just standing idle, too." Her voice was coaxing. "It hurts me so much to see it. I bought all that beautiful brocade from Ali Hassan to have a waistcoat made for you, but I have been afraid to trust it to any of the townswomen. A woman who lived under our own roof would be different, though. It would be a real help to me to have her, George. Could we do it? Of course, you would have to talk to her first and satisfy yourself of her honesty."

Dierdra held her breath waiting for the governor's reply. It was a long time in coming.

"So you think my vanity means more to me than justice?"

"You know I do not, George. I think justice means a great deal to you. As I said, the woman did serve her sentence. Now she is entitled to a chance to have a decent life again."

Burrington was silent. Then he turned on his heels and walked to the door.

"I shall have to think about it." He shot an angry glance at Dierdra. "You should have minded your own affairs, miss," he said as he walked out, slamming the door loudly behind him.

When he had gone, Madam Burrington sighed and sank back into her seat.

"Would you bring me my knitting, dear?" she said to Dierdra. "It is over there. In the top drawer." She nodded in the direction of the bureau.

Dierdra went over to the bureau and took out the knitting.

"Thank you, child," Madam said. She took up the knitting and worked for a while in silence. Then she looked up.

"Come, dear, sit down here again. I think we ought to have a little talk."

Dierdra sat down on the footstool near Madam's chair. As she gazed up she could see the little lines of worry that were beginning to etch themselves into the corners of Madam's eyes.

"First, I want you to stop fretting yourself about Mary Catten. She will be at work in our weaving house within a week, I am sure. As soon as my husband has had a little time to think he will realize that is the best solution all around. For many reasons. Not only because his own heart will tell him you acted properly, but because he will feel sorry for the poor woman if she is as frail and weak as you say."

"She is a pathetic thing, Madam," Dierdra said earnestly. "And I am absolutely certain she is innocent."

"And when George sees that for himself, he will want to have her here." Madam paused. "Besides, he is going to be thinking hard. If his friend Pagett, that vulgar man—" she shuddered—"is really responsible for the verdict, the best way to stop the rumors that are probably flying about is to bring her to Government House. That is also the best way to show people like the Kenyons they themselves should have brought their charges to court if they wanted them to be taken seriously. And obviously George is not unmindful of the fact that Mary Catten worked for Lord John Granville's mother. All these things make me feel positive that the governor will come around to our way of thinking."

Dierdra took Madam's hand and raised it to her lips. Her eyes glistened with tears.

"You are so good. And so wise."

Madam smiled and shook her head. "I am just a little more experienced than you, my dear. I have learned a little. And that is what I want to talk to you about—the lessons I have learned. For instance, I have found out that losing your temper is not the best way to win an argument."

Dierdra nodded ruefully. "That is a lesson I certainly have not yet learned."

"You still are young. And you have a high spirit—which is admirable. But losing your temper with George Burrington is the most foolish thing anyone can do. He has a quick enough temper himself; it is his worst enemy. You should know that by now, Dierdra."

Dierdra felt a flush rising to her face. Madam Burrington was right. She had behaved badly. She started to speak, but the older woman put up a warning hand.

"Mind, I am not scolding you, my dear. It is wonderful to have a warm heart and to be willing to fight for what you believe in. But you have to know how to fight. You have to keep your head. If George could only learn that lesson he would have a much easier time here. Most of his troubles spring from his temper. When he is in a calm frame of mind, he is a wonderful man. It is only when he has had too much to drink, or when he becomes upset. I know he will do the right thing about Mary Catten when he has had a chance to think. But you and I must make it easier for him, Dierdra, not harder. We must be kind and gentle. That is the only way. Sometimes the best way of winning is to appear to lose, you know." She laid down her knitting and looked for a long moment into the girl's remorseful face. "That is enough of that. Why don't you ring for Lillie and ask her to clear away our dinner things?"

Chapter XII

THE STRAWBERRY HILL AFFAIR

IN MID-DECEMBER, the weather suddenly turned warm, and the Burrington children spent several hours each day playing out of doors. Late one afternoon, Dierdra sat on a stone bench at the far end of the garden, while the children romped nearby. Their shrill voices formed a noisy background to her thoughts. On her lap lay the last letter she had received from Allin Killigrew. Like the others he had written since he left for William and Mary, it was a chatty, informal note; in the several they had exchanged during this time both of them, by unspoken consent, had avoided all references to their own relationship and to their conversation on the night of the Petersons' party. But soon Allin would be coming home for the Christmas holidays, and the subject would certainly come up then. Dierdra was looking forward to this time with eager anticipation; during his absence she had come more and more to realize how very much Allin meant to her. Perhaps now he would ask her directly to marry him.

She sighed, folded the letter, and looked about her. It was near sunset, and the waters of the sound glowed gold, reflecting the brilliant reds and oranges of the sky. The cypress trees on Batt's Island were a black line of sturdy sentinels stretching out to the horizon.

Suddenly the twilight hush was broken by Ann's excited voice.

"Miss Treffry, Miss Treffry, look who is here!" the little girl cried, and she came running up to Dierdra, pulling Allin along with her.

William followed close behind. "Mr. Killigrew caught my rabbit that escaped from the hutch!" he exclaimed. "Look!" and he held the creature out for Dierdra's inspection.

The girl's heart thumped wildly. "Allin," she said, her eyes flying over his tall form, "how wonderful to see you!"

"And how wonderful to see you!" A broad smile suffused Allin's dark face. He took both her hands in his and stood gazing at her for a long moment.

"Oh, Miss Treffry," Ann cried, her little face aglow, "William and I are so glad Mr. Killigrew is back. We love him so much. It has been much less fun to visit Lilac Farm since he went away."

"And I love you and William very much, too." Allin turned to the children, smiling. "Now that I shall be at home for a while, we will have ample time to play together—here as well as at Lilac Farm. But I wonder if I could talk to Miss Treffry alone for a little bit now?"

"Oh, yes, sir, yes. Come on, Ann." William grabbed his sister's arm and pulled her off.

Dierdra and Allin stood for a moment without speaking. Dierdra's heart was still thumping.

"Well," she said nervously, after a bit, "there is no use in just standing here, is there?" She made to sit down on the bench, but Allin's arms went around her in a long embrace.

"Dierdra, Dierdra, I've missed you so very much," he whispered.

"And I you." She buried her face in his shoulder. It was good to feel his strong arms around her.

Finally they broke apart. She sat down on the bench and patted the vacant space beside her.

"Come," she said, "sit down and tell me all about yourself. How are you enjoying college? I want to know everything."

Allin laughed and, spreading his coat-tails, sat down beside her. "I have written you practically everything already. I cannot think of a thing to add." He paused. "Well, there is one thing. I am still the same old Allin Killigrew, but I have let some of the chaps at college know I am Allin Gorgas, as well. That seemed the best place to start revealing the dreadful truth about myself." He laughed lightly. "And I have discovered that no one thinks the truth is dreadful, after all."

"I could have told you that a long time ago," Dierdra said softly.

"Could have? You did. But the nicest thing I have discovered is that I have two proud names, not just one. Gorgas and Killigrew are both respected."

"I knew that, too," Dierdra smiled. "But I want to hear about you, Allin, not your name. Letters cannot take the place of conversation. I want to know all about your studies, and all about the other fellows, and what you are planning to do."

"I am having a wonderful time, as I wrote you. I never knew there was so much to learn, or that I would have such a good time learning it. At first I was afraid I would be too far behind the other fellows, but all that reading seems to have stood me in good stead."

Dierdra laughed. "You make me feel like the wisest woman in the world. That is still another thing I knew."

"Well, perhaps you did not know this," Allin smiled and then his expression grew pensive. "I have not yet made up my mind whether to continue after this year. It is clear I can learn at home. And I am so much older than the others at college. But that is less important than the fact that my uncle has had a bad year. He could use my help here."

"Oh, Allin," Dierdra took his hand in hers. "Don't make up your mind about that too hastily. Give yourself a chance to be sure."

"But I have not yet told you the most important reason. When we talked that night at the Petersons', I said something I hope you remember. I asked you—"

The children's excited voices interrupted his words.

"But he is, Mother, he is. He's over here, with Miss Treffry," Ann was saying, and Madam Burrington appeared around the turn of the path, flanked by her small son and daughter.

"So he is, Ann, so he is," she said, smiling. "I did not want to burst in on you like this," she continued, to Allin, "but the children insisted that I come. They act as if they had not seen you for centuries."

Allin had jumped to his feet. He bowed low and kissed Madam Burrington's hand.

"Not quite centuries," he laughed. "I planned to come in and pay my respects after Miss Treffry and I had caught up on our news." He glanced fondly at Dierdra. "If you had been able to hold the children off one minute longer, you would not have had to make this trip."

"I am delighted I listened to them." Madam Burrington turned to Dierdra. "Do you know, my dear, that Mr. Killigrew has picked precisely the right time to come back home?"

Allin looked at her inquiringly.

"The governor has invited Chief Justice Gale and the members of the Council for dinner tonight. Young Mr. Middleton, of Virginia, was also supposed to come. He was due to have arrived this afternoon, for a conference with the governor. But he has been detained." She smiled. "He was going to escort Miss Treffry. Since he will not be here, I wonder if I could ask you to be her dinner partner?"

"Nothing would give me greater pleasure," Allin said. He pulled his watch from his waistcoat pocket and examined it. "But I had better leave now if I am to return in time. I will have to go back to Lilac Farm to dress." He bowed and walked quickly up the path.

Madam Burrington put her arm around Dierdra's shoulder. "There was something I meant to tell you the evening the governor and I came home. But in all the excitement about Mary Catten, I never did."

Dierdra looked at her but said nothing.

"It is about Mr. Killigrew," Madam went on. "In Virginia we heard that he is not Killigrew's son, but his nephew, that his father was Allin Gorgas and his mother Killigrew's sister."

"Yes," Dierdra said, "that is true. Allin told me about it last spring."

"As long ago as that?" Madam Burrington nodded thoughtfully. "Well, that explains many things I could not understand before." She paused. "I must admit that I had my eye on Mr. Dawson. But I certainly cannot criticize your choice—that is, if you have made it. Allin is a fine young man. We heard the most glowing reports about him in Williamsburg. It may take the people here some time to become used to his new name and the new position that will probably go with it. But if he continues to behave in the dignified fashion he has heretofore . . ." Gently she turned Dierdra around. "Come, my dear. We had best go back in now. I hope you will wear your sprigged muslin with the yellow taffeta petticoat tonight. It is by far your most flattering dress."

Dierdra came downstairs early, her skirts rustling and swaying as she moved. No one was in the drawing room yet, but she could see that Taphy had put it in order, for the fire burned brightly in the fireplace, and the candles in the wall sconces and the brass chandeliers had already been lighted. The delicate Aubusson carpet and the tapestry-covered walnut fireside chairs were bathed in the warm glow that spread through the room.

She walked over to the long mirror between the windows and stood for a moment, adjusting the curls that fell over her shoulder. She was still there when the governor entered.

"Ah, primping at the mirror, I see. A truly feminine trick!" His gruff voice was cordial.

Dierdra turned quickly and, moving away from the mirror, made a low curtsey.

"Well, we are guilty of the same thing," he laughed, and moved to where she had been standing. He turned slowly, the better to see to the adjustment of his purple brocade coat and his cream satin waistcoat. He pulled his lace cravat into place, and flicked an imaginary bit of lint from his satin breeks with a lace-bordered handkerchief. Then he pulled at his full-bottomed brown wig, which hung dark and heavy over his flushed jowls.

"And Castleton wanted me to pay for this thing," he said. "I suppose it will pass muster here, but I can tell you I would not have dared wear it in Virginia. It is a scandal what these people call workmanship. Look at that!" He stepped back from the mirror and turned to face Dierdra. "But I have one consolation," he went on, not waiting for her answer, "this waistcoat. I must admit that Mary Catten did a fine job on it. Those Kenyons were fools; a woman as skilled as that is hard to come by. Suppose she did take a few trifles now and then?" He turned to face the mirror again and bowed formally to his reflection. Suddenly he burst into a laugh.

"My wife tells me that young Killigrew, or Gorgas, or whatever his name is, is going to take Middleton's place at dinner tonight. She is starting him off in Edenton society, I suppose. I cannot wait to see the expressions on the faces of all my high and mighty Council member friends when they learn about him." He slapped his thigh. "I nearly exploded myself when they told me about it in Virginia." His expression became serious. "With training, that young man may turn into a gentleman. They are a fine family, you know, the Gorgases. But it is amusing. To think that Killigrew's shy son should turn out to be Gorgas' bastard!" Laughing uproariously, he walked out of the room.

Dierdra stood silently for a few moments after he left. She was furious, but she did not want to say anything to him. She had vowed, on the day of the argument about Mary Catten, never to lose her temper with the governor again. Perhaps he did have a kind heart, as Madam Burrington said, and possibly he was at bottom the just and honest man she believed him to be. But increasingly Dierdra had become irritated by his coarseness and his arrogance. She had known about these qualities all along, but in the past she had been much more easily able to throw them off, and to take his manner for what it was: a blustering façade that cracked under any pressure. The Eden will case was, she supposed, the beginning of her growing annoyance. Then there was the fight at the Petersons'. And then, of course, the Mary Catten episode. And now these comments about Allin. Dierdra shook her head. Somehow the worst of it was that all Burrington's noise and braggadoccio meant so very little, and that in every case, he backed down when the issue was joined. He would probably behave extremely well at dinner tonight and subject Allin to no embarrassment at all. She should not permit herself to become upset by him.

She sighed and hurried to the dining room, to make sure that everything was in place. The table was already set with the white china etched with scenes of the English countryside, and the Canton stemmed wineglasses. Michaelmas daisies and late purple asters made the centerpiece. Taphy had pleated the napkins and placed them in the stemmed goblets.

Dierdra's slim hand hovered over a glass. Should she take the napkins out and put them on the table? Better not. Taphy was proud of his ability to produce this fan-shaped decoration, and it would hurt his feelings if she meddled. With a shrug of her shoulders she left the room.

In the hall she met Madam Burrington coming down the stairs. The older woman looked beautiful in the brocade gown Mary Catten had sewn for her. She glanced into the dining room.

"Oh, dear. Taphy has made his fans again."

"Yes." Dierdra smiled sympathetically. "I wonder where he learned that trick?"

"From Governor Eden, no doubt," Madam Burrington said. "Well, the room will look like a country inn, but I will not mind. I find it rather charming. It is my husband I am concerned about. He is always so upset by this lack of elegance."

They had just entered the drawing room when the knocker sounded. They could hear Taphy's footsteps as he hurried down the hall, and his warm voice calling out:

"Mr. Chief Justice, sir, I bid you good evening. And your lady, too. Ladies, please to step upstairs, first door to the right. Gentlemen, put your hats and capes on that little settle in the back of the hall."

The Moseleys arrived shortly thereafter, Mary Moseley resplendent in her best taffeta dress, and the surveyor-general elegantly attired in a brocaded waistcoat, satin smallclothes and white silk stockings. The other Council members followed almost on their heels. Allin was the last to arrive.

When all the guests were assembled in the drawing room, with Madam Burrington and Dierdra, Taphy entered to announce the governor. The company rose as Burrington walked in, bowing graciously and smiling. In a few moments dinner was announced. The governor escorted Mistress Gale into the dining room, and the chief justice followed, Madam Burrington on his arm. Dierdra and Allin were the last couple in the procession.

"The governor seems to be in high spirits tonight," Allin whispered to her. "What do you think accounts for it?"

Dierdra was going to tell him of her suspicion that he might make Allin's story the subject of conversation, but she decided not to. They would deal with that problem when and if it came up. So she merely said:

"He is extremely pleased with his waistcoat. Mary Catten made it for him out of a piece of brocade Madam bought from Ali Hassan last spring. He loves elegance, you know."

Allin pressed her arm. "And I did not learn the story of that poor woman until my father told me about it today. It is exactly like you, Dierdra, to keep your sweetness and your good heart a secret from me." He smiled warmly at her.

Dinner was quite pleasant. To Dierdra's relief, everyone seemed already to have heard about Allin, and no one seemed to feel any difficulty or embarrassment about it. Dierdra felt proud not only of his behavior, but of the behavior of her dinner companions. The food, although simple, was good, and the conversation animated and gay. Once or twice Dierdra noticed Madam Burrington looking at her husband with some concern and, following the older woman's eyes, she could see that the governor was addressing himself to his wineglass more often than might have been considered strictly necessary. But his voice remained quiet, and he seemed to be in command of himself. When the meal was over, Madam Burrington rose to her feet.

"Ladies, shall we go to the drawing room? We will have our coffee there, and leave the gentlemen to their discussion."

In the drawing room, the women drew up chairs around the fire and began chatting about household matters. Dierdra, at Madam Burrington's request, poured coffee into the thin china cups. Penelope Lovyck came up to her and spoke softly, in her ear.

"That is the most exciting thing, about Allin! John told me before we came over. And that young man is more than a little bit interested in you, I could see that. How does it feel to have a choice of two handsome, eligible men? Anthony Dawson had his eye on you too, before he left. That was plain. How are you going to decide between them when he returns? Edward Moseley was telling me that he will be here soon; he had a letter from him the other day."

Dierdra was spared the necessity of replying; at that moment there was a loud crash, and a minute later Chief Justice Gale came striding into the room, followed by the other members of the Council. All of them looked furious.

"My dear," the chief justice said to his wife, his voice icy, "will you fetch your cloak, please. We are leaving for Strawberry Hill immediately."

"And will you get ready, Mary?" Edward Moseley said. "We are going, also."

The other men made the same requests, and the startled women, after throwing hurried glances at their husbands, quickly made their way upstairs. Madam Burrington rose and went over to the fireplace. She stood there quietly, a stunned expression on her fragile face. Dierdra ran out to follow the women. On her way down the hall to the stairs she passed the dining room. Through the half-open door she caught a glimpse of the governor, sitting slumped over the table. Allin was standing behind him, a firm hand under each armpit, trying to lift the older man to his feet.

The guests were gone in a moment and, as Taphy closed the door behind them, Madam Burrington walked slowly toward the stairs.

"I do not know what happened, Dierdra, and I do not think I want to. But I am beginning to believe I should never have left England."

"Let me help you upstairs," Dierdra said.

"No, no, my dear. You take care of yourself. I will be all right." And Madam Burrington, her head bowed, started to move wearily up the stairs. She had not gone very far when the door to the dining room was flung wide open and the governor emerged, staggering.

"You leave me alone, Killigrew, Gorgas—whatever your damn name is!" He flailed his arms wildly. "You, there, Taphy," he called to the servant, "you go down the street to Carter's. Tell him to make ready to go out with me. I have something to say to the chief justice. He may want to hear." He lurched down the hall and out the front door.

Taphy cast a pleading glance up at Madam Burrington, whom her husband had apparently not noticed. She was standing on the stairs, half-lost in the darkness. She seemed to be rooted to the spot. For a moment she did not move. Then she shrugged her shoulders and continued on her way. Dierdra started up after her just as Allin came out of the dining room. She wheeled round and ran down to him.

"Allin," she cried, placing a hand on his arm, "will you wait for me in the garden and tell me what happened? I want to be sure that Madam goes to bed."

He nodded and smiled woodenly, and she ran upstairs.

She arrived at Madam's bedroom to find the older woman at her dressing table, slowly and carefully undoing her elaborate coiffure.

"I simply do not know what to do, Dierdra," she said as she removed the last pin from her hair and began to plait it into a thick braid. "I am not strong enough for this."

Dierdra said nothing, but went to the closet and took out Madam's maroon velvet wrapper. The bed had already been turned down, and the flannel nightgown was laid out neatly across it.

"Let me help you to bed," the girl said. "No need to bother Lillie."

Madam Burrington nodded. She did not speak again until she had put on her nightclothes and was sitting up in bed. Then she sighed and said, tonelessly:

"This is the last straw, Dierdra. The very last."

Dierdra knelt by the side of the bed and took the older woman's hands in hers.

"The governor has just had a little too much to drink. It will all be forgotten by tomorrow."

Madam shook her head. "No, Dierdra. This time he has gone too far. The drinking and the fact that he loses his temper so easily—those things I have put up with. I even have defended his faults, as I did to you. But to do this in his own home to his own invited guests! I will not permit George Burrington to disgrace me that way, Dierdra! People feel sorry enough for me as it is. I will not have this added to it. I could not stand to meet their eyes." She shuddered, and an expression of disgust crossed her pale face.

Dierdra did not know what to say; she continued to kneel there, holding the older woman's hands in hers. After a while, Madam Burrington gently pulled them away.

"I think I will try to sleep now, dear. Would you snuff out the candle as you go?"

Dierdra found Allin in the garden, sitting on the same bench they had occupied that afternoon. He rose to greet her.

"Allin," she cried. "What happened? I have never seen Madam Burrington so upset." She sank down on the bench.

Allin reached over and took her hand, which lay in her lap. "Burrington was in liquor—that much I imagine you deduced for yourself," he started. "There was some conversation about the court session, the one when Mary Catten was tried, I suppose. Moseley said something about the whole thing being a disgrace." He shook his head. "Everything was going well up to then, but that man seems to delight in goading the governor. Well, anyway, Burrington asked him what he meant and he went on to say that the jury had been coerced. Then Gale interrupted to say that he was most disturbed about Philip Lancer's case, which was apparently scheduled for the same session of court as Mary Catten's, but which had been postponed for some reason. Then—" he sighed—"I'm afraid I added to the final explosion by asking about Philip Lancer. He is the Negro man they call Philander. It seems he is suing Thomas Harrow for his freedom. Harrow is the executor of the estate of Thomas Sparrow, and Sparrow had owned Philander. But Sparrow gave him his freedom a few years ago, before he died, because the black man saved two of his boys from certain death when their boat capsized in the sound during that big hurricane."

Dierdra nodded. "I remember hearing the story. But what has that to do with anything, Allin?"

"Patience, my dear, patience," he patted her hand. "I will come to it. The point is that when Sparrow died, Harrow insisted Philander was his property, and the old man is fighting to regain the freedom his master gave him. Well," he paused, "a case like this has all sorts of implications, Dierdra. It is the first time in our history that a Negro has sued a white man for his freedom, and it can lead to important consequences. Philander was the only free Negro in the entire province. Burrington was very much afraid of the outcome, and before he left for Virginia he forced Gale to have the case put off. He would like it never to come to trial. And tonight Gale said he felt the case should be brought to the Council instead of going to a jury, because all the juries seemed to be prejudiced." Allin stood up and began to pace slowly back and forth.

"Well, that threw Burrington into an absolute rage. 'That's your solution to everything, isn't it?' he shouted, and then started a long diatribe against the Council for what had happened in the Eden will case. He was pounding on the table with his fists and shouting. I'm surprised you did not hear him, Dierdra. He made enough noise to wake the dead."

"There was a din, but immediately afterward the chief justice came in. We had no chance to make any mention of it," Dierdra said.

"It was dreadful. Burrington was in his cups and he was in a foul temper. He grew angrier and angrier, and redder and redder, and finally he told Gale that he was not going to put up with any more insubordination, and the chief justice could consider himself removed."

Dierdra sighed and shook her head. "And tomorrow, when he has come to his senses, he will change his mind. I don't know what the matter with that man is, Allin." She was silent for a moment and then she added, "Poor Madam Burrington."

Allin grasped Dierdra's hand, pulled her to her feet, and drew her into the circle of his arms. "And what about you? I am afraid to leave you in the same house with that drunken beast!"

"You need not worry about me, Allin. I have very little to do with the governor. I just attend to the children's lessons and do whatever I can to help Madam. I am very fond of her."

"Well, I would like to see you out of here. What has just happened makes me even more doubtful about going back to college next year. Oh, my dear, I have missed you so much. I do not know how I can bear waiting three more years to ask you if you will have me." He laughed softly. "You interfere with my studies, too. I cannot concentrate when—"

He stopped as the sound of drunken voices shattered the still night air. They seemed to come from the direction of the stable yard.

"I'll have the horses saddled up, Carter," they heard Burrington call out. "You gather some of your friends from the water front. We'll go out to Strawberry Hill and tell that traitor a few things."

"That sounds like trouble," Allin said. "I'd better follow them. I will let them have a few minutes' head start, so they don't know I am on their trail." He ran down the path.

"Be careful, my darling, be careful," Dierdra cried out. But by now he was out of sight.

Chief Justice Gale had just reached his bedroom when he heard the sound of horses' hooves galloping up the roadway in front of his house. He took up a candle from the bedside table and hurried over to the window. His wife, who was already asleep, woke with a start and sat straight up, clutching the covers to her.

"What is it? What is the matter?" she called out.

"It's nothing, my dear, nothing. Go back to sleep," Gale said and, still holding the candle in his hand, hurriedly made his way downstairs. Through the window he had caught sight of Burrington, Dr. Carter, and a pair of strangers, who looked like some of the rowdies who were to be found hanging about the water front. Their sudden arrival, especially so soon after the scene at dinner that evening, certainly boded no good. As he descended quickly into the main hall, Gale could hear someone rattling the knob of his front door.

"Let me in, I say, let me in!" It was Burrington, shouting at the top of his lungs. He gave the door a tremendous kick, and it shivered under the impact.

"I have nothing to say to you, Burrington," Gale called out. "Any conversation between us can wait until tomorrow."

"I said let me in. Who do you think you are?" The rattling of the door was almost deafening.

"Want me to go in after him, your excellency?" The coarse voice was unfamiliar; one of the ruffians, Gale assumed.

"It's easy to get him," another voice cried, with a drunken laugh. "Like this, see!" There was a crash of glass as a stone smashed through the drawing room window.

Madam Gale came running down the stairs, tying her wrapper around her. Behind her were her personal maid and John, the chief justice's body servant.

"Have they gone mad?" she cried, running up to her husband.

"You had best stay out of this, my dear," he said. "Come." As he started to lead her back up the stairs a second stone was hurled through the window and Burrington's angry voice called out:

"I'll take care of you, Gale. One way or the other, even if I have to burn the house, or blow it up. When the governor wants to speak to you, you'd better come out. You are not the chief justice any more, you know. I am not even sure you will be a resident of this province much longer."

There was a burst of loud laughter, and then Carter's voice could be heard. "We will let them know who is in charge here, eh, George?"

The chief justice gave his wife a gentle shove up the stairs.

"Please, my dear, go back to bed. You are only making things more difficult. John and I will be able to handle this better alone." He looked over toward his body servant.

"Yes, sir, we'll handle it, never fear," John said.

Madam Gale permitted herself to be led upstairs by her maid, and the chief justice and his man made their way toward the drawing room, where a pair of French windows gave onto the gallery. The two men stepped out into the darkness.

"Burrington," Gale called out, "I am over here, on the gallery." He looked across to the path in front of the house. "You have had a drop too much, you know. We had better wait until morning to talk about this."

"There's nothing to talk about, damn your insolence," Burrington cried. "I just came to tell you again what I told you before. I'm in charge here, and you are out. You may have been chief justice once, but that was before I caught on to your tricks and your maneuvers to turn the government over to the Council."

Carter's loud laugh interrupted him. "I have an idea. Why don't we swear in a new chief justice right now? One of our friends here."

Burrington roared. "You think that's so foolish? The most ignorant oaf would make a better chief justice than that traitor. No one else would spend all his time trying to usurp my authority."

A loud voice rose above the confused babble: "I know how to make sure Gale won't keep the job!"

At that moment a stick of wood came flying through the air and hit the chief justice on the temple, knocking him unconscious. He fell heavily to the floor. His servant leaned over him, calling:

"Master, master! Is you all right, sir?"

With a clatter of hooves, Burrington and his cronies rode off; the game had gone too far and now they were frightened.

When Chief Justice Gale came to, he was still lying on the floor of the gallery. He opened his eyes to look straight into Allin Killigrew's face.

"What . . ." he began, but the young man silenced him.

"Don't try to talk now, sir. Wait until we get you inside."

Dawn found Chief Justice Gale, shivering despite his warm bathrobe, seated at the desk in his study. He was pale, and there was an ugly bruise over his left eye, but his mouth was set in an expression of determination. He had permitted Allin to help him upstairs—the young man had arrived too late to stop the attack, but just in time to give the chief justice first aid—and then, despite his earnest protests and his pleas to be allowed to stay until morning, Gale had sent him back home. There was no need to involve Allin in his personal difficulties with the governor.

Gale pulled a pile of paper to him and dipped his quill into the onyx inkwell.

The letter he was about to write would not be addressed to the Lords Proprietors, but it would come to their attention, he knew. Carkasse, his friend in London, to whom he was sending it, would undoubtedly show it to Lord John Granville, with whom he was on intimate terms. He must be very careful, therefore, in what he said.

He started to put pen to paper, then hesitated, and stopped. His tone must be calm, judicious, without rancor. At the same time it would have to make plain the outrageousness of Burrington's conduct and his arbitrary manner. Perhaps he should include mention of the difficulty he and the governor had had earlier in the year, when the naval officer of the port of Edenton had been impressed, arbitrarily, by the governor, for doing his duty in refusing to handle a cargo, and the collector of the Edenton port, Adam Cockburn, had been publicly insulted by Burrington for supporting him. The men had come to Gale for advice, and he had explained their rights to them. Burrington had been enraged, and had threatened to have the chief justice removed at the time.

And, Gale sighed, this latest episode with Philander had only strengthened the governor's resolution.

He started to write, but his pen was scratching and he stopped to sharpen it with a knife. At that moment, his servant entered.

"Master must be tired. I brought a little hot tea. That will ease your weariness."

"Thank you," Gale tried to smile but he could not. He picked up the teacup and downed the hot brew gratefully, in one gulp. "That does help," he sighed. "Leave the pot here, John."

The drink had refreshed him and he found himself writing with ease.

> "Prior to the general court, which began on the third week in October, the governor so grossly reviled and insulted me and so disturbed me and the assistant judges of the court, by threats and innuendoes, that, for fear of worse consequences, we agreed to put off some of the business pending until the next court."

Gale stopped writing and wiped his cheek with a large kerchief. Then he went back to his work. The scratching of his pen was the only sound that broke the dawn stillness around him. When he had finished his letter, he took a stick of wax from the box on his desk and lit a candle. He held it to the wax until it softened and then pressed the blob with his signet ring, sealed the letter, and placed it in the despatch box in his desk drawer. The despatch rider was due tomorrow; he would carry the letter to Virginia. From there, the *Victory*, sailing in a week's time, would take it to England. With it would go the memorials of complaint against Burrington for which Thomas Pollock had been collecting signatures ever since the day of the Petersons' party, the previous spring. There were two already filled out: one had been signed by all the councilmen save William Maule, just appointed to replace Reed, the other by many of the villagers and yeomen. Signatures for the memorial had not been as easy to obtain as he and Pollock had at first thought, but Joseph Castleton's severe punishment and the Mary Catten case had served to convince nearly everyone that Burrington was not to be trusted, and in the last weeks support for the demand that Burrington be recalled had snowballed.

The chief justice poured himself another cup of tea. In his mind's eye there rose a vision of London on a foggy winter morning. At a meeting in Whitehall, round a table in an oak-paneled council room, the Lords Proprietors were assembled to read the material. What would they do? Here the vision blurred and faded. Carkasse had already hinted in several letters to Gale that if Burrington were to be recalled, his place would be taken by Sir Richard Everard. Sir Richard, Carkasse had written, appeared to be a good man, and a gentleman, as well, very different in every way from the arrogant, vulgar and high-handed Burrington.

Gale sighed and, rising slowly from his desk, made his way downstairs to start a new day.

Chapter XIII

THE HOLIDAYS

THE MORNING after the Strawberry Hill affair, Dierdra woke to discover that Governor Burrington had left the house, bound on a journey whose destination nobody knew. Perhaps he had gone south, to New Hanover, or Bath, or Lilput, or even as far as Charleston, on the Ashley and Cooper rivers. Or perhaps he had gone north, to confer with his friend William Byrd, in Williamsburg.

"Not only do I not know, Dierdra," Madam Burrington said, when the girl came in to talk to her a little before noon, "I do not even care." The older woman was lying in bed, propped up on a mound of pillows. She looked particularly frail; her delicate face was drawn and haggard, and her expression was weary. "I meant what I said last night, and as soon as I feel well enough to get out of bed, I am going back to England." She shivered and coughed.

Dierdra was alarmed. Madam looked so ill, and there was such an unfamiliar note of bitterness in her voice.

"Let me send Taphy for Dr. Norcomb, Madam," the girl said. "When the children and I were out for our walk, we noticed him on the way to the King's Arms."

Madam Burrington nodded and sighed. "I am afraid you had better have him come over. This seems to be more than just one of my headaches."

By the time the surgeon arrived, Madam's condition had become much worse. Her face was damp with perspiration, and she tossed restlessly from side to side, moaning and crying out in pain. She was delirious and kept talking about someone named Donald, whom Dierdra had never before heard her mention. Once she whimpered, "Help me, Donald, help me. I'm falling further and further into the abyss! Donald!" And another time she cried in terror: "George! Keep away from me. You're drunk. I will not have your filthy hands on me. Go away!"

Mary Catten, who had come to Madam's bedside shortly after Dierdra, spoke softly to the doctor. Her voice was frightened. "I thought it was the quinsy, sir, and I know that you have to draw the abscess to a head to relieve the pain. So I had cook make up a flaxseed poultice. And we put hot salt bags at her feet and her back. With the blankets, they should be keeping her warm."

Norcomb nodded his leonine head. "You did the right thing, Mary. And don't worry, you and I together will pull her through. Although her fever is much too high for my liking." He turned to Dierdra. "Where is the governor?"

"I don't know, sir. We think he went to Charleston, but nobody seems to be sure."

"The swine! Gallivanting around the country while his wife is desperately ill!"

Little use though she had for Burrington, Dierdra could not let this unjust accusation pass. "He did not know anything was the matter, sir. He seems to have left before sunup." She frowned. "I know the quinsy is painful, but it is not serious, is it?"

"If it was only quinsy, I would not be worried. We can cope with that easily enough. But the woman has never been too strong, and now she is worn out, on the verge of collapse. That is why we must get this fever broken quickly. Otherwise, I cannot vouch for what may happen." Norcomb's eyes were troubled.

"She has had a good deal on her mind, sir, to upset her," Dierdra said.

"I know, I know," Norcomb nodded impatiently. "I heard about that Strawberry Hill affair at the inn this morning. The governor went tearing out there with his crony Carter and a couple of rowdies. They broke windows and knocked Gale unconscious with a stick they threw."

"I had not realized it was as bad as that," Dierdra said, her eyes wide with horror.

"Well, it was. That man must be out of his mind." Norcomb shook his head. "Mistress Treffry, I think that Mary and I had better go to work now. And as for you, I prescribe a short walk. You will have a great deal to do later, and the air and exercise will give you strength. Now, no arguments," he said as Dierdra started to protest. "These are doctor's orders. One patient at a time is quite enough."

Dierdra put on her red cloak and tied her fur-trimmed bonnet under her chin and started out on her walk. She crossed the Green to the water's edge, walked along it for a while, then turned up Rope Walk, and, when she had come to its end, made her way down the street beyond it. As she turned the corner, she came to the stocks and the pillory. A man and a woman sat in the stocks. She did not know the man, but she did recognize the woman: she had seen her walking along the water front with Mary Abbott, the lewd woman Dr. Carter was reputed to keep; the two hussies had no scruples about flaunting themselves before the eyes of respectable folk, and could be found swaggering along the water front at all hours of the day or night. Now the woman was wrapped in a blanket to keep off the chill winds, but even so she was shivering, and her face was blue with cold. Without doubt, she was a depraved creature, but Dierdra could not suppress a shudder of sympathy.

She hurried on, but stopped short when she came to the pillory. There was the barber, Joseph Castleton, standing immobile, his feet just touching the wooden boards, his head thrust into the wooden yoke. Dierdra ran toward him, her cloak billowing behind her.

"Keep away, mistress, keep away!" he called out through his chapped and frozen lips.

"Mr. Castleton!" Dierdra cried. "Why are you here?" Her eyes flew from his pinched face to his red and swollen hands.

He managed a rueful grin. "Haven't you heard, mistress? I asked the governor to pay me for a wig I made him."

"But I thought you served your sentence. Are you supposed to stand in the pillory forever?"

A bitter laugh escaped him. "As long as they can keep me here. They heard that men were gathering at my house to talk, and they liked that even less. Seems there's a law against talking."

"But what were you doing? Surely you have not been put here so long just for having a discussion, just for talking among yourselves. Did you make any trouble?"

"If there'd been any trouble, mistress, wouldn't you have heard? No, we were just having a talk over our difficulties. Talk's not illegal for the governor, but it is for us." The barber smiled wryly. "The law is a wonderful thing, mistress. It's like a piece of India rubber. There are all kinds of ways of twisting it."

"But how much longer do you have to stay here? You will be sick in this bitter cold."

"Only till sunset. That's not too long. Then the bailiff will unlock me and I'll be as good as new."

"Let me fetch you some brandy. Otherwise you will freeze to death."

"No, don't you do that. The guard will be back any moment. He just stepped over to the courthouse for something, and he will be here again before you know it."

But Dierdra did not hear him; she was already running down the street. It took her no longer than ten minutes to return to Government House, get from Taphy a bottle of the governor's best brandy, and run back to the barber. She had the bottle hidden under her cloak, but the guard was still away, and it seemed safe to give some of the strong liquor to him. She climbed up on the platform of the pillory. By standing on her toes, she was just able to bring the bottle to Castleton's lips.

"Here," she said, "take a big swallow."

He gulped down the burning liquor. "Thank you, mistress, thank you. That helps. I can feel it warming my vitals already. Now you hurry up and go before the guard gets back."

She tilted the bottle to his lips once more. "Take another sip. 'Twill help. I will be back later, and give you another." She hid the bottle in the bushes and walked sedately away; she could see the guard strolling again across the Green and she did not want to arouse suspicion in his mind.

When she arrived back at Government House, she found Allin waiting for her. The children had been excused from their lessons for the day, and were taking a walk with their nurse.

"We can talk up in the schoolroom, Allin," Dierdra said, and she led the way up the narrow winding staircase to the little room on the third floor where the children had their lessons.

"Have you heard about Madam?" she asked when they had arrived.

He nodded soberly and walked over to the blackboard. "Taphy told me. I do not wonder she's ill, after what happened last night." He picked up a piece of chalk and absently rolled it in the palm of his hand.

Dierdra's face was tense and drawn. "Everything seems to happen at once! Oh, Allin, I am so worried about her. Dr. Norcomb tries to be cheerful, but even he has to admit that he is disturbed. And the governor has gone off no one knows where!"

"With his tail between his legs, I hope," Allin said. "I suppose the news of what he did at Strawberry Hill has reached you by this time."

Dierdra nodded. "Dr. Norcomb told me. He heard it at the inn this morning, so it must be all over town by now." She paused and sighed. "But somehow what breaks my heart more than anything else is the children. With their father gone and their mother sick. And at Christmas time! I'm so disturbed I cannot really give them their lessons properly. It is as gloomy as the grave here now. Christmas is a time for children to be gay, and it is only a few days off. Those poor little things! I could cry for them!"

Allin looked thoughtful. Then a smile broke through his face. "Suppose I take them back to Lilac Farm with me. They can spend Christmas there. And you can come out and have dinner with us on Christmas Day. My mother—I suppose I will always call her that—has been preparing the feast for weeks now."

"Oh, would you do that, Allin? That would be wonderful!" Dierdra's eyes sparkled.

"Dick Chapman will be coming out, too," Allin went on. "He's been away for a few months, working on the property he bought down the river. He wants to have the house built in time for a spring wedding, and it's pretty wild up there, so he has been working hard."

But Dierdra did not seem to be listening, and noticing the troubled look that had crossed her face, Allin went over and put his arms on her shoulders.

"Now, my dear, what is it? I can see I have not solved all your problems. I wish I could, but Burrington's conduct and his wife's illness are beyond my help."

"I know that, Allin. You have been wonderful." Dierdra sat down on one of the children's little chairs. "No, this is something else. Just before, when I was out taking a walk, I passed the pillory. Joseph Castleton, the barber, was locked up in it. He was convicted at the last court session for speaking against the governor, but that had nothing to do with politics. It was because Burrington refused to pay him some money. Now, though, Castleton said something about men gathering in his house."

"So they've found out?" Allin's expression was thoughtful. "Well, it was bound to be discovered sooner or later. This is a political matter, Dierdra—a guild some of the artisans and yeomen have formed. It was their members who helped you with Mary Catten."

"Then it is my fault the barber is in the pillory!" The girl looked stricken.

"It is not your fault at all. You saved trouble about Mary Catten, you did not make it. You know very well those men would have done something desperate if you had not taken the action you did. And if it had not been the Mary Catten affair, it would have been something else. This problem of Burrington's conduct is coming to a head now, Dierdra. Things simply cannot go on like this much longer. My uncle wrote me that the situation was bad, but I did not realize how bad until last night. The chief justice told me that two memorials are being sent to the Lords Proprietors, demanding Burrington's removal. One from the Council members and one from the citizens."

Dierdra frowned. "I should have known. But the things that happened afterwards simply drove it from my mind. That day at the Petersons' party, Allin, before the governor fought with Tinseley and before you and I had our talk, I overheard Thomas Pollock and Chief Justice Gale discussing a memorial they were planning to send. They said they were going to ask your uncle to sign it, Allin. Did he?"

Allin nodded. "Not because he has anything personal against the governor. As a matter of fact, he believes him to be no worse than Eden, and better in many respects. But there has been so much dissension about him in the province, he says, that it would be best for everyone if he were to be removed."

Dierdra was just about to speak when she heard the clatter of the children's feet coming up the stairs. The door burst open, and they ran into the room, their little faces sparkling with health and cold.

"Miss Treffry! Mr. Killigrew!" Ann cried and, running over to Allin, she threw her arms around him. "Have you come to play with us?"

"I've come for something even better," Allin smiled. "To take you back to Lilac Farm with me, to stay there over Christmas. Then we will have all the time in the world to play."

"Oh, hooray, hooray!" And the children began to jump up and down and to run from Dierdra to Allin, kissing first one and then the other. When their first excitement had passed, Ann turned to Dierdra, her tiny face serious.

"But what will you do if we're not here to keep you company, Mistress Treffry?" she asked.

Dierdra smiled. "Don't worry about me. I shan't let you stay away from me too long. I will come out to Lilac Farm on Christmas Day to have a fine dinner with you and to give you your presents."

It was not until the day before Christmas that Madam Burrington passed her crisis. All that time, the house was like a tomb. On several occasions, Dierdra had gone to Madam's room and tapped softly on the door, and each time Dr. Norcomb had opened it a crack, shook his head doubtfully, and said:

"We are doing everything we can. But until the fever comes down . . ."

Once the door had been left ajar, and Dierdra had been able to catch a glimpse of the invalid. It was evening, and the room was dimly lighted by a bedside candle. Mary Catten was kneeling by the bed, holding Madam's hands in her small ones. The sick woman was turning from side to side.

"Don't go, don't go," she whispered, over and over again.

"I'll not leave you, Madam, never fear," Mary replied softly. "I'll never leave you. Everything will be all right."

That time, as Dierdra turned away, her eyes were filled with tears—not only for the governor's lady, but for her devoted little bondwoman, as well.

The next morning, however, Madam's fever was all but gone. Both the doctor and Mary Catten urged her to rest and talk to no one, but she insisted on seeing Dierdra.

"If I do not tell her what is in my heart," she said, "I will only become ill again. Please, doctor, please. I promise not to make it too long. But I must speak to her."

"If you insist, Madam. But only for a few moments—remember." Norcomb's face was drawn; like Mary, he had spent all his time in the sickroom, even sleeping there, on a little cot Taphy had brought in.

Mary went to find Dierdra. The girl was in her room, staring with unseeing eyes at the winter scene beneath her window.

"Madam wants to see you, mistress. She is really too weak to talk yet, but she insists on it so strongly that the doctor thinks it will do her more harm to deny her than it will to let her talk for a little while. But you won't let her keep you too long, will you?"

Dierdra shook her head and hurried down the hall to Madam's bedroom. She knelt down beside the bed and clasped the older woman's hand in hers. Madam still looked drawn and weak, but her color was no longer feverish, and her expression was more peaceful than Dierdra had seen it in a long time.

"You're better, Madam, you're better." Tears sparkled in the girl's eyes. "I'm so glad."

"You are sweet," Madam Burrington smiled weakly. "They don't want me to talk too much, Dierdra, but I want you to know this because it may affect your plans, too. As soon as I have recovered completely, I am leaving here, and taking the children with me. My mind is made up. We are going back to England. You can come with us, if you like. We would love to have you. But I will not stay here any longer. Not a single moment. I kept hoping and praying my husband would improve. I did what I could to make others understand his weaknesses and to help him out of the difficulties that drink and his bad temper brought him to. But nothing seems to do any good. Things have become worse instead of better. It is more than I can bear." Tears started to her eyes. "Perhaps I should be stronger, Dierdra. A wife takes her husband for better or worse, I know. But I simply cannot put up with it any longer."

"I understand, I understand," Dierdra whispered. "We will talk about it again when you are better. But not now. You are still too weak. I am glad you told me. I will think about it, too, and make up my mind. And now you go to sleep." She rose to her feet.

"Just one more thing, Dierdra. The children, how are they?"

"They are fine. They have been at Lilac Farm since you fell sick, you know. I was afraid it would upset them too much to be here during the worst of your illness."

Madam Burrington nodded. "That was the right thing to do. But now that I am better, perhaps they can come home. I am eager to see them."

"I will bring them home tomorrow." Dierdra smiled. "That will be Christmas Day, you know, and they will have collected all their presents."

Dierdra arrived at Lilac Farm late Christmas morning. The children were overjoyed to hear that their mother was better and that they would see her later in the day. And they were delighted with the presents the Killigrews had given them.

"Look!" Ann cried. "This doll. It's wooden. Owen made it for me. And Mistress Killigrew and Mistress Tamar sewed a whole wardrobe for her. See this pretty petticoat?" She lifted the doll's billowing skirt.

"And my wooden soldiers," William said. "Yeoman Killigrew carved them out and Allin painted them. There's a rifleman, and there's a cavalryman," he set the little figures before her on the table as he spoke. "It's nearly a whole regiment!"

"Not quite a regiment, William," Allin laughed. "But there are enough of them to keep you busy for a while."

"What about my presents?" Dierdra asked. "Aren't you interested in what I bought you?"

"More presents! More presents!" Ann clapped her hands. "What are they?"

"Open the parcels and you will find out," Dierdra said, smiling, and she held out two brightly wrapped boxes to the children. "This is for you, Ann, and this one is for William."

In seconds, the parcels were unwrapped.

"It's a little zither," Ann cried. "Just what I wanted!"

"And mine's a pistol! Bang, bang!" William ran through the room, decimating a band of imaginary Indians with his wooden gun.

"Come on and we can show them to Mistress Killigrew," Ann said, and the two children scampered out of the room.

Dierdra turned to Allin.

"I am in a quandary now, Allin," she said. "Madam Burrington plans to take the children back to England with her as soon as she is well enough to travel. She asked me if I wanted to go with her."

Allin grasped her shoulder. "You cannot do that! What did you say to her, Dierdra?"

"I have not said anything, so far," she replied. "Madam is still very ill. She may change her mind about the whole idea when she recovers."

"But suppose she does not?" Allin urged. "You cannot go back to England, Dierdra, you simply cannot. You know how much I need you."

She smiled. "I'm glad you do. And I have no intention of leaving. But what shall I do if Madam does go? I cannot live in Edenton alone."

"You can come out here to stay until the spring. Then I will be finished with my college year, and, if you will have me, we can be married."

"You know I will have you." Dierdra did not get a chance to go on; Allin's arms were around her, and they clung together in a long embrace. When finally they separated, Dierdra spoke again:

"But I do not want you to give up your education for me. I will wait, Allin, you know I'll wait." She went to the window that gave on the Chowan and stood gazing out at the choppy river. Then she turned to face him again.

"Dick and Tamar are coming up the path now. Perhaps we should not tell them anything until we have had a chance to talk a little more."

Allin was just about to reply when Dick and Tamar entered. There seemed to be a certain constraint between them; Dick's round face looked pinched and angry, and Tamar's tawny eyes were puffy. A lover's quarrel, Dierdra thought. I'm glad Allin and I are not the kind to have them.

"Mistress Treffry," Dick said, "it is good to see you again." It was obvious to Dierdra that the enthusiasm in his voice was forced.

"And it is good to see you, too, Dick. Allin tells me you are working hard to have your house ready for a spring wedding."

"Well, it may not be in the spring, Dierdra," Tamar said. "We've decided to postpone the wedding for a while."

"*You've* decided to, you mean," Dick said. His voice was angry.

"What's that?" A puzzled look crossed Allin's dark face. He turned to Tamar. "But you promised Dick . . ."

"Promises are made to be broken," Tamar interrupted, tossing her head. "And there is nothing more to be said. The wedding is postponed, and that's all there is to it."

"I wish you would talk to her, Allin," Dick spread his hands in a gesture of helplessness. "I do not understand what has come over her. Everything was all settled. I've been working like a Trojan to have the house ready in time, and driving my men like the worse kind of martinet." He shook his head. "I am thoroughly confused by the entire business."

"Don't worry, Dick, Tamar and I will straighten this out." There was a hard, set look on Allin's face. "I'll not have her acting like a spoiled child. Making plans and changing them . . ."

"How dare you talk to me like that?" Tamar turned on her heel and flounced out of the room, pausing at the door only long enough to fling back over her shoulder: "If you make me angry enough, I'll call off the whole thing."

Dick started after her, but Dierdra put a restraining hand on his arm.

"Wait," she cried. "Let me talk to her first. This sounds as if it needs a woman's touch."

She found Tamar in her room, staring sullenly out of the window at the bare winter landscape. There was a trace of tears in her eyes.

"So they've sent you to spy on me, Dierdra," she said, as she turned around.

"Come, now, Tamar. You know that is not true. What ever is wrong?" Dierdra asked gently. "This is no way to act. You've upset poor Dick. And on Christmas, too."

"Oh, Dierdra, I don't know what to do!" Tamar's defiant façade seemed to crumble. "If Dick doesn't love me enough to do the simple little things I ask him to . . ."

"I don't understand you, dear. He loves you a very great deal. Look at how disturbed he is right now."

"No he doesn't, Dierdra. He doesn't love me at all. If you only knew." Tamar sniffled and dabbed at her eyes with a muslin handkerchief.

She looked so young and so forlorn as she stood there! Why, she's nothing but a baby! Dierdra thought. She went over and put her arms around the girl.

"Come, now, tell me what the difficulty is."

"It's just that Dick doesn't love me. Even the way he kisses me proves it. He's so gentle. A man should kiss a girl differently when he loves her. He should sweep her off her feet, and kiss her with passion, as if he were going to devour her."

Such childishness! Dierdra thought. But an unpleasant suspicion crossed her mind as her own experience with Anthony on the day of the storm sprang into vivid recollection.

"How do you know so much about kissing, Tamar? Did Anthony Dawson . . ."

"Oh, no fear of that," Tamar sniffled. "He was never interested in me. No, that's not how I know. There are some things you just feel inside you. You do not require lessons in them."

"Now, see here, my girl, you listen to me." Dierdra deliberately assumed a severe and authoritative tone. "I am a year or two older than you, and I know what I'm talking about. It is time you got your head out of the clouds and started to look at things in a grown-up way. Richard Chapman kisses you tenderly because he loves you and wants to make you his wife, because he respects you, and because he is considerate of your feelings. His tenderness is the greatest compliment he can pay you. Especially now, before you are married. There will be ample time for what you call passion later."

"That is all very well for you to say. But it is not true. What about all the elegant London ladies who have affairs with men they have no intention of marrying? They think passion without marriage is much more fun. And everyone treats them with respect."

"Tamar Killigrew! Shame on you! How can you talk so admiringly about loose women? I suppose you look up to the girls in the lewd house, too!" Dierdra had not meant to be so sharp, but Tamar's words had shocked her into a loss of control.

"No, I don't look up to them," anger blazed from Tamar's eyes. "They aren't very clever. But I should not mind being one of these London ladies, and I should not mind having a passionate affair with a man of the world. I should not even have to worry about the consequences. I know all about how to take care of that. A witch woman who lives in the woods has ways of keeping you from having babies."

Dierdra's face had lost its color. She was speechless.

"So there!" Tamar said. Suddenly she burst into tears and flung her arms around Dierdra's neck. Great sobs wracked her slender frame.

"Oh, Dierdra, it isn't really that at all! But Dick is ashamed of me, I know it. He doesn't love me as he should."

Dierdra did not know what to do. She patted the sobbing girl on the back and murmured consoling words. But she was utterly confused. When Tamar's sobbing had quieted down, she led her over to the bed.

"Sit down, dear, you need not talk until you feel up to it."

"But I am so unhappy, Dierdra! When Dick came home from Virginia and said we were going to live here after we were married, instead of along the James, as we had planned, I could not but think he was ashamed to have me meet his elegant family, because he believes I am not good enough for them."

Poor little thing, Dierdra thought, it is so close to the truth, and so far away. But she said nothing, simply stood waiting for Tamar to resume her tale.

"But I said nothing to Dick about what I suspected, because I thought perhaps I was wrong and he would be angry. And anyhow, I thought he would realize in time that I can be just as elegant as any of the Virginia ladies." She stopped to blow her nose and wipe her tear-stained eyes. "Then, when I heard about Allin the other day, well, I thought that would prove to Dick that we were every bit as good as he is, and he would be happy to take me up to his family on the James. And I thought we would live there, and I would be a great lady. I always have wanted to live an elegant life, Dierdra!" She looked at her friend pleadingly. "I always have wanted to get away from this poky little village and all its poky people. But before I heard about Allin's real father, I thought I would never have the chance. Now I do, though. After all, my cousin is a Gorgas. And my parents always said I look like my father's sister, Allin's mother. And if she was attractive enough to catch the eye of a very well-born man, and he even wanted to marry her . . ." She paused, and there was a childish defiance in her voice when she resumed. "Well, perhaps I'm not as beautiful as she was. But I would rather be the mistress of some elegant gentleman than a little housewife, hidden away on the Chowan River, where nobody ever comes, and there's nothing to do. If Dick is too ashamed of me to take me out in society . . ." She rose from the bed and went over to the window again. "No, Dierdra, I simply will not let him treat me this way. I am too young and pretty to be shut up in some little house far away from anything."

Chapter XIV

THE PROPRIETORS ACT

THE GOVERNOR returned to Edenton the last day of January. By that time, the wave of excitement that had followed in the wake of the fall court term and the Strawberry Hill affair had somewhat abated. To many of the people, politics and government were matters for little more than gossip, and those who were seriously interested had reason to believe their problems would soon be at an end. Edward Moseley lost no time in outlining to his friends the contents of a letter he had received from Chief Justice Gale, who had left the province almost immediately after the governor's attack on him, and had sailed for England on the very same packet that was carrying his memorandum to Carkasse. Gale's information—that the Lords Proprietors would meet late in January, and that Burrington's removal at that time was a virtual certainty—spread from the Council members and soundside planters to the Chowan River yeomen, and from them to the artisans, merchants and craftsmen of the Edenton Guild. With Burrington on the way out, there was no further need for protests or petitions or secret meetings and it was, therefore, to a relatively peaceful town that the governor returned.

But the peace of the village did not extend past the door to Government House; his excellency had been home only two days when Madam Burrington told him of her intention to leave him. She, Dierdra, and the governor were in the dining room having dinner when Madam said:

"The doctor feels that a sea voyage would be good for me. I plan to sail for England very shortly. William is old enough to be in school now."

At her words, a red flush crept up Burrington's neck and over his face. But for the moment he said nothing. Madam's eyes were fixed firmly on her plate.

"I have written to Lucy Howard, at Williamsburg, asking her to secure passage for us on the *British Prince*. It sails next month."

"I see that you felt no need to consult me about this matter," Burrington said coldly. "For how long, may I ask, do you intend to be gone?"

Madam took another mouthful of the trifle cook had made to tease her appetite; although she was by now fully recovered from her illness, she was still thin and pale, and Dr. Norcomb insisted that she try to build herself up.

"No, George, I felt no obligation to consult you. I am returning to England for good."

The governor was struggling for control. "By God, Madam, am I to understand that you have joined my enemies?"

Madam's calm, remote voice went on. "You are to understand anything you wish. I have merely said that I am returning to England for good, and taking the children with me."

"Are you trying to goad me into anger, Amelia? Well, you will not succeed. I am determined to keep my temper, no matter how great the provocation."

Madam looked up from her trifle, an expression of polite interest on her delicate face. "Ah, you have turned over a new leaf. Good. I approve heartily. I believe folk should keep their tempers."

The governor glared at her and opened his mouth to speak. Then, abruptly, he closed it and, jumping to his feet, flung his crumpled serviette on the table. He turned on his heel and strode out of the dining room, slamming the door behind him.

Madam looked at Dierdra. "I am truly sorry to have subjected you to this unpleasantness, my dear. I had my own selfish interests at heart; I hoped George would offer me an apology for his recent behavior. That would have helped a bit. But . . ." She paused. "Do you want to come to England with me, Dierdra? You never did say."

Dierdra looked down at her clasped hands for a moment. Then

she spoke slowly. "No, thank you. I have no one in England any longer. All my friends are here, in America."

Madam nodded, and a smile lit her pale face. "I have an idea. Why not come to Virginia with me? You can stay with me until I sail, and we can speak to my friend Lucy Howard. I think she would very much like to have a companion, a friend who could assist her. Her husband is a member of the governor's staff, and she holds an important position in Williamsburg society. Lucy is always busy, always entertaining, and she has much more to do than she can possibly take care of by herself. The house is full all the time; either there are visitors from abroad, or delegates to the House of Burgesses, who usually take their wives to Williamsburg with them when the meetings are held." She paused. "Unless, of course, you would rather stay here, in Edenton."

"No, no, Williamsburg sounds like the ideal answer."

This time Madam's smile was knowing. "I thought you would feel that way. The college is in Williamsburg, as I remember." She rose from the table, steadying herself by placing her hand on the back of her chair. "Mary Catten can come with us, too. And there will be no difficulty about getting to Virginia; Thomas can drive us up in the coach and then bring it back here for the governor."

"Then you have really made up your mind to go?" Dierdra asked.

Madam Burrington nodded vehemently. "I am even more convinced than I was before. Do you know who my husband's companion was on that mysterious trip from which he has just returned? That boor Dr. Carter." There was bitterness in her voice. "Oh, no, Dierdra. I have put up with a great deal and said nothing. But this time George has gone just too far."

Dierdra rose from the table and was pushing her chair back into place when Taphy entered.

"It's Mistress Peterson, Madam," he said. "I showed her into the drawing room."

"Thank you, Taphy. Will you serve our tea in there?"

Dierdra and Madam Burrington found Patience Peterson

standing at the window, examining with great care a French enameled music box she had taken from the little side table on which it usually stood.

"Such a pretty thing!" She smiled embarrassedly. "I could not resist looking at it in the light. Although how much light one gets on a rainy day like this . . ." Her voice trailed off.

"It was a wedding present. Do be seated, Mistress Peterson. Taphy will bring us tea."

Mistress Peterson carefully seated herself in a petit-point-covered chair, spreading her skirts artistically around her. "I really should not have anything. I am becoming much too stout. But I find it so difficult to resist things I like, and I am exceptionally fond of tea." She sighed, and then spoke with prideful resolution. "But I shall take only one spoon of sugar. Only one." She cast an appraising eye over her hostess. "I envy you, Madam, I really do. You seem slimmer every time I see you."

"I've been ill," Madam Burrington said. "That keeps one slim." She smiled ruefully. "But I can hardly recommend the method. Will you pour, Dierdra?" She gestured in the direction of the tea things, which Taphy had just set down on a table.

Patience Peterson nodded sympathetically. "Yes, I heard. I am delighted to see you recovered." She looked fixedly at the large diamond ring on her right hand, which was draped gracefully over the arm of her chair. "Poor thing! You *have* had a difficult time! I must tell you what is in my heart, Madam, I must. Not about political matters; they interest me not at all, and I admit that I pay very little attention to Enar when he talks of government affairs. Why, I barely remember when it was he told me the governor was to be recalled. That's how little interest I take in *that* subject."

She paused, and Dierdra shot a glance at Madam Burrington. The governor's wife was sitting bolt upright in her chair, a distant, withdrawn expression on her face. Mistress Peterson must have seen it, too, but it did not deter her; she went right on.

"But personal things, things about people—well, all women take an interest in them. And when Enar told me about your husband's trip to Charleston and said that Dr. Carter had taken that lewd woman of his along to keep him company while the governor was busy on his affairs—I felt I simply had to come over and tell you how shocked I am, and how upset. Even though it was raining so badly, I had the boy bring the carriage round right away." She leaned forward. "I want you to know, Madam, that you have my deepest sympathy."

Madam put her teacup on the table and rose to her feet.

"Mistress Peterson, I am sure you will understand if I ask to be excused. I hope you will feel free to stay as long as you like, and to examine any of the curios that may take your interest." She moved quickly and quietly to the door and left the room.

Mistress Peterson turned to Dierdra, who had also risen. "Well, I never!" Her voice trembled with indignation. "Imagine talking to me like that! To me! Very high and mighty she is, I must say, for a woman whose husband is in disgrace and about to be dismissed from his office. Enar says there have been enough petitions for his removal to sink a sailing vessel. And no wonder: a man who consorts openly with lewd women and even takes them with him on his trips!" Her face was growing redder by the moment. "And when a respectable woman comes to offer her sympathy! And in this weather, too! Why, I could have caught my death of cold! All I can say is . . ." But apparently she could say nothing: she turned on her heels and flounced into the hall.

Dierdra did not wait to summon Taphy, but opened the front door herself and stood watching as the woman stalked off down the garden path, while her Negro servant, holding a large umbrella over her head, hurried to keep up with her.

When Mistress Peterson's outraged back had disappeared into her carriage, Dierdra ran upstairs and knocked on the door of Madam's sitting room. She entered to find the older woman standing in the middle of the room, her face white, her hands clenched.

"How many indignities am I expected to put up with? To learn from a woman like Patience Peterson that my husband is about to be recalled! To have her coming to me with her false sympathy and her crocodile tears! It—"

"Madam, Madam," Dierdra put her arm around the older

woman's shoulder. "Try not to be so upset. It cannot be good for you. You've been sick. Let me fetch Mary Catten; she will help you to bed."

Madam Burrington shook Dierdra's hand from her shoulder. "I am not going to bed. I am going to Virginia, and I expect to be on my way before sundown."

"But Madam—"

"You cannot stop me, Dierdra. My mind is made up. Mary Catten can pack the children's things." Madam went swiftly to the mantel and pulled the bellcord to summon her maid.

Dierdra had never seen the woman display such anger and such furious energy. She ran from the wardrobe to the bed, tearing dresses from their racks and flinging them in a heap on the counterpane. When Lillie, the maid, appeared, she was sent first to fetch Mary Catten and then to the attic for packing boxes.

"Madam, please, I beg of you," Dierdra pleaded. "You know Patience Peterson is nothing but a gossip. It is not like you to pay attention to malicious rumors."

Madam turned swiftly to face Dierdra. The red brocade dress she held over her arm rustled. "That is precisely why I have to go away. Her stories may all be false, but by now I am so disturbed I am inclined to believe them. If I have to listen to this kind of thing much longer, I will lose all confidence in myself. How can I tell what to think any more? And now, to have every spiteful housewife in the Albemarle whispering about me from behind her fan!" She stamped her foot and threw the dress on the bed. "How dared he? How dared he? I will never forgive George Burrington for putting himself—and me—in this position!" She whirled around. "If you plan to come with me, Dierdra, you had better begin packing your own things."

Dierdra left the room and walked along the hall to the winding staircase that led up to the classroom. She wanted to think. Madam must not go now; it would be the worst possible step she could take. Her health was still precarious; very likely she would break down again before she arrived in Virginia. And now, of all times, she must stay with her husband. If the governor was to be sent back to England, it would speak more heavily against

Madam than against him if she were to leave while he was in the midst of difficulties. People would accuse her of deserting him in a moment of crisis; the humiliations to which he had subjected her would be all but forgotten in a surge of indignation against her disloyalty.

But who could persuade her to stay? Why, oh, why, did these emergencies have to occur when Allin was away? Even Anthony Dawson would be a help, but he had not yet returned from England.

She was halfway up the stairs when an idea came to her. She paused, her hand on the banister, and then turned around and flew downstairs and out of the house, stopping only long enough to pick up her cloak from the rack in the front hall.

Goldsmith Coltrane was seated at the desk in his study when Dierdra entered. Her cheeks were red from the wind and the rain, and she was out of breath from hurrying.

She looks like a little girl, Coltrane thought, as she dropped into a chair and began telling him her story.

"You were the only person I could think of, Mr. Coltrane," she concluded. "I have little sympathy for the governor, myself, and I understand how Madam feels. But if she leaves him now, what will people say? Things are going so badly for him. Everyone says he is to be recalled."

Coltrane looked at Dierdra with his sad, dark eyes. "Yes, my child. Of all times, she must not leave him now. His recall is all but certain, and since she has waited this long . . ." He took up his beaver and threw a long blue cloth cape over his tall, spare frame. "Come child. Let me talk to her. Perhaps I will have some influence."

Together they hurried across the Green to Government House. At the North Gate, Dierdra stopped.

"I'll slip in by the side door, sir. If Madam sees me with you, she will know I brought you over. It would be best for her to believe you just happened by."

Coltrane smiled. "Such a pretty face and such a sharp mind!" He turned the corner and entered the garden from Broad Street, while Dierdra stepped in through the gate near the weaving house and went into the residence through the side door. She had just hung her cloak on the rack when Burrington emerged from his office.

"Miss Treffry, have you seen David Elton?" he asked.

"Not since yesterday, sir. I understood he was going to Norfolk for a week."

The governor scowled. "So he was. I had forgotten. Well, you will have to do it, then. You write a fair hand. I require to have some letters copied. In here."

Dierdra followed him into his office. From the desk, which was piled high with books and documents, he picked up two pieces of paper.

"This is to be copied in my book," he said, handing her one of the sheets. "And this is a letter I have just written. It is to go to Virginia by messenger, but the man will not be here for another hour, so you have ample time. Use Elton's room." He sat down in the high-backed chair behind his desk and nodded his head in the direction of the door leading to the secretary's small cubicle.

Dierdra went in and closed the door behind her. Seating herself at Elton's oak table, she sharpened the quill and began to copy the first letter in the governor's book. It was from William Byrd. Her eyes skimmed the contents quickly, but they were arrested by the last few paragraphs, and she read them with care.

> I think, by some samples I have known in that country, it would cost a pretty deal of trouble to bring it into order, and a lesser spirit than yours would never be able to effect it. People accustomed to live without law or gospel will with great reluctance submit to either.
>
> In the meantime, I wish you all the success in the world in bringing the chaos into form and reducing anarchy into regular government.
>
> In doing so, you will deserve to have your statue erected or, which perhaps would be better, to have your salary doubled. With all good wishes, William Byrd.

Dierdra read the paragraphs again. It was difficult for her to reconcile Byrd's obviously high opinion of Burrington with the dislike of him in North Carolina, and with the evidence she herself had seen of his vulgarity and arrogance. If the note had come from anyone other than Byrd! But he was universally acknowledged to be the greatest of all the Virginians, and one of the most distinguished leaders of the New World. One could not toss his opinion aside lightly. Was it possible that Burrington, despite his glaring faults of character, was in fact what Byrd considered him to be: a man of some greatness and of broad vision, struggling against a group of small-minded, stubborn people, capable of seeing only their own immediate interests, and completely blind to the problems of the country as a whole? Perhaps the governor's answer would contain a clue. She read it carefully as she copied it out.

Honorable William Byrd II, Western James River, Virginia.

Dear and Honored Sir: You will remember that I told you shortly after I first came to North Carolina, that the Lords had instructed me to have the Council and Legislature set a fixed salary of seven hundred pounds annually, out of a permanent fund. I hoped, since I was forbidden to accept any presents, to obtain it out of quit rents.

The Assembly has refused, so far, to adopt such a plan, so I am entirely without salary since I have been in North Carolina.

This is in answer to a facetious sentence in your letter: 'to have your salary doubled.' Tell me, good sir, can you double nothing?

To get away from nonsense: I think no government could have carried out my instructions to keep the peace, with a people who are by nature subtle and crafty to administration, who can be neither outwitted nor cajoled, who have always behaved insolently with their governors, who maintained that their money could not be taken from them, save by appropriations made by their own House of Assembly, a body that has always usurped more power than ought to be allowed.

As to the matter under discussion the last time we talked together, I have written confidentially to friends in London. So far I have received no answer. Be assured that I shall advise you as soon as I have an answer to my inquiries. The Crown has its secret ways of arriving at facts, as you well know. In the meantime, I can only wait, and I am not good at waiting, impatient fellow that I am.

Dierdra had got this far when she heard a knock on the door of Burrington's office.

"Come in," the governor's gruff voice called out.

It was Coltrane; the goldsmith's distinctive tones came clearly through the closed door that separated her from them.

"May I have a few words with you, your excellency?"

"If you have not come to press me to cover my loan," Burrington said. "You know my financial circumstances are straitened, to say the very least."

"I have not come about that." The goldsmith paused, then spoke gently. "I have just been visiting with Madam. I found her in a very distressed frame of mind."

The governor snorted. "Hah! That's nothing new."

"Madam has been consulting me about a voyage to England," Coltrane went on. "I believe you know that she is not obliged to depend on you for funds; her family has issued bills of credit for her to draw on whenever she wishes. She now tells me that she wants to leave here within the next month. And I might add that I had the greatest difficulty in persuading her to postpone her departure that long; she insisted, at first, that she wanted to leave tonight, and it took all my powers to persuade her to stay at all."

Dierdra heard the scraping of a chair across the floor and then the sound of pacing footsteps.

"She threatened to leave at dinner," Burrington said. "But I did not believe her."

"I am afraid you should have, sir. She is quite serious, I give you my word."

"Go back and talk to her again, Coltrane. She relies on you. She will listen to you."

"About financial matters, yes. But this is different."

There was a long silence, and then the governor spoke again.

"I tell you, Coltrane, she must change her mind. I cannot have her leave now. Do you think her illness has affected her?"

"Perhaps in the sense that it has made it more difficult for her to . . ." the banker's voice trailed off in a cough. "If you were to examine your own conduct, sir . . ."

"My conduct?" Dierdra could sense the embarrassment behind Burrington's bluster. "Yes, I suppose it would have been better if I had been here when she was ill. But how was I to know she would become ill? And I simply had to go to Charleston. Grave matters depended on it." He paused; when he spoke again his voice was subdued. "I should have told her I was going. It was inconsiderate of me to leave without any notice to her. I am afraid I am sometimes thoughtless."

"Such a confession would be cold comfort to Madam, sir." Coltrane's voice was icy.

The sound of footsteps ceased, and the governor spoke loudly and angrily. "If I have my faults, I am no different from anyone else. Amelia herself is not an angel, no matter what she may think." He paused. "But we must stop her from going. I simply cannot have her leave me now. The situation is much too delicate. Far too much is at stake. Far too much. If she only knew . . ."

"I doubt if even you know how delicate the situation is, your excellency. The village may have seemed quiet since your return, but many people are still indignant about the Strawberry Hill affair. And they are not satisfied with an explanation that lays your conduct to the bottle." He paused. "Particularly when you ran off the very next day. You may have had urgent business in Charleston, but I cannot believe you had to take Carter with you. Madam tells me Mistress Peterson was here not an hour ago, bursting with the news that Mary Abbott also accompanied you. How do you think it makes her feel to have to listen to that?"

"She has had to listen to gossip before." The governor tried to shrug off Coltrane's question. "Scurrilous rumors are part of the price one pays for a position in the public eye. I will not stoop to discuss the question of Mary Abbott. But I had to have Carter with me. I thought I might need medical attention. I have been feeling rather ill lately."

"You have a right to any explanation you choose to offer," Coltrane said drily. "But the Edenton folk care very little about your explanations. They care about your actions. Are you aware that two memorials have already been sent to London, requesting your removal? One of them is from the Council, the other from the settlers—merchants, artisans, craftsmen, yeomen, plantation owners . . ."

There was the noise of a fist banging down heavily on a desk. "My God! Have things gone this far? And so quickly?"

"That is precisely how far they have gone. You are in great trouble, sir, and you might as well face it."

"So petitions have been sent," Burrington interrupted. "I suppose the Proprietors will act on them." His voice was thoughtful.

"I cannot speak for them, sir. But . . ."

"Everard will replace me, I imagine. He has always wanted the post." The governor spoke softly; it sounded to Dierdra as if he was thinking out loud. "I wonder how much time I will have. Six months, at least, I should imagine. And in six months . . . She must give me that time, Coltrane, she simply must."

"I have pointed out to her how impolitic it would be for her to leave now . . ."

"Impolitic! Disastrous! I will do anything. Tell her that, anything. If she only knew how important it is!"

"I cannot promise a thing beyond this coming month." His voice was firm. "But if you will come with me to speak to her, and give her some security for your future conduct, we may be able to persuade her. She does not want to admit her marriage is a failure, sir."

"I will give her any security she wants. I'll even sign a document. She need have no fear of my conduct, none at all. It will be impeccable. I promise. But she must not leave. If she does, it will ruin everything, destroy all my work and effort." He paused. "Coltrane, if she will give me these six months, she can have anything she wants from me. I will be a new man."

The Lords Proprietors had held their meeting in London, on January 21, 1726. A letter of complaint against the governor, his personal conduct, and his illegal procedures, was read; it was signed by nine of the ten Councilors appointed by the lords to be of the governor's Council. The letter of complaint from the settlers was also read into the record.

Not all the Proprietors were present at the meeting; the Lord Palatine was in Ireland on a government mission. But the assembled lords voted unanimously to remove Governor Burrington from office and to replace him by Sir Richard Everard, Baronet, who had requested that he be permitted to succeed the present governor. Although the decision was binding, it was agreed that its execution should be postponed for a period of some six months, until the Lord Palatine had returned from his trip and added his approval.

Of all these facts, and of the time of his probable departure, George Burrington was duly notified, in a letter which arrived at Edenton late in February, shortly before Madam Burrington planned to leave. When she saw it, she agreed to remain with her husband until the date of his recall.

Chapter XV

THE RETURN OF SPRING

IT WAS EARLY in March when Anthony Dawson returned to North Carolina—almost a year to the day since he had first set foot in the New World. But this time, as if to make up for its late arrival the year before, spring had come early to the Albemarle. Already, the sap was rising. The birds, seeking their summer homes, filled the forest with their chatter and calls, and pecked at the nuts of the chinquapin trees. The air was rich with the smell of fresh earth; in preparation for an early planting, the farmers were plowing, turning over the fallow winter earth to receive, in time, the seeds that would send forth their sharp green shoots. This was the season Anthony loved the most, and the season that now seemed to him to hold the very spirit of the New World.

And this year, spring had a special meaning for him. For he had come back to North Carolina to stay, to build his permanent home on the Chowan River acreage he had taken up before he left for England. His months there had taught him many things. Although he had derived some pleasure from the festivities of the London season, they had at the same time served to demonstrate to him that this world of fashion and flirtation was no longer his. To a man who had known the adventure of war, the perils of philandering were far too tame. To a man who had been in the thick of the battle of colonization, gossip about preferment and position was trivial, at best. In every way, the life and vigor of the New World made the old seem artificial and effete.

Anthony's personal desire to settle in North Carolina fitted in perfectly with his family's decision, which, arrived at only after long conferences and much thought and, taken together with the certain knowledge of Burrington's eventual recall, made his presence in the province even more urgent.

Anthony entered the common room of the King's Arms to find himself surrounded by a noisy and enthusiastic crowd of merchants and artisans.

"Ah, Mr. Dawson!" Martin Trewilliger, the farrier, called out. "A pleasure to see you back, sir."

"And a pleasure to be back, Martin." Anthony shook the man's hand.

"You've come to give Old Bunger another lesson in wrestling, I take it," said Nate Trewilliger, Martin's cousin; he was the hostler who had made Anthony's skillibegs.

"I had forgotten Old Bunger," Anthony laughed. "But since you remind me . . . Boy," he called to a potboy, "some Madeira for everyone. We'll drink the wrestler's health."

Above the burst of approval there rose an unfamiliar voice.

"And after the toast to the Bunger, whoever the devil he may be, a round on me, for His Majesty, the King."

"Fair enough," Anthony cried. "And I'll stand one for the Lords Proprietors."

"No, no, not on my last day here. I'm off for home in the morning, and I hate to waste good wine on those bloodsuckers!" The stranger's voice was scornful. "We rid ourselves of ours, and if you're wise, you will free yourselves of yours. Why, even your governor has no use for those London dandies. And I say it who knows!"

The potboy arrived, and the men began milling around him, reaching avidly for the glasses of wine on the tray he carried. Anthony stole a look at the stranger. A tall, angular, red-haired man, he was obviously deep in his cups; his face was flushed and he was unsteady on his feet.

"Who is that fellow?" Anthony asked Martin. "I cannot remember ever having seen him before."

"A visitor, sir. Name of Simmons. From South Carolina—Charleston. A merchant, he says, although what he sells I've yet to learn. Been here a couple of days now. Sober and sensible as you please until last night. But then you should have heard him. Drunk as a lord, and going on about the Proprietors all evening.

'What do you want them for?' he kept asking. 'We know all about those fellows in South Carolina. We had old Johnston, you know, and we learned all the tricks these scoundrels can play. They get you in a vise,' he says, 'and squeeze and squeeze until the blood runs. But we cut old Johnston's horns,' he says, 'and you can do the same thing. Governor will help, too.' He must have said it fifteen times."

"What do you think he meant when he said the governor would help?" Anthony asked.

"Oh, that was just talk, I make no doubt," Martin replied. "But his help wouldn't mean a thing, anyway. He's been recalled, you know, sir. Just staying around until the new governor comes to take his place. And that will be a good riddance to bad rubbish, if you ask me." He smiled. "Although I must admit old George had been behaving beautiful for the last month or two. Had he been like this all the time . . ."

"Yes, I heard he would be leaving," Anthony said.

"What I've always thought, sir—" Martin began, but Anthony interrupted him; he had just caught sight of Yeoman Killigrew and Dick Chapman entering the room.

"Will you excuse me, Martin?" he asked. "I want to talk to Mr. Killigrew and Mr. Chapman." He made his way through the noisy crowd to the doorway.

"Anthony, you old scoundrel!" Dick wrung his hand enthusiastically. "We thought we would find you here. When did you arrive?" His pleasant face was wreathed in smiles.

"Dick! And Mr. Killigrew! I arrived just a few minutes ago." Anthony clapped them each on the shoulder. "You look fine, sir," he said to the older man. "And you," he turned to Dick, "you look simply marvelous. Thinner and taller and stronger."

"Muscle, my dear fellow, muscle." Dick laughed. "Clearing land and building a house—those are tasks that would put muscle even on a dandy like you."

"Dandy!" Anthony retorted in mock anger. "Dandy indeed! Now that I am back to stay, I will be clearing my own land, and building my own home, and planting also. And I wager I will have it all finished in half the time it took you."

"I'll take you up on that wager, Mr. Dawson," Killigrew said, smiling broadly, "Dick is as fine a worker as you could ever hope to meet. You'll need go far to outdo him."

"Now, now, Mr. Killigrew," Anthony shook his head, "you must not let your prejudices run away with your judgment. Just because this young man is going to be your son-in-law—"

"I think I see a free table over there," Dick said, nodding toward a corner of the room. "Shall we sit down and have a drink?"

"Fine," Anthony said. Why, he wondered, had his friend changed the subject at that moment? And was he mistaken, or had both Dick and Yeoman Killigrew looked unhappy at his last words?

By now they had reached the vacant table. While Dick was giving their order to a potboy, Anthony turned to Killigrew.

"Well, now, you must tell me everything that has happened since I left. Young Chapman has been the most abominable correspondent. I think I have had only two letters from him since I left for England. How is your family?"

"Mistress Killigrew is fine," the older man said, "and so is Owen. Allin is up at college, you know, and enjoying it, from what he writes us."

"Allin at college? Dick never wrote a word about it. How pleased you must be; I remember you wanted him to go."

"Aye," Killigrew nodded. "It was always my fondest wish."

"But what made him decide to do it?" Anthony asked. "It seemed to me that he was very much against the idea when you spoke of it."

"So he was," Killigrew said. "But he changed his mind. Decided to take his rights."

"Rights?" Anthony was puzzled.

"I think perhaps you ought to tell Tony the whole story about Allin," Dick put in. "I have to admit I wrote him nothing about it."

"Ah. Then it still be a secret to you, Mr. Dawson? Well, I'll be happy to tell you. And it's better you should hear it from me than from the town gossips, who will have it all wrong, no doubt. Although the gentry has been fine, and taken no more notice than if it happened every day. Mayhap that be why Dick did not write you about it; he may be used to this kind of thing." Anthony waited impatiently as the yeoman drew his pipe from his waistcoat pocket, lit it, and took a few reflective puffs. "Allin is not my son, Mr. Dawson," he finally said. "He's my sister's boy, although my wife and I raised him from a babe. His name is Allin Gorgas, according to the law and set on the rolls, for all that he was born out of wedlock."

"Gorgas? That's a great name in Devon," Anthony said. "Is Allin of the Devon Gorgases?"

Killigrew nodded.

"Of course, of course," Anthony said. "There was an Allin Gorgas. He died when I was still young. But I did not mean to interrupt you. Do go on, sir."

It took some time for the entire tale to come out. When it was over, Yeoman Killigrew took a long swallow from the tankard of ale the potboy had brought him. Then he spoke again.

"That's the way it was, Mr. Dawson, and a sad story, too. My sister was not a bad girl, only young and full of love. Gay, with never a care in the world. And Mr. Gorgas loved his Mary very much, and was a pitifully sad young man when he came to our cottage to ask her to marry him and found that she had died giving birth to his son. He sat still as a church image and said not a word. Then he got up and went away, but the very next day he came back and made arrangements for me and my woman to keep the babe. That's the way it was, Mr. Dawson." Killigrew heaved a long sigh.

"But it has had a happy ending," Dick put in. "So don't look so sad, sir."

"So it has, so it has," Killigrew said. "And now I think it be time to talk of your plans, Mr. Dawson. You are back to stay, eh?"

Anthony nodded. "Yes. And I must start working on my property. Moseley did so little with it, it is still almost virgin land. I foresee a great deal of work, especially if I am to have a house up soon, and do any planting this season."

Dick took a long swallow of ale. "You should have very little difficulty building the house, Anthony—at least, if my experience means anything. The artisans are a highly skilled lot, and very efficient. And the neighbors will probably help out with the carpentry and the other construction work. They pitched in with a will for me. Yeoman Killigrew tells me they always do."

The older man puffed thoughtfully on his pipe. "Aye, the neighbors will help. But you must start soon. With the early planting this year, they will not have too much time to give you. You began your work late in the fall, you know, when there was little to do on the farms," he added, turning to Dick.

"No one can be more eager than I to get to work quickly," Anthony said. "So we should have very little trouble on that score." He ran his fingers through his hair. "But I have another problem. I stopped off in Virginia on my way here, and bought a few slaves. But not enough for planting the fields, and I must plant soon if I am to have any crops this fall. I do not know where to find more men, though, unless I go down to the slave market in Charleston."

"Let me think." Killigrew scratched his head. "I'm not too familiar with slaves, myself. I own none, as you know. I don't understand the blacks, and I cannot take to the idea of owning human souls, no matter what the color of their skin. I feel more comfortable with the bondmen."

"Why not do as I did, Tony?" Dick put in. "Advertise in England. You can obtain bondmen that way, if you pay the fare for a man and his family."

"I fear I've no time for that now," Anthony said. "It would be months before anybody arrived here."

"That's the truth." Killigrew drew his brows together. "Let me think a moment. African slavers do come in every once in a while. I can ask around and find out if one is due any time soon." He paused. "Ah, here's an idea. Philander." Briefly, he told Anthony the story of the Negro freeman. "His case against Thomas Harrow has not been settled yet, and I have the feeling that Harrow would be glad to let him go at a good price, and have him off his hands. Long as Philander is around, Harrow is afraid the court may give him his freedom, and that way Harrow would have not a penny. And Philander would jump at the chance, too. He would make a fine foreman for your field hands."

"I shall talk to Harrow in the morning, then," Anthony said.

"And I'll ask among those I know." Killigrew rose. "I'm not the only man in Chowan Precinct." He held out his hand. "I must leave you now, Mr. Dawson. I have to see Goldsmith Coltrane about some matters of credit. Now that you are back, I shall expect you to come out and have a meal with us at Lilac Farm. We will have something to tempt your appetite, I promise." He turned to Dick. "Likely I will see you again before you leave. But if not, I hope you will try not to worry."

When the yeoman's sturdy form had disappeared from view, Anthony turned to Dick.

"What say we go up to my room and talk a bit?"

Dick nodded, and the two young men made their way up the stairs to Anthony's suite. The Englishman's mind was busy. What had Killigrew meant about Dick leaving? Was there any connection between that and the gloom that had descended on both of them at his quip about Dick's approaching marriage? And should he ask Dick directly, or wait for the younger man to volunteer?

Dick answered all his questions for him as soon as they had arrived at the sitting room of Anthony's suite. Flinging himself on the sofa with an air of discouragement, he said:

"You might as well hear about all the Killigrew family skeletons at once, Tony. Tamar and I seem to be at the end of our engagement."

Anthony looked at him in surprise. "What? What has been happening? Why didn't you write me about it, Dick?"

The brown-haired young man sighed. "I would not even have known where to begin. Women! I simply cannot understand them!"

"The proper place to begin is at the beginning. Now then, let's have it." Anthony sat down opposite his friend.

"Well, first there was that trouble because I told Tamar we were going to live here instead of in Virginia. You remember that, Tony, don't you?"

Anthony nodded. "But I was sure she would get over it," he said.

"For a while it looked as if she had. From a short time after you left until just about Christmas, everything was going along smoothly. I was working like a demon to have the house and the property all ready for a spring wedding. It was supposed to be early in June. And then . . . Damn me if I can understand what happened to her!"

"Let me hear it, Dick."

"It all started when Allin came home at Christmas time. Suddenly she took it into her head to postpone the wedding. And she has refused to give me a single sensible reason. Every time I've asked her, she says something more mysterious. First she hinted that I didn't think her good enough for me, and was ashamed to take her to Virginia. Tony," he looked at his friend pleadingly, "how could I tell her my father is opposed to the marriage? It would have broken her heart. And her family's, too. Then she turned around completely and started to hint that I wasn't good enough for her. She wants me to be more daring, she says, and more sophisticated. I'm no London gallant, Tony, and she knew it from the beginning. But now she wants me to be some kind of romantic cavalier, who writes poetry to his lady's eyes, and fights duels to defend her honor, and seduces her, too. She talks the most idiotic nonsense you can imagine."

"Then perhaps it is better the engagement should be canceled," Anthony said thoughtfully. "It sounds to me as if you would be thoroughly unhappy with her."

"I probably would be," Dick sprang to his feet and started pacing the room restlessly. "But more unhappy without her. Dammit, Tony, I love the girl. When she's herself, she is the sweetest, gayest, most beautiful . . . But now she has some sort of bee in her bonnet and I cannot for the life of me understand what it is. So I'm going away for a while, Tony. Up to Virginia, to help my father with the spring planting. Perhaps if I'm gone she will come to her senses. I simply do not know what else to do, Tony. I'm at my wit's end." He threw himself down on the sofa again and stared moodily ahead of him.

Anthony felt a wave of pity for his friend. "I wish I could help, Dick. But I am even more in the dark than you. Did you do anything to upset her?"

Dick shook his head. "What could I have done? Her family understands no better than I. And it was an especially merry Christmas. The Burrington children were staying at Lilac Farm, and Dierdra came out. And Allin had not told Tamar or Owen about his father up to then. That was the time the news came out, and they learned that they were connected with an important family." He shook his head again. "No, it confounds me utterly." He rose to his feet. "So I shall take myself to Virginia for a month or two. I have a choice between that and liquor and loose women. The girls at the lewd house are pretty enough, and I suppose they know how to make a man happy. But they were no help to me at all, even though I gave them the pleasure of my company once or twice." He smiled wryly. "But that kind of life is not for me, Tony."

Anthony did not know what to say. He walked over and patted his friend awkwardly on the shoulder. "It will all be all right, Dick. You'll see."

"I doubt it. I doubt it very much. Well," he took a deep breath and drew himself to his full height, "I'm off now. I have to ride out to the plantation and pack some things. I want to get an early start tomorrow."

When Dick left, Anthony rang for Smalkins to prepare a bath for him, and a change of clothing. He wanted to go over to Government House, to pay his respects to Burrington. He had just finished stripping himself when Smalkins entered his bedchamber.

"Sir, your bath is laid." The valet led the way down the hall to the room that had been set aside as a bath. Anthony squeezed himself into the tin tub, while Smalkins poured cold water from a copper bucket over his well-soaped body.

"I am going out, to pay my respects to the governor," Anthony said. He had finished bathing and was drying himself on a large towel. "I will order dinner when I come back. You can have the evening off, if you wish."

"Thank you, sir. But, begging your pardon, why pay your respects to Burrington? From what I heard below stairs just now, he is on his way out."

"So he is, Smalkins, so he is. But he is still the governor, and will be until Sir Richard arrives. The governor's office is entitled to respect, no matter who holds it."

"I suppose so, sir." Smalkins shook his head. "He must be a strange one, that Burrington. They were saying below stairs that he'd been a terror the last few months before it was known he was to be recalled. But ever since the news came through, they say, butter wouldn't melt in his mouth. No more drunken rampages. No more ordering people about. No one trusts it, but everyone says it's a seven days' wonder."

An idea struck Anthony, chasing from his mind for the moment his concern about Dick. These words of Smalkins, confirming as they did Martin Trewilliger's earlier comments; the red-haired merchant, Simmons, with his talk of Burrington's dislike of the Proprietors; the events which, Anthony knew, were marching steadily toward their inevitable conclusion in England . . . Surely there was a pattern here. Could it be that all the time he had been in the employ of the Lords, Burrington had been secretly working for the Crown?

He nodded. Of course, of course. That must be it. How better account for all the otherwise inexplicable aspects of the governor's behavior? How better construe his friendship with William Byrd, that arch-enemy of proprietary government, and Byrd's respect for him? How better explain his arrogant treatment of the Council members? How better interpret the dilatory way he had handled so many pressing problems: the tobacco tax, the shipping laws, the dividing line with Virginia? Burrington's apparent incompetence was in all likelihood part of a well-thought-out plan, directed toward making the settlers so dissatisfied with proprietary government that they would welcome a sale to the Crown, and toward making North Carolina such a burdensome and unprofitable enterprise for the Proprietors that they would be eager to dispose of their holdings. And—Anthony smiled wryly to himself—one had to give the devil his due: there was every probability that the plan would succeed, at least in good measure.

Anthony arrived at Government House to find that Burrington and his family had left a few days earlier, for a week's visit to Bath. But, Taphy told him, Mistress Treffry was at home, and he showed Anthony into the drawing room, where the young man waited eagerly for her arrival. In a few minutes she came running in, both hands extended.

"Anthony," she cried, "how good to see you!" She was wearing a lemon-yellow dress, which served to add even more sheen to her sleek black hair and more sparkle to her deep blue eyes. Anthony felt a stab of unhappiness. Here was the only girl he could ever really care for—and she was in love with another man. And if ever there had been even the faintest chance that he could have won her from Allin, that chance surely had disappeared with the dramatic story of the Black Cornishman's birth. . . . He kissed her hands, one after the other, and then held her at arm's length.

"Dierdra, you look beautiful! More beautiful than ever!"

"Why, thank you, sir," smiling, she made a deep curtsey. "You have been away so long, I had forgotten what a gallant you are."

"But this is the truth," he protested, "not gallantry."

"Then I thank you even more. But sit down, do, and tell me all about yourself." She motioned him to a chair.

"There is really very little to tell," he said as he sat down. "I went to England to report to my family on the situation here, and I came back as soon as my business was finished. The only news is that now I have come back to stay. I am as enthusiastic a convert to the New World as you, Dierdra."

"I am not at all surprised. But I am delighted. I always hoped you would be." She smiled warmly at him.

"And now that I have given you my news, suppose you give me yours. I am sure that a good deal has happened here since I left."

"It certainly has. Let me see, where shall I start?" She frowned and sat looking pensively ahead for a moment. "Well, first there was Mary Catten's trial," and she went on to tell him that story, and the story of the Strawberry Hill affair, and of Madam's threat to leave his excellency just at the time the news of his recall, although still a rumor, was becoming known. "But now, thank heaven," she concluded, "everything is calm and serene. Mary Catten is here, and happy, and a great help to Madam. Chief Justice Gale has returned to England. And Mr. Coltrane and the governor, between them, were able to persuade Madam to stay. The governor gave her his solemn promise that he would behave himself, and he has been living up to his word, I must say. You know, Anthony—" she leaned forward—"I always believed that he was fonder of her than he appeared to be, but I never realized how very deep his feelings went. Why, he is hardly the same man. If love ever changed anybody . . ." She paused. "Although I think something else may also be involved; I accidentally overheard a conversation between him and Goldsmith Coltrane, and it seemed to me that Burrington had political reasons for wanting Madam to stay and for improving his behavior. In some way, his reform is connected with the news of his recall, I feel sure."

Anthony nodded. "The governor is not a simple man, Dierdra, and I would be very much surprised if his conduct was governed by simple motives." He rose and went over to stand in front of her. "And now, what about you? You are not planning to return to England with the Burringtons, are you?"

She shook her head. "No. Of course, Madam has offered to take me. But . . ." she fell silent.

"But what?" Anthony urged.

Dierdra sat for a moment without speaking. Then she said, "I should think you might have guessed, Anthony. I am going to be married. To Allin Killigrew—or Gorgas, if you prefer."

Anthony smiled. "I had my suspicions. But that is delightful news, Dierdra! And what a fortunate fellow Allin is! To have you and a distinguished family, too! I saw his father earlier today, and he told me Allin's story." He paused. "Tell me, when is the happy event to take place?"

"We are not sure as yet. There are so many things to be settled.

First of all, whether Allin is going to stay on at William and Mary. If he does, the wedding will have to be postponed for quite a while."

"Does Allin want to stay?" Anthony asked. "In his position, I think I would rather leave."

Dierdra smiled and looked down at her lap. "Well, he *does* say he would prefer to be married soon. But I am not convinced he should give up college. Of course, the final decision is his. In any event, the wedding cannot take place until the Burringtons return to England; I would not want to leave Madam alone with the governor. He is so unpredictable, you know; I am far from positive this reform of his is permanent. And Madam is too frail and sickly to tolerate any more of his antics. She was dreadfully ill last winter."

"I can understand your feelings." Anthony returned to his chair and sat down. "Dierdra," he said after a moment, "I want to ask your advice. Since you are to be Allin's wife, I imagine the members of the Killigrew family have taken you into their confidence."

She looked at him inquiringly.

"I am speaking about Tamar," he went on. "Dick told me that they have been having a great deal of difficulty."

She nodded. "The girl is so confused, Anthony." She sighed. "It's all this silly business about classes. Tamar takes it much too seriously. I am very much afraid that if something does not happen soon to bring her to her senses, she will find herself in a great deal of trouble. I've tried to talk to her, but nothing seems to help. Allin will be back for the Whitsun holidays, and I hope he will have some influence on her."

"I hope so, too. Poor Dick is dreadfully upset. Well . . ." Anthony rose. "I should be going now. I want to be out on my property early tomorrow morning, to start clearing land for the house. So much needs to be done!"

"I can imagine." Dierdra, who had also risen, extended her hand to him. "I have an idea, Anthony. While you are at work building your home, I shall begin to look round for a mistress for it. Now that you are back here to stay, we shall have to find a wife for you."

Anthony smiled faintly. "I am afraid you will find that a fruitless quest. I fear I am going to remain a permanent bachelor."

Chapter XVI

MR. SIMMONS

A FEW DAYS later, as he was returning to the village from a trip to his property, Anthony's eye was caught by an unexpected flash of color in the murky brown of a swamp off a back country lane. He reined in his horse, dismounted, and picked his way gingerly through the mire to the spot that had attracted his attention. There, his body sprawled in an awkward position, his face half-buried in the slime, his skull bashed in, lay the body of the red-haired stranger, Simmons, who, true to his word, had left Edenton the morning after Anthony's arrival. The young man's first impulse was to pick up the body, sling it over his saddle, and take it into the village with him. But a moment's thought dissuaded him. This was no accidental death; only a vicious and deliberate blow could have produced such damage to the man's skull. Murder was a problem for the law. Anthony ran back to his horse, spurred the animal to a gallop, and rode directly to the sheriff's office in the Edenton courthouse.

The news spread quickly, throwing the entire village into an uproar. The only murder in all of Chowan Precinct in the last year had been the result of a fight between two drunken sailors. But Simmons' death was not just the tragic outcome of a brawl. The man had been robbed. No papers or money were found on his body, and in his saddlebags, still slung over the horse the sheriff's men discovered grazing quietly a few miles up the path from the swamp, there were only some clothing and a little note-book, from which all the pages had been torn. If an armed robber was prowling the countryside . . . Villagers and planters double-locked their doors at night, and the militia took turns in patrolling the area.

At the coroner's inquest, Dr. Norcomb testified that the

wound had probably been inflicted with a club, and the splinters in the man's matted hair strengthened this belief. But although the sheriff and his deputies combed the swamp, they could not find a single trace of the murder weapon. No one seemed to know anything more about the man than his name and the fact that he came from Charleston, and since no address had been found, and the governor was still away and could not be consulted, the body was finally buried in the open field outside the East Gate. No other untoward events occurred, and in a week the excitement had simmered down.

But Anthony was not satisfied. This, he was sure, was something more than a simple case of robbery. There had been something mysterious about Simmons' visit. If only one could find out something more about the man, if only there were some facts . . .

The facts came shortly thereafter, when Ali Hassan called on Anthony in his rooms at the King's Arms. The merchant was accompanied by the young lad who acted as his servant. The boy set down the bundle of material he carried, salaamed, and left.

"Sir," said Ali Hassan when the door had closed behind his helper, "I have some information for you. But we must be sure of absolute privacy."

Anthony had never seen the man's face so serious. "No one else is here," he answered, "not even my man."

The merchant went to the door and called for his boy, who was going down the stairs. The lad returned, and his master gave him a brief order in Arabic. The youngster nodded in reply, and sat down cross-legged outside the door, where he commanded a view of the hall in both directions.

"Mr. Dawson," said Ali Hassan as he closed the door, "I have learned something about the man who was killed. In the first place, he was not a merchant, but a barrister, a man of fine education. Doubtless he had good reason for the masquerade. But the fact is that he was a man of substance, on very good terms with some of South Carolina's leading citizens. Indeed, he was an intimate of the governor. He knew Burrington well, too. He came up here from Charleston by water, on the *Sea Sprite*. As soon as he arrived, he took a room at the inn and bought a horse, and almost every day he rode out on the Virginia Road. Each time he did, the governor rode out shortly afterwards, also alone, and in the same direction. Simmons would go out to the woods, about six miles beyond the Red Lion Inn, and the governor would meet him there. They talked for an hour or more each time." Ali Hassan smiled and shrugged his shoulders. "Alas, I am remiss, Mr. Dawson; I do not know precisely what they spoke about. But I do know that on two occasions papers were exchanged; the first time Simmons gave something to Burrington, and the last time they met, Burrington gave something to him. If I may be allowed to hazard a guess, I would say that Simmons was carrying a communication from the governor of South Carolina, which Burrington answered."

Anthony let out a stream of air through his teeth. Then he nodded thoughtfully. "This fits in all too well with something I have been thinking. It explains a great deal."

"I think it explains Mr. Simmons' death," Ali Hassan said soberly.

Anthony looked at him with interest.

"Let us take matters in order, Mr. Dawson," the merchant said, ticking the items off on the fingers of his delicate brown hand. "First: Simmons was apparently engaged on some sort of secret business with Burrington. They met several times to transact these affairs. Second: As Simmons' visit in Edenton drew to a close he began to make speeches against the Proprietors, and to hint openly that Governor Burrington shared his aversion to them."

Anthony nodded. "I heard one of those speeches."

"Ah." The merchant shook his finger. "But I will wager you did not hear the things Mr. Simmons said late in the evening the night before he left. He changed his tune then. He was very far gone in liquor, and was sitting alone in the common room, over a bottle of rum, talking to himself. 'These are valuable papers,' I heard him say, 'very valuable. What would they be worth to Lord John?' And he threw back his head and began to laugh."

"So he was going to betray his trust, eh?" Anthony asked.

"That we will never know. Perhaps he would have thought better of it had he lived." The merchant sighed. "But someone else, I am sure, overheard Mr. Simmons and decided to take no chances on what he would do."

"But the governor had already left for his visit to Bath when Simmons departed," Anthony said, shaking his head dubiously.

"I have said nothing about the governor, sir. I do not believe he would do such a thing. Violence is in his character, yes, but only when it is released by drink. And, as you may have heard, he has not taken a drop since the news of his recall became public. No, this crime, I am convinced, was planned and executed by someone else. I have wondered if our landlord, deVoe . . ."

Anthony was silent. What about deVoe? The landlord had always been among Burrington's admirers. He stood behind the bar in the common room, and certainly could easily overhear any conversations. He was mistrusted and disliked throughout the village; all the people believed him to be a spy for the governor. deVoe . . .

At that moment, there was a slight cough in the hall, and Ali Hassan swiftly undid the bundle of fabrics. He spread a bolt of velvet over the back of the sofa and draped a long piece of Venetian brocade over his shoulders. When, a few seconds later, a knock sounded at the door, he was discoursing on the merits of the materials to Anthony.

"Come in," Anthony called, and deVoe entered, carrying a bottle wrapped in straw.

"Sir, a shipment of this rare Spanish wine came in on the *Sea Sprite* a few days ago. I brought some to you the evening you arrived, as a welcoming gift, but when I knocked, I found neither you nor your man here."

"Very thoughtful of you, deVoe." Anthony's lips smiled, but his eyes were cold. "Very thoughtful, indeed."

The landlord bowed slightly to Ali Hassan. "I would have sent a bottle to you, too, sir, but I understand you do not drink."

"My religion forbids it, sir. But thank you, nevertheless." The merchant turned to Anthony. "Then you will take the ivory and the rose brocade?"

Anthony nodded. "Yes, I think so. I will be out on my property on Friday. The house should be far enough along by then so that if you bring samples of the materials for draperies . . ."

"An excellent idea, sir. I will see you on Friday, then." The merchant bowed and withdrew.

As the door closed behind Hassan, deVoe, who had been standing quietly near the window, said:

"So you are serious about your plan to settle here, Mr. Dawson?"

"Did you think I was not?"

"Sir," deVoe replied, "that was just in a manner of speaking. I asked only because, if you do expect to stay, I may be able to perform a small service for you."

"Indeed?" Anthony spoke coldly. There was something unpleasant about the landlord's ingratiating manner.

"Yes. It occurred to me that you might need men to help you work your land, and I happen to know that a ship has just come in from Africa, carrying slaves. Captain Kellogg is an old friend of mine, and I can vouch for his honesty."

"Thank you, deVoe. I do need field hands. Where can I find Kellogg?"

"His ship is anchored a few miles upriver." deVoe rubbed his hands. "You follow the Virginia Road to the turnoff near the Peterson place."

Anthony nodded. "That should not be too difficult to find. I think I will go to see him right now."

When Anthony and Philander, whom the young Englishman had purchased from Thomas Harrow the day after his conversation with Killigrew, arrived at the spot deVoe had described, a gay sight met their eyes. The slave ship lay at anchor in the river, and on the beach, frolicking and taking their ease, were its cargo, a group of strong and healthy-looking young men and women. The men wore calico togas and the women bright-colored calico cloths, draped over one shoulder and held in place by beaded belts. Some of the women carried small children on their backs; the youngsters were wrapped in the folds of their mothers' clothing, and the arrangement of the draperies exposed the women's bare black thighs.

Two men squatted in front of a driftwood fire, one of them holding across his knees a slab of wood with small shells attached to the ends of highly polished iron tongues. The man raised and lowered the shells with quick, expert fingers, and they tinkled plaintively as they hit the iron tongues. The other man was beating out an exotic rhythm on a small drum suspended around his neck by a leather thong.

Some of the younger girls were dancing, their bare feet sliding gracefully along the sand, their bodies twisting and turning in rhythm. The younger men, happy at their release from months of imprisonment in the ship's narrow quarters, were running up and down the beach, jumping and leaping, their muscles rippling as they moved.

Anthony and Philander dismounted and walked down the path to the riverbank. Two of the men, in particular, attracted Anthony's attention. Tall and well-built, the gay fezzes on their heads and the caste marks cut into the flesh of their foreheads and cheeks indicated that they belonged to a Mohammedan tribe of East Africans, whose members were known for their strength and intelligence. They would make fine field hands.

Seeing Anthony approach, Captain Kellogg made his way up the beach to greet him. The slaver was a heavy-set man, with jowls and a pendulous lower lip. Anthony thought there was something familiar about him, but he could not immediately remember where, if ever, he had seen the man before.

"Good afternoon, sir," Kellogg said.

"Good afternoon," Anthony replied. "Landlord deVoe said that I might be able to buy some men from you."

Kellogg smiled, showing stained teeth. "Aye, deVoe and I are old friends. Had some fine adventures together in the old days."

Recognition came suddenly to Anthony: this man had been one of the crowd at the King's Arms the day he had arrived in Edenton.

"Haven't I seen you before?" he asked.

Kellogg smiled nervously. "I think not, sir."

"Now I remember," Anthony said, fixing his piercing eyes on the slaver. "You were at the King's Arms the other day. But I understood deVoe to say you had just arrived here."

"Oh, well, now you mention it—" Kellogg avoided Anthony's eyes. "Yes, I was here for a day or so. I left my ship down in South Carolina and came up here alone on some business. To find out whether it would be worth my while to bring the ship up. I discovered it would be," he added hastily. "And then I went away again. But now I'm back, and if it's good workers you want . . ."

Anthony could barely repress his distaste for the man's shifty manner. "That was my purpose in coming," he said coldly.

"The best blacks that have ever been brought to this country. I feed my people good on the voyage, and none of them is scrawny or weak. The women are fine breeders, too. Just look them over." He raised his voice and shouted a few words in some native dialect. The drumbeats ceased, the plaintive tune was silenced, and the dancing girls stopped their gyrations. Their garments dropped to the sand, and they stood naked, their bronze bodies glistening against the sunlit sky.

"Ha, see them now," Kellogg ran his tongue over his lip. "Choose any one of them and you'll have women for work by day and pleasure by night." He leered knowingly. "Real pleasure. Satisfaction guaranteed." He poked Anthony in the side with his elbow. "Wouldn't recommend them if I didn't know from personal experience. A slaving captain has to have some relaxation." He laughed raucously.

A wave of disgust swept Anthony; he was tempted to turn on his heels and leave. But what would that accomplish? Anyone he bought would be better off with him than with this creature. He fought down his revulsion and spoke through clenched teeth.

"I want field hands," he said shortly.

Kellogg shrugged his shoulders. "Every man to his taste."

Anthony nodded in the direction of the two men he had noticed earlier. They had stopped racing and now stood together, next to a tall, slim girl who also had the distinguishing caste marks cut into her face.

"Two brothers and their sister. The best of the lot, save one," Kellogg said, pointing to a tall Negro, with wide, heavy shoulders and a narrow waist. "He's the best. Simba, the lion, he is. Swears he's a king." He slapped his thigh. "A king! How will it feel to own royalty, sir? Make me an offer for the four of them. I'm selling them as a piece, not separate."

"How much?"

"As I say, they're the pick of the basket. Good and strong and hard workers. One hundred and fifty pounds for the four."

"Fifty," Anthony replied.

"I can get fifty for the woman alone. Look at that shape, sir!"

"I said fifty for all of them," Anthony spoke coldly.

In the meanwhile, Philander had gone down to the beach, where he examined the slaves with a practiced eye, punching and pounding, inspecting arms and chests, running his hands over legs and ankles, as one would examine a horse for purchase. When he returned, he spoke to Anthony.

"Those four are the best, master, but there are two other men and a woman who will serve you well."

Anthony nodded. "I trust my man, Kellogg. I will give you a hundred and fifty pounds for the seven."

Kellogg cried out in anguish, but in the end he succumbed, and Philander led the new slaves to Anthony's property, where the huts of the quarters line had already been built.

On Friday, Anthony rode out to his land. He had chosen his house site carefully: near the beach, not far from the turn of the river. Around it was primeval forest, heavy and thick and tall. A mile or more beyond, Indian Creek cut into the forest, forming a boundary line between Anthony's land and Peter Parker's. Below was the site of the old Indian village, on high ground above the wooded riverbank.

When he had been in London, Anthony had read a description of the first trip made by white men up the Chowan River. Recorded in Richard Hakluyt's book, first published in 1600, it told the story of the voyage Anthony's ancestor, Sir Richard Granville, had made from Roanoke Island in 1585 when, with his two small ships, he set out to explore the river and buy corn from the Indians. True, the colony Sir Richard established on the island in the broad, quiet stream had failed; Hakluyt's book told in full the harrowing tale of the attack by the Chowanoke Indians, which had all but wiped it out. But it was the first British settlement in the New World; this spot, on the Chowan, was the very core of England in America.

As he had told Edward Moseley nearly a year before, it was a matter of both pride and pleasure to Anthony to know that the land on which he was going to live was the same land his ancestor had explored more than a hundred years ago; now, as he watched the craftsmen at work, he found the ring of their axes on the tall trees and the tap of their hammers on joists and beams as beautiful as the sweetest music. He walked over to the bank and sat down, gazing over the deep, quietly flowing river. There were herons in the reeds at his feet, cardinals and mockers and wrens in the trees. Above, an eagle soared, high and proud and strong, as if to reach the sun. He heard the bark of a fox, and then the moaning of hounds in full cry. Some yeomen must be hunting through the forest. He lighted his pipe and sat smoking.

Suddenly the sound of hammer and saw ceased; the workmen had stopped for their midday meal. They found seats for themselves on the stumps of trees or on the grass and began to eat slices of bread and meat and to drink ale from stone mugs. The Negro slaves sat some distance away.

Anthony heard the sound of horses' hooves, and looked up to see Ali Hassan, astride a black stallion. He rose and went over to greet the merchant.

"Good day, Mr. Dawson," Hassan said as he dismounted. "I have come, as I promised, with your drapery samples. I have some news, also."

Anthony looked at him inquiringly.

"Just as I was leaving the village, I heard that Tom the Tinker had been arrested for Simmons' murder," the merchant said. "He seems to know something about it; they found a few shillings of the man's money in his pockets. He is being held in the gaol dungeon, and they threaten to keep him on bread and water until he tells what he knows. There is a rumor that if he will not talk, they will hang him by the thumbs to see if his tongue will come loose then."

"Tom the Tinker?" Anthony frowned. "That half-daft little fellow who sits down on the Green singing songs to the children?"

The merchant nodded. "Yes. He has a weak brain, poor thing, and I doubt very much that he had anything to do with Simmons' death. But even if he did, this will not be the first time a servant has paid for the crimes of his master."

Anthony shook his head. "I cannot believe that poor Tom had anything to do with it. Tom is a gentle soul, who would not harm anything or anybody. We may never be able to verify our suspicions about this murder, Hassan, but we cannot permit anyone to suffer unfairly. We must do something. But what?" He fell silent.

"If I may suggest, sir?" Ali Hassan spoke softly. "Tom trusts no one. He loves the children but, he says, men become evil when they leave childhood." He smiled faintly. "And that, I think, is spoken like a wise man rather than a fool." His expression again became grave. "But one man, sir, Tom trusts. If you were to confide in this gentleman, and tell him what we think, he might be able to find out what Tom knows."

"Who is the man, Hassan?" Anthony asked. "Do I know him?"

"I believe you do, sir. Edward Moseley, the surveyor-general."

"Of course I know Mr. Moseley," Anthony smiled. "And I have no hesitation in confiding in him. He is Lord John's representative on the Council, you know."

Hassan nodded. "Then you will speak with Mr. Moseley about this matter?"

"Indeed I will."

"Good, sir, good. And now to our other business. I have brought some samples of the brocades you looked at the other day. Perhaps you will be able to make a decision on which ones you want. They are in here, sir," and the merchant took several small swatches from a fold of his aba.

Anthony shook his head in despair. "You know, this absolutely terrifies me. I feel quite confident about the construction of the house, and the landscaping of the grounds. But this . . ." He shrugged his shoulders. "Furnishing a home is a woman's business."

"Do you really want a woman's advice?"

Anthony wheeled around to look into the tawny eyes of Tamar Killigrew. She was dressed in a dark blue riding habit and she held a crop lightly in her hand. But her horse was nowhere in sight.

"Tamar! Where did you come from? You move as quietly as an Indian. I heard not a single sound."

The girl smiled. "I left my horse up at the bend of the river and came the rest of the way on foot. I have a very light tread. Aren't you pleased to see me?"

"Of course I am," he held out his hands to her. "Delighted. I was planning to visit Lilac Farm very soon. You know Ali Hassan, don't you?"

Tamar nodded. "My most elegant dress was made with some silk I bought from you. I copied a London pattern."

"I am pleased to hear it." Ali Hassan smiled. "And now that a lady has so fortunately arrived to help you make up your mind," he said to Anthony, "I shall leave my samples with you and return to the village. You can step into my room at the inn any time you like, and tell me which fabrics you have decided on."

"Thank you so much for coming out," Anthony said. "And tomorrow I will take care of that other matter we discussed." He shook the merchant's hand. When the man had mounted his horse and ridden off, he turned to Tamar. "You arrived at the perfect moment. I need your advice badly."

Tamar dimpled. "So you see! I was right to come out today, instead of waiting for you to come to Lilac Farm. But I can only help if I can see what the house is going to look like. This," and she waved her riding crop in the direction of the wooden skeleton that was beginning to rise under the expert hands of the workmen, "may mean something to you, but it only confuses me."

"That can be remedied in an instant." Anthony laughed. "I

have my architect's plans and a picture of the completed house. They are in the little shack over there." He nodded toward the hut on the beach that Edward Moseley had built when he owned the land. "Just one moment." He started off.

"Oh, wait. Let me come with you. That will be less bother," Tamar said, and, walking swiftly, she caught up with him.

When they reached the little hut, Anthony threw the door open and stood aside for her to enter.

"How adorable!" she said as she stepped in. Her eyes darted over the tiny, neat room, passing swiftly over the deal table and chair in its center and coming to rest at the cot that stood under the one small window. "Oh, you can stay here overnight," she said, as she walked over to the cot and sat down on it. "Quite comfortable, too." She bounced up and down, testing it. "It must be wonderful here at night. I wish I could see it. And when the moon shines in through that window, I'm sure it is too romantic for words." She looked at him from under her long lashes.

Now, what the devil is she up to? Anthony thought. But aloud he said only, "Here are the plans, Tamar, on the table."

Slowly she arose and walked over to stand at his side. She looked down at the prints he had spread out.

"Now really, Anthony," she laughed. "Those cross-hatches confuse me just as much as the construction outside. I'm not an architect, you know. I am a girl." And she moved closer to him.

"This is the picture," he said, taking up another sheet.

Tamar saw a two-storied building with outflung wings and a wide gallery running all around the first floor.

"How elegant!" she cried.

"Do you like it? An architect in London drew up the plans for me."

"Oh, how could I help it? A London architect!" She clasped her hands and looked up at him. "I've never seen a more beautiful house. This is the kind of place I hoped Dick would build. But his is just a shack compared to this." Her tawny eyes searched his face.

"I have not seen Dick's place yet. I hear he is in Virginia."

"His is just a shack," she repeated, "just a shack. I told him I wanted a really elegant house, but he has no taste at all, and he knows nothing about elegance, even though he did spend time in London." She pouted. "But you do, Anthony." She turned to face him, her back resting against the edge of the table, her hands flat on it. She arched her body toward him. Her tight jacket molded the curve of her breasts. Her eyes were shining and her parted lips were moist. "You know about everything, Anthony. You could teach me, if you wanted to. You are the most worldly man a girl would ever want to know."

"I know very little about fabrics, though," Anthony said, keeping his tone as light as possible. "You were going to help me choose them, remember?"

"Oh, fabrics!" She tossed her head. "We can choose the fabrics later. We have all the time in the world. But now that we are here alone, in this adorable little place, and . . ."

"Now look here, Tamar!" Anthony spoke sharply. "You and Dick Chapman are engaged, and Dick is my close friend."

"If that is what bothers you, you can stop worrying right now. Dick and I are finished, finished. We never should have become engaged in the first place. Anthony . . ." She held her arms out to him.

Anthony stepped aside to avoid her embrace. He could feel his poise deserting him. What was he to do with the girl? And did she herself know what she was doing? The picture of the child-like Tamar playing the role of siren brought a wry smile to his lips.

Tamar saw it and took heart.

"Many people think me quite pretty, you know," she murmured, turning her shoulders slightly, "and if Dick had been any kind of man at all, he would have discovered that I have a lot of fire and passion. I must be like Allin's mother, my Aunt Mary. She was full of fire."

"Tamar!" Anthony said sternly, "that will be quite enough. More than enough, in fact. You are a very pretty girl and I feel sure that you will make Dick a fine wife. Save your fire for him, after you are married."

"Oh, why are you so cautious? You're nearly as much of a

stick as Dick." Her tawny eyes flashed. "We would be right for each other, Anthony. I know. I can feel it."

"I have to go back to work now," Anthony said abruptly. "Excuse me, Tamar." And he strode to the door, flung it open, and walked swiftly out of the little hut.

Tamar stood for a long moment without moving.

"I don't care," she murmured, "I don't care. I shan't be put off. I know that if he would only kiss me once . . . just once . . ." Slowly she turned, and walked out of the hut.

Chapter XVII

TOM THE TINKER

THE ARREST of Tom the Tinker created indignation of massive proportions throughout the precinct. The people of Edenton were particularly outraged; the tinkle of Tom's little bell and the songs he sang as he went from house to house, crying his wares, were part of the life of the village. The children were his special friends; they followed him on his rounds and sang with him:

"I'll mend your pots and pans,
I trade for jellies and jams,
I'll make the old new
For a penny or two,
I'll mend your pots and pans."

Almost every day, when he had finished his work, Tom could be seen sitting on the Green, a group of rapt youngsters gathered at his knees to hear his tales and ditties, and when they heard that Tom had been arrested, the children's anger knew no bounds. They congregated outside the gaol to demand his freedom, banging on tin pans, whistling, and stamping their feet. When the sheriff and the gaoler went out to see what was happening, they were met with such a deafening roar that they were glad to retreat to the security of the gaoler's office.

"Young hoodlums!" the sheriff said the second day of Tom's imprisonment. He had to raise his voice to make it heard above the din that rose outside; the children had come back again to demonstrate their rage. "Hoodlums!" He wiped his face with a dirty bandanna and sat down heavily in the chair at the gaoler's desk.

"That's as may be," the gaoler said, "but I have a feeling for them. Tom is their friend, and I don't believe he is any more guilty of this crime than I am myself."

"I have evidence against him. Good evidence. We found the man's money on Tom, remember?"

"You found a few shillings. Simmons had more than that with him, I wager. And what if Tom did take a coin or two from the body? I can name you twenty others in this village who would have done the same thing. And probably not reported it, either. But they would have been clever enough to conceal the money. Poor Tom hasn't the wit."

" 'Poor Tom,' he says," the sheriff mimicked his colleague's tone. "Can I trust you, Burnett?"

The gaoler looked at him inquiringly.

"One minute." The sheriff arose and went over to the window. "Scat!" he cried to the children outside. "Time's up for today. You can come back tomorrow. If you go now, I may let you visit with Tom the next time."

"Honest?" one boy's voice called out.

"You promise?" cried another.

"I gave you my word, didn't I?" the sheriff said. "You go now, and you can see Tom tomorrow. Scat!" He waited at the window until the crowd of children had dispersed. Then he returned and sat down again at the gaoler's desk.

"There, now I can hear myself think. But if they have any idea they are going to see Tom tomorrow . . ." He narrowed his eyes. "I'll tell you something, Burnett, if you can keep a secret. Somebody led me to Tom. Pointed the finger. And from what that person said, certain high quarters here have no objection to Tom's arrest."

"Who was it told you?"

"Never you mind who it was. The arrest has been made, and Tom is in gaol. And there he will stay, as long as he goes on sitting there, never opening his dummy face, and with those coins in his pocket. He's as likely guilty as anyone else in the village, after all."

The gaoler shook his head. "It seems all wrong to me, all wrong. Higher up or no, if the man is innocent, he shouldn't be in gaol. I should like to know who put you on to Tom. That's the man I would investigate, if I was you."

"You would, would you? Well, I'm the sheriff, not you. And I must say you are pretty chicken-hearted for a man in your job." The sheriff eyed his companion contemptuously.

At that moment, there was a knock on the door and Edward Moseley entered.

"Mr. Moseley." The sheriff rose to his feet. "What brings you here, sir?"

"I would like to see Tom the Tinker." The surveyor-general spoke firmly. "Alone."

"Well, now," the sheriff said heartily, "if we can let the children see him, I suppose we can let you see him, too." He looked at the gaoler, who nodded in agreement. "Go fetch the man, Burnett. I'm off to my own office now." He and the gaoler left together.

In a few moments, the gaoler returned. Tom shuffled along slowly behind him, his freckled face streaked with tears, his wiry red hair standing on end, and his pale blue eyes watery.

"You can talk in here, Mr. Moseley," the gaoler said. His voice was not unfriendly. "No one will disturb you." He closed the door behind him and left.

"Well, Tom," Moseley said when the two men were alone. "You sit down right over there and tell me what happened, and we will have you out of here in a wink."

"I didn't do it, Mr. Moseley, I didn't." The little man's expression was woebegone, and there were sobs in his voice.

"I know that, Tom. You are the most gentle soul I have ever met. But we must find out who did; then you will be freed. You must have seen something . . ."

Tom shook his head. "What should I have seen in that swamp, Mr. Moseley? Not a thing. When they arrested me, I would have told 'em, if I had seen anything. I don't trust 'em, but I'm afraid of the gaol, and I would have told them."

"You know, Tom," Moseley said soothingly, "I wager that if we talk this over calmly together, you will discover that you know more than you think. Shall we try?"

Mutely, Tom nodded.

"Well, then, when you arrived at the swamp, what did you see?"

Tom wrinkled his brow. "Nothing. Just poor Mr. Simmons lying there, with his head all smashed in. I bent over, and saw he was dead, and there was a couple of shillings near him, so I took them. And then I started to run away. I was that scared! Could have been me, you know, because of the red hair. Mr. Moseley," he turned his terrified gaze on the surveyor-general, "you think that's why they did it? Thought it was Tom, because of the red hair, and wanted to kill me?"

"Of course not, Tom," Moseley said gently. "Nobody would want to harm you. You just keep calm and think back to the day you found him. On your way to the swamp, or coming back, did you meet anybody? Any strangers?"

Tom shook his head. "No, sir, no strangers."

"Anyone you know?" Moseley urged.

Tom's face was bewildered. He wrinkled his forehead and looked fixedly at the ceiling.

"People I know? I'll have to remember hard. I know so many folks. Everyone in Edenton. Let me think . . ." He bit his lip. Then he nodded, and a smile crossed his freckled face. "It was early in the morning, it was, and I saw Old Eph, Killigrew's bondman. He was driving a cow back to Lilac Farm. Fool thing wandered loose, he said."

"That's fine, Tom, fine," Moseley encouraged him. "Now think some more. After you met Eph, what happened then?"

"I'm thinkin', Mr. Moseley, I'm thinkin'. But don't rattle me all up; Tom thinks slow, you know." His frown deepened. Then he went on, speaking as much to himself as to his friend.

"Eph and I, we talked about the dratted cow for a minute or two, and then I walked on. I was singing a new song I know." He began to hum. "But that ain't important," he added hastily, "I was walking along and, and . . ." he paused and scratched his ear doubtfully.

Moseley was trying desperately to conceal his impatience. Was there no way of speeding up this slow brain? But Tom was right; if he was pushed too hard, he would become completely confused. He smiled. "I am proud of you, Tom, very proud. You have a good memory."

"Thankee, sir. Well, let me see. There was one of the fishermen who was late getting out. Jeff Dale, I think, because he is late so often. And . . ." Tom heaved a loud sigh of relief. "That feller from the slaver." He nodded. "Yes, sir. Kellogg. I knew there was someone else. Drunk, he was, and reeling along. He was going back to town when I was going out. Must have been out drunk all night. And he was all muddy. Probably so tipsy he'd fallen down more than once. Didn't even stop to say hello to me."

"Kellogg, eh?" Moseley kept his voice calm. "Are you sure?"

"Oh, yes, sir, Mr. Moseley. Sure as I can be. I've seen him at the King's Arms more than once. He and landlord de Voe are real friendly. And my, he was drunk!" Tom shook his head in disapproval. "Bright and early in the morning, too, with the air smelling so good and the birds singing! Drunk!"

"Have you told anyone else that you met him, Tom?"

"No, sir, no." He shook his head. "Nary a soul."

"Well, you just forget all about it now, and say not a word to anyone. It will be better that way. And you have nothing to worry about, Tom. You did nothing wrong, and in a very few days you will be down on the Green again, singing to the children."

"You mean that, sir?"

"I certainly do. You trust me, Tom, don't you?"

The little man nodded vehemently. "Only one I trust is you. 'Cept the children. They are my friends, too."

"You have many friends, Tom. And all of them will do what they can to help you. I am going to give the gaoler some money to buy you some ale, and you will be out of here before you have drunk your fill."

Anthony was in the sitting room of his suite at the King's Arms when Edward Moseley arrived. Early that morning he had asked the surveyor-general to visit Tom and find out what he could about Simmons' murder, but although he had said he believed

Tom innocent, he had not confided all his suspicions to the older man. It would be time enough for that after he had learned what, if anything, Moseley had discovered from his talk with Tom.

"Kellogg, eh?" Anthony said thoughtfully when Moseley had finished his story. "A friend of deVoe's. And a brute, if ever I have seen one. This fits in only too well with my theory, Mr. Moseley."

"I would be very much interested in hearing what you think," Moseley said.

"Ali Hassan and I have reason to believe that Simmons was acting as a messenger for the governor of South Carolina. We know that he and Burrington met in secret several times during the course of the man's visit here, and exchanged papers. Further, we believe that when Simmons had completed his mission and had Burrington's papers in his possession, he began to think about betraying his trust and selling the papers to an interested party, rather than delivering them to South Carolina. We believe he was killed to frustrate that plan. The papers were taken from him, and I am inclined to think, they are by now in the hands of the governor of South Carolina. We will never know precisely what they were about, but I have a fairly good idea."

"You think Simmons was acting as Burrington's agent, then?" Moseley asked. "And when the governor learned he had betrayed him, he had him killed? I would put nothing past the governor, of course; it seems entirely possible to me."

Anthony shook his head. "I do not think Burrington was implicated in the murder. After all, he was not here when it occurred. But deVoe, and Kellogg—those two would stoop to anything. And it all fits in so neatly. Kellogg returned to South Carolina to join his ship immediately after the murder; he must have delivered the papers then. Burrington would, I am sure, have wanted the papers taken from Simmons, but I do not think he would have gone as far as murder to get them."

"I suppose he would not." Moseley ran his fingers through his hair. "But deVoe is his friend and Kellogg is deVoe's. So indirectly, even though he was not here when it occurred, he is responsible for the murder. By the way, he seems to be back now. I saw his coach driving up to Government House as I was on my way over here." He paused, withdrew his pipe from his waistcoat pocket, and lit it. "But what kind of papers can have led to murder?"

Anthony rose from his chair and began to pace the room.

"Ah, now you have hit on the real question, Mr. Moseley. And my answer, I fear, will be as distasteful to you as it is to me." He stopped for a moment in front of the window and stood looking out over the Green and the waterfront. The sun was at its zenith, and a wedge of wild fowl, flying high above the sound to their northern feeding grounds, showed black against the blinding gold.

"Do you remember," he went on, turning to face his guest, "that when I came here last year I told you that some of the Proprietors were giving serious consideration to the idea of selling their land to the Crown?"

Moseley nodded.

"On my trip to England, I learned that most of them have already decided to do that. It may not be today or tomorrow, but there is no question that it is going to happen. I know this disturbs you, sir," Anthony said as he saw an angry flush rise to Moseley's face, "but there it is. The province has never returned a penny, as you know. Most of the Proprietors are quite uninterested in the New World, and much prefer money in their pockets to unprofitable property on their hands."

"You did say this might happen," Moseley said, resignation in his voice. "I suppose it was inevitable. But I believe it to be a serious mistake, sir. This is fertile land. Our settlers are hard-working, decent people. With proper government . . ."

"I agree with you completely, Mr. Moseley," Anthony interrupted. "But what can we do? At least, on my visit to England, I was able to persuade the members of my family not to sell. The Granvilles have decided not to give up their grant, no matter what the other Proprietors may do. So there will be some proprietary land here, in any event."

"But no proprietary government," Moseley put in.

"No, no proprietary government. But, for those who live on Granville land, the comfort of knowing they can depend on us to protect their interests." He paused. "And now, sir, let me tell you what in my opinion this has to do with the governor and with Simmons' murder. I believe that Burrington, together with the governor of South Carolina and with William Byrd of Virginia, has been plotting for the sale of North Carolina to the Crown. The papers he exchanged with Simmons undoubtedly were a part of this plot."

"Blackguard!" Moseley burst out, "unprincipled scoundrel! It serves him right that he is being recalled."

"The governor's conduct has not been exemplary, I must admit. But the immediate problem is to have Tom the Tinker released from gaol. And I believe we can enlist the governor's help in that endeavor. I am sure he has his reasons for the about-face he has recently made; I gather he is much improved since the news of his recall. We may never be able to bring Kellogg or deVoe to justice, but at least we can see that Tom does not suffer unnecessarily. I doubt Burrington even knows about Simmons' murder yet, and I would like very much to be the one to tell him. I am most curious to see how he will react. If you will excuse me, Mr. Moseley, I shall walk over to Government House right now."

Anthony found his excellency in an affable mood. He talked at length of his visit to Bath, of the news that had come in the late mail from London, and of his pleasure in hearing that Mr. Dawson planned to remain in North Carolina. He was disturbed, he said, that the dividing line between Virginia and North Carolina had not yet been settled, and spoke of the difficulties this caused.

"With things as they are, neither province can collect taxes, or write out clear deeds for property along the border. I am eager to have this matter in order before I leave, Mr. Dawson, and it would please me if you would consent to act as one of our representatives on the Boundary Line Commission. I plan to appoint

Mr. Moseley and Mr. Lovyck, also, and I hope you will agree to serve with them."

"I am honored, your excellency. But I am not a surveyor, and I have had very little experience. . . ."

"No matter, no matter. Mr. Moseley will be in charge. The Virginia commission has already been appointed. Mr. William Byrd, with whom you are acquainted, will head the group, and Mr. Harrison and Mr. Dandridge will act with him. It should be a congenial company."

"I shall be happy to serve, sir, if you think I can be of assistance."

Burrington nodded and smiled. Then he rose from his chair and pulled the bellcord on the wall behind his desk.

"Let us drink to your success, Mr. Dawson. Taphy," he said, as the servant entered, "some glasses and a decanter of Madeira." He turned back to Anthony. "You *do* know that I will be leaving here soon, Mr. Dawson, do you not?"

Anthony nodded, but said nothing.

"When I first received the news," the governor said, "I was quite disturbed. But, on thinking it over, I have changed my mind. I am sorry that the settlers have not understood what I have been trying to do, and have, therefore, thought badly of me. But I fear that no governor, meeting these problems, could keep the regard of those he governed. To preserve order among a people who do not understand the subtleties and intricacies of government, and to do it without the protection of the Crown—" he shook his head—"it is a well-nigh impossible task. And to bring prosperity to a land-locked province whose only access to major seaways is through Crown colonies—it is almost laughable to imagine that possible. Virginia and South Carolina simply tax us out of trading with England and the Continent." He paused. "Mind you, Mr. Dawson, I am not trying to exonerate myself. Undoubtedly I have done a few things I should not have. I am not the most patient man in the world. But I wager Sir Richard will find the task of governing no easier than I. Mr. Dawson, I may tell you in confidence that the real fault here is neither the people nor their governors, but the very fact of proprietary government."

Anthony remained silent.

"Yes," Burrington went on, nodding reflectively, "history, I think, will bear me out. You mark my words. This colony will have to go under the Crown, sooner or later. And there it will stay, to everyone's advantage."

"And yet you came here to represent the Proprietors, sir."

"So I did, Dawson, so I did. And with the intention of doing the best job possible. But do you know I have not received one penny of salary in all the time I have been here? And, because I have taken up property to give me some income, they call me a land-grabber! Yes, Dawson, I have been blocked at every turn, not only by the settlers, but by the Proprietors themselves. Only Lord John, of all of them, takes the faintest interest in the province. The rest of them, without exception, think of nothing but hunting and the London season."

Taphy came in with the wine and set it down on the desk. When he had left, the governor said:

"Yes, Mr. Dawson, the governor is in an untenable position here, caught between the upper and the nether millstones." He rose from his desk and poured the wine. "And now, sir, to more pleasant topics. I hope you will tell me what news there has been in the village since Madam and I left for Bath. We have been back only a short hour or so, and I have not yet had an opportunity to catch up with affairs here."

"Then you have not heard about Simmons, the merchant?" Anthony spoke casually, but he kept a close eye on the governor's face.

"Simmons?" Burrington's eyes narrowed. "I do not think I know whom you mean." But he was a poor actor; nervous concern was evident in every movement of his face.

"He was from South Carolina, sir, and he visited in Edenton for a few days. I found his dead body in a swamp some few miles out of town the day after he had left to return home. He had been murdered."

Burrington's hand shook, and the wine in the glass he held spilled over to form a spreading purple blot on his cream-colored waistcoat.

"Great God!" He set the glass down on the desk and began to pace the room rapidly. "Who did it? Who did it? And why?"

"Tom the Tinker has been arrested, sir," Anthony kept his voice calm and quiet. "But I can hardly believe he is guilty. He has neither the wit nor the malice. The entire town is outraged, and the children have been gathering in front of the gaol and taunting the sheriff. Tom did take a few shillings from the dead man's body, but no more than that, I feel sure. Not a single paper was found on the man, not even identification. Not a man alive but has some papers with him. Tom did not have them; the murderer must have taken them."

"Does anyone know what kind of papers he was carrying? Have they been found?" There was desperation in the governor's voice. "Who could have done it? Who? Stealing his papers . . ." He pounded his fist in his open palm. His face was white with anger.

"I have no proof, sir," Anthony went on, slowly and deliberately, "but if I were the sheriff I would have questioned Kellogg, the slaver, that friend of deVoe's. He was seen on the morning of the crime on his way back to town from the swamp where Simmons' body was found. And he left shortly thereafter for South Carolina. He has just returned from there."

The governor stopped pacing. Slowly the color returned to his face, and an expression of relief showed in his eyes. "I see, I see, deVoe's friend Kellogg, you say? And he did go back to South Carolina?"

"So I have been told."

Burrington nodded. "Kellogg," he said. He returned to his desk and sat down. "Would you excuse me now, Mr. Dawson? I have some urgent business to attend to. And I wonder if on your way out you would mind asking Taphy to come in."

Anthony nodded and left. By the time he reached the front door, Taphy had entered the governor's office, and Anthony could hear Burrington's loud voice saying: "Bring deVoe over here immediately. Immediately. And if Captain Kellogg is in town, I want to see him, too."

Anthony smiled as he closed the door of Government House behind him. This visit had confirmed every one of his suspicions. And he was sure that Tom the Tinker would be out of gaol before very long.

Chapter XVIII

THE AUCTION

THE GOVERNOR lost no time in making sure that Tom the Tinker was released from gaol; early in the morning of the day after Anthony had visited him, he stormed into the sheriff's office at the courthouse, and a half-hour later Tom was free to make his rounds again, the familiar tinkle of his little bell sounding merrily through the village streets.

The speed of Burrington's action, following so swiftly on his return, provided the villagers with as much of a conversational feast as did his words to the sheriff, which had been overheard by a group of loungers, passing their idle time outside the courthouse.

"A couple of shillings in his pocket is no evidence against anyone, particularly a simple-minded, harmless fellow like Tom," Burrington was reported to have roared at the astonished sheriff, "though even that poor devil has more brains than you; if you had the sense God gave geese, you would have known Tom couldn't be guilty. Or did you do it to arouse the children? Perhaps you thought the time had come for another Children's Crusade?"

The sheriff had murmured something—too softly for the avid eavesdroppers to hear what it was—and then Burrington's outraged bellow had blasted itself into their eardrums.

"*Please* me? *Please* me? By God, if I am still here come November, I will see to it that you are not *made* sheriff again. You are a disgrace to your office! You cannot solve a murder by arresting the first man in sight! It was robbers of some sort killed Simmons, that's obvious. And they escaped because you are so inefficient. As long as I am governor here, things will be done in a legal way! People will not be arrested simply to suit your whim and provide scapegoats for your own blundering! That will please me, and only that, regardless of what anyone might have told you!" The door had slammed loudly enough to give the crowd beneath the sheriff's window a chance to disperse. But Burrington, striding rapidly across the Green, did not fail to notice with some pleasure that the little knots of people, apparently engaged in their own pursuits, were eyeing him with new respect.

At the common room of the King's Arms, Tom, the sheriff, and Burrington provided the only topic of conversation for days, and it was notable that landlord deVoe, who displayed a sudden access of generosity and stood drinks for the entire crowd several nights in a row, was among those loudest in his praise of the governor and in condemnation of the sheriff. But the dramatic resolution of Tom's case was soon supplanted in interest by another event: One day in late April, during the spring Drag Hunt, Enar Peterson was killed by a fall from his horse.

Villagers and planters alike were shocked by the news, not only because Enar had been so generous with his considerable wealth, but also because his unaffected simplicity and kindliness had made him genuinely well-liked throughout the province. But Mistress Peterson's behavior soon took people's minds from their sorrow over Enar's death and provided them with a new store of discussion. For as soon as her first show of grief had subsided, and while she was still observing the mourning period, the widow announced that she was auctioning off her new plantation on the Virginia Road and returning to Maryland, where one could live, as she put it, in "a more selective society." She retained an attorney, William Reed, to look after her interests, but she paid scant heed to his suggestions.

"Since you are going to sell your other land holdings directly," he said to her one afternoon as they sat in his office discussing the problem, "I fail to see why you want to auction the plantation. It is a valuable property, and it would undoubtedly bring a good price. The people would prefer that, too. After all, when you leave here, a great deal of money will be leaving with you, and if the plantation and its furnishings are auctioned off piecemeal to small purchasers, rather than sold as a whole to one wealthy buyer, there will be even less chance of new money coming into the province to make up for what you are taking out. It will work a hardship on the people. And your husband was very fond of them, and always said he owed his wealth to North Carolina and its settlers. I imagine he would have liked it if you stayed here. But failing that . . ."

"Oh, Enar would never have expected me to remain in North Carolina. He knew what a sacrifice I made when I came here in the first place. And now that he is gone . . ." She dabbed at her eyes with a tiny square of lace. "I have no understanding of money matters, Mr. Reed. But I know that I want an auction. Auctions are exciting. Everyone will come for miles around, and it will be a big event. My final party. And the lower classes will appreciate the opportunity to be entertained by me." She paused. "Do you think you could get an auctioneer from Virginia, Mr. Reed? A tobacco auctioneer, perhaps? They simply fascinate me. I can barely understand what they say."

"That hardly seems an advantage, madam," Reed put in. "You might find you were giving your property away." But his heavy sarcasm was lost on Mistress Peterson. She gazed past him, her eyes sparkling.

"Yes, an auction. It will be thrilling. I wish I could wear white instead of black; it is so much more becoming to me. And," she rose and straightened her skirts preparatory to leaving, "I hope you can have things under way soon. I want to be back in Maryland in time for the summer races."

"I shall make every effort, madam," Reed said. He opened the door to let her out. She won't wear the willow long, he thought as he returned to his desk. Some poor fellow in Maryland, who has no inkling of her existence as yet, will find himself swallowed up as soon as she arrives there. He has my sympathy. Even with all her money.

The auction took place on a sunny day during the Whitsun season. The birds were caroling in the pine trees. The woodland was green. Wildflowers bloomed at the edge of the forest and along the hedge rows that divided the plantation. Red trumpet vine, the farmers' scourge, had run up trees and fences, and was growing rampant in the untilled fields.

People arrived in gigs and carriages, Devon carts and oxcarts, and on horseback; more than two hundred men, women and children were at the plantation by early morning. An auction without a barbecue was unthinkable, and Mistress Peterson was determined that this one would be talked about with admiration for generations. Two great pits had been dug at the edge of the North field; two steers were roasting in one and in the other, a half-dozen pigs, wrapped in wet towsacks, lay baking in the live coals. Plantation Negroes turned the meat and stirred great iron pots of black-eyed peas. Cakes and pies and steaming cornbread were brought out from the kitchen, set twenty yards away from the main house. Negro women cooks, borrowed from the kitchen of the Red Lion Inn, and wearing bright calico dresses and red bandannas on their heads, stood behind long tables made of sawbucks or planks to serve the feast. Waiters hurried about, placing ewers of ale and cider on the long tables. Platters of beef and pork, hot from the pits, followed.

Two men had come down from Williamsburg to conduct the auction. They were slick, swift and brittle; their manner was calculated to befuddle and confuse the country folk, who were deliberate both in their ways and in their speech. Madam stood on the west gallery, talking with the auctioneers. She wore a black dress with a little Mary Stuart cap and a white band about the face. She was elegant even in her widow's weeds.

"I want all the folk to have enough to eat," she said, "so the auction will not begin until they have finished their dinners."

"That will run it very late, madam," one of the men protested. "I would suggest that you begin right now."

Madam shook her head. "No, no. It shall be as I say. No bidding until after dinner."

"But, madam," the second auctioneer added his protest, "it will take hours to sell the horses and stock, let alone the plantation."

Mistress Peterson looked at him coldly. "You will auction off the plantation as I wish you to. I have hired you. I am paying your fee. And the work will be done according to my wishes." She paused, then added, more gently: "Besides, it may not take as long as you think."

The first auctioneer shrugged his shoulders, the second spread his hands, and Madam's eyes followed them as they walked off together. They disappeared around the corner of the house and she turned to look out at the crowd on the lawn. Among all the throng, a man's tall figure stood out. Mistress Peterson went to the rail of the gallery and called out:

"Mr. Dawson, Mr. Dawson! I must talk with you; do come over here."

Anthony, who had just arrived, looked up and, spying her, joined her on the gallery.

"This is certainly a festive occasion, madam," he said, bowing. "Everyone in the province seems to be here."

"It *is* crowded. But I wanted to talk to you about something else. How could you believe that you could hide your secret from me?" She wagged a coquettish finger at him.

"I beg your pardon?" Anthony was mystified and momentarily disconcerted.

"Now, now, you need not be coy with me, you know."

"I am sorry, madam, but I simply do not know what you are talking about."

Mistress Peterson shook her head. "You *are* a difficult man, Mr. Dawson. I had not thought it of you, and it is very naughty, indeed."

"Believe me, madam," Anthony spoke earnestly. "I have no idea of what you mean. This secret you accuse me of having must be a very deep one. I have even kept it from myself."

"Do you mean to tell me that you are not the person who has empowered Mr. Little to bid for him?"

"I beg your pardon?" Anthony's expression showed his puzzlement.

"Well, well. And I was simply positive it was you. Who else is there in Chowan Precinct with the taste to appreciate this place?"

"It is a superb property, madam. But I have my own land, you know. My house is nearly finished, and I hope to start planting soon. I have no intention of expanding my holdings at this time."

"But who can it be, then, Mr. Dawson? Somebody intends to purchase this entire property, including the stock and the house-furnishings, and has retained Mr. Little to bid for him. Mr. Little dropped a few hints that could have pointed only to you. 'A young gentleman, of good family,' he said, 'who lives here and is very well regarded by everyone. Unless you want far too much, Mistress Peterson,' he said, 'he will buy the entire plantation.' And Mr. Little told me that the purchaser would keep it in a style of which I would be proud. Now, who else could that possibly have been, Mr. Dawson? It must be you, it must be. Come, now, confess it."

"My dear lady," Anthony smiled, "you flatter me. I only wish I did live up to that description. But I am afraid it is not I."

"I simply do not understand, then," Mistress Peterson shook her head in bewilderment. "It cannot be anyone else."

"But it very obviously is. And we shall find out soon enough, I imagine. When is the auction to begin?"

"In a short while. The folk have nearly finished eating and I told the auctioneers to begin the bidding immediately after that. You need not stand down on the lawn, Mr. Dawson. I have set up seats on the South gallery for the gentry, so that we do not have to mingle with the rabble."

"May I leave you for a moment, madam?" Anthony said. "My friend, Mr. Chapman, should be here by now. He has just returned from Virginia, you know. And we should like to take a look at your livestock. Both of us are interested in bidding for farm animals."

"Go right ahead, Mr. Dawson. But do not be too surprised if Mr. Little outbids you."

Anthony smiled and made his way across the crowded lawn, searching for Dick. But the young man was nowhere in sight. Edenton men and women were strolling about: barristers, physicians, merchants—all were there. A group of artisans stood by themselves. The yeomen were moving toward the stables to appraise the mules and work horses. The young sports were at the stables, too, attracted by the hunters and racing horses. And in the pasture, several men were looking at the sheep, nibbling the tender young grass. In a cleared field, some farm lads had organized a game of bandy ball, played by kicking a blown-up bladder weighted with dried peas. The bladder rattled gaily as it bounced along. There was a clamor of voices, the men's tones husky and deep, and the women's higher pitched and more musical. The auction had taken on a great air of festivity. Everywhere Anthony went there were excited, gesturing knots of people. But Dick was not among them. Nor did Anthony see Dierdra or Allin or any of the others of the Killigrew family.

By the time he returned to the lawn, the auction had already begun; a crowd of men and women, thirty or forty deep, was milling about the auctioneer's block. Anthony took a place on the rim of the circle.

"I see the sale has already begun," he said to his neighbor, a stout, cheerful-looking yeoman.

The man nodded. "Livestock is all gone. Little bid in all of it, horses and all. He must be acting for some wealthy man."

"Did he give the name of his client?" Anthony asked.

"No. I fancy he will hold that back until the plantation is sold. That's what I'm waiting about for. I have no interest in buying this place. I have ample land of my own, in Bertie."

The auctioneer took his stand on the block. After he had stated the size of the plantation, the plantation house and the other general information, he announced that the furniture would be sold at private sale. His singsong chant spread above the crowd.

"What am I offered? What am I offered? The finest plantation near the village of Edenton. Five hundred acres of cleared, fertile land ready for spring planting. What am I offered? What am I offered?"

The bidding began. Thomas Harvey made the first bid, which amounted to no more than what the raw land had cost, and was obviously an opening gambit. Other bids followed quickly, until the original bid was doubled by the Perquimans planter, Newby. Harvey raised the bid and Newby sang out a response.

Little still had not bid, but presently his voice was heard in a bid that astonished everyone.

The auctioneer repeated the figure, and sang out: "What am I bid, what am I bid, what am I bid?" The last phrase was spoken with such rapidity that the words were as one.

People looked from one to another, surprise on every face. An unheard of price!

"Last call and fair warning," came the auctioneer's shrill voice, "going once, going twice, going thrice . . . Gone!" He hit the table with his hammer. "Sold to Mr. William Little, of Edenton, to be paid in English bills of credit."

Everyone talked at once, and a voice from the back of the crowd made itself heard above the tumult.

"Give us the name of the buyer, Mr. Little."

Little consulted with the auctioneer for a moment, then mounted the auction block. He raised his hand for silence.

"The Peterson holdings, plantation, cattle, horses and sheep, all have been sold to Allin Gorgas, Esq."

A burst of handclapping broke the stunned silence, followed by a buzz of excited chatter. Anthony's neighbor, the short, cheerful-looking yeoman, poked him enthusiastically in the ribs.

"Whoever would have thought it?" he asked. "Killigrew's Allin. Buying one of the finest pieces of property in the whole district? And right out from under the noses of the wealthiest gentlemen! I tell you, sir, this is a wonderful country!"

Anthony smiled. "Allin is a fine man. He deserves good fortune."

"Likely the plantation will be his bridal gift to the Treffry lass. It's all over that the two of them are to be married."

Anthony nodded. The man was undoubtedly correct; from the very moment Mistress Peterson had told him of Little's intention to bid, Anthony had suspected that Allin was the lawyer's client, and that the Peterson plantation was to be his and Dierdra's home after their marriage. He murmured his excuses to the yeoman and went off to look for Allin and Dierdra, to offer them his congratulations.

He found the pair on the gallery of the house. Mistress Peterson was fluttering excitedly over them.

"So now we know who Mr. Little's mysterious client was,"

Anthony heard her say. "And to think that all the time I suspected it was you, Mr. Dawson," she added, as he mounted the steps.

"Even though I told you it was not," Anthony said, smiling. He turned to Allin and extended his hand. "I hope you will accept my congratulations, sir. Not only for your purchase, but for the happy event which, I understand, is soon to come."

Allin grinned broadly, his white teeth gleaming. "I believe I am the luckiest man in the world, Dawson."

"I think you probably are. I have known Dierdra ever since she was a child, and I have always believed that the man who finally won her would be fortunate indeed."

"How very kind of you, Anthony." Dierdra smiled.

"He is only speaking the truth," Allin said as he took her hand.

Anthony nodded. "Allin is not only fortunate, he is wise."

"So there is to be a wedding here soon!" Mistress Peterson exclaimed. "Why did you not tell me? If I had known, I would have postponed my departure for Maryland. I am very fond of weddings. You do plan to have a large party, don't you?" she asked Dierdra.

"Probably not," Dierdra said. "Matters are still indefinite. Allin has to go back to college, you know, to finish out his term."

"Although I am sure it will be a complete waste of time." Allin smiled. "I have not been able to concentrate on my studies for months now."

By this time, Edward Moseley and Mr. Little had caught sight of Allin and were hurrying up the gallery steps to speak to him, and in the excitement that followed, Anthony was able to slip away unnoticed.

Quickly he made his way down the path to the river. He needed to be alone. He had thought himself resigned to losing Dierdra. Obviously, however, he was not; the tenderness that glowed in her eyes when she looked at Allin had given him a deep hurt. He must have a while to himself, to put his emotions in order, to bring himself under control.

Moodily, he stood gazing out over the quiet river. On its far bank was a pocosin, dark and mysterious; the first tender green of spring decorated the tops of the tall cypresses at its edge. Birds sang in the deep forest. Water birds dove into the still waters of the river for fish, and eagles planed high in the sky.

Suddenly the peaceful silence was broken by the sound of footsteps, and Anthony turned to see Tamar running down the path toward him.

"I've been looking all over for you, Anthony," she said, breathlessly. "Martin Trewilliger saw you start down here, and he told me."

"Good afternoon, Tamar. I am just on my way back. I have to leave for my plantation."

"Don't go yet, Anthony, don't go," Tamar implored. "I must speak to you. And you have been avoiding me for weeks now. Why, Anthony, why?"

Her childish voice grated on his ears; now, of all times, he was in no mood for her flirtatious silliness.

"I have not been avoiding you, Tamar." By dint of great effort, he managed to keep his voice even.

"Yes, you have. You know it as well as I."

"I have been very busy with the spring planting, Tamar."

"If you had wanted to see me, you would have found the time. There are the evenings, as well as the days. I believe you are afraid of me."

"Please, Tamar!" Her chattering was rubbing his nerves raw.

"Yes, you are. Afraid of me." She paused. "You think I have designs on you."

Anthony looked at her in astonishment. What else was he to think? But he said nothing.

"You think I want you to marry me. But that is not on my mind at all. How could I expect us to be married? You don't even know what I am really like."

By now impatience had overwhelmed him. "I know perfectly well what you are like, Tamar." The words were out before he could stop himself. "You are like a silly, spoiled baby. You think that all you have to do to get what you want is to scream loud and long enough. Well, life is not like that. There are many things we want we cannot have. You had better start learning that right now. Otherwise you will be a little idiot all your life. I feel sorry for the poor man who marries you!"

Tamar stared at him wordlessly for a moment. Then she burst into tears.

"How dare you, how dare you?" she cried. "You're mean and rude and I hate you! I would not have you if you were the last man on earth. You're . . ." her words were drowned in sobs.

"Then we are in agreement," Anthony said coldly. "Neither of us wants the other. Now wipe your nose, and stop sniffling, and try to act like a grown woman."

As he reached for the handkerchief in his waistcoat pocket, Dick Chapman appeared around a bend in the path. One look at Tamar's tear-stained face and Anthony's angry expression, and he leaped headlong to a completely erroneous conclusion.

"Tamar!" he cried and, turning to Anthony, "How could you? How could you? You were supposed to be my closest friend! You must think you are still in London, where every woman is fair game!"

"Don't, Dick, don't!" Tamar whispered through her sobs. "Oh, what shall I do?" And she turned and ran stumblingly away, crying as if her heart would break.

"Tamar, Tamar, it's all right. Everything is all right. Come back here," Dick called, starting down the path after her. He overtook her quickly and took her by the arm, but she shook herself free and, sobbing, continued on her way alone.

Anthony stood rooted to the spot; he had not moved when Dick returned. The brown-haired young man looked at him with contempt, and his voice was icy.

"I never would have thought it of you, Anthony. To take advantage of the girl when you know how wrought up she has been for the last few months. It's the most despicable thing I have ever heard of." And, turning on his heel, he stalked off.

Anthony started to call after him. Then he changed his mind. This was hardly the moment to tell Dick the truth. Better to be thought a rake for a while than a boor forever. Surely, Dick would soon realize how wrong he had been.

Anthony smiled wryly. Well, at least something had happened to take his mind off Dierdra.

Book III

Chapter XIX

THE WEDDING

ALLIN'S PURCHASE of the Peterson plantation on the Virginia Road left only one question still unsettled between him and Dierdra: when and where would their wedding take place?

"Perhaps you ought to come up to Virginia with us when we leave here," Madam Burrington said one evening a few weeks after the auction. She, Dierdra, and the governor were sitting in the Government House library after dinner. "There is a rector in Williamsburg, and he could perform the ceremony for you in the chapel there. I imagine we will be going at about the same time Allin's college year is finished."

"We've thought of that," Dierdra said. "But it would be very difficult for the Killigrews to leave Lilac Farm, and it seems a pity to have the wedding without them. After all, they are Allin's parents in every sense but one."

The governor looked up from the book he was reading. "It's a scandal, a shocking scandal. Not one preacher in all of Chowan Precinct. Scarcely a one in the whole province. I'd like to have a pound for every couple living together as man and wife who have never been rightly wed. The Society for the Propagation of the Gospel for Foreign Parts has tried to obtain men for the province, I suppose, but it has had little luck. It would be much easier to keep order here if we had a minister."

Madam Burrington looked at him thoughtfully. "But there is a minister in Bertie Precinct, is there not?" she asked.

"And how many miles away is that? He never comes here. And how many of the Edenton folk ride over to attend his services?" Burrington's voice was rising.

"I know, my dear, I know," his wife said in a conciliatory tone. "I was only thinking that he might ride over to perform the marriage for Dierdra and Allin. That is," she turned to Dierdra, "if you'd like."

The girl nodded, her eyes sparkling. "Oh, yes, that would be wonderful. I hadn't known there were any ministers in the province at all. If I had . . ."

"Bailey arrived only a short while ago," the governor interrupted. "He comes from a Devon family with which I have been acquainted for many years. As a matter of fact, it was largely my influence that persuaded him to take up this position." He nodded several times. "He thinks a great deal of me. You know, that is not a bad idea at all, Amelia. It would do no harm to let the folk here see what a preacher looks like. If anything is to change them from their godless ways . . ."

Madam Burrington smiled. "Now, George, not so quickly. This is Dierdra's and Allin's decision, not ours."

"I'll write Allin about it this very evening," Dierdra promised. "I'm sure he will be delighted to know we can be married here."

Governor Burrington rose from his chair. "When the time comes for the Crown to take over—and it will not be too long before that happens—one of the first tasks will be to find ministers for every precinct in the province. It's fine that the vestry has started building a church here in the village, but who is to preach in it, I should like to know?" He shook his head. "I shall write to my London friends about it right now." He turned on his heels and left the room.

A short time later, Dierdra excused herself and ran upstairs to write to Allin. If he agreed, they could be married at Lilac Farm by the end of June. By then, the Burringtons would probably have left. And if they had not, it could only be a few weeks more at the most, and the governor had kept so faithfully his promise of reform that Dierdra felt no compunctions about leaving Madam Burrington alone with him.

Allin fell in with the suggestion gladly. The governor arranged for the Reverend Mr. Bailey to come to Lilac Farm to perform the ceremony, and when he learned that Sir Richard would not be arriving in Edenton until July, he insisted he be permitted to give Dierdra away. As her employer, he said, he felt that he stood *in loco parentis*.

The day before the wedding, Owen sat on the long gallery at Lilac Farm, watching the Reverend Mr. Bailey rehearse the ceremony with a very nervous bridegroom. Allin fumbled his lines repeatedly, and repeatedly dropped the ring.

"We should have been married in Williamsburg. Then no one would have seen me make a fool of myself. I am certain I shall do something absolutely idiotic."

"Sir, you have nothing to do but repeat the words after me." The minister's gaunt face was grave but his eyes twinkled. "Come, sir, try again."

Allin groaned. "I'm so befuddled! I can barely hear what you are saying!"

"Now come on, Allin, once again." Owen laughed. "I, Allin Gorgas, do . . ."

Allin turned to his foster brother. "That's all very well for you, Owen. This isn't your wedding. Just see that you remember the ring, and hand it to me at the proper time."

And in the sewing room at Government House, Tamar sat with Dierdra as Mary Catten put the finishing touches on the cream-colored taffeta gown she had stitched with loving care.

"You're going to be the most beautiful bride in the world, Dierdra! The most beautiful!" Tamar exclaimed.

The dark girl smiled. "And the most nervous. I am just happy that it is to be a small wedding."

"Now then, Mistress Treffry, turn a bit." Mary Catten was kneeling on the floor, checking the hem line of Dierdra's gown. "Just a trifle longer here, don't you think so, Mistress Tamar?" Dierdra looked down, and the bondwoman sighed and shook her head. "Now, mistress, you keep your head up and look straight ahead. When you bend like that, the gown hangs all higgledy-piggledy."

Dierdra straightened up and stood rigid, her arms at her side, her eyes fixed firmly ahead of her. "I've never been so worried about a dress in my entire life!" she exclaimed.

Tamar giggled. "And I'm supposed to be the flighty one!" Suddenly her pretty face darkened. "Oh, Dierdra, how will I ever face Dick tomorrow? I haven't seen him since the day of the auction. If you only knew what a fool I made of myself over Anthony Dawson then! And even before. I don't know what possessed me!"

"Tamar, Tamar!" Dierdra cried and, forgetting completely that Mary Catten was still kneeling at her feet, ran over to clasp the blond girl in her arms. "I've waited so long to hear you say this! Dick has been in agony for months now." She paused. "Anthony told me what happened; he thought perhaps I would talk to you about it. But I just could not bring myself to. I haven't told the story to a soul, not even Allin. Poor Anthony is dreadfully upset. He is too much of a gentleman to tell Dick about it, and there has been a real coolness between them ever since that day."

Mary Catten coughed softly. "I think I know now what needs to be done. If you will take off the gown, mistress . . ."

"Mary!" Dierdra exclaimed penitently. "I'm so sorry!" Hastily she slipped out of her wedding gown and into her yellow muslin. "Come, Tamar," she said as she fastened the last of the buttons. "We can talk in my room."

Tamar nodded mutely, and the two girls made their way in silence to Dierdra's bedchamber. Once there, Tamar sat down disconsolately in the chair and buried her blond head in her hands.

"Dierdra, Dierdra, what am I going to do?" she asked, her voice despairing. "Anthony was absolutely right. He said I acted like a spoiled child. And I did, I did. I'm so ashamed of myself. I do not even have the courage to confess to Dick what an idiot I've been."

Dierdra dropped to her knees next to the chair. "There, there, Tamar," she said soothingly. "Things are not as bad as you paint them. It may be difficult to tell Dick the truth, but once you do, everything will be all right again. Learning to apologize is part of growing up. Allin and I discovered that a long time ago." She smiled in recollection.

"But how can I, Dierdra, how can I?" Tears were running down Tamar's cheeks. "I will never be able to bring myself to tell him what a baby I've been, and what silly ideas were running through my head. How can I tell him I thought he was ashamed of me, and would not take me to Virginia for that reason? Or that I hoped he would become jealous and love me more if I persuaded Anthony to pay some attention to me? I know I'm not very bright, Dierdra, but a child would have shown more sense."

Dierdra thought quickly. Evidently Tamar did not yet know of Mr. Chapman's opposition to his son's marriage to her. Certainly, it would hurt her feelings to learn about it now, but perhaps that hurt would be helpful. There was no better way of showing the girl the depth of Dick's feeling for her; after all, if he had not truly loved her, he would have given in to his father's wishes. If Tamar was ever to grow up, this was as good a time as any for her to begin.

"Tamar," she said gently, "you have been very foolish in many ways; I cannot deny it. But in one respect you were not far from right, and I think you should know about it. Dick has never been ashamed of you for a single instant, but his father was most unhappy when he heard there was to be a marriage. That is why Dick wanted to settle here. He wanted to save you from any unpleasantness. He was even willing to give up his own family to do it. And he would never have dreamed of hurting you by telling you the truth."

Tamar sat silent, her eyes cast down, her hands folded in her lap. After a moment, she got to her feet and walked slowly over to the window. Unseeing, she gazed over the brightly blooming garden. The flowers and trees were flecked with the golden rays of the sun. A mockingbird was singing in the branches of an oak. When finally she turned to face Dierdra, there was a new look of dignity on her pretty face.

"Then I owe Dick not just one apology, Dierdra, but two. One for putting him off, and flirting with Anthony, and another for not recognizing how gentle and considerate he has been. I'm going to ride out to his plantation this very instant and tell him how sorry and ashamed I am. I owe Anthony an apology, too, and my thanks for bringing me to my senses." She paused, and the familiar impish grin crossed her face. "I will be swallowing more pride than I ever thought I had. I hope I'll still be able to fit into the dress I made for your wedding!"

The wedding day dawned bright and sunny, and the breeze that rustled through the early morning stillness gave promise that the weather would be pleasantly cool, even at high noon, when the ceremony was to take place.

Dierdra rode out to Lilac Farm in the governor's coach with the Burringtons and their two children. Her face was flushed and radiant, and the cream-colored taffeta set off the sparkle in her blue eyes and the sheen of her blue-black hair. Madam Burrington was beautiful in blue silk, little Ann charming in her white organdy, and William, in his beige satin, was nearly as elegant as his father, who had dressed for the occasion in his most splendid London clothes.

As the carriage rolled up the path to Lilac Farm, Mistress Killigrew hurried out of the house to greet them, her gray taffeta rustling as she walked. Her husband, solemn and dignified in his Sunday suit of fine broadcloth, followed.

"Oh, Dierdra," Mistress Killigrew exclaimed as the bride stepped out of the carriage, "thank the good heavens you are here! Allin is as nervous as a cat. He keeps saying you aren't going to come, and he wants to see you right now."

"But he cannot see the bride before the wedding," Madam Burrington put in. "The groom never can. It would be bad luck."

"So I have told him, over and over," Mistress Killigrew shook her head in despair. "But I fear he's past all reason now."

"And what bridegroom is not, on his wedding day?" The governor laughed jovially. "I believe that was the most frightening day of my entire life. Eh, Killigrew?"

"Aye, your excellency," the yeoman nodded. "I was not even sure I would stay alive long enough to get to the church."

"Well, someone will have to tell Allin that his bride has really come," Mistress Killigrew said, "else he is likely to burst."

"May we tell him, may we?" William asked hopefully.

Little Ann jumped up and down in excitement. "Yes, we will tell him!"

"That's a splendid idea," Dierdra said. Her heart was pounding, but she managed to keep her voice calm. "I am going up to Tamar's room. I have to arrange my veil. Oh, I'm as bad as Allin! I wish it were all over!" She flew into the house and upstairs.

At last the time for the wedding arrived. The Reverend Mr. Bailey took his place at the altar which had been set up on the lawn, under a giant sycamore. The guests were grouped to the right and to the left. The Killigrews stood erect and smiling, Dick and Tamar beside them. Anthony was next to Madam Burrington and her children, and the other guests—the Lovycks, the Moseleys, Goldsmith Coltrane and the families of two of Yeoman Killigrew's neighbors—formed a semicircle behind them. In the third tier were the bondmen and bondwomen, Mary Catten, Phenny and Taphy.

Allin and Owen stood facing the grassy runway. Dierdra, her hand resting lightly on Governor Burrington's arm, moved gracefully across the greensward.

"God bless you, my dearest," Allin whispered, and he went to her side even before the minister gave the signal. He had the look of a man bewitched.

"If only our sweet Mary were here," Yeoman Killigrew whispered to his wife, "then I would have nothing more to ask for."

She nodded, and tears filled her eyes. "She'd have been a proud woman, she would, to see her son grow up so tall and strong and handsome, and to marry such a fine girl."

The simple ceremony was soon over and Allin, his eyes shining with love, took his bride in his arms. There was a tremulous smile on her lips and her happiness overflowed in tears.

Yeoman Killigrew's voice broke the silence. "Come, fair ladies and gentlemen," he cried, "let us drink a toast to the bride and groom in good Cornish cider."

The guests made their way to the tables that had been set up near the house, where there were cider and ale and plates of Cornish goodies: meat pasties and saffron cakes. When the last toast had been drunk, and the bride and groom had quietly slipped away, Anthony felt the pressure of a hand on his arm and heard a masculine voice saying:

"Tony, I want to apologize to you."

Anthony looked up to see Dick Chapman and Tamar standing near him.

"No, not you, Dick," the girl said, "it is I who owe you an apology, Anthony. I cannot tell you how ashamed I am." Anthony raised his hand to cut her off, but she refused to be interrupted. "I don't want only to apologize, though, I want to thank you. If it had not been for you, I might have gone on being a little idiot forever. And then I would have lost Dick completely. But—" she turned her sparkling eyes to Dick—"he has forgiven me, and now everything is fine between us. And we have you to thank for it. You and Dierdra."

Anthony extended his hands to both of them.

"I am so glad. Truly I am."

"I am, too." Dick was grinning from ear to ear. "And now that Tamar has said her piece, Tony, I want to apologize, too. I had no right to lose my head like that, and to make such accusations against you."

"Any man in love would have done exactly the same thing." Anthony patted his friend on the back. "And besides, Tamar is a very pretty girl." He paused. "Now, you two, I want to hear about *your* wedding. When will it be?"

Tamar dimpled. "You're the one who has to decide that. We did not want to ask Mr. Bailey until we had made our apologies to you."

"Just one moment," Anthony said in mock anger, "I will not have you make me responsible for postponing the happy event. The minister is over there, Tamar, talking with your father. You take yourselves right to him, and don't you dare come back here until everything is settled."

Dick smiled. "Yes, sir." His face sobered. "We expect to go up to his church in Bertie, Tony. There has been so much confusion about this wedding already that Tamar and I thought the best thing would be just to slip away and have the ceremony performed quietly. Will you come up with us, and be my best man?"

"Will I? I would never speak to you again if you had not asked me. Now, off with you, and make the arrangements." Placing a hand on each of their shoulders, he turned them in the direction of the minister and gently shoved them toward him.

Anthony stood for a while watching the young couple as they spoke to Mr. Bailey; when he turned back he saw Governor Burrington approaching him.

"Dawson, I wonder if you would do me a favor?" Burrington asked.

"Certainly, sir," Anthony replied. "If I can."

"Ever since you first arrived here, over a year ago, I have suspected you of concealing something from me. And now that my departure is imminent, I want to ask you about it."

Anthony was silent.

"When I was still in England," Burrington went on, "I met Lord John several times. Indeed, it was he with whom I had my dealings before I came over here. And from the very moment I first set eyes on you, I was struck by your great resemblance to him. I have believed for a long time that you are a member of the Granville family. Now, tell me the truth. Am I correct?"

There was nothing to be gained by denial. "Yes, your excellency," Anthony said. "Lord John is my cousin. My full name is Anthony Dawson Granville."

"I knew it, I knew it." The governor slapped his thigh. "And I presume you were sent over here to report on me?" His voice was even, but Anthony could sense an undertone of resentment.

"Not on you, sir, but on our interests in the province," Anthony said. "We Granvilles have never been convinced, as, apparently, have many of the other Proprietors—with some prodding from other sources, I believe—" and he shot the governor a piercing glance—"that these holdings should be sold to the Crown. We have always believed that they could and should be made profitable to their owners."

"Only a fool would say that the land is not fertile," Burrington's voice was rising, "but that does not mean it can be made profitable under proprietary government. Indeed, events have made it quite clear it cannot be." He paused, and when he spoke again, it was more calmly. "Mr. Dawson, I hope you will believe me when I say that I came to the conclusion only with the greatest reluctance that the province should be sold. But the situation does not seem to me to admit of any other solution. Either anarchy or the Crown—those are the alternatives. I am deeply sorry you and I should be in disagreement about this matter. But since we are, I think it better to have things out in the open."

Anthony started to speak, but was interrupted by Edward Moseley, who had come up in time to hear the governor's last words.

"I, too, think disagreements should be brought out into the open," he said heatedly. "But I notice, your excellency, that you never troubled to make the views you have just expressed known to the Council. This is the first time I have ever heard them from your lips. Do you call that honest dealing?"

"Mr. Moseley!" Burrington's face was an angry red, but his voice was steady. "Do you think the Council has dealt honestly with me? Withholding my salary from me, so that I have not received a penny in all the time I have been here? Overriding my every action? Scheming behind my back to have me recalled? Why, sir, you made up your minds to oppose me before I even arrived here! Your enmity helped drive me to the conclusion I finally reached."

"Gentlemen, gentlemen!" Anthony attempted to stem the flow of angry words. "This is a wedding, a happy occasion. It is hardly the time or place for a quarrel."

But Burrington would not be deterred. "I am not quarreling. I would not stoop to that. But I am not a fool, and it is time Mr. Moseley should know that I have been on to his game for quite a while, and that I feel no need to apologize for anything I have done. I am as interested in helping the province as he. But I have seen its problems as part of the larger picture of the New World as a whole, and this view has determined my actions. Unlike you, Mr. Moseley, I am not a small-minded person."

"I am glad you think so well of yourself, sir." Moseley's voice was icy. "Especially since no one else does."

"So you believe me to be isolated, eh, Moseley?" Burrington's voice was rising. "Well, I am not. I have powerful friends, very powerful. The next time you and I have dealings with one another, you will find that out for yourself. And make no mistake, sir, we will be dealing with one another again, and in the not too distant future." And the governor turned on his heel and walked over to speak to Yeoman Killigrew.

"And what does he mean by that, do you suppose?" Moseley asked Anthony, his eyes on the governor's retreating back.

"It is quite clear, I think," Anthony said. "The governor does not expect his work for the Crown to go unrewarded. I wager that when the colony is sold, it will have as its first Crown governor one George Burrington. And you had better get used to that idea, Mr. Moseley."

Chapter XX

A GOVERNOR LEAVES AND ONE ARRIVES

Governor Burrington and his family left Edenton without fanfare. No red carpets were rolled from the Government House garden to the coach, no trumpet blared to announce their departure. Dierdra had wanted to come in from her new home on the Virginia Road to bid them farewell, but Madam had protested that she found leavetakings painful, and preferred to make her departure quietly. And so only the servants and a few of the villagers—some fishermen, the town watchman, and the lamplighter—saw the governor and his family board the *North Star* as the first streaks of false dawn showed in the eastern sky.

The captain was on deck to welcome them, holding a lanthorn high in his hand to light the way up the gangplank. When his passengers had been shown to their narrow cabins, he gave the order to set sail. The sailors climbed aloft, the sails caught the dawn breeze, and the *North Star* was on her way to Virginia.

As the ship began to move, Burrington emerged from his cabin to stand at the rail and watch the little village recede into the distance. Slowly, the ship moved out of Edenton Bay into Albemarle Sound. Here the wind was sharp and steady, and the sails flapped and filled. The *North Star* slipped down the waterway toward the Atlantic, past the soundside plantation houses: Moseley Point, Strawberry Hill, Sandy Point, Greenfield. At Drummond's Point, the sun was over the eastern horizon.

When the *North Star* reached Pirate's Hole, beyond the Outer Banks, another vessel approached it from the Atlantic. The two ships dipped ensigns as they crossed: the old governor of North Carolina and the new were greeting one another. For among the passengers on the inbound ship was Sir Richard Everard with his family.

It was early afternoon before the vessel anchored in Edenton Bay. The July day was hot; the province was still suffering from a long spell of drought and higher than normal temperatures, and the few clouds that hovered in the sky, giving promise of rain, had so far brought only more humidity.

At Government House, the servants were waiting impatiently for Sir Richard's arrival. All morning long, Taphy and Mary Catten had been busy directing them at their work, clearing out the old, making ready for the new. Madam had offered to take Mary back to England with her, but the bondwoman preferred to remain in North Carolina. She and Smalkins had struck up a warm friendship, and when Anthony suggested he would take over her bond and put her in charge of his household, she had accepted with alacrity. Today was to be Mary's last day at Government House, and she was determined that the new governor would find his home in perfect order when he arrived. The house had been scrubbed clean and sweet. All the white paneling had been washed and rubbed down, and the windows, with their small panes of blown glass, sparkled and shone.

In the kitchen, the cooks were basting the roasts and hoping they would not dry out before Sir Richard and his family arrived. Small Negro boys were running from the woodshed to the kitchen, carrying sticks of pine and oak: "Pine to burn, oak to hold."

Taphy was dressed in his very best, the Eden livery, and his bearing was proud as, hearing the sound of the governor's coach, he opened the front door and hurried down the steps.

"Sir, your honor, welcome to Government House, your new home. Madam, welcome, and welcome to all your family."

"What's your name?" Sir Richard asked as he stepped out of the carriage. The new governor was tall and spare, but there was a sense of strength in his thin, wiry frame. His face was long and narrow, his penetrating blue eyes were set deep under heavy brows, and his nose was high-bridged and long. His wide, firm lips held no hint of humor. He did not wait for Taphy's answer, but turned to help his wife arrange her wide silk skirts, so that she could descend from the coach gracefully. Behind her came her daughter and son, the girl a pretty thing of about eighteen, the boy, tall and handsome, about a year older. As they emerged from the coach, the young people looked around curiously at the crowd which had gathered on Broad Street to watch the new governor's arrival.

But their father gave the townsfolk only a brief glance and then took his wife's arm to lead her into the house.

"Should you not acknowledge your subjects, Richard?" she said. "After all, they have come to greet you."

The governor turned, removed his hat, and made a stiff bow. But he said not a word until he had again taken his wife's arm.

"Come, my dear, come," he murmured then. "Let us go inside. You must be weary. I am sure I am."

Lady Everard laid her hand lightly on the governor's arm and walked toward the stoop. She moved with elegance, in a rustle of skirts and a flutter of scarves, the faint perfume of violets following her. When the young people had run up the steps behind her, Taphy closed the door.

Once inside, the Everard family stood in the hall looking about them. The girl, Amanda, shot a discouraged glance at her brother, Richard, and both of them laughed ruefully.

"So this is the new world of opportunity!" The girl's light young voice filled the hall. "If this is the best it has to offer, we would as well have taken a tenant house in Hertfordshire. 'Twould have been no worse."

Her brother sauntered down the hall, glancing casually into the rooms. "You are quite right, Amanda. It's a poor place, by God. I should have stayed in London and read my law at the Temple."

Sir Richard turned to face his son. "That will be quite enough from you, sirrah. Your opinion was neither asked for nor wanted. Come, madam," he said to his wife, "let us go upstairs and find your room. Your maid will be here in a while to settle things for you."

As they turned to mount the stairs, Lady Everard halted.

"Do look into the drawing room," she said to her husband. "See how brightly the sun shines in on the paneled walls. It is not an elegant place, but it is rather cozy. Like a country retreat. It may not be too frightful."

The governor's frown cleared somewhat. "Yes, indeed. It is a small place, almost a miniature, but I suppose it is pleasant enough in its way."

Richard shrugged as he and his sister followed their parents up the stairs. "Everyone to his own taste," he muttered, loudly enough to be heard. "If I had my choice, I'd rather have a sixteenth-century cow barn in Hertfordshire."

"That will be quite enough of that, Richard!" His mother spoke sharply. "It is perfectly true that Carolina is not Hertfordshire or London. But your father is the governor here, and you will have a very distinguished position. You had better conduct yourself as befits it."

"Hah!" Richard laughed under his breath. "From what I've heard of North Carolina, that would really be casting pearls before swine. And I've heard, too, that the governor and his family have no position in society at all. These ruffian Carolinians have a habit of making trouble for their governors. How else did we come to be here?"

The following morning, Anthony Dawson entered the Council chamber in the courthouse and found a seat near the window. The room was crowded; the news that Sir Richard would meet with the Council had spread quickly, and a large number of villagers had come to see their new governor in his first official appearance.

Sir Richard entered the room promptly at ten o'clock. He was dressed in the latest London fashion: a knee-length broadcloth coat of dark blue over an embroidered brocade vest, satin smallclothes and square-toed shoes with silver buckles. There was fine lace at his neck and sleeves; his elegance barely escaped dandyism.

As the Council members and spectators rose to do him honor, Anthony scrutinized the governor with some care. The square turn of his jaw, the firmness of his mouth and the hard look in his eyes all bespoke a determined, even a stubborn man. He will not be easy to influence, Anthony thought.

Chief Justice Gale, who had been reinstated by the Lords Proprietors to the position from which Burrington had removed him, and who had arrived in North Carolina on the same ship that carried the governor, rose to make the welcoming address for the Council.

"When I was in London," he said in his slow and dignified manner, "I had the pleasure of meeting with Lord John, Palatine of the Lords Proprietors. He asked me to convey his greetings to his people in North Carolina, and his sincere good wishes for their welfare. It is his pleasure to send you as your rightful governor and administrator, Sir Richard Everard, Captain General and Admiral, a man of proven worth in matters of government." He bowed in the direction of the governor. "I am happy to present to you, your excellency, the members of your Council."

Everard rose from his high-backed governor's chair and bowed slightly to the Council members.

"Gentlemen, I bring you greetings from the true and absolute Lords Proprietors of North Carolina, who have honored me by appointing me your governor. I have in my possession a paper confirming my appointment, which I shall put in the hands of your chief justice, for safekeeping. As I take it, this is an informal welcome by my Council. The public greeting will be later, at a celebration to which all the people of the province will be invited. Until that time, I shall only say that I am happy to be here in North Carolina. I hope I shall give the people a satisfactory administration according to the law. I thank you." The governor bowed again and sat down in his high-backed chair.

The Council members rose, their hats under their arms, bowed deeply, and remained standing until the governor had made his way to the retiring chamber behind the Council room.

Anthony left the courthouse with Edward Moseley, and the two men stood chatting for a moment on the steps.

"How does Sir Richard impress you, Mr. Moseley?" Anthony asked.

"Very well, so far. He speaks briefly, and to the point. And he has dignity—something for which the governor's office has not been noteworthy these last two years."

Anthony smiled. "That is true enough." He paused. "I have been thinking about the Boundary Line Commission, Mr. Moseley. Since we have not done any work yet, I wonder if Sir Richard will want to appoint an entirely new group."

"I doubt it very much," Moseley said, shaking his head. "The Virginians have postponed the work so far, not we. Actually, I am rather pleased about that; it has given me time to finish my map of North Carolina, which should be a valuable guide for us when we begin. But more than that, I must confess, I think of the map as my mark on the history of the province. It has been a monumental undertaking, sir, monumental. There are eight sections, and it covers all the known features of the land, from the seacoast to the mountains, rivers, creeks, villages, crossroads and mill runs. I do not think I have left out a single detail. Now all that remains to be marked is the dividing line with Virginia. I plan to see to it that the first act Everard signs is to order the commission to get to work. I hope that he will add to it, also, by appointing Chief Justice Gale and Mr. Little to serve with us. Those two, with you, me, and Mr. Lovyck, should make enough of a match even for that old fox, William Byrd. If I know him, he will try to bring the dividing line as far down as he can."

At that moment, Chief Justice Gale joined them. He had put off his robes of office and was now attired in somber colors. He greeted Anthony cordially, his eyes twinkling.

"Well, young man! To think that I had to travel all the way to London to find out something you could have told me here! But I must say, Lord John is proud of your ability to keep a secret. And—" he turned to Edward Moseley—"I am proud of yours."

Anthony smiled. "At first there was very little to be gained by revealing the truth. But now, it seems, there is very little to be lost."

Gale's expression became sober. "So it seems, so it seems. Lord John told me that he had done his utmost to prevail on the other Proprietors not to sell their holdings, but that it was a hopeless task. They are determined to let the Crown have the land. The memorial of sale has not yet been drawn up, but Lord John expects that it will be, momentarily. It will have to be submitted to Parliament and approved in a special act." He sighed. "I was sorry to hear the story."

"No more than I, sir," Moseley put in. "But, as I have told myself over and over in the last few months, we should hardly have expected anything else. After all, most of the Proprietors are simply not interested in the province."

"Did you and Lord John discuss Governor Burrington at all?" Anthony asked. "I have written him my beliefs on that subject, but he has sent me no answer."

Gale nodded. "We did, indeed. And we are inclined to agree with you that Burrington was working for the Crown. It is unfortunate that such talents should be put to such evil use; Burrington is an able man."

"Sir Richard seems to be competent," Moseley said. "Did you become well acquainted with him on the trip from Virginia?"

"Fairly well. I find him a difficult man to understand. He is quite reserved, in the first place, and then he seems to have a rather dilatory attitude toward this engagement. Whenever I endeavored to tell him anything about the province, he put me off. And yet, everyone in London speaks so highly of him."

"He probably knows he will not be here very long," Moseley said, rubbing his forefinger against the side of his nose. "Oh, well, time will tell."

"And on that note I shall leave you gentlemen." Anthony smiled. "Since I have my fields planted and my house built, I begrudge every moment spent away from my home." He bowed to the chief justice. "I hope you and Madam Gale will do me the honor of dining with me at Stowe very soon."

"Stowe? Is that what you call your plantation?" the chief justice asked.

Anthony nodded. "That is the name of my family's estate in Devon, you know. I have a sentimental attachment to it." He smiled and made his way across the Green to the King's Arms, where he had stabled his horse.

As he passed through the common room, he overheard snatches of conversation from the merchants and artisans who were gathered there. In one corner, a yeoman from Bertie was describing the case of a conjure woman in his precinct, who had been arrested with her youthful assistant for digging up a child's grave to get its dust to make into a salve for a love philtre. But most of the talk was about the new governor. Martin Trewilliger was violent against him.

"I could tell from one look," he was saying, "one look. No better than Burrington, I'll wager. Even worse, mayhap. Stiff-necked, and stubborn as a mule. Ice water runs through his veins."

Elkin, the cordwainer, took a more moderate view. "Now, don't you damn the man before he has had a chance. He seemed all right at the Council meeting."

"Huh!" Martin snorted. "And what about yesterday? He'd not even have greeted us on the street if his lady had not given him the order."

"What did you think of her?" It was Joseph Castleton, the barber. "She looks to me fair determined, herself. Back like a ramrod. And those eyes! Nothing escapes her."

"It's the boy I didn't like," Elkin said. "Did you see that arrogant stare?"

"I tell you," said Martin, shaking his head, "I don't trust Everard. I don't trust him one bit. This will be the third of the governors I have known in my time—all sent out by the Lords Proprietors. Eden, he was a pirate, and there's no denying it. And Burrington—well; he wasn't too bad when he was not in liquor. But when was that, I should like to know, except in the last few months? And now this one! Brrr!" He shuddered. "If I never before thought we should go under the Crown, I think it now. Mayhap King George would send an honest man to govern us."

Anthony smiled wryly at these words. Would Martin like Burrington any better as a Crown governor? Or would he like any governor at all, no matter who he was, and no matter whom he represented? Where, Anthony wondered, did one draw the line between a love of freedom and a resistance against any and all authority?

By this time, he had passed through the inn and was crossing the courtyard on his way to the stables, where Smalkins should be waiting with the horses. At first, as he entered the stalls, he could see nothing, but as his eyes became accustomed to the darkness, he caught sight of Smalkins standing some distance inside the stable. The man beckoned to his master, a finger to his lips, and then motioned toward the horse stalls at the far end of the building. Baled hay, halfway up to the roof, made a partition dividing the great room in two, but a wide crack between the bales gave a clear view of the stalls beyond and of the three men standing there: the landlord, deVoe, Captain Kellogg, and Tom the Tinker. As Anthony tiptoed up, he could see that Kellogg was shaking Tom violently.

"Did you tell them? Answer me that. Did you tell them?" He struck Tom across the face with the back of his hand. Tom whimpered, a strange, animal sound, like a beaten dog.

"Come on, now, speak up." deVoe's voice was threatening. "I'll cut off your ears if you don't." He aimed a vicious kick at Tom's shins. "Burrington's gone, now, you know. You have no more protection."

"Mr. deVoe, Mr. deVoe," Tom's voice was no louder than a whisper, "I didn't mean anything, I didn't. Let me go, let me go, please!"

"Oh, the devil with this," Kellogg muttered. "No sense in talking to the dummy. Even if he hasn't said anything up to now, there's no telling when he might. I'll just get rid of him, as I did of Simmons." He pushed Tom heavily in the chest, and the little man fell to the floor, where he lay sobbing and gasping for breath.

"That's your solution to everything, isn't it, Kellogg?" deVoe said roughly. "You weren't supposed to kill Simmons, either. Just knock him unconscious and take the papers to South Carolina. I was trying to do the governor a favor, not to stir up a hornet's nest."

"Tenderhearted, aren't you? And unselfish. Don't make me laugh. You must have expected a pretty penny from Burrington. Catch you watching out for anyone's interests but your own."

"Oh, shut your mouth! Of course I expected the governor

would do a little something for us. After all, Simmons was likely out to cheat him and he should have been grateful to us. I thought the governor was a gentleman. Ptew!" He spat. "Fine gentleman he was. Not only did I make sure his papers were delivered, but when you went too far and killed Simmons, I found him a first-rate suspect, so the whole case could be buried dead as a dormouse, and there would be not a single thing to worry about. But then his excellency suddenly becomes the soul of honor and righteousness, and has the dummy released. Ptew!" He spat again.

"I have no time to stand here and listen to your whining," Kellogg said contemptuously. "It's done, and over with. Your friend Simmons put up a fight, so I had to kill him. And I tell you that as long as this creature is alive," and he kicked at Tom with the toe of his heavy boot, "you and I will be in danger. We have to get rid of him. That's all there is to it. We might have been safe while Burrington was here; he wouldn't have dared let anything happen to us lest the story of his double-dealings would come out. But Everard is a different kettle of fish. What do we know about him? And who would believe you if you said you were an altruist?" He peered venomously at the innkeeper. "I've had enough talk. I'm going for my gun." He turned and started for the corner.

Anthony had heard enough.

"I'll take Kellogg," he whispered to Smalkins. "You take deVoe."

The two men crept quietly forward. Luck was with them; the bullies had their backs turned, and it was but the work of a moment to spring on them and stun them with heavy blows to the neck.

"Rope, we need rope," Anthony panted. "Smalkins, you fetch some. And Tom, if you can pick yourself up, you run for the sheriff. I'll stand guard here."

Smalkins hurried off, returning with the rope just in time. The ruffians were beginning to regain consciousness, and they lay on the floor groaning and cursing. Between them, Anthony and Smalkins managed to tie the men's arms and legs, and when the sheriff arrived, soon afterward, he led the bound men to the gaol.

The news spread rapidly through the village, and the people were in a fury. So these were the two men who had committed the crime for which poor Tom had been imprisoned! The mutterings and curses along the streets boded no good for deVoe or Kellogg, and the sheriff, frightened of what might happen, put an extra guard around the gaol that night and arranged to take his prisoners secretly to the Norfolk prison for safekeeping after the arraignment, which was to take place the next day. With Anthony and Smalkins to testify against them, there was no question but that the prisoners would be found guilty by the court when it met in the autumn. But the people were impatient. Autumn was months away.

Late that night, the sheriff and his deputies started out of town with their prisoners. But they had gone no further than the stockade gate when a crowd of masked men moved in on them and, dragging the prisoners from their horses, tied their wrists behind them and flung them into a cart. They bound the sheriff and his deputies to the postern gate and rode back into the village with the criminals.

They made straight for the public gallows and walked the first of their prisoners, deVoe, up the wooden stairs to the platform. A rope with a noose hung from the gallows tree. Silently, one of the masked men adjusted it around the landlord's neck. Then, when all was in order, a loud voice called out:

"In the name of the people of Edenton, we commend you to the mercy of God."

The moon came out from behind a heavy bank of clouds and the light fell on a black figure dangling from the gallows. Kellogg shrieked and cursed as the masked men pushed him up the steps to stand under the noose from which his companion had already been cut down. He, too, was quickly put to death, and both corpses were strung up from the same gallows tree, to be left swaying in the hot breeze of the midsummer night.

Far up Broad Street, at the turn of the Virginia Road, the watchman's lanthorn bobbed up and down. "Two o'clock in the morning and all's well."

And in the shuttered farrier's shop, a group of dark figures stood around the brightly glowing forge. Stripping the dark cloths from their faces, they burned them on the fire.

When Sir Richard heard of the hanging, he sprang into immediate action. Every house in Edenton was searched, to no avail, and the watchman was given strict orders to arrest anyone found on the streets after midnight.

"I will not have the law flouted," Sir Richard told the sheriff. "I want the scoundrels discovered and brought here. How dare they do this to their governor?"

But the culprits were never found.

Chapter XXI

CORNWALL PLANTATION

Dierdra called her new home Cornwall. The very name was nostalgic, carrying with it the memory of the high, rocky cliffs of her native land, of the angry Atlantic beating against its rugged shores, of its wild moors, and of the stones, set in wide circles, that had been the temples of worship of the strange, primitive people who had once lived there.

Although it did not take her very long to settle into the ways of a country housewife, Allin, familiar since his childhood with farms and farm life, enjoyed teasing her gently about her naïveté, and his particular favorite was the story of the day, shortly after their marriage, when she had stood, riding crop in hand, at the gate, calling coaxingly to a couple of straying porkers: "Here, piggie, here, nice piggie, here." Dierdra took his affectionate joking in good grace; she loved Allin, and he loved her, and she was happy to be his wife. She loved his strength, his frankness, his earnestness. He was a passionate man, urgent, yet tender, and nearly every morning she would wake to feel his hand on her shoulder and his eyes fixed devouringly on her face. How good it is, she would think to herself as she smiled at him, to be so loved!

For her pleasure, and as an outlet for his own energies, Allin had built a race course and a jumping field and often, in the early morning, she would look out of the window of her bedchamber to see him putting his hard-mouthed, spirited stallion, Black Magic, over the hurdles. She feared for him, sometimes, as she watched the stable men set the bars higher and higher for the jump. But Black Magic always took the five-barred gate with ease.

Dierdra's greatest joy was to watch her husband at his work

—leaning over the fence of the lot and keeping an eye on the cattle as they moved in from the pasture to the shelter of the barn, stable and byre, or riding across their acres or, at the beginning of the day, assigning the chores to the slaves and farm workers. Once, when she was out riding, she had caught sight of him, his coat off, his shirt sleeves rolled up, hammering out a horseshoe on the anvil in the blacksmith shop.

Allin was a hard worker and a careful farmer, and Dierdra knew he would make a success of their new estate. But for this first year, it would not be easy. The hot, dry spell that had started in July was still with them in early September. All summer only occasional light showers had fallen, and now eighteen long days had passed without rain. The bushes along the creeks were dry and the straw brown as in winter. In the fields, the corn shriveled and dropped, the cobs only half-filled. There was a mere half-crop of grain. Tobacco was sorry. Only cotton thrived under the blazing heat of the sun and promised a bumper crop. The yeomen were filled with gloom—another bad harvest.

One morning, dressed in her blue lawn peignoir, her dark hair hanging in two braids over her shoulders, Dierdra sat on the gallery eating her breakfast. As she looked down to the lawn, she saw two mockingbirds drinking in the fountain. They held their wings away from their sides and ruffled out their feathers, as though they were too hot to endure the feel of them next to their bodies. Even the birds are protesting, she thought.

At that moment, Allin came out on the gallery. He had been up and working since dawn; now he had changed his clothes and was ready for his second breakfast. He bent to kiss her lightly on the forehead, and Dierdra could see a worried look on his dark face.

"I am afraid you married a sorry farmer, my pet. We will not make enough money this year even to pay expenses. The tobacco is too poor to be acceptable for the Virginia market." Sighing, he sank into the chair opposite her and lifted his cup of chocolate to his lips. "We should have a market of our own, here in Carolina, so that we would not be so dependent. Anthony Dawson and I are meeting with the governor about it at eleven. We have spoken to him before; he said he agreed with us, but so far he has done nothing. I am very much afraid he is not going to be a good governor. He is extremely dilatory, and in addition he has already antagonized a number of the soundside planters."

Dierdra nodded. "I know. Mrs. Moseley told me the other day that her husband says he finds it almost impossible even to see Sir Richard."

"That's true enough," Allin said. "He insists that everyone must make an appointment with him in writing. That is what Dawson and I had to do. Whatever else can be said about Burrington, he was always available to the people. Sir Richard has been here more than two months, it has been drought weather all this time, and we had to plead with him to give us this appointment. He does not seem to understand how serious it will be if the crop fails again after the bad harvest last year, and he has done nothing to help the situation."

"I am afraid Sir Richard understands very little about the problems of farmers and planters," Dierdra put in. "Mrs. Moseley told me that the Everards are city folk. Lady Everard's only topic of conversation, she says, is the elegant company she used to keep in London. And the children, Mary says, are even worse. Especially the boy. He quite looks down on us."

Allin smiled wryly. "If that gives him any satisfaction, he is free to do it, of course. I wonder when our governors are going to learn that Carolinians do not like to be patronized?" He took his last sip of chocolate, wiped his lips with his serviette, and rose. "I must leave you now, my dear. Dawson will be waiting for me." He kissed her on the forehead and started down the steps to the rack, where Black Magic was pawing the earth. On the last step, he paused.

"By the way, when I was in Edenton the other day, Martin Trewilliger told me he heard that Governor Burrington is in Virginia. Apparently, he never went to London at all, but has been staying with William Byrd, at Westover."

Dierdra looked up in astonishment. "Never went to England?"

Allin shook his head. "It seems he has also made several trips to Charleston, to confer with the governor there. It all points to just one thing. He expects that the province will be sold to the Crown very soon."

"How do you feel about this matter, Allin?" Dierdra asked.

"That is a difficult question to answer, my pet. I know that many of the planters are in favor of proprietary government, and are very disturbed to think that the Crown will be taking over. But the village folk feel that Crown government will be an improvement, and I am inclined to think there is some merit in their arguments. The Crown might find it easier to keep order. The hanging of deVoe and Kellogg, for example. That kind of lawlessness should be prevented, and the Proprietors seem powerless to do a thing about it. And there is another thing. With North Carolina an island of private ownership between two Crown colonies . . ." He paused, his eyes thoughtful. Then he looked up at her and his face broke into a smile. "But I must not waste my time with you talking about such somber matters. We are together, and happy, and nothing else really counts." He ran back up the steps and leaned over to kiss her cheek. But his lips found her mouth, and the light kiss became something more, strong and passionate. When finally he drew away, his voice was husky.

"I think you are trying to keep me from my duty," he said. "If I do not leave you now, I never will." He ran his finger tips gently down her cheek and descended the steps again.

Dierdra watched him as he mounted the stallion. The horse was skittish, and jumped sidewise, throwing Allin against the rack. Startled, he cheekstrapped the animal and mounted with a rush, raking his spurs against the horse's flanks as he landed in the saddle. Black Magic took the bit between his teeth and ran, throwing his great head from side to side. He raced down the path and across the meadow and was almost at the woodlot before Allin finally brought him under control. The groom, who had come up from the stables just in time to witness the scene, shook his woolly grey head.

"Master going to take a fall one of these times. I know it, I just do. That horse is purely devil inside."

Dierdra went back into the cool, shuttered house. She felt disturbed. She had been afraid of Black Magic from the moment

Allin bought him, and although she had seen no show of temper from Allin since the day of their quarrel at the old Indian camp more than a year before, she still had a vivid recollection of how fierce his anger had been then. She shuddered to think of what might happen if the rebellious stallion were to goad his master into rage.

Allin and Anthony had arranged to meet at a private room of the King's Arms, whose management, after deVoe's hanging, had been taken over by a Virginia tavernkeeper named Giles Martin. Allin arrived to find Anthony already there, deep in conversation with Mr. Coltrane, Edward Moseley and John Lovyck.

"I do not understand you gentlemen," Coltrane was saying. "You could not abide Burrington, and now you are beginning to find fault with Sir Richard. The man has not even been here three months and already you have discovered a whole catalogue of deficiencies. Have you ever asked yourselves if the fault may not be partially yours?"

"It is well enough for you to defend the governor, Coltrane," said Moseley. "You are not obliged to sit on the Council and look at that cold, stony face day after day."

"Moseley is right," John Lovyck chimed in. "Do you like him, Coltrane?"

Coltrane held up his wineglass to the light and examined the golden bubbles that clung to its sides. It was a moment before he spoke.

"Gentlemen, I do not have to like the governor to respect his office. I admit we have had some sorry specimens here, but try to think from their side of the fence for a moment. They come here to find antagonism and resentment. We have not always been as helpful as we should, and there is no gainsaying that. I think we are perhaps too jealous of our freedom, and fearful that the governor may take away some of our privileges."

Anthony spoke for the first time. "I must admit that there is some truth in what you say, sir. And when the Crown takes over, we will probably have to learn to adjust ourselves to a loss of freedom. But that is only part of the story. When a governor removes himself from the people to the extent that Everard has, it is extremely difficult to achieve anything at all. Today will not be the first time that Gorgas and I will have spoken to Sir Richard about a tobacco market here in North Carolina. And I will be very much surprised if we accomplish anything more than we did at our first meeting."

"Have you thought at all about a more convincing method of approaching him?" Allin asked. "I confess I find myself at a loss. When he looks at me with those cold, uncomprehending eyes of his . . ."

"So you can understand how we feel at the Council meetings, eh, Gorgas?" John Lovyck asked.

Allin nodded. "I can, indeed." He turned to Anthony. "It is getting on to eleven. We had better go."

"I suppose we had." Anthony rose from his seat.

The two young men found Sir Richard in a little house in the Government House garden, which he had converted into an office. The room's bare neatness contrasted as sharply with the cluttered disorder in which Burrington's office had been kept as Everard's frozen calm did with his predecessor's hot-headed impatience.

"What brings you gentlemen here?" the governor asked after they had seated themselves on the cane chairs in front of his table.

"We wish to speak to you about establishing a tobacco market here in the province, sir," Anthony said. "You may remember that we mentioned the matter earlier."

"So you did, Mr. Dawson, so you did. And, as I remember it, I told you I would take the matter under advisement."

"Sir Richard—" Allin leaned forward in his chair, his expression intent. "I am afraid we have not made clear to you the urgency of the situation. The drought and the heat are going to make for a very poor harvest this year; every farmer in the precinct expects to take a loss on his crops. And with the tobacco unacceptable for the Virginia market, as it doubtless will be, things will be even worse. But if we could dispose of the tobacco here—"

"Am I to understand that you want a market at which to sell inferior leaf?" Sir Richard interrupted.

"Not inferior, your excellency. Not as good, perhaps, as we would like, but not inferior."

"You know, sir," Anthony put in, "that farming is our principal activity here, and a bad season works a great hardship on the entire province. If the crop is poor, the farmers have no money with which to make purchases, and then the artisans and merchants suffer as well."

"Thank you for that instructive little lecture, Mr. Dawson." Sir Richard's voice was heavy with sarcasm. "However, even a man like myself, whose experiences have been in the cities and, as an admiral at sea, cannot fail to have learned what you so kindly told me."

Anthony could feel his temper rising, but he managed to keep his voice calm. "I am sorry if I have offended you, your excellency. I spoke only to give emphasis to Mr. Gorgas' words. This is a matter about which both of us are seriously concerned."

"His words needed no emphasis. I quite understood them. And, as I told you, I have the matter under advisement. You will hear from me when I have made my decision."

"But two weeks from now it may be too late," Anthony urged. "The problem is immediate and pressing."

"If the dry spell keeps up much longer, everything will be lost," Allin added.

"I cannot possibly be held responsible for the weather, gentlemen," the governor said icily. "I have told you that you will have my decision when it has been made."

Anthony shrugged and started to rise from his chair.

"Just one moment." Sir Richard's cold blue eyes were fixed piercingly on his visitors. "There are one or two things that should be understood between us before you go. I did not come here to be instructed in my duties by my subjects. I am quite competent to decide what needs to be done, and if I am in need of advice as to how to proceed, a Council has been appointed for that purpose. I will not be harried and pressed into premature action, particularly by people whose only concern is their personal prosperity. Do not think for a moment, gentlemen, that I am unaware of the fact that both of you have extensive holdings here, that this is your first year of active farming, and that, therefore, you are particularly eager for a good harvest. As I said before, I am not responsible for the weather. Good day, gentlemen." And Sir Richard picked up a piece of paper from his table and began ostentatiously to read it.

"Well, we cannot count on much from Sir Richard, that's evident," Allin said as the two young men started back to the King's Arms to get their horses.

"It certainly is." Anthony shook his head. "I wonder what makes him so antagonistic to us? It almost seems as if he had some kind of personal grudge."

"I wish I knew," Allin sighed. "It probably is not personal, though. He has been having trouble with the Council, I imagine. John Lovyck and Moseley made it clear that they do not like him at all. And doubtless he knows he will not be here much longer. And, in addition, his administration began with an illegal hanging. That's hardly calculated to put a man in good humor."

"And in a sense I'm responsible for that hanging. After all, it was I who caught Kellogg and deVoe." Anthony stopped and nodded his head several times. "You know, Gorgas, I would not be at all surprised if that had something to do with the governor's attitude."

"It is possible, of course. And it's an interesting situation. A governor being angry with a citizen because he solved a crime." Allin laughed wryly.

By this time they had arrived at the King's Arms. As they mounted their horses, a sudden gust of hot, damp wind arose, shaking the leaves off trees and raising little tongues of dust and dirt from the hard-trampled earth of the courtyard.

Allin smiled. "Well, perhaps nature will solve our problems. That feels to me like rain. We certainly can make use of it."

Allin arrived back at Cornwall to find his old Negro slave, John, frightened and worried.

"Hurricane weather, master," he said, "better batten down."

"Nonsense," Allin laughed. "A heavy rain, perhaps; I think that very likely. It will be a boon. But it is still much too early for hurricanes."

"Hurricane, I say. Better you batten down, master," the old Negro repeated. "Look," and he pointed to the barnyard. The chickens and ducks and geese were huddled together in small circles. In the pasture, the cattle had closed in and stood back to back, facing the wind. Birds fluttered nervously about, uttering shrill cries. The sky was overcast, and white clouds scudded across the horizon.

Allin frowned. These were hurricane signs. And a bad storm would ruin the crop completely.

"I'm afraid you may be right, John," he said. "Give the orders, will you?"

John nodded and ran off to the quarters line.

The next day, the wind was from the southeast, and Allin studied the falling barometer with concern.

"Sir," his overseer, Gillis, said, "if we don't move quickly, the wind will beat down all the crops that ain't took up yet. The cotton in the south field ain't been picked, and it will be beat into the earth. I doubt it will be any good after the wind is past. And that's about the only crop we can count on, Mr. Gorgas."

Hastily, Allin ordered the slaves into the field, and they worked feverishly all day, picking cotton against the rising wind.

"Master," John said as the last bag of cotton was brought into the barn, "I smell that storm. It's strong in my nostrils. I've seen the devil ridin' in the storm at St. Croix and the Islands, and he's ridin' up there now, in those black clouds." The old man waved his arm toward the southeast. "He's there, master, waitin' to pounce on the wicked and tear them from the earth into the sky. I can smell the sulphur strong."

It was midnight when the hurricane wind hit in full force, roaring in with a noise like the booming of forty cannon. Trees shook and bent double, and the younger ones snapped with the quick, staccato sound of artillery.

Dierdra and the household servants ran from room to room, to see that the hurricane shutters were secure. Allin hurried out to the stables and stayed there all night, calming the terrified horses. At dawn he fought his way back to the house, arriving weary and breathless from his struggle against the wind. He stumbled into the living room and fell into a chair, too exhausted to speak. His linen shirt was in ribbons, and he was soaked from head to heel.

Dierdra hovered over him, wiping his face and arms, stroking his thick black hair.

"Allin, Allin," she cried, "thank God you are here. There was such a crash just before you came in!"

Allin raised his arm, showing a long gash from wrist to elbow.

"It was the hickory on the lawn," he gasped. "I just escaped the outer limbs. Dierdra, I thought it was the end of me."

She threw her arms around him and clung to him in terror and relief.

"My darling, my darling," she murmured, over and over, "my darling."

Noon found them in the quiet of the dead center of the storm, and they went out on the gallery to see the damage. There were fallen trees everywhere—uprooted oaks, pines snapped in the middle, the hickory tumbled on its side, its branches digging into the earth. Trunks were lying on one another in a tangled mass. A wide path had been cut across the lower plantation, and the woods beyond were a shambles. The stables still stood, but many of the outbuildings were flat. The fields were knee deep in water. The swamp at the edge of the plantation was a jungle of entwined trees and branches, a horrid, evil place, where serpents hid, ready to strike, where miasmic vapors curled into the air, bringing fever and death.

The slaves came slowly out of their shacks on the quarters line. The children raced in the wind, shouting with laughter, while their elders fell on their knees, thanking God for delivering them from the storm demon.

But by midnight, the tempest was upon them again; the backlash, whirling in from the northwest, brought a solid sheet of wind-driven rain that beat relentlessly on the sodden earth.

Dierdra sat beside Allin in the drawing room, mute and terrified, hanging desperately on to his arm. Her face was white, her eyes enormous. Never had she heard such a furiously raging storm. The shutters banged crazily back and forth, and candle flames gutted and were blown out. The slaves had run into the house in the last upturn of the wind, and they were huddled in the dining room, wailing, praying, weeping, singing, and calling on the Lord for help. Some stood with their arms up-raised, defying the devil of the storm.

"Satan, go away," they cried, "the Lord will get you. Go away, go away!" Their voices mingled eerily with the passion of the wind and the rain, and Dierdra's terror and panic increased by the moment.

Dawn finally arrived, and with it, the hurricane passed, and the sun rose to reveal in full the horror of desolation that had been wrought: flattened buildings, flooded meadows, ruined crops, fallen trees; the earth had been beaten and subdued.

Allin and Dierdra stood on the gallery and looked out at the storm's handiwork. "Thank God, thank God," Allin said, as he put his arms around his wife. "We have come through it safely. All our people are alive. We have weathered a mighty hurricane together, my love. I believe it is a good omen for our life together."

Dierdra raised her face to his. "I hope so, Allin. With all my heart, I hope so."

Chapter XXII

THE WIND CHANGES

GOVERNOR EVERARD had arrived in Edenton in July. What enthusiasm there had been for him at the beginning of his administration was quickly dampened by his cold, forbidding manner and his lack of interest in the province and its settlers. His unconcern seemed even more shocking after the hurricane; the storm took several lives and ruined crops and property throughout the province, but Sir Richard's first reaction was irritation because the holocaust had cost him his office: a tree in the Government House garden had crashed, shattering one side of the little house to smithereens.

It was not until December, however, that feeling against the governor became strong enough to result in memorials to the Proprietors requesting his immediate recall. The event that brought this about was preceded by all sorts of rumors concerning former Governor Burrington: that he had moved from Virginia and taken up residence on a property he owned in Bertie; that he had been seen entering Government House late one night by the town watchman; that he had been closeted with Edward Moseley at Moseley Point for several hours; and that he and Chief Justice Gale had had an altercation at the courthouse reminiscent, in some respects, of the Strawberry Hill affair. And Burrington's sudden and unexpected reappearance, it was said, was intimately connected with the charges of misconduct against Sir Richard which the Reverend Mr. Bailey was to present in a remonstrance prepared for the winter session of the Inferior Court.

For weeks before the document was to be read, the town buzzed and clacked: at tea parties and supper parties, in the common room of the inn and at the meetings of the Edenton

Guild, the remonstrance and its probable contents were the sole topics of conversation. If the governor had—as he was, apparently, to be charged—attacked a man of the cloth, he must be a heathen and unfit to rule the people of North Carolina.

The council room was packed the day the remonstrance was to be read. Many more people had come than could be seated, and the overflow, unmindful of the late December cold, milled about on the Green in front of the courthouse. If they could not witness what was to take place, they wanted to be the first to hear about it.

Anthony, Allin and Dick had arrived together in the village early enough to be assured of good seats, and all of them leaned forward eagerly as Chief Justice Gale rapped for order and motioned Will Badham to read the document. It was evident that the little clerk found the task distasteful; he spoke so low and haltingly that Gale had several times to admonish him to raise his voice.

"The remonstrance of the Reverend Thomas Bailey, of Bertie Precinct, reads as follows," Will said and, adjusting his spectacles nervously on his nose, read from the sheaf of papers in his hand.

" 'On the ninth of November, Sir Richard Everard came to my house in Bertie Precinct and I had a two-hour conference with him in my own chamber. He at once began to cast reflections on the late governor, Captain George Burrington, and when I showed my dislike at his words, Sir Richard, with an abundance of heat, said that I stood precarious as a minister and that it was within his power to prevent my preaching in Edenton to the people.

" 'I answered humbly that I had done nothing unbecoming to my ministerial function, but had attended diligently to my duties, collecting more people to hear my sermons and baptizing more people and children than any other minister in the province. I told Sir Richard further that I had been invited to come to Bertie by the vestry, and that I had worked peaceably with that body and with our former governor, George Burrington.' "

Badham stopped to turn a page, and in the silence the spectators could hear the sound of heavy footsteps in the corridor outside. The doors were thrown open, and a loud voice called out: "Make way for his excellency, the governor of the province of North Carolina."

The governor entered, followed by his son, and automatically the entire assemblage rose to its feet. Sir Richard, a commanding figure in his red plush breeks, long-skirted broadcloth coat, brocaded waistcoat and full, dark-brown wig, paused to shoot a sharp glance at Bailey, who was seated alone at the end of the first row of chairs. Thin, almost cadaverous in his shabby clericals, his large hooked nose making his other features seem much too small, the minister was a sorry contrast to the elegant Sir Richard. His deep sunken eyes followed the governor as he mounted the dais and sat down in his high-backed elbow chair.

"Proceed, pray, Mr. Badham," Sir Richard said, nodding graciously, "I am sorry I interrupted."

The clerk, even more nervous than before, lifted the paper and began to read again.

" 'After a time, the governor became more moderate, but still he leveled his discourse against Captain Burrington. I expressed uneasiness, telling him I knew no harm in Mr. Burrington and I could not speak with another's tongue. I told Sir Richard further that if I could not obtain his favor without speaking evil of a man I knew no evil of, I must despair of obtaining it at all. Sir Richard was calm then, and invited me and my wife to his house in Edenton.

" 'Accordingly, we set out, arriving there on Thursday morning. On Saturday I met with the members of the vestry and asked leave of the pulpit for the next morning. They said I was welcome.

" 'I then received, by one of the governor's household, an invitation for a dish of chocolate on Sunday morning, and I waited on Sir Richard at that time. I had pleasant entertainment, excepting only some scandalous and gross reflections on Governor Burrington.

" 'After this I left and went to the church, which was locked. Mr. Parris came along and I asked him who kept the key. He said that it was in the keeping of the clerk of the court, and that he would fetch it. I waited, and he returned without the key, saying that the governor had it. I therefore went to the governor, finding in his company one Dr. Carter, a man of vile character and lately condemned at Williamsburg for cursing King George and Mr. Drysdale, the governor of Virginia.

" 'I said to the governor, "Sir, the congregation waits at the church, and I beg that your honor will please let me have the key."

" 'Flinging the key on the floor in a great rage, Sir Richard cried: "I will let you know who is governor here!"

" 'I answered that I knew his honor was the governor and I hoped his honor knew that I was a priest.' "

As Badham read these words, there was a stir in the courtroom and a low murmuring. "That took courage, to talk back to the governor that way!" one man whispered to his neighbor. "Aye, that it did," came the reply. But Bailey took no notice of the admiring words and glances; his eyes were fixed firmly ahead, and he sat quietly, his hands clasped in his lap.

"Let us have no interruptions," the governor said loudly. His face was an angry red. "You will proceed, Mr. Badham."

The paper trembled in the clerk's hands, and he had to clear his throat several times before he could make his voice loud enough to be heard.

" 'The governor said I would go to prison if I preached, and I answered that I would try to preach, nevertheless, as it was my duty to do, and that I had no doubt God would defend me. Accordingly, I went to the church, where I then found the door open, and I went in and read Divine Service and delivered a sermon to the people.

" 'The next morning a warrant was issued against me by Chief Justice Gale on the complaint of Governor Everard. To prison I would surely have gone, had not Governor Burrington's compassion and love for the clergy prevented, by offering bail, which was accepted.' The document is signed, 'Thomas Bailey.' "

Badham sat down, and the audience began once again to whisper and murmur in subdued voices. But suddenly something happened that threw the courtroom into near pandemonium. The doors at the back of the room were flung open, and George Burrington, a hard smile on his lips and a determined look in his eyes, stalked down the aisle to take the empty seat next to the minister. Chief Justice Gale banged his gavel repeatedly in a futile effort to restore order, but the excitement among the spectators grew rather than diminished. There were long whistles and loud cries and a steady buzz of wondering conversation; under this was the sound of chairs scraping along the floor as people were trying to move into positions from which better to stare at Burrington's burly frame. In the excitement, only a few people noticed Sir Richard rise from his chair, shoot a contemptuous glance at Burrington, and, beckoning his son to follow him, leave the chamber by a side door. As the governor made his exit, Burrington arose, reached into his waistcoat pocket, and pulled out a document.

"I beg leave to have this deposition entered into the records of the court," he said gruffly, handing the paper to Will Badham. The sound of his voice accomplished what the chief justice's gavel had failed to do, and a hush, almost as loud as the previous din, fell instantaneously on the courtroom.

Badham turned and offered the paper to Chief Justice Gale, who glanced at it, nodded, and returned it to the clerk.

"Very well, Mr. Badham. You will read the paper aloud, so that it can be legally entered into the record."

Badham's voice was becoming increasingly lower with every word he uttered; the spectators sat forward in their chairs, straining to catch his mumbled words.

"This document is an affidavit, sworn before Edward Moseley by Captain George Burrington of Bertie Precinct. It is relative to the Reverend Thomas Bailey's remonstrance, and it reads as follows: 'I, George Burrington, being duly sworn, do depone as follows: That I was present when a warrant for Mr. Bailey's arrest was sworn by Sir Richard Everard before Chief Justice Gale, that the said Mr. Bailey was treated by the governor with base and scurrilous language such as I have never before heard given to a clergyman by any official of the government, and that the said Mr. Bailey, notwithstanding such treatment, did give modest and respectful replies to the questions put him by Chief Justice Gale. Nevertheless, the aforesaid Mr. Bailey, whom deponent knows of his own knowledge to be a devout and honorable clergyman, was threatened to be sent to prison if he would not appear at the General Court, and deponent verily believes he would have been so served, had not bail been given.' "

Chief Justice Gale did not even wait for the clerk to read the signature on the document; banging his gavel loudly, he called out:

"It is now twelve of the clock. This court is hereby recessed until half after two."

Anthony leaned across to speak to his companions.

"Burrington certainly chose the most dramatic moment for his entrance. He must have been standing outside waiting."

Allin nodded. "The man is foxy, of that there is no doubt. It makes quite a picture, doesn't it: a governor who habitually drank to excess, whom I saw with my own eyes egging on a couple of rowdies to throw rocks through the windows of the chief justice's home, who connived behind their backs to sell out his employers' interests and violate their trust—to emerge now as the champion of religion and honor!"

"And the worst of it is that people's memories are so short," Anthony said. "I wager the entire village thinks he has always been a hero."

"The only person I feel sorry for," Dick spoke slowly, "is Mr. Bailey." He shook his head. "He seemed so proud of his accomplishments and so hopeful about his own future the day Tamar and I went up to his place to be married. Do you remember, Tony?"

Anthony nodded and glanced over to the front of the room, where the minister still sat. Burrington was standing a little distance away, surrounded by a crowd of admiring townspeople, but there was not a soul near Mr. Bailey; he was utterly alone. Anthony rose from his chair.

"Poor devil," he said, "to be in the middle of this kind of thing. We ought to go over and encourage him."

The three young men walked over to the minister.

"Good morning, sir," Anthony said. "May I tell you how very much I admire your courage? It takes great bravery to do what you are doing."

"Mr. Dawson speaks for all of us," Dick put in, and Allin nodded.

"Thank you, gentlemen, thank you." The minister's thin fingers moved restlessly over his face and there was weariness in his deep-sunken eyes. "It was not an easy decision for me to make. It would have been so much more simple to hold my tongue and pay the small fine that would probably have been levied against me in the General Court." He sighed. "It would have been simpler, yes, but it would have been against my conscience. I meditated and prayed for many days over this matter and finally the Lord came to me and told me I must speak out, even though it be against his excellency, the governor of the province. After all, gentlemen, little David stood up before the giant Goliath and defeated him."

"The people are with you, sir," Allin said, "and very angry at Sir Richard. I do not know what this will mean for his position here."

"Believe me, Mr. Gorgas," Bailey's voice was earnest. "I did not take this action to do the governor harm. I took it to defend the church. Perhaps another man would have listened silently to Sir Richard's attacks on Mr. Burrington, and more than once I have asked myself if I should not have shown more Christian forbearance in this regard, and have wondered if I acted from vain pride in speaking up. But I have known Captain Burrington for many years, even before I came here, and I have always found him a God-fearing man." He looked up at the former governor, who was by now making his way out of the room, still surrounded by a little knot of admirers.

"Captain Burrington may on occasion be somewhat intemperate," Bailey went on, "and inclined to impatience. But he is a man of honor and dignity, and I did not feel I could sit by and hear him unjustly attacked."

At this moment, Chief Justice Gale entered from the retiring room and beckoned Anthony to him, a disturbed expression on his aristocratic face.

"Dawson," he said, drawing the young man aside, "I am deeply distressed by this morning's events. Burrington has turned a straightforward legal problem into a Roman circus; whatever decision is reached in this matter can only create further disturbance." He shook his head slowly. "And I am the more distressed because I now see that unwittingly I have been responsible for some of the difficulty."

"What do you mean, sir? None of this is your doing."

"I should have tried to dissuade Sir Richard from swearing out the warrant. And I did not. When I saw that George Burrington was Mr. Bailey's supporter, I leaped immediately to the conclusion that Sir Richard's accusation was true: he said that Mr. Bailey was in liquor when he requested the keys to the church. I believed him implicitly, and agreed that he was right to withhold admission to a house of God from a drunken preacher. The entire matter is most upsetting, most upsetting. I had hoped that we would have some peace here, for a while, at least." He sighed deeply.

"I wonder—" Anthony began, but he was interrupted by a babble of voices from outside, rising in volume by the minute. The five men dashed to the window that gave on the Green; this was the direction from which the noise had come.

A fantastic sight met their eyes. There, in the center of a ring of fascinated spectators, stood Governor Everard and former Governor Burrington, each with a drawn rapier in his hand. Burrington's voice rose above the noise of the crowd.

"It will be a pleasure to fight you, sir," he shouted. "You are a damned heathen and a liar, and no more fitted to be governor of this province than a hog in the woods. I need no seconds; I'll run you through like butter!"

The men in the courtroom ran hastily out onto the Green, arriving there to hear Burrington's voice raised in taunting fury.

"Come on, sirrah, come on. Come and fight. Unless you are afraid. In that case, I'll gladly fight your son instead." He shot a contemptuous glance at young Everard, who was standing silently behind his father, his face pale, his mouth a thin line.

"I'll do my own fighting, damn you for a drunken swine!" Everard cried.

"On guard, then!" Burrington called, and lunged toward his opponent.

The fight began. Burrington, a big man, was heavy with the rapier, thrusting and lunging rapidly, and retreating just as rapidly. But Everard was no mean swordsman. More subtle in his endeavours, he kept dancing out of reach of his opponent's rapier; his graceful retreats and advances aimed as much at tiring Burrington as pricking him.

Anthony and Allin managed to elbow their way through the circle of onlookers to the center of the ring.

"Sir, I beg you," Allin called out to Sir Richard, "do not debase your office in this way."

"You keep out of this, Gorgas! What would you know about a gentleman's obligations?" young Everard cried. There was a loud chorus of protest from the spectators.

"Leave 'em alone. He deserves what he's going to get!" one man shouted. "Run him through, Captain Burrington, run him through!" called out another. "He's a yellow-bellied coward!" came from a third.

Anthony turned to face the crowd.

"Are you mad?" he exclaimed. "Are you no better than bloodthirsty animals?"

"They ain't made you governor yet, Dawson," a coarse voice yelled.

Suddenly the gaunt figure of Mr. Bailey appeared in the center of the ring.

"In the name of God and the church, gentlemen, this fighting must stop. Get you home, good people, get you home, lest you burn in hell for your savagery and bitterness. Vengeance is mine, saith the Lord. It is not for mobs and savages. Get you home!"

Burrington lowered his rapier and turned to face the crowd.

"My own honor demands that I fight this man," he called out. "But since the minister has said that my obligation to God forbids it, I will stop—for now, at least. Listen to the Reverend Bailey, good people, and leave." And he elbowed his way through the press of people to the King's Arms, Mr. Bailey following him.

Slowly, the crowd began to break up and the people straggled off, in little groups of twos and threes, to their homes and shops. Sir Richard did not move, but stood silently, a grim expression on his face. His son came over, took him by the arm, and led him off to Government House.

"Come, sir," he said as they moved away, "you will truly debase your office if you remain for another moment in the presence of these rogues." He shot an ugly glance over his shoulder at Allin and Anthony. "You told me yourself that you neither trusted nor liked them."

"Insolent pup," Anthony muttered.

"Yes." Allin frowned. "But I feel sorry for the poor devil. To have such a father . . ."

"It is not only his father," Dick said. "He is a nasty little pup himself, and treats everyone with contempt."

Allin smiled wryly. "Sometimes people use contempt as a mask, to hide their own fears, as they can use shyness, or pride. I ought to know. No, I do not like young Everard, but I feel sorry for him."

Chief Justice Gale, who had been standing in silence, turned a white face to the young men.

"In my sixty years, I have never seen anything like this. Never. It is as if a madness had descended on the entire village. I am at a loss, gentlemen, at a loss." His shoulders sagged as he walked slowly back to the courthouse.

Silently, Anthony, Allin and Dick started toward the King's Arms, where they had left their horses. The common room was filled to overflowing, and from the snatches of conversation they overheard, it was clear that Burrington was the hero of the hour. In one corner, Martin Trewilliger and some of his friends were laboring earnestly with pen and paper, writing up a draft of a memorial to the Lords Proprietors requesting Sir Richard's recall. Through the open door to one of the private rooms, Anthony saw Arthur Goffe, a member of Burrington's Council, seated with two of the representatives in the biennial assembly. Goffe's voice was loud and clear as he said:

"The lords must know that the aspersions that have in the past been cast on Governor Burrington are false, and that they discredit not only him, but all of us in North Carolina. Our paper to them must make this clear. The honor of the province is at stake."

"Burrington has won his point, no doubt of that," Allin said as the three young men crossed the courtyard. "And more—he has hastened the sale of the province to the Crown. The Proprietors will be even more anxious to be rid of it once they hear of this."

"And I wonder how the Crown will enjoy its new property." Anthony smiled wryly. "Well, we shall find out soon enough."

Chapter XXIII

THE HIGH JUMP

ONE MILD AFTERNOON, shortly after the turn of the year, Penelope Lovyck packed some clothes and toilet necessities in her saddlebags, mounted her brown mare, Susie, and rode out to Cornwall to spend a few weeks with Dierdra and Allin. The day before, John and the other members of the Boundary Line Commission—Anthony Dawson, Chief Justice Gale, Mr. Little, and Edward Moseley—had left for Williamsburg, whence they and the Virginia commissioners were to set out on the Dividing Line Survey. John would probably be gone for over a month, and since Penelope did not relish the idea of spending all that time alone in the house in Edenton, she had gratefully accepted Dierdra's invitation to stay at Cornwall during at least part of John's absence.

Dierdra looked out of the drawing room window to see Penelope riding up the driveway to the house. She threw a light wrap over her shoulders and ran outside, arriving at the upping block to find that one of the grooms had already helped Penelope dismount and was now leading Susie to the stable.

Dierdra kissed her friend warmly.

"How good to see you!" She turned to the groom, who had just emerged from the stable. "Will you take Mistress Lovyck's saddlebags into the house, Zeke, and ask Esther to take them to the south bedroom and unpack them?" She turned back to Penelope. "I hope you will be comfortable there. It is not a very large room, but it is bright and cheery!"

Penelope smiled. "I'm sure I shall be. It was so kind of you and Allin to invite me to come."

"We are delighted to have you, Penelope, you know that. Would you like to freshen up a bit?"

"I think I would. I always feel a bit grimy after riding."

Dierdra led the way back to the house and upstairs to the cheerful bedroom.

"It is simply charming," Penelope said. "Do keep me company while I change, Dierdra." She took off her riding habit and put on a green wool dress that brought out the reddish glints in her brown hair. As she was putting the finishing touches to her toilet, she noticed that Dierdra was looking out the window.

"What do you see down there?" she asked.

Dierdra turned, smiling. "My husband. He and Dick Chapman are out on the jumping field with young Richard Everard. Allin heard that he missed jumping practice, so he invited him to use our field. Allin feels sorry for the lad. People have been very harsh on him since that disgraceful duel between his father and Governor Burrington."

Penelope stopped brushing her long bright hair.

"Allin shows more charity than I would, Dierdra. Young Everard is an arrogant fellow." She paused. "Perhaps I should not say this, but . . ." her voice trailed off.

"What is it, Penelope?"

"Well, John has told me some of the things the boy has said about Allin. He cannot avoid seeing him occasionally, you know; young Everard goes everywhere his father does, even to the Council meetings. He has spiteful comments to make about everyone, but he seems particularly to dislike Allin and Anthony Dawson. He says that if it were not for them, his father would have rid the province of Burrington once and for all."

Dierdra sighed. "It is easy to understand why that scene at the duel upset him, and I suppose it is only natural that he should talk a bit wildly. After all, the people have no use for him or his father, and he must know it. But I cannot say it makes me feel specially friendly to him." She paused. "Perhaps now that we have taken the first step to repair the breach, he will improve. I must say he was very gracious when Allin asked him to come out. Almost pathetically grateful."

Penelope went over to the window and looked out. "He seems a good horseman," she said. "Just look at him fly over that gate!"

Dierdra's blue eyes darkened. "Allin has had them put up another bar. I do wish he would not make it so high. Especially with that horse. Black Magic has a hard mouth and he's nervous and wild. I do not like him one bit. I wish Allin would sell him. I have asked him to, but he simply will not listen to me."

"Now, Dierdra," Penelope patted her friend on the shoulder. "Allin is an expert horseman. He will not try anything he shouldn't. When you have been married as long as I, you will learn that men like to do things their own way. And they are much happier and easier to live with when they are allowed to. The only arguments John and I ever have are when I interfere with his affairs. He becomes simply furious."

"Allin does not become furious," Dierdra said, "just stubborn." She sighed. "I suppose you are right, Penelope. For all his gentleness, Allin does have a temper. I shall never forget the one time I saw it." She paused. "In any event it will soon be time for tea so they will not be at it much longer. If you are ready, we can go down now."

Penelope nodded, and the two young women made their way downstairs. Dierdra gave the order for tea and then turned to her friend.

"Shall we go out and fetch them? It isn't too cold."

As they crossed the lawn toward the jumping field, Dierdra saw the groom putting another bar on the gate. Her face darkened.

"He has never put it so high before," she said, almost in a whisper. "What ever has gotten into him?"

Penelope said nothing, but as they neared the jumping field and she caught sight of Richard Everard's face, a suspicion began to cross her mind. There was something in the young man's expression she did not like. Was he egging Allin on, in the hope of out-riding and out-jumping him, and of proving that the governor's son was a better horseman than his host?

By now the bar had been set into place. Everard spurred his horse, and the animal took the jump easily and gracefully. As he rode back to the starting point, he called out:

"Now, Gorgas, let's see that black devil of yours do as well!"

Allin laughed and spurred Black Magic on. The stallion made a run for the gate. He moved swiftly and evenly and it seemed sure he would take the jump with no trouble at all. But only a few feet from the gate, he stopped short, almost throwing Allin from the saddle.

Everard laughed.

"You call him a jumper?" he cried. "One bar more and he panics. Out of my way, now! I'll show you how a gentleman's horse takes it!" And once again he took his mount flying over the gate.

Penelope stole a look at Dierdra's face. It was white, drained of all color.

"Ignore him, Allin, ignore him," she whispered, "he is only an arrogant little snob."

But it was obvious that Allin's temper was rising. His mouth was set in a grim line and his eyes were narrowed to slits. Once again he dug his spurs into the stallion's sides and the huge animal ran headlong for the gate. And once again he came to a jolting stop only a few feet away.

"Forget it, old boy," Dick called out. "Six bars is too much for any horse!"

"Not for Black Magic!" Allin's voice was hard, and he tugged at the reins to turn his mount back to the starting point. Black Magic tossed his head in anger.

"That's it, Gorgas!" Everard shouted. "Teach the beast!"

"Don't, Allin, don't!" Dierdra cried. "He's wild with rage! He'll throw you!" She started to run toward the field.

The picture of the next few moments never faded from Penelope's mind. There was the flat, winter-brown meadow and the forest of green pine trees beyond it. There were the sheep drinking at the little stream behind the white fence. And there was the great horse, again pounding toward the gate, angry and wild, his head swinging from side to side.

Then there was the jolting stop at the gate, and the black body twisting suddenly sideways to fling Allin headfirst onto the hard-trampled earth of the jumping field. There was his cry of anguish, and the horse's whinny, and Black Magic dashed wildly off while Allin lay, twisted and unmoving, on the ground.

Dierdra grabbed Penelope's arm. "I must make his bed ready. Send someone for the doctor! Quickly! Allin! Oh, dear Lord!" She turned and ran headlong back to the house.

Penelope dashed across the meadow.

"Fetch the doctor, someone! Ride for Dr. Norcomb!" she called as she ran.

"You go," Dick shouted to Richard Everard. "I'll take care of Allin."

By the time Penelope arrived at the spot where Allin lay, Dick had gently lifted the unconscious body onto the shutter a groom had brought from the stable. A little Negro boy came running out, carrying a bucket of water and a sponge. Penelope knelt beside the shutter and washed the blood and dirt from Allin's pale face. She felt for his pulse. It was faint, but steady. Out of the corner of her eye, she could see that one of the grooms had caught Black Magic, and was leading him back to the stable.

"Everard has gone for the doctor," Dick said grimly. "If he doesn't make it in time, I will kill him." He spoke through clenched teeth. "Rotten little swine! He wanted Allin to take a fall!"

"Or give up," Penelope said. With her handkerchief she wiped off the little trickle of blood that ran from Allin's temple. "Why did he have to invite him here, why?"

Four of the stable men came hurrying up. Slowly, they lifted the shutter and slowly they started across the meadow toward the house, walking carefully so as not to disturb their burden. Dick and Penelope walked at either side, their eyes never leaving Allin's pale face.

When they were only a few steps from the house Dierdra came running out to meet them.

"His bed is ready," she said, her voice strained and tight. "Is he . . ." She stopped, unable to bring herself to say the words.

Dick put his arm around her slim waist.

"Steady, Dierdra, steady. He has had a bad fall, but he will be all right. Everard has gone to fetch Dr. Norcomb."

Under Penelope's direction, the stable men gently shifted

Allin's inert body from the shutter to the bed. Then they backed quietly out of the room.

As he closed the door behind him, the last one spoke.

"He will be all right, mistress," he said. "He's strong, Master Gorgas. And we will pray for him."

Dierdra weakly smiled her thanks and hurried over to the bed, where Dick and Penelope were pulling off Allin's riding boots. Blood was still flowing from the gash in his temple, and Dierdra ran to bring a basin of cold water and a cloth. She knelt beside the bed, gently wiping away the blood.

"How could he have done it? How could he?" she whispered under her breath.

"The horse went wild, Dierdra," Dick said, "no one could have kept his seat."

"I begged him to get rid of that horse. Everard . . ."

"Now, Dierdra, hush," Penelope said. "It's Allin we have to think of."

Dick looked up at Dierdra's drawn face. "Allin will be all right. But you are pale as a ghost."

"I'll bring her some brandy," Penelope said and she went swiftly out of the room.

Dick pulled a low chair to the bedside. "Sit down, Dierdra," he said. He took her gently by the shoulder.

"Perhaps you had better ride over to Lilac Farm, Dick, and let them know. They will want to be here. Penelope will stay with me. And the doctor will be coming very soon, I'm sure."

"All right." Dick patted her hand awkwardly. "Don't worry, Dierdra. Everything will be all right." At the door he turned. "Tamar is visiting with her parents today, so I will not have far to go. We will be back in ten or fifteen minutes."

Dierdra nodded listlessly. She took Allin's hands in hers. The wound in his temple had stopped bleeding and it seemed to her that he was breathing more easily.

"Please, God," she whispered.

In about fifteen minutes, the Killigrews arrived.

"Let me spell you, my dear," Mistress Killigrew whispered. "You must be worn out."

Dierdra raised her eyes and shook her head.

"No, I want to stay here, with Allin. I want to be here when he opens his eyes. But it is a comfort that you are here, too." She got up from the chair. "You sit down," she said. "I'll kneel over here."

Yeoman Killigrew cleared his throat. His voice was gruff. "Our boy will be all right."

"Of course he will," Owen said, in his quiet voice.

Tamar patted Dierdra on the shoulder. Her pretty face was stiff with grief.

The door opened and Dr. Norcomb came in. He touched Dierdra's arm gently, turned, and spoke to Dick. "Pull back the curtains, Chapman. I must have more light. And will everyone leave for a moment except young Mr. Killigrew and Mr. Chapman. They can help me take Mr. Gorgas's clothes off so I can examine him properly."

Tamar and her parents tiptoed downstairs, while Penelope led Dierdra into her dressing room.

"Take off your frock and your stays, dear," Penelope urged. "That way you will be more comfortable while you wait. It may be several hours before Allin regains consciousness. Where is your wrapper?"

"Hanging behind the door," Dierdra said. "Take the blue one. Blue is Allin's favorite color." She sat down on the stool in front of her dressing table and buried her head in her hands. After a moment she wiped her eyes and stood up. "I am forgetting my duties. Will you ask the housekeeper to look after food for our guests? And she will have to make up some extra beds in case the Killigrews and the Chapmans want to stay the night." As she spoke, Dierdra took off her dress and stays and pulled her wrapper around her.

There was a knock on the door, and Owen's quiet voice called softly:

"The doctor says you can come back in now, Dierdra."

Dierdra patted her hair into place with a tentative little gesture and ran swiftly to the bedroom. Allin lay unmoving on the bed, the comfort pulled up to his chin. There was a wide white bandage on his head. Dr. Norcomb motioned her to the low chair that stood at the bedside.

"Sit down, girl, sit down. It will be a long night's vigil for us."

She looked up to see a worried expression on his kind face.

"What is it, doctor? He will be all right, won't he?"

Norcomb shrugged his shoulders. "I cannot tell. That gash on his temple is worse than I first thought. He must have fallen very heavily indeed." He paused. "But he is young and strong, and you and I will see that he has every chance."

Dierdra wanted to speak but she could feel the sobs rising in her throat. She took Allin's hand in hers and, blinking back her tears, looked straight ahead, to the window. Through the open curtains she could see the moon rising over the dark pine forest. Soon the night sounds would begin: the lowing of cattle, the scurrying feet of small animals, the owls' hoots. The moon brightened and Dierdra heard a fox bark and, from the kennels, a hound lifting its mournful voice in reply. Allin neither moved nor spoke. The room was deep in silence.

Dierdra did not know how long she had been sitting when she heard a long, low sigh, and felt a sudden heaviness in the hand that lay in hers.

"Dr. Norcomb!" she cried, but, even as she spoke, she knew it was too late. She bent over and kissed Allin's cheek.

"Go with God, Allin, go with God. . . ." The words of the old Cornish leavetaking had come to her lips automatically.

Allin's body was taken to the little chapel that had been Mistress Peterson's pride and joy when the house was built, only a few years before. The death watch began, two people always keeping guard over the body. Allin was as handsome in death as he had been in life. As he lay there on the bier, covered with a black pall, the tall candles that burned at his head and at his feet sent dancing shadows over the strong contours of his face.

Dierdra stood looking down at him for a long time. Then she turned and stumbled back into the house and to her bedroom where, a few minutes later, Penelope found her standing at the window and gazing out over the early morning landscape with unseeing eyes.

Penelope went over and put a gentle hand on her shoulder and Dierdra began to sob. Then, straightening her back, she said in a flat, unbelieving voice:

"It is over now, Penelope. All over. There is nothing more to be done."

Penelope shook her head. "There is much more, my dear, much more."

"You mean the funeral?" Dierdra's voice was still expressionless.

"That, and the wake. People will be coming from all over the province and even from as far away as South Carolina and Virginia. That will be for three days, and they will eat and drink and talk, and we must be prepared. Mary Catten has come over to help. A funeral attracts folk, Dierdra, just as Market Day does, or Muster Day. Didn't you know?"

Dierdra looked bewildered. "I must have forgotten. When my parents were killed . . ."

"I shall have to write out the notice," Penelope spoke briskly; she could see that Dierdra was on the verge of breaking down, and she wanted to forestall it. "It will be put on a parchment scroll, and my old slave Gabriel will carry it from door to door, to let the people of the village know. Your bondmen will carry the sad news to Bertie and Perquimans. Hundreds of folk will come over. That is the custom of our country."

Dierdra's shoulders dropped. "If that is how it must be."

"Yes, my dear, that is how it must be." Penelope rose. "I am going into the village now. Dick will drive me. I will attend to everything. And when I come back, I will bring some things for you. I have the mourning bonnet and veil I wore when my stepfather died. Do you need a black dress? We could lengthen mine."

Dierdra's eyes widened. "No, I will not wear black. Allin hated it. I could not do that to him."

"But you must." Penelope spoke firmly. "It is the custom."

Dierdra shook her head. "No black, Penelope. Allin was my

husband and I loved him and I am going to do what he would have wanted. A wake, yes. But no black. Blue was his favorite color. I shall wear blue." She paused. "My mind is made up, Penelope. Don't try to dissuade me. I shall wear blue. Everyone who loved Allin will understand."

"Aye." It was Mistress Killigrew, who had entered as Dierdra was speaking. "That is what our Allin would have wanted. She was his happiness, was Dierdra, and he would not have liked to see her in black, all cast down and sorrowful."

The day of the funeral dawned clear and cold. For two days, folk from all over the province had been arriving for the wake. In the dining room, the tables groaned under the weight of the food, and in the carriage house were the kegs of ale that had been brought over by Groggins, of the Red Lion Inn, and by Giles Martin, of the King's Arms. The bare lawn and the house were crowded with people. When Governor Everard and his family arrived, the folk drew away from them. There were muttered curses and some of the villagers ostentatiously turned their backs. Although nothing could ever erase her bitterness against them from Dierdra's heart, she and the Killigrews received them with quiet dignity.

The Burringtons came, too. Madam kissed Dierdra's cheek and whispered:

"My dearest girl, my dearest girl. What can I say?" There were tears in her eyes.

Burrington spoke gruffly. "He was a fine man, young Gorgas."

Martin Trewilliger had sailed across the sound to Bertie and brought the Reverend Thomas Bailey back to read the service. When he arrived, the minister clasped Dierdra's hand in his, compassion in his deep sunken eyes.

"Our mortal happiness is all too brief, mistress, all too brief."

The grave, lined with soft, fragrant pine, had been dug on the plantation burial ground not far away from Enar Peterson's, already overgrown with ivy. The joiner had made the coffin with expert care and the hinges were Martin Trewilliger's most careful work.

Slowly the funeral procession crossed the lawn. The Reverend Mr. Bailey came first. Then there was the wooden box in which Allin rested, carried on the shoulders of four strong young men. Next came Dierdra, holding her slim body erect and tall, and the Killigrews, and Owen, and Dick and Tamar. Behind them were the hundreds of mourners.

As she made her way to the grave, Dierdra thought back to the evening—so long ago, it now seemed—when, not far from this very spot, Allin had told her of his parents, of his love for her, and of his hopes for both of them. It was all over now, the hopes ground into the earth beneath Black Magic's heavy hooves. All over. Finished. She lifted her head to hear the minister's voice.

"I am the resurrection and the life. . . ."

Slowly the coffin was lowered into its bed of pine boughs.

Chapter XXIV

THE DIVIDING LINE

THE FIRST PART of the Dividing Line Survey had been completed without too much difficulty, but now an arduous task lay ahead: to run the line through the reaches of the Great Dismal, the huge, forbidding swamp that stretched from a few miles beyond Norfolk Town all the way to the Western Mountains. There were islands of dry land in the Dismal, on which settlements had been built, but for the greatest part of its still uncharted length, the swamp was not fit for human habitation. Legend had it that strange, supernatural creatures inhabited it; the truth was that its habitable stretches were a haven for runaway slaves and for debtors and criminals who had managed to cheat the law and lived among the Borderers, an ignorant and uncouth lot who, in exchange for offering the refugees safety, took the greatest share of the meagre crops they managed to raise.

A large team of men would be necessary to run the line through the Dismal, and the Virginia and North Carolina Commissioners had separated the day before, to provision themselves for the trip and to find chain-bearers and packers to accompany them. They were to meet at Norfolk, a pleasant little village on the Elizabeth River, with straight, well laid-out streets and stoutly constructed houses. There were wharves curving out into the three branches of the river, and more than twenty brigantines and sloops lay at anchor. The inn was clean and cheerful and, after dinner, John Lovyck and Chief Justice Gale sat down to a bitterly contested game of backgammon, while Edward Moseley and Will Little pored over the map and plotted the next day's journey.

Anthony retired early. With his men, Philander and Smalkins, he had been out riding and exploring the countryside the whole day, and he was tired. If he was to be at his best when they started out for the Great Dismal, he would need a good night's sleep.

He came downstairs the next morning to find William Byrd of Virginia sitting alone, drinking his morning chocolate and reading from a volume of Tillitson's Sermons as was, Anthony had discovered, his regular custom.

"Good morning, sir." Anthony said.

"Dawson!" Byrd looked up. "Good morning. Sit down, sir, and join me."

Anthony pulled up a chair and sat down. From the window he could see a slough. Two men were fishing from a small skiff.

"I have a letter from my friend Lord Peterborough, from London," Byrd said. "Delivered by hand by one of my servants. It arrived at Westover only a few days ago. Lord Peterborough writes that your family is fighting the rest of the lords against the sale of North Carolina."

"I have not had news from my family for several months," Anthony replied. He did not wish to pursue the subject.

Byrd looked at Anthony out of sharp, inquiring black eyes. But his glance found no response. He pushed his cup aside and lit his pipe.

"Well, Dawson, now that we have the first part of the work out of the way, we can move on to the real problem: this vast stretch ahead of us. You know this is not our first attempt to run the line through this area. But last time there was so much discussion and disagreement that we all gave up and went home." He paused. "Your Mr. Moseley was not much in the wrong then. He found fault with our quadrant on the district survey, and now it appears that there was an error of nearly thirty minutes—either in the instrument or in those who used it. We Virginians were in error, I must admit."

Anthony beckoned to the slovenly waiter and the lad came over, wiping his greasy fingers on his leather apron. As Byrd ordered breakfast for both of them, Anthony ran an appraising eye over this man with whom he had spent so much time in the last weeks. The Virginian was not tall, but he had an undeniable air of leadership and elegance, and managed to look fashionable even in his hunting clothes: leather breeks and jerkin, and a knit cap bound with a bright silk kerchief. He took the last sip of his chocolate and wiped his lips elegantly with a rough linen napkin.

"We have brought a clergyman with us for the work. The Reverend Peter Fountain. He will have much to do."

"A clergyman?" Anthony's expression was puzzled.

"Yes indeed." Byrd nodded. "To marry the folk who are living in sin and to baptize their children. The Borderers live in utter godlessness, Dawson, utter godlessness. It is a scandal."

As Anthony was about to reply, Edward Moseley entered the room.

"Gentlemen," he said, "everyone is packed and ready to go. What do you say to starting off? If we leave now, we will get to the Dismal before nightfall, and have time to pitch camp. The packers and chain-bearers have left already, by the land route. We will go by boat. The pirogues are already at the wharf."

At nightfall, after a long paddle up the river, they reached the camping ground. Quarters had been prepared for them in an old barn. The Virginians occupied the loft, and bedded down on piles of hay, while the Carolinians slept on the ground floor. The packers and chain-bearers, to the number of about twenty-five, had found places outside. The surveyors were quartered in the barn, with the commissioners.

They started out early the next morning. The weather was raw, and there was a light drizzle. The bedding and other necessities had been made up into packs for the men to carry on their backs, and the Carolinians had enough victuals for about two weeks; the Borderers had insisted it would take no longer than that to traverse the great swamp.

The entire party started off with light hearts. Commissioners, surveyors, packers, chain-bearers—all were in good spirits. The Reverend Mr. Fountain led them in a hymn, and the great adventure had begun.

Anthony walked with Edward Moseley. Almost at once they were entangled in stiff briars and gall bushes. When they had gone a quarter of a mile into the Dismal the ground became full of sunken holes and slashes, and the going became extremely difficult.

"This is going to be worse than we thought," Moseley said. "It will take twelve men to carry the chains and clear a path for us."

"Perhaps we should give the men a chance to rest," William Byrd called out. "There is some firm land up ahead, and we have only moved forward half a mile in the last three hours."

Moseley nodded, and a halt was called. In a half hour, rested and refreshed, they took up the journey again. But by nightfall they had covered only another half mile.

"The men can do no more." Moseley shook his head. "Twelve of them can only make a mile and a half a day. This looks like a three months' task, instead of a maximum of thirty days."

The next day was no better, or the next, or the next. The bog they traveled had no firm ground, and with every step they sank deeper into the muddy earth. A man had but to lift his foot, and water sprang up instantly to fill the hole. They fought their way through reeds ten feet high, and their legs were held and gashed by briars. No breeze came to refresh them; even now, late in January, it was hot and breathless. But on they struggled, behind the enthusiastic Byrd, who still managed to look fresh and rested.

"You have to admire the fellow," Edward Moseley said grudgingly to Anthony. "He does not know how to quit."

Since they had entered the deep swamp, the surveying party had not seen another living creature, bird or beast, insect or reptile. The eternal shade that brooded over the mighty bog, holding off the sun, made no proper habitation for life. The verdure rested the eye, but the foul damp and the rotting vegetation corrupted the air. Not even a vulture flew overhead.

It was over two weeks before they reached firm land. The Carolinians' provisions had been exhausted days before, and the men had been living on nuts and berries. But here they found a settlement where they were able to purchase fresh supplies of food. Men, women and children came by the dozens to be baptized.

"I have done some of God's work today," Mr. Fountain said, "but not a couple has asked me to marry them."

A great flock of cranes flew overhead, squawking loudly. They roosted nearby for the night, a sentinel bird guarding the flock from the highest tree. The liquor ration had long since been used up, and one of the carriers brought in some Angelica plants to make a dram. Boiled in water, it made a kind of aromatic cordial —not as good as rum, but better than nothing. The men had their first good night's sleep in weeks.

But the next day, when the party started out, the land turned to swamp again. And the pattern was repeated for week after week. Days on end slogging through the miasmic vapors of the Great Dismal—footsore, weary, with not enough to eat and no sign of life. And then the occasional clearing with its settlement of Borderers, runaway slaves, debtors and criminals.

They had been out two months. To Anthony it seemed the men were too exhausted to go on. And one day, when they had reached a clearing, fifty miles beyond the last inhabited settlement, the Carolina Commissioners met together under a giant pine tree to talk privately.

"We have done enough," Moseley said. "About a hundred and seventy miles, from the Currituck inlet to the south branch of the Roanoke River, and then on into this trackless swamp. I do not know what you gentlemen think, but I am ready to call it quits. It will be a long time before settlers move out this far. If we have had such difficulty making the journey—and with a party of trained chain-bearers, to boot—how will they reach here?"

Gale nodded. "The main part of the dividing line has been settled. We have done a yeoman's chore, and, it seems to me, satisfied our orders and carried out our responsibility."

"Do you not think we should write down our reasons for leaving?" Anthony asked. "That will keep the record clear."

William Little nodded. "When we get back to Edenton. Gale and I, as the legal experts, can draw up the document."

"Then it is agreed," John Lovyck put in. "We will leave in the morning."

When Byrd heard this news, his aristocratic face became tight with anger.

"You undertook a responsibility, sirs. And you have failed to carry it out. But we Virginians will go ahead. And we will hold your province to the line as we draw it all the way to the Western Mountains."

"You can write out your arguments, Mr. Byrd, as we are going to write out ours," Christopher Gale said. "His Majesty and the Lords Proprietors can then decide between us."

And early the next morning, the Carolina commissioners left for home.

Anthony arrived back at Stowe on a pleasant afternoon in early April. Faint greens were beginning to lace the trees, and the lawn in front of the house was spotted here and there with sharp shoots of grass.

Mary Catten was waiting at the door.

"Welcome home, Mr. Dawson, welcome home!"

Smalkins led his horse off to the stable, and Anthony went into the house. He stood for a long moment in the center of the entrance hall and looked around.

"How wonderful to be back, Mary!" he exclaimed. "This house looks more beautiful to me than the most elegant palace." He strode into the drawing room and, with a deep sigh, sank into a comfortable chair.

"Sit down, Mary," he said, motioning her to a seat, "and tell me everything that has happened. Has it been a peaceful winter?"

The little woman's face darkened, and she spoke slowly.

"Except for Mr. Gorgas, sir."

Anthony looked at her uncomprehendingly.

"Did you not hear?" she asked.

"I've been in a swamp for the last two months, Mary, and have heard nothing. What about Mr. Gorgas?"

"Ah, that was a sad thing, sir," and slowly she told him the story of Allin's death. He listened in shocked silence, and when she had finished he sat staring ahead for a long moment.

"Mistress Gorgas—how is she?" he finally asked.

"She took it very hard, sir, very hard. For a month or so, she barely spoke. Mistress Lovyck stayed with her, and Mistress

Killigrew went to see her often, and Mistress Chapman, too. And I went to comfort her as often as I could. But she was without life. You know, sir, I could not help thinking of her name—and the prophesy that came true: 'Dierdra of the sorrows.' So young, and lost so many near and dear to her." She sighed.

"Is she still at Cornwall?" Anthony rose from his chair. "I will ride over right now."

Mary Catten nodded. "Yes, sir. She will be glad to see you, I know. She has asked for you many a time."

At the door, Anthony turned. "Will you have Smalkins ride over to Mr. Chapman's and tell him I would be honored if he and Mistress Chapman would have dinner with me tonight?"

"Of course, Mr. Dawson. I will send him right over."

Dierdra was sitting in the drawing room at Cornwall when Anthony arrived. There was a sewing basket on the small table beside her, and she was edging a white lawn handkerchief. She jumped to her feet as Esther came in to announce Anthony's arrival.

"Dierdra, my dear," he said as he entered the room. She held out her hands to him and he clasped them in his.

"Anthony! I am glad to see you again." She smiled, but her face was thin and drawn. "Sit down, do, and we will have some tea and talk about old times." She motioned him to the big comfortable chair near the window, and started toward the smaller one opposite it.

"Dierdra," he said, and holding out his hands, again took hers. "Let me first say what I must. I just heard the dreadful news from Mary Catten, and I want you to know how shocked and heartsick I am, and how I grieve for you. If there is anything I can do, anything at all . . ."

"I knew I would have your sympathy, Anthony. And I am grateful, deeply grateful. All my friends have been more than kind to me; without them, I do not know if these last few months would have been bearable." She smiled wanly. "But it has not been easy, Anthony. Every room in the house has memories, every inch of the grounds. And I cannot help thinking of a prediction of tragedy that was made to Allin and me, long ago, at the old Indian camping ground. . . ." Gently, she withdrew her hands from his, and, walking over to the bellpull on the side of the mantel, rang for the maid. When she had ordered the tea she turned to Anthony again.

"Now, do sit down, and let us talk of more cheerful things."

They chatted about Anthony's work on the Dividing Line Survey for a while; when they had finished their tea, Anthony brought the conversation back to the topic that interested him most: Dierdra herself.

"You have not yet told me your plans, Dierdra."

"I can make nearly any plans I want," she smiled ruefully. "You know, Anthony, I am a woman of means now. Allin left me this plantation, and we own it all, free and clear. And the income he had from his father's estate—that belongs to me, too." She paused. "I did not want to accept it at first. I felt it should all go to the Killigrews. After all, they did so much for Allin, and we were married such a short time—not even a year. But they did not want to take it. We had quite an argument," she laughed softly, "but finally we came to an agreement."

"And what was that?"

"Owen will take over the management of the property, and we will share and share alike on its earnings. The Killigrews finally agreed when I pointed out that unless I were to sell the property, I would have to have a man to run it."

"That is true enough, of course," Anthony said, "and with Owen in charge, you will have the best man possible."

Dierdra nodded. "So that has all been arranged. He has already started to lay plans for this year's crops; he rides over every day from Lilac Farm." She paused. "The only real problem is that he cannot move in here. People would talk, and it would be most improper. But since I will not be here—"

"Will not be here?" Anthony interrupted. "Where are you going?"

"I am telling you this story in bits and pieces, am I not?" Dierdra sighed. "I am going back to England. Roger will be at home, on leave. It is so long since I have seen him."

"But you will be coming back, won't you?"

She shook her head. "I don't know. I have not made up my mind yet. I do not feel up to the decision."

"When are you leaving?"

"In two weeks. On the *British Prince*, from Williamsburg."

"We shall miss you, Dierdra. All of us. And we will be waiting eagerly, and praying for your return." Anthony rose. "I will leave you now. Perhaps you will let me ride over once or twice before you go. I may be able to give Owen a hand with some of his tasks."

"Do come, Anthony, whenever you can. I am always happy to see you."

The sun was beginning to lower as Anthony rode back to Stowe Plantation. The sky was washed in gold, and along the quiet road, the evening sounds began to make themselves heard. The scampering feet of small animals, the cricket's chirp, the plaintive calls of the wood dove—they all formed an accompaniment to his thoughts. Dierdra must not go back to England for good. It was still too early to hope.

He arrived home to find Dick and Tamar already there. They greeted him warmly, and sat chatting in the drawing room.

"Dierdra told me she was leaving for England," Anthony said.

Dick nodded. "When first she said she wanted to go, we tried to dissuade her. But on thinking it over we came to the conclusion that she is doing the right thing. She says she does not know whether she will return, but we are all sure that she will. A few months in England, away from all the faces that remind her of her grief, and she will have the perspective she needs to remember that they remind her of her happiness as well. She is young. She should marry again. And I am sure she will be ready to, when she comes back. Allin would have wanted it, I know."

"Dick is right," Tamar said. "She will come back. This is her home. We need her here, and she needs us. And I have a husband for her, when the time comes," and she looked at Anthony and smiled her old impish grin.

"Tell me what has been happening in the village?" Anthony

said, hastily changing the subject.

"There is not much to tell," Dick said. "Except that everyone is waiting for Everard to leave. No one feels the slightest doubt he will be recalled. After Allin's death, the feeling against him has risen even higher. The whole tragic accident was really his son's fault. I cannot count how many memorials were sent against him." He paused. "There has been a good deal of speculation as to who will take his place. Everyone suspects it will be Burrington, and everyone is so busy talking about that—the villagers with pleasure, the gentry rather more unhappily—that no one has given much thought to the fact that we shall all be under the Crown pretty soon, and shall not be living on proprietary land much longer."

"But we shall be," Anthony said. "We shall be on Granville land. Our stretch runs from here to the Virginia border, and as far inland as the Western Mountains." He looked up to see Smalkins at the door.

"Dinner?" he asked. The valet nodded, and Anthony, Dick and Tamar went in to the table.

Chapter XXV

THE GRANVILLE GRANT

AT LAST the day arrived for which Anthony had been waiting so long, half in hope and half in regret. The notice that an extraordinary public meeting was to be held had been sent by messenger to every precinct in the Albemarle, and people had descended on Edenton from all corners of the province.

Anthony stood on the courthouse steps, looking down over the crowd that milled excitedly about on the Green. The women, in their brilliantly colored gowns and big, flowery hats, made the men in their dark coats and brocaded waistcoats, seem somber looking and almost dowdy. The July day was hot, but none of the people seemed to mind; they were in a fever of anticipation so high as to have burned out anything but the need to have their curiosity satisfied.

How would they feel when they found out, Anthony wondered, and he turned in astonishment to hear Chief Justice Gale answer his unspoken question. The old man had come out of the courthouse and was standing beside him.

"There will be rejoicing all over the province tonight and, who can tell, perhaps even, for a little time, peace. But I do not know how long it will last, Dawson, I do not know. I hope for all our sakes that the new dispensation will bring an end to lawlessness and disaffection, and to tyranny as well. But I am an old man, and I have learned long since that hope is usually the sire of disappointment." He paused and grasped Anthony firmly by the shoulder. "Hope and trust are, however, two different things. I *hope* that the rest of the Carolinians will act as they should in discharging their obligations, whether as citizens or as leaders. But I have *trust* in you, young man, and I know that you will do what is right in the performance of your new duties."

"I shall do my best, sir, my very best."

From the direction of Government House there came a long roll of drums, and the militia, in the scarlet of His Majesty the King, marched smartly across the Green. Behind them was the Governor's state coach. It drove up to the courthouse and Sir Richard Everard mounted the steps, to the beat of the drums, and took his place in his high-backed chair. He was dressed in grey satin, with white breeches, white silk stockings, and silver-buckled shoes. His wide black beaver had a long grey plume, which fell below the black curls of his full-bottomed wig. He gave the order for the review to begin.

There was a salute of muskets and the sharp command, "Attention! Columns right!" and the militia passed in review. When the last maneuver had been executed, officers' swords snapped into scabbards, and the soldiers lined up on the side of the Green, Sir Richard stepped forward.

"People of the Albemarle, I bid you listen carefully to Chief Justice Gale." He sat down again, and Gale stepped forward, his red robes fluttering in the hot summer breeze.

"My Lord Governor, members of the Council, citizens! I now have the distinction of introducing to this great assemblage Colonel Anthony Dawson Granville, whom you have known as Anthony Dawson.

"He will read a proclamation that has been sent to him by his cousin, Lord John, Palatine of the Lords Proprietors of North Carolina, on a matter of grave importance to you, and to your children, and to your children's children."

Anthony stepped forward. He wore a long dark coat, with braids and buttons, a modest tan silk waistcoat and a broad beaver without plumes. He began to read from the paper he held in his hands.

" 'We, the Lords Proprietors of the province of North Carolina,' " he read in a strong voice, " 'send greetings to you, its people, and inform you of the following change of ownership of the province.

" 'The Lords Proprietors, hereditary owners of the whole of

North Carolina have sold the titles of the land therein to the King's Crown. The province will be from now and henceforth under the jurisdiction of His Majesty the King of Great Britain and all islands.' " Anthony paused a moment and then went on: " 'With the exception only of one eighth portion of the province, lying alongside of the Virginia line, from the Atlantic Ocean to the South Seas. This property will remain under the ownership of the Carteret, Bath and Granville family, and will be known as the Granville Grant.' " Anthony paused again. "This document is signed by Lord John, Palatine of the Lords Proprietors, under his seal."

For a long moment the crowd was silent, the full meaning of his announcement still unclear. Then there was a wild burst of handclapping, and cries of "Long Live the King!" and "Long Live the Granville Grant!"

Chief Justice Gale stepped forward again. He held up a hand, and the crowd came instantly to attention.

"A new governor has been appointed under the Crown," he said, "and will be arriving to take up his duties soon. The official welcome for Governor George Burrington will take place on Muster Day."

The crowd went wild. Hats were flung in the air. People danced and sang. No one noticed as Sir Richard left the Green and made his stately way to Government House or as he and his son mounted their horses and rode up Broad Street, through the North gate, into the Virginia Road.

In inns and ordinaries, men drank wine and ale and cider and toasted King George, Lord John, Governor Burrington, and North Carolina, a new free country. Those who had kept their heads found out from Anthony that their ownership of property would not be affected by the new arrangements; both Crown land and Granville land would continue to be held as they were formerly. New property, to be taken up on the Granville Grant, would be administered by Anthony, as land grant agent, from an office to be set up in Edenton.

Anthony made his way to the King's Arms, where he found Edward Moseley and Goldsmith Coltrane closeted in a private room.

"You Granvilles will grow rich, I know," the surveyor-general said. "But I still wonder what will happen under the Crown, and with Burrington as governor."

Anthony shrugged his shoulders. "It will be as much our responsibility as anyone's. And I can tell you, gentlemen, I feel my own responsibility keenly."

"We know you do, lad," Coltrane said, "and we know you will do an honest job. North Carolina will pull through, Proprietors or Crown, good governors or bad. We may have our reservations about Burrington, but the people are behind him now. And as long as he conducts himself properly, and has their support . . ." He broke off. "I almost forgot. I have a letter for you. It came a few days ago, from Mistress Gorgas, in Cornwall, but she asked me to hold it for you until the great day had come. The news of North Carolina was known in Cornwall, it seems, before it was officially known here."

Anthony tried to conceal his impatience as he took the letter from Coltrane's long fingers. But he made a poor job of it.

"Take your letter and run." Moseley laughed. "You can speak with us any time."

Anthony nodded and strode out of the room. He put the letter in his waistcoat pocket; he would not read it until he was back at Stowe. The trip back on horseback was the longest he had ever taken. But at last he was at home.

He stood on the bank of the river and opened the letter.

"Dear Anthony," he read. "Cornwall is beautiful, but not half so beautiful as my true home, North Carolina. Not until I arrived here did I realize how much I loved the New World. So I am coming back soon, very soon, to all my friends. And I hope that they will think of me as they did before, and as I think of them, with love."

Slowly, Anthony put the letter back in his pocket. He looked across the river to the dark fringe of the cypress pocosin and smiled. Soon she would be here with him, Dierdra, whom he had always known should be his. . . .

He thought of the long roll of Granvilles who had loved the land, and whose heir he was. From the time of William the Conqueror, down through the long ages, they had nurtured the land, and the land had nurtured them. "To receive, one must give. Do not take from the land, without giving in return." The great Sir Richard Granville had said this. And the others who came afterwards, they were all the same: Sir Bevil, and the Queen's General—the love of the land transcended all else in their lives.

He started back to the house. The Spanish moss that hung in long festoons from the giant oaks swayed gently in the summer breeze. Smoke from kitchen fires in the cabins of the quarters line and in the great house curled slowly upward toward the sky. When Dierdra came, he would walk with her as he was walking now, across his land, their land, where they had their home.

He stopped walking, bent down, and laid his hand on the earth. It seemed to him to throb under his touch, like the beating of a great heart. Summer was here, the season of richness. . . .